Eve's Garden

Glenda Bailey-Mershon

Twisted Road Publications LLC
Tallahassee, Florida

Twisted Road Publications LLC

.

Copyright © 2014 by Glenda Bailey-Mershon
All rights reserved
ISBN: 978-1-940189-04-8
Library of Congress Control Number: 2013957251

Printed in the United State of America

www.twistedroadpublications.com

Dedication

For my grandmothers,
Canna, Ophelia, Nancy Adeline, Amanda, Betty, and Lavinia,
whose wisdom carries me;
for my Aunt Thelma, who loved me when I needed it most;
for my singular sister, Gail; and our beautiful mother, Easter,
whose longing made me try;
for my friends Carolyn, Debby, O.J., and Donna,
who showed me how to enjoy being a girl, and how to survive it;
they and all my girl cousins keep my girlhood alive;
and for my nieces, who hold open the door.
We are home.

Acknowledgements

Writing for me is a balance between solitude and community. The support of many people helped Eve's Garden to thrive.

My first writing group, which needed no name but resulted in a wonderful brew of tea and stories, included Linda Mowry, Julie Sass, and Clara Johnson, who read and improved the very first version of this book. You will always be my sisters.

Many Romani scholars and activists helped me envision Evangeline's world. I especially want to thank Drs. Ethel Brooks and Petra Gelbart, who make learning real. To Kristin Raeesi and Sonya Jasaroska, I am grateful for so many conversations and multiple reality-checks. I carry your voices with me, phenia.

There are no words to describe the debt I owe to Connie May Fowler, for her generous advice and contagious love of getting it right, and for the writing communities she sustains, especially the St. Augustine Writers conference and the Remembering Blue Novel Seminar, where *Eve's Garden* truly came to life. Alligator Point will always be a home of sorts for me, and my compatriots in the seminar, Terri Chastain, Tricia Bratton, Brad Kuhn, and Darlyn Finch Kuhn, will always be family. Connie May asked the question that led to an afternoon encounter with Evangeline along a dusty Florida road. This book flows from that point.

No writer can work comfortably without the support of family. I am fortunate to live with a husband and son who respect both our similarities and our differences; without their love and consideration, I would be smoldering debris.

I am fortunate also to share the twisted road with Pat Spears, Sandra Lambert, and our valiant publisher, Joan Leggitt. For fourteen years, I have enjoyed the support of my friends at Jane's Stories Press Foundation.

I have tried to put all these many gifts to good use. Where I have failed, the blame is mine alone.

GBM

Blossoms

Eve, 1973: The Garden

July's heat has boiled North Georgia into syrup dusted with dried red clay. Even the sky sweats, faintly blue at its crest, faded yellow-green around its rim, the color of work jeans washed so many times, the indigo and grease have formed a compromise.

Despite the swelter, this solitude is what I need. I finger the hard edge of the envelope in my pocket as a barn swallow slips across my path on the tar-sticky road.

"Hello, old friend. Come to watch me take the plunge?" The bird glides across our orchard, its grey wings blending, its red throat pulsing, against the hatched bark of persimmons. I follow, veering around the blackberry thicket, where my nightmares began. By the time I jump, landing on the far side of the ditch in the shadow of the orchard, the swallow has become a moving comma, dipping and soaring over the trees' waving limbs. Tangled, crooked branches spring out from the deep-cut trunks, embracing a chunk of sky the way my family revolves around my mother, whom everyone trusts, who holds the truth the way some people hold a dubious gift. All these years, I thought silence was her spear, when it was really the tent that sheltered us all.

Broom straw crunches underfoot and a crosswind whips my coat as I make my way through the labyrinth of cherries and peaches toward the ridge. When I reach the ring of firs guarding my grandmother's garden, the trees that bear the fruit of queens, I stop and slide my finger again across the crisp stationery in my pocket.

"Make your choices and live with them," said my friend. Trouble is, my choices—the people and places I love—are here, where I don't want to be. I am less a queen than a restless traveler in a still landscape.

Whirring wings thrash the air. The barn swallow flashes overhead, flits its tail once as if to lead me on, then disappears over the hill. By the time I gain the crest, it has tucked itself under the eaves of Grandmother's house, its "su-seer" whistling up the slope.

"I know, things look different from your perspective," I reply. When I reach the inner circle of firs and slowly turn to face the way I came, intending to celebrate having passed through the orchard without being overwhelmed by grief, a spark of iridescent wing— so different from the muted swallow—distracts me. The crow tracks toward the Tyndalls' clapboard walls, its mate hopscotching to a pokeweed patch along the ditch.

An old rhyme counting crows comes to mind:

One for sorrow. Two for joy. Three for a girl. Four for a boy. Five for silver. Six for gold. Seven for a secret never told.

A secret never told. Two secrets set me on this path, one ending in sorrow, one in joy. It has taken me years to solve the riddles. And now that I've unraveled them—what?

"Swallows mate for life," Dad said. They may fly anywhere, migrate thousands of miles, and still remain a team. And crows? No, crows stay put. They defend their nests and their territories from all comers. My mother has been our crow.

"Crows are good gardeners," Granny Burnett said to me once, when I was helping weed her corn. "They sow and reap very well."

Which am I, I wonder, a defender, a gardener? Crow or swallow? I don't know. If I did, I would have known earlier what to do about the man I love and how to think about the past in a way that doesn't twist my insides like the treetops pin-wheeling below me.

The crow calls from the west, where the Chinaberry rises golden-green over the Tyndalls' patched tin roof, its lower branches swooping to accommodate small climbers. Ears straining against the fickle wind, I can almost hear the chatter of girls from its leafy crown.

Evie, 1950: Fairy Tales

"Give me your hand, silly. I'll pull you up." A child reached down to me from the notch between two branches. Sunlight seeped through the leaves, melting into her eyes. At three, I knew about fairies from reading books with my dad, and I thought this girl in the tree might be one. A fairy, or a sprite.

Suddenly, my mother lifted me and I was flying, bare feet scrabbling for a hold. I reached out to grab a limb, anything, to stop my forward motion. Two little hands grasped my elbow and tugged me upward.

"Come on," the fairy giggled, an instant before I felt my body come to rest securely in the vee where she was braced, back against the rough bark. I looked down to see our moms below, laughing, their arms around each other's waists.

"I told you we were going to meet a friend, Evie. This is Beverly." My mother nodded toward the girl with eyes like leaves. A friend? I pulled a shoot off the tree's nearest arm and stuck it to the sprite's forehead. She giggled like a puddle splashing with rain. Maybe this wasn't so scary after all.

I pulled another leaf from the tree and plastered it above the three green eyes. Then laughter bubbled from my belly, too.

By the time I was five, I knew that Beverly wasn't a fairy, but she was a year older and more daring than me, and that was as good as having Tinker Bell for a companion.

My brother George, who was fourteen, couldn't be bothered. "Don't you know anything?" he'd say when I asked a question, ruffling my thick ponytail till it stood arched like a squirrel's tail.

Beverly had no brothers or sisters at all. "How'd you learn how to climb a tree?" I asked her once.

She slumped her shoulders toward her ears. "Dunno. Tried till I got it right."

I was her willing pupil. She taught me how to make dolls from string and cornstalks, and how to sneak cookies from her mother's kitchen, counting Willeen's steps down the hall to make our escape. Our existence was charmed, as long as we kept out of the way of my mother's sharp eyes and Carl's temper.

"Don't rile your Dad," was Willeen's constant admonition. The Chinaberry tree in the Tyndall's back yard provided perfect cover.

Yet when Willeen registered Beverly for first grade, we learned how far we lived from Fairyland.

"I'll run away and come live with you." Beverly hooked her legs over the branch below me, steadied herself with hands on either side of her hips, and flopped over, head jerking to a stop a few inches above the ground.

"Can't I wait for you at Granny's?" I stashed my doll in the notch farthest from Beverly's baby, who had a tendency to hit and knock others out of the tree. That left my hands free to place tiny cups into their rose-patterned saucers. We left one tea set stashed in a hollow knot on the first branch, ready for our weekly Saturday parties with our "babies." This was my favorite game, one Beverly consented to only if she could name the next. And her games were always exciting.

Like the day before. As usual, our moms had left us with Beverly's Granny Burnett while they worked the first shift. Granny shooed us through her feisty Rhode Island Reds and tried to keep us away from Old Fred, who lived in the south pasture of her farm. As soon as her back was turned, Beverly slipped inside the iron-framed gate and teased the bull, waving and stomping till he veered toward her at a gallop. Knees flexed, I waited at the entrance while she dashed out and slammed the gate behind us. Maybe next week, I would be brave enough to flag the bull myself.

Today's news threatened to put an end to all that.

I watched Beverly haul herself back up to sit on the branch opposite me. "Nope, you aren't going to Granny's in the mornings like we do now. They're gonna send you to some place in town, while I go to the country school. I heard Mama tell Dad about it last night." Again, she fell backward, head and arms sweeping out of sight.

Careful to move gently, so as not to wobble the teacups, I leaned over to watch her blonde hair trailing in the red dust. My mouth puckered with envy. Now that I was big, I could lift myself into the tree, but I hadn't yet had the nerve to hang by my knees. I called down to her. "You don't know the way to our house. You'll get lost. And your Dad will be mad."

Beverly knifed her knees toward her nose and flipped off the limb, nearly dashing all our crockery to the ground. "You cross the train tracks and go where you see the mill smoke." She brushed shaggy locks out of her eyes, bracing one foot against the trunk to climb back up. "And Dad's always mad. So what?"

"I'll ask my mom and dad. They'll do something." Confident that my parents could take care of anything, I poured rusty water into each cup, careful not to spill a drop.

⌘

Why couldn't I go to school with Beverly?

Dad scratched his thinning hair while he lugged a grocery bag up the steps and explained that a man from the School Board made that decision. Until I was old enough for first grade, I'd go to Miss Marva's kindergarten in town. "You'll learn to read better. Won't that be fun?"

"I want to learn with Beverly!" I screeched.

Dad dabbed at my tears with his handkerchief while Mom put away the food and started supper. She did not turn from rinsing potatoes at the sink to see my bottom lip poked out. "Go ahead— march right up to Superintendent Jackson's office and tell him you have to go to school with Beverly out in the country."

"I will!" I promised. Mom drove me over to the School Board building. On the third step, I looked at that long flight of stairs leading to the office and turned around, dragging my doll behind me to the car where Mom was waiting. "I think he's too busy today. I'll come back." I made my voice sound polite, as Mom always urged me to do.

"Whenever you want to come, I'll drive you." She swept our old Pontiac into gear and swung its nose toward the mill village.

On the first day of school, my father found Beverly scuffling up the road near our house. I was in awe of her courage, but by the time we drove up to the sagging front porch where Willeen and Carl waited, my parents had almost persuaded me to settle for seeing each other every Saturday.

"You'll both be busy with school," Mom reasoned, holding me by the shoulder in the front yard.

Beverly hollered while Carl dragged her up the steps by the elbow, "I don't want to live in the country with you!"

"Wait a minute, Maisie, Frank." Willeen turned and went into the house. My parents glanced at each other, then mounted the steps and sat down on the edge of the rocking chairs.

Within a minute, we learned that Carl meant to convince Beverly with a belt. Soon as I heard her scream, I ran inside and hovered outside her bedroom, wailing right along with her, ignoring my mother's calls. Sharp thwacks came through the closed door.

"Do something!" I urged my parents through the screen. Finally, my dad got up, came into the hall, and tried to pull me back toward the car.

I jerked my arm out of his grip. "You never hit me that hard!" My mom and dad at most gave me a swat on my behind for sins like running into the street.

I looked to the grown-ups for an explanation. Dad dug his hands into his pockets and stared at birds lining a telephone pole as if he could find an answer in their chatter.

My mother spun slowly and confronted me. "Evie, we cannot march into other people's houses and tell them what to do. Law says Carl has a right to discipline his daughter. She'll be all right, later. Come on, get in the car. Now."

Willeen came out with a box of canned tomatoes and handed them to Mom, then opened the screen door and slipped back inside. Mom put the tomatoes in the back seat and stood, hands on hips.

Beverly's screams had turned into whimpering. I held my hands over my ears and slid into the front seat, sobbing. We rode the dirt road home, me jostling between my parents' knees, all of us staring straight ahead out the windshield, until Dad spoke.

"You need to tell us if Beverly's planning something you know is wrong."

I squelched my sobs enough to answer him. "Why was it wrong? Carl's always mean to her. If you'd let her live with us, she wouldn't run away, and Carl couldn't hit her any more." Why didn't my parents see the matter as clearly as I did?

"Evie, what if Beverly had gotten hurt? Wouldn't you be sorry if you didn't tell us what she was doing?" When Mom agreed with Dad, I knew I'd better think again. They always stuck together.

"You want me to be a tattletale?" George had taught me that telling on others was the worst thing I could do. I never told on him, not even when he put firecrackers in Dad's toolbox and exploded it in the driveway.

"If we took Beverly, the police would take her back. And they might put us in jail. What good would it do you if Dad and I had to go to jail?" Mom had a point. Still, I couldn't see any sense in the way grownups figured right and wrong.

"You could get a … what do they call, them, Dad? A law—" I couldn't get my tongue to say the word Dad had just read me last week, something about men getting together to make rules for people.

"A lawyer." His tone made it seem like the word tasted bad in his mouth.

"Lawyers cost a lot of money." Mom patted my leg as she explained. Usually, her touch calmed me, but I was mad that it seemed all right to her for Carl to beat Beverly. She was a scaredy-cat. Otherwise, she would stop him. I lay down with my head in Dad's lap, drawing my feet up so they wouldn't rest against my mother's thigh, and listened to the road rumbling beneath us.

My parents probably thought I was asleep, and maybe I was, till I heard my mom's voice ring with irritation. "Willeen needs to work harder to keep Carl in line. She promised her mother to look after her. I don't see that letting Carl beat her is taking care."

Dad answered in a whisper. "I can't make Carl see the light. He's convinced she'll turn out like her mother." I snuggled against him, and then I did fall asleep, though not before wondering why Granny Burnett made Willeen promise, and why Carl wouldn't want Beverly to be like Willeen.

Whenever I thought I had my mother figured out, she surprised me. The next time Carl took out after Beverly, it was a Saturday. Frost nipped our legs in the Tyndall's bare front yard. Mom and Willeen huddled inside sweaters while they rocked on the Tyndalls' porch, sorting dress patterns. Beverly and I were gathering our toys, about to make a dash for the Chinaberry tree, when Carl came storming out of the small hutch he used for a workshop and grabbed Beverly by her gingham collar. With one hand, he prodded her toward the house, while he stripped his belt from his pant loops with the other.

"I told you to leave my tools alone," he snarled.

Left standing in the red dirt, my arms full of a tea set and two dolls, I looked to my mother in panic. For one long second, her deep olive eyes focused on me. Then she leaned over and whispered to Willeen, who got up quickly and clomped across the porch in her black oxfords, slamming the screen door behind her. Pretty soon Carl came out and huffed off in his pickup.

Willeen returned to her seat beside my mother, her jaw set. "He remembered some chore he had to do at church." She turned her attention to me. "Evie, Beverly won't be able to play today. She has to stay inside till dinner."

I tried to signal my gratitude to my mother by giving her a big, toothy grin. She didn't look my way as she picked up a pattern envelope and rifled through it. "We'll go in a minute, Evie, soon as I find the bodice piece for Willeen."

When the women were engrossed once more in their discussion, I unstuck my feet from the clay and sidled around the house. Beverly was waiting for me at the window to her bedroom.

"What happened?" I whispered.

She leaned her nose into the saggy screen, making a rough impression in its rusty wires. "I borrowed his big knife to cut vines so we could swing in the tree. I was going to show you when he jerked my head off."

"You used a knife? We're not supposed to touch sharp tools!"

"Next time I'll make sure to put it back right where I found it. I didn't cry. Mama made him stop." Beverly shrugged and pushed the screen out further with her fists.

I thought about telling her that Mom had said something to make Willeen spring into action, but I thought better of it. Mom didn't want me to brag.

"Does it hurt?" I touched the outline her nose had made in the screen.

"Nope. He only got in a lick or two. 'Sides, I'm a big girl." Beverly crooked her arm to show me her muscles. Maybe those weren't tears making her eyes shine.

She was even braver than my mother, to take Carl's licking without crying. "Well, I won't ever tell on you," I vowed.

To my mom I muttered a thank you as we got in the car.

"For what?"

The sharpness in her voice made me hesitate, but finally I said, "For helping Beverly."

"It's not a good idea to get involved in other's people's family problems. Unless you have to." She turned her attention to the road, clearly finished with the topic.

Even her graces she preferred to go unnoticed.

After that, we saw fewer stripes on Beverly's legs. Still, we took care to avoid Carl, playing as high in the Chinaberry as we could climb. Inside, we stuck to her bedroom, or to the kitchen, if Willeen and Granny were cooking.

We devised a campaign of sulking until our mothers promised that we could have sleepovers almost every Friday, all year long, and in the summers we could spend two weeks of Bible Camp at our Methodist Church, followed by two weeks at the Tyndall's Holiness Vacation Bible School. On holidays, and Saturdays when the mill was running, Granny Burnett would still pick us up and take us to her farm.

"Is it a deal?" I eyed my mother, hesitant to accept the truce.

"It's a deal." Mom stared back, her eyes steady. She'd never broken a promise yet.

Beverly's shrug put an end to our agitation. "Running away wasn't likely to work, anyway. Not till you have a car, I guess."

I resigned myself to facing school alone.

If it were not for the chill on a September morning when I was seven, I might not have discovered the hole in my mother's heart.

"She's excited. It's her first time helping with the harvest." Dad tilted his wood chair back on its legs and nodded at my half-eaten breakfast.

"Go get your sweater. It'll be cool." Mom cleared away my plate. Crumbs from my toast and jam lay on the stoneware next to an untouched mound of scrambled eggs, yet she didn't scold me. I hopped down from my seat and ran for my room, afraid Dad and my aunts would leave without me, and I would miss my chance to climb the ladder—"First rung only!" my father had answered to my plea—and eat persimmons fresh off the tree. Once the orange fruits came into the house, they were reserved for the jelly my mom doled out to us and gave away as presents only to people she really liked, unlike the jars of cherry and peach preserves that went to all our neighbors and acquaintances.

On my way back to the kitchen, I spied the locket on my mother's dresser. Usually, she wore it around her neck, mostly hidden underneath her clothes. I had just clicked it open to the two portraits framed inside, when I heard a gasp behind me. Mom stood in the doorway, drying her hands on her apron. The gesture became a wringing motion that went on for minutes while I wondered how much trouble I was in. Then she walked slowly to the bed and sat down.

"Bring it over here," she said. I sank down beside her and handed her the locket. "That's my mama and papa. Your grandparents." Her voice seemed to catch a little. I peered at the yellowed photos inside the golden bezel. Down my grandmother's back trailed a mass of shiny, dark locks. On the other side, my grandfather seemed paler, more ordinary.

"The ones who made the orchard?"

Mom nodded. "They're gone," she whispered.

There was something about Gramma's swooping brows that reminded me of both my mother and myself. And her hair resembled my own dark, clotted curls, but perhaps it didn't have the red sparks I shared with Mom. I could see our eyes weren't the same. For mine were grey, almost as clear as glass, except for some coppery bits. The eyes in the photograph glistened like the jet beads on my Aunt Tally's bracelet, the one she let me play with when I got fussy. I glanced at Mom's face, every feature pressed together like the leaves of a book, her olive eyes a note withheld, and knew I shouldn't ask more.

She snapped the locket closed, brushed off her apron, and rose. Her voice was not cross, though it wound tight as she sent me to help load baskets into the truck. She turned at the door. "Your Grampa James planted those trees for your Gramma Evangeline, brought them down from her folks' place in the mountains. Be careful."

Careful with the trees or careful not to get hurt? I wasn't sure which she meant. I could think of about a million more questions, but I scurried to do as I was told.

My aunts worked from the far end of the orchard row, while my dad and I moved steadily toward them, me picking the low-hanging branches and scouring the ground for fruit that had no worms or smooshy parts as Dad picked from the middle rungs of the ladder. Midway down the line, he stopped and sipped water from a Mason jar, wiped the brim with his white handkerchief, and handed it down to me. I drank, then put an orange-brown berry into my mouth and bit down. That first taste of persimmon made me pucker—sharp, at once juicy and fleshy, almost a perfect balance between bitter and sweet. I held a small amount on the tip of my tongue, exploring the tingly taste and bumpy texture. You could either love raw persimmons or hate them. I loved them.

"I want to live out here and eat these all the time." I grinned at
Dad and popped another between my teeth. "Why doesn't Mom want
to come with us?"

He resumed picking. "Can't make a living out here, Hon. Mr.
Applewhite bought all but ten acres from us. Not enough left to farm.
Don't like the country much, anyway." I waited for him to answer my
question. He moved the ladder to the next tree and climbed up to a
branch full of golden balls.

So I thought about it while watching my flame-haired Aunt Talitha
hike up her skirt and pin it between her knees as she leaned over to
dump her small pail into Aunt Vinnie's bigger bucket. They reminded
me of a picture I'd seen of two curly-haired girls sifting sand at the
beach. Only Aunt Vinnie was mopping sweat from under her auburn
hair and bickering amiably, as usual, with her sister. "Tally, if you only
pick a half-pail every hour, we'll never get done."

Idly, I tracked a caterpillar making its lazy way up a trunk. My
fingers snagged on the unevenly patched bark, which brought to mind
the sideways quirk in my mother's smile when I'd asked her if she were
coming with us. She simply shook her head and the smile disappeared
from her bow-shaped lips.

Silence did not apply to her snappish sisters. They talked about
their younger days, mostly about picking berries, or Ruv, the old
Greyhound they'd owned, or dishes their mother made. Mom mostly
listened, a faraway look on her face.

And there was something else. When they thought I was out of
hearing, they slipped into a language I didn't know.

"Just some words our mother brought from the mountains," my
aunts would say when I suddenly entered a room. "Ask your mother,"
was their answer, if I asked for a translation.

"Oh, it's an old saying," Mom would say.

Three against one is not even odds.

Yet, when I didn't tell about Beverly planning to run away, my parents had said you shouldn't keep secrets. Surely, this was a secret about my grandparents and whatever made my mother so sad? My mom, who insisted I "do the right thing," wasn't telling something she knew, something I was pretty sure was awfully important.

"Mom doesn't tell the truth, so why do I have to?" I hadn't meant to say it out loud. A long silence told me I had. Looking up, I saw my dad with his hand nearly touching a ripe orange persimmon, staring, not at me, but at my aunts. They looked at each other like this right before someone told me off and sent me to my room.

I waited for someone to tell me to stop sassing. Quiet, broken only by bee hum. Like they had forgotten how to talk. My aunt Tally was … crying? No, that was probably anger in her eyes. It came out of her mouth cold and flat. "Not telling everything you know is not the same as telling a lie."

Her voice struck me like an icicle. Something bubbled through my chest and soured my stomach. Hot water splattered on my eyelashes. Aunt Vinnie grabbed me up and cuddled me tight. I blinked with confusion. My aunts often disagreed, usually not when I had done something wrong. Yet here was Vinnie whispering fiercely in my ear, "Your mother loves you within an inch of your life. Don't you ever forget it. Anything she does, she does for you."

I wrapped my arms around her and buried my head in her hair, letting the sun penetrate my lashes enough to create a vivid red blur through her soft curls. Of course, my mother loved me. But why didn't she tell me about my grandparents?

Dad always seemed to know what I meant. He leaned close to my face so I could see his clear blue eyes. "Your mom loves this orchard because her parents planted it. She misses them, that's all. Now, don't you go asking her about it. It makes her sad to talk about that time."

Tangled in a warm web of love, I lay against my aunt's shoulder and let questions float around me like insects struggling against the mysterious spinner at its center. Mom's words both held and snared me. *They're gone.* Where did they go? All around me, fruit lay rotting in the late sun.

Evangeline, 1919: Roots

As we clatter down Rabun Bald, I keep looking back to watch the persimmons swaying in the wagon bed.

"Thank you for bringing the trees from home."

Mr. James, beside me on the seat, nods and aims his blue eyes straight ahead.

We spoke little to each other, even after my mother accepted his offer. I was too busy to get to know him, while I bathed her and pressed her to drink Aunt Juba's healing tea. And then, once Mama gave her last breath to the still meadow air, there was the journey to think about. Now, here we are, together, jostling down this mountain, no other living beings for miles around. Except for the hens I brought in Papa's old rabbit cage, the trees, and Papa's horse, tied behind the wagon. And Ruv.

I hurried so, to say goodbye to the folks in the cemetery behind Grandpa's smithy, and to gather what I could carry from the cabin, that I almost forgot Ruv. He bounded out from the barn as I stacked baskets and burlap bags in the wagon bed. I guess he had his own goodbyes to make. I planned to take him onto the seat beside me, but when I saw the frown on Mr. James's face, I pushed Ruv back down, signaling him to follow. And he did, loping easy as a deer to the wheels' pace, his long Greyhound legs pounding gracefully behind us.

Now, I sense him gone, so I look back. Birds flush from a copse away from the road. There's Ruv, cantering back to our trail, a rabbit in his teeth. I look back again, and the quarry has disappeared. Only a faint scrim of blood shows around his jaw.

Greyhounds will keep you in meat if times are hard. With my father, Ruv brought down deer and wild boar, dragging the carcasses home in a harness Papa rigged. A rabbit is no more than a mouthful to him. He will hunt more when we make camp.

Again, I look around and cannot see the dog for many minutes. I try not to cry out, but Mr. James senses my concern. In a moment, he halts the wagon, climbs down, and begins to check the horses' hooves for stones, though I felt no change in their gait.

I get down from the seat by myself and amble back to look for Ruv, as if seeking a place to relieve myself. I find him just around a curve in the forest, nursing a stone out of his paw. He limps with me to the wagon, where I dig out some salve from the saddlebag, and plaster the bloody spot where his teeth teased out the intruder. Mr. James busies himself about the team, until I climb back onto the seat. Ruv resumes his place behind the wagon.

A short time later, we stop beside a little stream. Mr. James hands me down. I place my hand on his shoulder, steadying myself, and feel a tremor go through him. Is he afraid of me? A man of thirty, scared by a sixteen-year-old girl? Those blue eyes—not all blue, but lightly gray, like a summer sky gathering clouds—are hard to read. Where do you come from? I wonder. Where did he come from? I had not thought to ask.

I jump lightly to the ground. He looks surprised, perhaps thinking I might float down to touch the earth. After a moment, he claps his black hat on his sleek brown hair, thin fingers sweeping the brim.

"We'll stop here for dinner. Do you need a fire?" He nods toward the wagon bed, where I have stowed inside burlap bags every ham left in the smokehouse, and all the canned goods we can fit. I didn't want the wolves and neighbors to get them. In one basket rests the cold chicken Mrs. Garretson gave us this morning. I lift it out and place it beside a bag of potatoes on the ground.

At my elbow, Mr. James still waits. I nod, figuring he likes his meals hot, or he would not ask. I will have to guess at everything, for he does not talk much.

I've known quiet men before. My cousin Paulo could be silent like this, barely lifting his head when Papa spoke to him. He would sit down beside the fire and not speak a word for an hour, but that felt all right. He would point to a bird nesting in a hedge, or a cloud scudding over the crest of a hill. He was *with* you. This one, I'm not sure where he goes in his head, but he goes there alone.

I bustle to find my pots in the jumble of baskets and rolled blankets in back of the wagon. I don't want him to think he has struck a bad bargain. My mind wanders to what else he may expect, but I straighten my neck like a proud romni. Mama would not give me away to a bad man, not even with her lying there gasping for breath. I prepare the meal, thinking about the last few days.

The night he came to our door, hat in hand, seeking a meal, I could see he was poor. On his way to a new church, he said, where the people had promised a small farm to make his living on while he preached for them. I looked over his shoulder toward the Garretsons' place. Mr. Garretson had already paid his daily visit to check on us. When my eyes returned to the stranger's face, I saw nothing but patience in his blue eyes. My papa always told us, take a chance on a doctor or a preacher, if you have to choose.

"You can stay in the barn." Afraid he would think me unkind, I added, "My mama is sick. She doesn't sleep well."

He looked through the open door to the bedroom, where he could clearly see my mama, her face pale, hands slack against the coverlet, the blue-threaded one she had made herself as a bride. *Even a blind man can smell the death in this house*, I thought. He stood, silent, near the door, while I went to the kitchen.

I came back and laid a sandwich on the table. He took it, along with his hat. "I reckon that bay horse I saw on my way in and that cow could use a little hay." He held onto the leather tie we used for a lock, so the closing door wouldn't make a sound.

The next morning, when I came out to feed the hens, I found him sitting on the porch step. "I gave them some corn." He tilted his head toward the hen house, but did not even glance my way as he rose. "I'll chop some wood now."

I made another sandwich and left it on the porch, along with a glass of cold milk from the tin pail that I found there, the freshly-drawn cream rising already to the top.

As Mama lay dying, he stayed to help, days after his new congregation expected him. On the second day, Mr. Garretson showed up before noon to bring me some corn meal. The stranger and he shook hands, their eyes wary.

When Mr. Garretson stared pointedly at me while the preacher turned away, I shrugged. "He's a preacher. His horse needs another day's rest."

Our neighbor frowned. "Maybe you should come to our house. We'll carry your mama, too. I promised your brothers I'd look out for you. I'd have been here earlier, if the plowing hadn't taken so long."

I smiled to let him know I understood that a man can't be in two places, though it made me sad to think how impossible it would be to do as he suggested. "It hurts Mama when I change her bedclothes. She wouldn't survive a move. We're okay. There's no harm in him. He'll soon be on his way." Even as I spoke, I knew my brothers would not accept such an excuse for being alone with a man who wasn't related. Why wasn't I worried?

Mr. Garretson stalked away toward my mama's room. He returned, shaking his head. My mother must have told him she wasn't worried, either. Grumbling about checking with his missus, Mr. Garretson ambled away.

Only once did the preacher speak to me about anything other than chores.

I had come out on the porch for some fresh air and to get a look at the full moon rising over the creek, where Papa and my brothers liked to fish. I did not even see him sitting there, until he spoke. I swung around to find his face gleaming in the shadows.

"This farm's been looked after well."

I waited, but he said no more.

How much should I explain? I wondered. "My brothers worked the farm while my Papa ran the blacksmith shop." I nodded toward the small building alongside the barn. The stranger held his pipe in one pale hand and waited.

"The police arrested Papa in New Orleans for fighting with a gad—" I stopped myself from using the Romani word for outsiders" —with a drunk man who grabbed me and tried to pull me into a bar. Only Papa never hit the man. He tried to reason with him while my brothers pulled me away. The drunk swung at Papa and missed and fell face first on the floor, but he told the officers that Papa gave him the black eye when he wouldn't give him money. My brothers brought me home. When Papa didn't return after a few weeks, the oldest, Tomas, went with some folks we know who came by on their way West. They were hoping that together they could get Papa out of jail." I didn't mention Aunt Juba or the others in the caravan, or that they took along money to bribe the jailer, if they had to. Eight months had passed since they left.

Still the stranger waited, taking one long pull at his pipe.

"When Tomas, too, stayed away—" I stopped. What must he think of my family leaving us alone here? Yet what choice did my brothers have?

"The other brother went to find them both?" His voice was gentle. "So you been working the place by yourself?" The pipe in his hand sent a long stream of smoke flickering over the porch railing.

I was embarrassed by the praise he hinted. "The Garretsons next door helped with the rest of the crop, and Mr. Garretson took it to mill for me. It's been enough." *Till now*, I thought, but didn't say it. Still, I reckoned he could see the hay getting low and no new crop set in the field.

We didn't talk much more after that, just pleasantries and the weather, but I felt his eyes on me whenever I made his meals. He didn't make me feel dirty, like that drunk in New Orleans. That had been the only time I went with Papa and the boys to a wedding party. My mama was too frail to travel, so she raised me settled. I wished I'd never gone.

One morning, a few days later, I came into the bedroom and found the preacher man kneeling beside the old spindled bed. Mama looked so small, shrunken, under the bedclothes. Her hands rested on his head as if *she* were blessing *him*. She lifted her dark eyes like burning embers to look at him, and I could see the centers already growing dim. She said one word. "Yes." He rose quickly, without looking at me, and left the room.

"Come here, Evangeline." I knelt on the bare planks beside Mama's bed, and she blessed me, too, her long hands cupping my face. I hated to see her beautiful hair, once thick and red-tinged like a maple in autumn, now spread--dry and brittle--over the linen pillowcase. I stroked her beautiful fingers, the only part of her still fleshy and full.

"Your father may not be back for years. You are brave —" She shook her head, just a little, when I started to protest, and coughed for several minutes, while I held her hands. "—but a romni alone on a farm? The gadje will come and take everything from you. Better to belong to a gadjo who knows God than to one of them young soldiers who only drink and tell war stories. When your grandpa settled here, he thought they would get used to us—" Her rasping breath barely stirred the bedcovers.

I tried to make her stop talking. "Mama, I can take Papa's horse and go find Aunt Juba and my brothers. Don't fret. I will dress in Papa's clothes...." I babbled, saying anything to keep her from worrying.

With her outstretched hand, she gestured toward the big mahogany chiffarobe in the corner. I could guess what she wanted me to fetch. Opening the burnished wood door, I reached in for the small chest carved of rosewood and ivory, and brought it back to the bed. Mama opened it, brought out her heavy gold roped chain with its oval locket. She thrust it into my hands. "Your papa will no longer be o baro rom. Leaders aren't supposed to get in trouble with the law. He may not be able to find a good rom for you. And he may not return for a long while. ... Take this and Papa's vest with the gold buttons. Go with the preacher. Make him a good wife. It is the only way." She coughed until she was too weak to speak.

The next evening, Mama asked us to take her to the meadow where the wildflowers bloomed. The preacher man carried her like she was a great bouquet and laid her gently on the blue-threaded coverlet I had spread on the ground. She told me once that on her wedding night she and Papa had danced in this meadow, kicking up fireflies from the grass. Now they flew toward a crescent moon that came rising over the hill.

Like a good romni, she met her Maker underneath a sky just turning dusky with stars. "Ash Devlésa, shey." Stay with God, Daughter. She breathed those words to me and said no more.

My nose leads me back to the basket Mrs. Garretson brought. If the hens mind being packed side by side with a dead one of their kind, they make no more noise than usual. I check the damp burlap around the cuttings I took from Mama's pomegranate trees, add some more water, and resettle them among the persimmons.

As I gather greens to place in the pot with the chicken and potatoes, I try to guess where my family is. One day my brothers may return from the West. They will bring back the farm and make the smithy glow. Or else they will sell it and go back to the new life they have found. What will they say when they find our mama gave me in marriage to a gadjo, an outsider? Will they be kind, like Vashti Garretson?

I walked over to tell her about Mama's death and that I would marry the preacher. Vashti hesitated only a minute before offering her parlor to us. And there we stood this morning, him in his one good shirt and his black coat, me in the cherry red dress Mama made for me last winter, saying our vows to the Justice of the Peace who lives down the hill. I was so nervous I hardly listened to the words. Mr. James paid the man a dollar and drank whiskey with him and Mr. Garretson in the front room. Vashti took me into the kitchen, brought out a bottle of sherry, and gave me a thimbleful.

"You're a married woman now. I guess you can have a little liquor." She looked soberly at me for a moment before lifting her own glass. "Sastimos!" She said it softly, firmly, like she gave me a blessing instead of wishing me health.

I smiled.

Only then did she let herself smile. "You know about my mother?"

"Mama told me not to mention it unless you did. And now here I've gone and done the thing that made your mama marimé—I married a gadjo. I wish I knew what my Papa would say." The wine suddenly tasted bitter. I put down the glass on the pecan sideboard.

Vashti reached out to cup my elbow. "Your mother did not shun me, though she knew the kris that ruled against my mother sent us away because they didn't trust my father. Still, no rom here would marry me, till John came to visit from down South. Your father is the baro rom here. Surely he would not ban his own daughter for marrying outside the group?"

I shook my head. "I don't know. I only know that Papa said I must do as Mama wants. She thought perhaps he would not be baro anymore, even if he returned." I swallowed hard and tried to see in Vashti's eyes the answer to the question that tumbled from my lips. "I think for a gadjo, he is not bad?"

My neighbor looked toward the parlor like she could see through the walls. "You've married a good man. He must have seen a lot, being a traveling preacher, yet he's gentle and careful with you." She cocked her head and peered at me. "Are you afraid of what may happen tonight? Did your mother tell you what to expect?"

I nudged the wine glass with my finger. "Mama talked to me about how to remain pure so that evil did not visit my family and about giving birth. About how to run a household and be clever with money. I wish she had told me more about … well, about what takes place between husbands and wives." In my family, sex was an open secret. We knew from the time we were little that men and women loved each other in bed, but no one discussed exactly what they did. "I'm sure my mother thought there would be more time to tell me."

Vashti drew me to a seat at her table. "Ask me, Evangeline, whatever you want. I've only been married two years myself, but I reckon I know enough."

I stammered, "Will it hurt? And how exactly do I make him happy?"

"Well, you can start out letting him look as much as he likes. You may feel embarrassed, at first, but you're beautiful, so why wouldn't he be happy?" Vashti advised me to let my husband show me what he wanted. "It's simple, really. Let him guide your movements. If he's gentle, it will only hurt a little the first time, and, after that, you may find you like it. I do." She looked directly at me, her eyes so soft that I believed every word she said.

Mr. James appeared in the doorway. "We'd better go if we're to get down the mountain before dark." He twirled his hat in his hands. It made me feel a little better to see that he looked nervous, too.

"I'm ready," I said, and rose. My legs shook, but they held me. Vashti hugged me tightly, for a long time. Eventually, Mr. James cleared his throat, and I turned. Together, we three walked out to the wagon piled high with our things.

My eyes weighed the goods we would bring with us. I realized I would never see again my mother's clock with its lovely golden chime or the lacquered table my papa had built from the walnuts that grow along our creek. Or the creek itself, its willows swaying on a moonlit night. My vision blurred as I looked toward the cemetery where Mama lay.

I gave Vashti our cow. She's far behind me now, along with everything else I have ever known.

❦

Stirring the stew helps me tear my mind away from those I left behind, those in the old graveyard, those traveling somewhere out beyond these mountains.

Ruv barks nearby. I note he waits at the edge of the clearing until the preacher man brushes past him, carrying a rabbit with the dog's teeth marks still evident on its neck. So Ruv let him take the game. The man comes over to the fire and gently lays the rabbit next to me, on a burlap bag I had spread out to hold my spoons.

I did what Mama said. I married him.

I'm his, now. This is the only way.

❦

The first time we lay together, Mr. James would not even look me in the face, though he gathered me up when he was finished and held me as you would a doll. I felt like I was drowning in a bottomless river, my breath crushed. I held on to him, and he to me, and we rocked together, stranded on some invisible sea.

Now, with our child tickling inside my womb, it's as if we've made a pact to start over, the two of us. I think he may have been in the War, for there's a long ugly mark that slashes from his right hip down to his knee, and sometimes he mutters in his sleep in a language I can't understand. Short, sharp barks, like giving orders. All he's told me is that he came down the New River on a longboat from someplace in Ohio.

The words "Roma" and "Gypsy" have never passed my lips to him, nor his to me. The most he has asked is whether I was raised Christian. Mr. James has no notions about race. He believes every word in that Good Book of his applies to all of us, and trusts that others will follow it, the way he does. If they don't, he is sure a good talking-to will bring them to the Light.

The day we first came, the farm was overgrown with saplings and bracken, and the house fairly crawled with field mice. Not a crop set in any field. We had no livestock, except the few hens I brought, and Papa's horse. We survived the first year on Mama's hams, the game Ruv brought in, and the vegetables I could harvest quickly. We used the hens' eggs sparingly, so the flock could increase, and now we have both the eggs and occasional pullets.

As soon as I had the house in order, I set about putting in an herb and vegetable garden near the house, using a rusty hoe I found in the barn to break clods. Mr. James planted the persimmons on the southern slope of our hill. The pomegranates are growing into saplings under a hay mulch near the barn, until I can find the perfect spot for them. They need sunshine and shelter from harsh winds. Mr. James says he'll add cherries and peaches to the orchard as we can afford them, or, if we can, get seedlings from neighbors.

That first day of digging the herb garden, the stubborn dirt had all my attention, until a man appeared around the corner of the cabin, a small fellow with a reddish mustache and one droopy eye. I brushed the dirt from my face and extended my hand to him, but he didn't take it. His eyes moved from my face to the diklo tied over my hair. Then, without saying anything at all to me, he put down some seed packets and a bag of potatoes by the back door and left.

I had seen him at my first church service here, but I didn't learn till later that he was Peter Dockhart, our closest neighbor.

My biggest concern was the women in the church. I needed them to like me so our life here would be peaceful. The night before his first sermon, I spoke to Mr. James about what we could expect.

"The women may not accept me." I ventured a word while he still had his back turned to me. He never undresses facing the bed. I make sure to get my nightgown on before he comes into the little room off the kitchen that we use for sleeping. Vashti's advice aside, I think Mr. James feels better about what we do if he cannot see me clearly.

"They'll like you well enough when they come to know you." He took off the silver cross he wears every day and hung the chain over the slat of a chair.

"You know what I mean. " He stood listening, trousers unbuttoned, but held in place by his big, careful hands. "What if they reject you because of me?" I said to his back. If they turned us away, I had decided, I would urge him to go west to find my brothers. Roma might not refuse a romni, even with a gadjo husband. And there are plenty Roma who like a good sermon.

Mr. James let his pants drop and slid quickly under the quilt before facing me. "They will see what I see. A woman doing God's work."

"What do you know about God's work for women?" I took a chance on teasing him. He waved his right hand at me. The long scar where the boar tusked him gleamed in the light from the small window, whiter than the mark on his leg.

He and Ruv broke into the cabin that day, his cheeks pale and his shirt, soaked with blood, wrapped around his right arm. I had stared dumbly for a minute, never having seen his bare chest in the light before. Then I walked quickly to him and unwrapped the shirt. The wound ran deep.

I made him lie down and cleaned the jagged cut where the animal had splayed open the skin. He gasped once as the alcohol drenched the slash. "Can you hold still if I stitch it?" He did, making one groan only when the needle first bit into the red under-flesh. I ground sage leaves, St. John's Wort, and bayberry into a paste, which I made into a poultice dampened with ginger brew, and plastered it over the swollen ridges. Throughout the night, and for the next few days, I changed the dressing every three hours or so. Ginger tea mixed with ground ginseng root helped to strengthen him.

He now waved the hand in front of my face. "It never got infected. God sends us the knowledge to save us, and the people to use the knowledge." I pushed my face into the pillow, pleased that he valued the woods lore that Aunt Juba had taught me.

And he was right, to a degree. Some of the women are still suspicious, but most have learned I can be useful. I make my poultices and tonics for them, too. But I thought they would never warm up. I could hear their buzz behind me each Sunday as I walked down the aisle and took my place in the front pew.

In the beginning, when I came to Bible study, no one spoke to me. The second time, Mrs. Dockhart, leading the discussion, pointedly stared my way, talking about the heathen who resists God. "God said the wicked would deny him, and so they do, keeping their own ways. Worshipping idols."

I stood under the wooden cross hanging over the door. My knees knocked under my skirts, but I knew I had to answer her or slink away, so I rose and said, "My grandparents came from Scotland. My family has been Christian from far back. We lived in a little community that didn't have a church, but Mama led Bible study every Sunday, and sometimes we had visiting preachers." I sat back down.

I didn't mention that my mother also kept the old ways, bringing herbs and flowers in from the woods to lay at the feet of Sara e Kali and photos of our ancestors. Or that my father felt the best church was God's earth. The whole truth is not always needed to bring people to the light. And worshipping one god does not prevent one from honoring others.

After that, some of the women smiled politely at me as they left service. Mary Avery even asked me to help her with the littlest ones during the sermon. Still, some, like Mrs. Dockhart, whisper behind my back. Their uncertainty about what I am keeps them from doing worse. Only Mary and Sissy Applewhite, who live close by, have become friends of sorts, trading recipes and fruit from our trees and sometimes bringing their children for me to watch while they drive into town with their husbands.

Only one woman—Hilda Redding, the storekeeper's wife—had the nerve to ask me if I told fortunes, too. That's how I knew some had guessed what I am. I replied kindly to her, though I wanted to make her hold out her palm then and there, so I could spit into it. "No, none of the women in my family read fortunes for strangers." I fixed her with a cold eye to see if she would redden. She did.

Truth is, Aunt Juba and some of the other women I know will read your fortune, if you offer them money. But they will tell you only what you could see yourself, if you watched yourself as carefully as they do.

Evie, June, 1958: Secrets and Dreams

"Why don't you look it up?" Beverly said. "You know a few words." She pointed in the direction of the public library as we passed it on our way to buy new saddle oxfords at Rutherford's. My mom and Willeen had given us money and told us to get shoes while they shopped for groceries.

I stared down at the scraped toes of my summer slippers and thought of the warm smell of oiled leather at Rutherford's. "Yeah, I figured out a few. Dosta! That's the sound Mom made when Vinnie poured too much sugar into the jam, the same word she uses when Tally makes her laugh so hard she cries. I figure it means 'Stop!' or maybe 'Enough!' Can we make it to the library *and* the shoe store before ten?"

"Never know till you try! C'mon, Headlights!" Beverly dashed off across the square in the direction of the library.

"Stop calling me that!" Fearful someone would hear, I hissed into the vacuum she left behind as she flew. Two boys zipped by on bikes as I scurried to keep up.

Beverly slowed up long enough to fling another taunt, this time in a stage whisper. "Well, you don't have breasts yet, but you've got those big ole grey eyes like car lamps." She circled her eyes with her thumbs and forefingers as she ran backward. It's a wonder she didn't tumble into the junipers around the Civil War cannon.

She was too fast for me to catch, so I slowed my pace and fumed. This past year, in eighth grade, my status all through grade school as "Teacher's Pet" had changed into a nickname with a more hateful tint: I heard "Professor Know-it-All" in the halls more frequently than my real name. "Headlights," if it fell into the hands of some of the meaner boys, would finish me for good as a freshman.

Beverly waited for me on the top marble step of the courthouse basement, where they kept the books. One look at my face told her she'd gone too far. "I'm sorry, Evie. I was joking. I'd never call you that in front of … them." She nodded at the boys parking their bikes under the nearby elm, chatting about some baseball game, apparently oblivious to us. I realized with relief that I didn't know them.

The big walnut doors opened to a wall of lemon-scented shelves, the air a swirl of glittery dust. I headed for the alcove facing the stairs, where a row of dictionaries lay open like mammoth bones in the sun. This was my territory. "Maybe Italian, like the folks who live out past the orchard. You know, the ones who work at the quarry?" I started with the first tome, checking every spelling I could imagine. Nothing. Not French. Or Spanish. Definitely not German.

The rail-thin librarian shook her head at me when I asked if she recognized anything in my notes, then went back to typing out titles on manila note cards.

"Maybe it's a language they made up," Beverly offered as we exited the shoe store.

"Yeah. It's an idea, anyway." I brushed a tiny mark from the toe of my new brown oxfords. "Don't think I've forgiven you. If you call me that again, I'll make up a name you'll never live down." She tossed her hair. We both knew I could do it. And that I wouldn't, anymore than she would shout that ridiculous nickname to the world.

"Evie, don't eavesdrop." Mom almost always knew when I lurked around the hall corner. Ever since the library search, though, I had vowed to solve the mystery, lingering within hearing distance every time my aunts visited.

The best way was to work alongside them and hope one of them let something slip.

Because her husband, Uncle Milt, owned an appliance store, Aunt Tally didn't have to work at the mill, like Vinnie and my mom, but all three sisters kept big gardens, and one of them always needed help processing the excess piles of zucchini and cucumbers and onions. And there was the orchard fruit, too much for any one set of hands. All of it made its way to our house for paring parties.

I'd come from school into a flood of earth scents and chatter that was half-English, half-whatever-it-was. They'd stop speaking when I entered. My mom would greet me, then shift her attention to whatever task lay to hand. Aunt Vinnie would purse her rosebud mouth, while Aunt Tally's brightly painted lips became a zippered bag to which she couldn't find the key. Three against one. Always.

Still, I was eager to lend a hand, hoping for some nugget to fall into the conversation. Rarely, I'd be rewarded.

"Yek," Tally might, say, holding up her pitiful harvest of one misshapen eggplant or oversized tomato. Or Vinnie might murmur, "nice tookay" when Mom passed her a cloth to dry her hands. *One. Thank you.* My phonetic list grew.

For a while, I considered we might be Jewish, like the Pearsons, who ran the department store. They didn't hide, though some folks talked about them as if they should. I'd heard they had to go all the way to Anderson to go to synagogue. Besides, our prodigious consumption of ham seemed to argue against it. Something always stopped me from showing my list to my teachers. If Mom and my aunts took so much trouble to keep it from me, there must be a reason.

As for details about my grandparents, they were sparse.

"She came from up around Towns County in the mountains," Mom told me. And then sent me to ask Dad to come to supper. When Mom said a topic was finished, that was it. Disobeying resulted in long stares from both of my parents and an even lengthier period of silence, during which I was asked to reconsider in my room. I did not disobey, at least not intentionally.

Once, I caught Aunt Vinnie on a particularly loquacious day. "Papa was a preacher. In fact, the church that Beverly goes to now was his, once. Of course, it was Methodist, then, like him. He used to preach all over the hills, though." Turning my head in surprise to see how my mom would react to this cast-off gem, I caught a nod from her to my aunt, as if to say, *Good. Stop there.*

If I tried to drag more details out of them, both my aunts shook their reddish curls and replied as one. "We don't remember. You'll have to ask your mother if you want to know more." Both of them, buttoned up tighter than my last year's winter coat. My mother was their unquestioned leader. She was like a big closet with no light inside. Anything you found you touched by accident, and, even then, you were lucky if she acknowledged it. My aunts were the hinges that made the door swing tight. Just once, I longed to be let in for more than a peek.

Once we outgrew tea parties and tagging bulls, figuring out what the grownups weren't telling us was a favorite game for Beverly and me.

The weekend before my first day in high school, we were returning from taking some tomatoes to one of the Tyndalls' neighbors when Beverly veered into our orchard. She bounced on her heels and squinted at the fruit trees climbing the slope. "How come your mom keeps this place? I mean, you'd think she'd sell it."

I took the plum she offered. "You know they don't tell me much."

Beverly scratched through her layers of thick, blonde waves and kept bouncing. "Because your grandparents died? Heck, Mama and Granny are always going on about Grandpa John and Gramma Myrtle, what they wore, what foods they liked, boring stuff like that."

I picked two more plums and tossed one her way. "Aunt Vinnie says words are like dollars to Mom." A ladybug tickled my arm. I

brushed her carefully into my palm and set her on the ground.
"Gramma grew herbs, I think. Tally and Vinnie are always going on
about how to make some remedy, or that stew with Gramma's special
spices."

Beverly flopped onto the parched grass. She was wearing her
junior cheerleader tee shirt, the one she'd gotten at the end of cheer
camp. Two whole weeks out of our summertime for a camp I couldn't
attend. Too clumsy. I turned away to examine a caterpillar crawling
up a milkweed stem, scolding myself for hoping my friend would get
grass stains on her shirt and never be able to wear it again. I forced
myself to tune into her stream of questions.

"What the heck's the big secret? Who took care of them after
your grandparents died? And don't you have an uncle—where is he,
now?"

I collected facts like acorns and considered them, one by one.
"Mom went to work in the mill to make money to raise Uncle Paul
and my aunts. Right after she married Dad and they sold the farm. I
know that much. I haven't seen my uncle since I was little. He trains
horses and travels a lot. He writes to Mom, though. And he sent her a
tablecloth from Mexico."

Beverly stuck her tongue out with a bit of ripe fruit peel on the
end, deep red like Rudolph's nose. We both giggled.

I sat down beside her and turned my palms out. "Did I tell you
that your church used to be my granddad's church? Aunt Tally said
they were baptized in the river." Grass prickled through my skirt, so
that I shifted my weight.

Beverly jumped to reach a branch laden with small orbs. She
settled for rattling the leaves instead of taking a fruit, drifting down to
the ground in a perfect cheer posture. "You don't want to go to our
church now. Remember when Brother Rice jumped over that bench?
You cried for hours!"

"Yeah, they're a little loud for me." One tumultuous Holiness
Sunday sermon, years ago, had scared me so badly that Willeen had

taken me out, screaming and hollering. Since then, my mother picked
me up from our visits on Saturday evening, so I wouldn't have to go
to the Tyndalls' service. At Vacation Bible School, we sang hymns and
painted ceramic animals. No one shouted.

Beverly tossed a leaf and watched it float to earth. "Well, I
wish I could wear dresses hemmed to my knees and dance, like you
Methodists. That's sinful, Dad says." Light flared in her bottle-green
eyes. She raised her hand, testifying. "It starts with short skirts, hose,
and makeup, and listening to rock 'n' roll—the Devil's music—then
riding with boys in cars. Next thing you know, they ship you off to
the McPherson Home for Wayward Girls." She commenced to jitterbugging furiously, careening around the weed-choked pasture, arms
waving, knees bent, swiveling from the hips. "Look at me! I'm sinking
into sin before your eyes." She threw her head back and belted out
"Tutti Frutti," hips swishing at each "lop-bam-BOOM."

I jumped up to join her, enjoying the buzz of being a little bit bad.
My parents might not be strict about religion, like Beverly's, but they
wouldn't approve of making fun of it, either. I swished my skirt with
all the abandon of a safe rebellion.

Beverly stopped suddenly, sat down hard on her rear, and grabbed
some broom straw, so dry its tiny seeds spilled out between her long,
flat fingers like Rice Krispies into a bowl. "How come they avoid
answering all the important questions?" She shook a straw until it let
go its last offering. "No matter how many times I ask, Willeen won't
explain what dancing to rock 'n' roll has to do with getting pregnant."
Her eyes took on the color of river stirred to mud. "I sure can't find
out for myself. Dad won't let me near any boys. I can't even date till
I'm seventeen and a junior. Preacher Allen says early dating makes
Jezebels out of girls."

My shoulders through the blue cotton shirt felt like a hot griddle.
Suddenly sleepy, I flopped down, lay back, and raised my arm to
shield my eyes from the sun. "Emily Glassinger, in George's class, got

pregnant, and her folks sent her away to New York for an operation. She came back without the baby." Seeing Beverly's puzzled frown, I added, "When George told that story, Mom sent me down to get eggs from the neighbor. All I know is there's something you can do about it, if you have money." I would have enjoyed holding up my end of the conversation, for a change, if my back weren't itching so furiously from the dry broom straw. I sat up and pawed at it with both hands.

Beverly rose and stood, rocking from the toe of one foot to the heel of the other and back, her eyes a suspicious slit. "If there were something you could do about it, Doc Brown would know. No need to go away. Maybe that girl lost her baby, that's all."

I settled the hem of my shirt around my hips. "Because you're not *supposed* to do anything about it. You know, original sin, Eve and the apple and all that stuff. If you get pregnant without being married, I think you're supposed to accept your punishment, have the baby, and get saved again."

Her shoulders deflated. "Well, at least your mom told you how you get a baby. All I know about sex is from watching Old Fred and the cows in the field. Well, Willeen tossed me a pamphlet about 'Now That You're Married,' but she wouldn't say much about it. Dad would have a conniption if she did."

"Yeah, Mom answers questions if I ask, but it's only … information. She doesn't like it if I ask about how she met Dad, for example, or what they did on dates. Can you imagine her teaching me how to flirt?" My mind drew a blank even thinking how such a thing might look.

Beverly crowed. "Can you imagine Willeen?" She pantomimed Willeen's long face sucked into a pucker. For a second we sounded like two birds cackling over the field.

"Yeah, well, you've got Mary Alice," I gasped, still laughing. "Wish I had an aunt that young and pretty. She had a trail of guys following her every move before she and George got together." Among the things I most envied Beverly was her dark-haired aunt, Willeen's youngest sister, who was in the same class as my brother, George. They'd been dating on and off ever since their senior year. Homecoming Queen and Cheerleader wins Football Hero: right out of central casting for all the sappy romances we saw at the Emily Theater in town.

Beverly dragged herself to her feet. "I'd settle for *one* guy trailing me. What I really want is to dance. That's all. Dad thinks I want to run off with boys. You'd think they'd trust us by now."

"Why wouldn't my parents trust me?"

My face must have looked peeved, because she reached down to help me up. "I mean, when they don't talk about something, either they don't trust you or there's something they're ashamed of." She waved a beckoning hand at me. "I'm sure your grandmother was a perfect angel. Come on, Evie. Mom will be home and expecting us to help with dinner."

As close to an apology as Beverly could manage. I rose and started after her, till a breeze stirring the branches enticed me to close my eyes and let the orchard brush against me, its scents overflowing my body from head to toe. Why did my mom avoid this holy place? And why wouldn't she tell me, whatever the reason? She had explained carefully how men and women got together to make babies. She answered every question I dared to ask. Except about our orchard and the people who made it. No reason to think they'd done something my mother was ashamed of, so maybe she didn't trust me with the truth. Some deep, dark truth—about what?

Overhead, the branches rubbed together, whispering as if they had the answer, if I could only understand their tongue.

Evangeline, 1928: Seeds

Four men lounge on the Gossip Bench of Redding's Grocery while the girls and I rush beneath the overhang. All but one wear stained coveralls. Rain drops slip from my nose as I nestle Tally with her blanket into the wagon, freeing my hands to fumble in my bag for a penny each for Maisie and Vinnie. They take the coins I hold out to them and hurry inside toward the candy counter.

My skirt clings to my legs. Adjusting it would probably make the men stare harder. The one with the missing hand says in a loud whisper to the baby face sitting next to him, "Might as well be pickaninnies."

The teenager places one scuffed boot on the porch railing and cocks his hat over his eyes, like he owns the place. I know his name is Lewis Allen. He hides out here during the day with his maimed uncle, because his dad is a mean man who takes a whip to Lewis if he doesn't plow straight. Some say the uncle's accident happened because Old Man Allen sent his little brother out to check hunting traps and didn't look for him until the next morning, after he'd struggled all night to free himself.

I lift Tally and walk toward the door, cradling her against my throat. We're almost there when Lewis rises from his seat, spits off the low porch, and chuckles to his friends, "There's the Gypsy queen. Reckon she might slide down my pole if I ask her real nice?"

Soon as I see him open his mouth, I call out to the girls, "Remember: Look, don't touch!" to drown him out. Maisie immediately places her hands down by her sides, but Vinnie points to all her favorites under the long glass counter.

As long as my girls do not hear, I can bear his meanness. Before I open the screen door, the bastards have stopped laughing and resumed their loud argument about cotton prices and how large this year's crop will be.

On the threshold, I pause for a moment to get my bearings in the gloom. Mr. Redding stows barrels of pickles and sausages in the center aisle, where no light penetrates from the windows set high over the back counter, so I have to be careful not to swish my skirts against the merchandise. Even if I no longer believe that everything below my waist is impure, like the old ones did, habits my mother taught me die hard.

Now that my eyes are adjusted, I catch sight of Maisie's blue skirt, and Vinnie's rose one, her slip always hanging because she pulls on it so. Tally squirms to get down and totters over to press her nose against the long walnut counter. She lets the bigger girls choose, then squeals until they give her a taste. At nearly three, she rules the roost, mostly because her sisters give in to her.

I walk to the center of the long counter and stand in a warm pool of sunlight from above. Hilda Redding, her thin, auburn hair piled high on her head, looks up with that pinch-mouthed glare of hers from behind the worn wooden surface. She's engaged in a mild quarrel with a customer, a tall lady with straggling gray hair, who wants two pounds of flour for the dozen eggs she's trading. Keeping one eye on the girls where they run back and forth, debating the merits of different candies, I wait. After a minute, the tall woman exits down a different aisle. Mrs. Redding gives me a tight smile, making sure I know she knows I'm there, then turns and walks away.

Mr. Redding climbs down from the long ladder he uses to reach the upper shelves, and covers for his wife, calling out, "That's right,

Hilda, you have to count the eggs in the icebox. I'll wait on Mrs. Grey while you do that." His wife does not bother to acknowledge him, but continues walking toward the produce.

"How are you today, Mrs. Grey? I bet the girls know what they want. I'll wait on them first. Then we can visit." He gives me a wink and moves to the candy counter. I don't think he's flirting with me, but I doubt that would comfort his wife. My mother warned me that gadje always think Romani women are seducing their husbands. She said that's because we don't blame them for being male and that passes for seduction to men whose wives believe in Immaculate Conception.

I'm acquainted with few men, but I know that some, like Lewis on the front porch, have evil intentions. Mr. Redding, I think, is a kind man who likes to make women happy by paying attention to them. He listens patiently to each girl. Vinnie changes her mind twice before accepting a small bag of spearmint and lemon drops. She passes one of each to Tally, who pops them both into her mouth at once.

Maisie makes her spit one out before asking for two chocolate squares, two lemon drops, and two peppermint sticks. She gets an extra bag from Mr. Redding, puts one chocolate square and part of one peppermint stick in it, and hands it to Tally. "You've already tried the lemon," she points out. Tally sputters and grabs the bag.

Mr. Redding moves over to stand in front of me. "That should keep them busy for a little bit. What shall we talk about today, Mrs. Grey?" He says this with a shy smile, which has nothing of the wolf in it.

"How are your children?" I ask. He launches into an account of his son's college studies, but I'm distracted by the feeling that his wife is staring at my back.

Mrs. Redding would choke me if she could. She has a good husband, two children, both old enough to help, though one is away at college, and money enough to buy her own dresses and hats at the department store in town. But I can see by the way she always wears pearl earrings, even when slicing cheese and chopping ground meat, that she expected more out of life.

I know that the only reason she has not shunned us completely is that she doesn't know where Gypsies come from. "Why, she's no darker than the Italians who work at the quarry," I heard her whisper to Mrs. Dockhart as we were packing baskets for the poor in church. "Her parents are from Scotland, and that's in Europe, too. I don't hold with treating those Italians like Negroes. Though they use so much garlic they all smell."

Her confusion means my girls are safe, and they can go to the nice brick school rather than to the shack reserved for the "colored." If that is wrong, I hope Del will forgive me. But Mrs. Redding has one thing I don't—she is white, beyond doubt—and that one thing is worth more than everything I have, if she chooses to make it so.

Mr. Redding's patient tone stirs me back to the present. "Do you need any piece goods today, Mrs. Grey?"

I ask him for cloth, thread, flour, and nails for Mr. James. He makes small talk about the weather and crops while he measures, cuts, and stacks. It does not matter if I only smile and nod occasionally. I don't pay much attention to the footsteps coming down the aisle until a hearty laugh from behind makes me turn.

A man with broad shoulders, a gray moustache, and a wide smile inclines his head toward a pretty young woman. Her blonde hair gleams in the light drifting through the dusty windows and her eyes match her dress, the color of grass. She smiles at him. They seem to be sharing some private joke. He pats her hand, draped casually over his arm.

"Well, Nettie, you might be right. I bet her husband does have some liquor hid in the barn!" The man throws back his head and roars again with laughter. When he spies me, his eyes narrow, suddenly keen. I think he might swoop down on me like a hawk. In a way, he does. He scans my face and the diklo tied like a bandanna across my head, then reaches out, grabs my hand, and begins to pump it. "Could this be the woman we've heard about? Mrs. Grey, I presume?"

"Father, you've startled her!" The daughter frowns at him and smiles at me in quick succession, and bats his hand away, replacing it with her own gentle touch.

"Mrs. Grey, I'm Nettie Evans. This is my father, Dr. Robert Evans. We're neighbors. We've heard that you are an herbalist, and we've been meaning to stop by to see you. It's so nice to run into you like this."

The doctor sweeps off his hat.

Uncertain how to proceed, I admit, with caution, "I learned herbal lore from my aunt. She could take care of most things, except badly broken bones. And plagues, of course, scarlet fever and such."

"None of us can do much against the deadly germs, but the day is coming!" The doctor twirls his brown fedora on two fingers of his right hand. I am mesmerized, watching the red-tipped feather on the band go round and round. "Meantime, I don't follow my colleagues' insistence that traditional lore is always wrong. In the hands of a good practitioner, an elixir from the forest can take care of many a minor illness. But that's not why we wanted to meet you." His words seem to rush out, then suddenly halt. He looks at his daughter, as if his time has run out.

"My father means, we want to talk to you about helping some of our patients."

The doctor interrupts to brag, "My daughter just graduated from Columbia Medical School in New York. She's going to help me with the women's side of my practice, pregnancy and children and such. But there are so many breeding women in this area, she has her hands full. That's where we're hoping you can help." Again, his words gush wide, like a raging stream. Without meaning to, I take a step back to avoid being splashed.

"Father, I'm afraid we've overwhelmed Mrs. Grey." Nettie Evans has the clearest eyes I've ever seen, like the calm water I saw once in a mountain lake. There is no greed, no duplicity, no hesitation in her. I take to her immediately. But there is something in common with her father, on second glance: a certain bobbing motion in her eyes that matches her father's frantic pace.

I realize I need to say something. "No, you haven't overwhelmed me, except by your compliments. I don't know what I could do for you. Did you want me to make some of my tonics for your patients?"

"No, no. We want more than that. We want a midwife."

The doctor's wide ruddy face makes me wonder how old he will be when he drops dead of a heart attack. Surely no one so forceful can live long, throwing himself headlong against the weight of the world.

I try to wrap my mind around his words. A midwife? To gadje? My mother complained about how unclean they are. But Mr. James and I need money to buy the farm. What would it be like to have a job?

Nettie hurries to explain. "We've heard that you make teas and such to help women with their monthlies and that you have helped some give birth, and we thought you might have a rapport with the women of the area. We would train you to handle all kinds of births, of course."

Is it her mention of such a private condition here in the middle of the store, or the thought that local women might value my advice, that strikes me dumb? Still, if some women, like Hilda Redding, treat me like a germ they can catch, it is true that quite a few women have sought out my mixtures lately, and that I've attended Mary Avery in her last two confinements. I would like to be something in the community besides "that Gypsy the preacher brought home."

I draw in my breath to steady my voice. "I would have to talk it over with my husband." I hope that is enough to give me time to think.

The doctor is not a man to give up easily. "The good preacher, I hear, is a reasonable man. Surely he'll say yes."

"Father, we have to give the Greys time." Nettie turns to me with a dimpled smile. "Perhaps you and your husband and your girls"—she smiles at the children peeking from behind my skirts—"could come to dinner at our house on Sunday evening? I've been meaning to attend your husband's service. I hear he has a fine grasp of the Bible. Perhaps you could come home with us after church?"

"I'll ask Mr. James. Tonight."

She seems puzzled for a moment. "Oh, Mr. James is your husband. I see." I blush. Nettie Evans's forthright manner makes me feel old-fashioned. I guess that she doesn't have a husband, and, if she did, she would not call him "Mister." She's still staring. Does she think me too young at 25 to birth babies? Surely she can't be much older.

Whatever she's looking for in my face, it appears she's found it. She turns to her father and reminds him to buy tobacco. Mr. Redding bustles to fill the order and take the doctor's money. Nettie charms me with a wide smile. "Shall we say this Sunday? You'll let us know if that won't do. In any case, we'll come to hear Reverend Grey."

I stammer out as she turns briskly away, "I think you'd better come to us. It will be easier, with the children." I bow my head to indicate the knot of babies holding onto my skirt with their sticky fingers.

Her father replaces a leather pouch in his suit pocket and swivels toward his daughter. "Nettie, we have to be at that meeting about the new hospital at one."

Nettie Evans nods to me again. "Sunday, after church, then."

Before I can say more, they are gone in a mix of green dimity and gray serge.

Mrs. Redding joins her husband behind the counter. In front of me I find a neat stack of articles and Mr. Redding's smiling face. "A fine man, Doc Evans. And a lady doctor, imagine that." Hilda sniffs and places her back to me. Her husband pretends not to notice her rudeness. "Mrs. Grey, I think that's everything. Did you want me to put this on your account?"

I pick up the fabric and the smaller items and place them in the basket I carry over my arm. "Yes, that's all, Mr. Redding. Thank you. Come, girls, we have jam making to do at home." I can feel Hilda Redding's penetrating glare on my back. Every woman in the vicinity will know what Doc Evans asked me. With surprise and a little thrill, I find that I don't care in the least. I am inclined to do exactly what he wants.

But will Mr. James agree? My mother would not have needed permission. She handled most of our money affairs. Romnya are taught to do that. But Mr. James, I have learned, likes to be consulted. Surely, birthing babies is God's work.

My thoughts run to the future. We have wanted to buy the farm outright from the church, so we will have something to pass on to our girls. Mr. James is earning extra money from the mountain congregations, who can't find regular pastors, and are thus willing to meet any day he can come to them. With that, plus my earnings, we might be able to do it sooner rather than later.

Some women in the neighborhood do visit to ask for my mixtures now. Will the others—Hilda Redding's crowd—accept me as a midwife?

I shoo my girls past the Gossip Bench, empty now, except for one old coot nodding off in the corner, his hat pulled low over his face. As we walk, the girls kicking up dust till we look like a herd of small beasts storming down the road, I mull over my good fortune.

◦◦◦◦◦◦

Tally has fallen asleep in the bed of the little wagon, her sticky fingers entwined in her red hair. Later, I will have a time of it trying to keep her still while I comb out the knots. Vinnie runs ahead to gather Queen Anne's lace at the edge of our long drive. Her hair is matted, too, sugar sprinkles shining among the dark strands. Maisie walks beside me and the wagon, her signal that she has something to say. She is so like my mother, not only her dusky hair, but her grave eyes and serious manner.

"Dr. Nettie is pretty." Maisie's voice is decisive, sure.

"Yes, she is," I agree.

"I've never met a woman doctor before."

"Me, neither."

My daughter tilts her dainty, pointed chin to look at me. "I didn't know you were an—" She struggles to get the word out. "—an herbalist. What does that mean?"

"Oh, it's just a fancy word for someone who makes medicines out of plants and roots." I wait. Is that what has her staring down at her shoes? Probably not, for she kicks at an old piece of horse collar embedded in the dirt for a minute before falling in beside me.

"Mama, are you a witch?"

Her sudden words snatch my breath. I try to read her expression, but she's walking with her face turned toward the ruts at our feet. "Why do you ask, daughter?" Did she read something odd into the doctors' words?

"Well, people say that sometimes." Her big moss-colored eyes shine at me.

"Who says that?" Perhaps those old men said something I didn't hear?

There's a vee-shaped wrinkle above her nose. "The kids at school. Well, it's really the Dockhart boys. They say that you probably dance under the moon every night with all the other witches."

"I see." It's hard not to smile at such a notion.

"They say you're a Gypsy, and that's the same as a witch."

I look to where Vinnie has stopped to examine the contents of the ditch under a copse of young turkey oaks standing like scarecrows in the autumn sun. Maisie trots along beside me as I pull the wagon into their shade.

"Well, are you?"

"Which?"

"A witch?"

"No."

"A Gypsy?"

I stop. The sound of family laughing around the fire comes to me like a distant memory. "Maybe not any more," I say. Maisie waits, staring somberly up at me. I have to protect her against lies. Yet how much is too much for her to hear?

I look into her eyes and see the wise child that she is. "Come. Let's sit in the shade. The sun is hot for September, and we still have a way to go." I drape the blanket over the wagon sides to shelter the baby, catch Vinnie, brush the hair out of her eyes, and pat her behind. She skips off to chase a butterfly. "Thank goodness the sun has dried most of the puddles already." I sit between the root arms of the old oak tree, its leaves too dense to allow the ground to get wet in a brief shower, and wait for my eldest to sink down beside me. When she is settled, I begin.

"Being Gypsy—or Romani—people call us Gypsy because they think we are from Egypt, but we are really from India—is about family—lots of family, aunts and uncles and cousins and grandparents, too. About knowing how to survive. I don't travel any more and my kumpania—my group, my family—is off somewhere else—where, I don't know—so it's been a long time since I lived like a Romani woman, a romni."

Maisie's eyes were huge, mossy and brown at once like the stones in the brook that sings at the bottom of the hill. "I'm an Indian?"

"Not that kind of Indian. The kind from India. Where the big elephants live. Only half. Your father is Scottish." I'm not sure if she's seen either India or Scotland on a map.

"Oh. That must be far. How did you come here?" She takes a rock from her pocket and turns it, end over end, in her palm. I have seen her do this countless times when she is listening.

"I was never in India. Nor my father nor my mother nor my grandparents—your great-grandparents. And none of our people for many years before that. We left India long, long ago. My grandfather and my grandmother came from France. They met in England and came here before I was born, before my mother was born."

"Why?" she says the word slowly and carefully, working the stone's many sides.

"They could not find a place to settle. Roma roam. That's what they have to do." I know there is much I cannot yet tell her. About all the Romanies hunted down in cold blood in Europe, the suspicious fires in our wagons at night, about the police who try to make Roma settle down in the poorest parts of town, where not even the dogs want to live. About my grandmother and how she lost two fingers on her right hand as a punishment for running away from a slaver. I feel my way through the stream of my family's story, looking for solid ground, for stepping stones that will help her understand, without frightening her or making her resentful. "After traveling very far, my grandparents found land they loved in the mountains and bought it."

I wrap her hand in mine. "You see, a long time ago, in France, a young man showed a wonderful talent for the fiddle and the guitar. With his brother, he formed a band, and they played everywhere. For parties and just for fun in the park at night. People would put money in their hats and they came all the way across town to get them to play for their weddings. The brothers made enough money to buy a building and bring all their aunts and uncles and cousins to live there.

"Then one night something awful happened. A man threw a rag soaked in oil into their bedroom window. The young man—Stephane—grabbed his wife and took her out of the building. He went back in to get their two babies, but he could only find one. His brother, his uncles, his cousins came to help. No one could find the smallest one." I hurry on, wondering if I have said a thing too sad for her to hear. She is still listening closely, her fingers moving quickly over the stone as it rolls in the cup of her hand.

"The young man went wild with grief. He tried to find another place for his wife and child and the rest of the family, but no one would rent or sell to them."

"Why?" Maisie's olive eyes swirl with shades of the forest.

"Because they were Roma, and some people think Roma are bad."

"Why?" Now she frowns, and I know I have confused her.

I watch a swallow wing its way back toward our barn and think about how to answer my wide-eyed little girl. Maybe she can understand from her own experience. "Is there someone in your class who is smaller, or unusual, or different in some other way?"

It does not take Maisie long to consider the small group, perhaps twenty children, who study in her one-room brick schoolhouse. She wrinkles her nose. "Daisy Allen smells bad, like she doesn't bathe. And Willie Wallace has an eye that rolls around." She covers one eye and rolls the other in a circle.

"I see. And do the other kids make fun of them?"

"Yeah," Maisie laughs. "They call him Wall-Eye Willie. And her, Nasty Daisy."

"And do you call them those names?"

I wait. My eldest grows somber and hangs her head. "I did, once. Willie was mean and took away my ball at recess. "

"What happened?" My eyes find Vinnie still chasing butterflies, with her sash now dragging in the dust. She will need a bath when I get her home. At my feet, Tally stirs in the wagon, her lips puckering as if sucking on candy.

"He cried." Maisie bows her head still lower.

"How did that make you feel?" Though I can see quite clearly that she feels ashamed, even now. My heart warms with pride that my daughter understands the wrong.

"Worse. I let him keep the ball." She twists the rock in her hand.

"Is there someone who's different, but not in a bad way?"

Maisie squinches her eyes to think about it. "There's Willeen Burnett. She's really tall. And she doesn't like to talk much. She has pretty hair and eyes, and she likes to listen. I told her my whole story about the pig and the cow that go off to school together, and she said it was good. But some of the kids say she's creepy. She's so quiet, you never know she's there."

"Well, that is exactly how some people treat Roma. Because we look different and our ways and clothes are different. Not bad, just different. We roam because we cannot go back to our real home— too many wars, too many people moving in after we left—and so we must travel in the lands of other people. Sometimes people try to keep out people they don't understand. And if something goes wrong—someone gets robbed, say, or a garden is trampled—they say the Gypsies did it. Maybe one of their own people did it themselves, but Roma are easy to blame, because they are always strangers."

Maisie's head bobs. Her voice grows loud with excitement. "I know! Ray Billings told the teacher Tom Harden stole Annie Sloan's cap, but Ray took it—I saw him!"

"Well, sometimes people who want to avoid blame, point to the one no one likes or knows." I place my arm around her slender waist.

"Everybody knows Tom, but most people don't like him," she agrees. "He can't spell, and he walks like this." She jumps up and walks a few paces, dragging her left leg.

"Well, there you have it. It's called scapegoating. And I hope you will remember that if someone tries to blame Tom or Willie or Daisy for something they did not do. Look a little further for the culprit."

"But, Mama, I don't understand why Gyp—Roma move so much or why you don't live with your family."

I sit her down again beside me and tell her very simply how my father was jailed for a fight he did not start, and how my mother died and left me alone. I try to explain that, because people can be mean, it is perhaps best not to tell our whole story. I look deep into her eyes to see if she understands.

Her eyes are steady. She reaches over and pats my arm. "I won't tell. Did you cry?" She looks at me with so much sympathy, I nearly cry right there.

"Yes. But I married your father and got you and Vinnie and Tally, and now I'm not lonely any more."

"What happened to the man whose baby died in the fire?"

"He decided to leave that place and come to England. That was your great-grandfather, Stephane Lefevre. His wife was named Evangeline, like me. When they came to England, they changed their last name to Lee. Later, they came to America with his two brothers. One of them married my Aunt Juba, whose family had been here a long time. Her nephew, Tomas, became my father after he married my mother, Lavinia."

"Vinnie's name!"

"That's right. And they had my brothers, Tomas, named for our father, and Stephane, named for our grandfather."

"Who am I named for, Mama?"

"Oh, daughter, you have the happiest name of all. You are named for a story my Mama told me about Maisie, the fairy queen."

She rubs one leg with the other foot and considers. "Fairies are beautiful, aren't they? I'm not beautiful, not like Dr. Nettie. But fairies can make people happy, can't they? Grant them wishes?"

"Yes. They can. And they are all beautiful in different ways, as people are. As you are lovely in a way that's different from the doctor."

Maisie rises on her tiptoes and sprinkles me with imaginary dust. "I grant your wish, Mama. Your family will come back." She gives me her gentlest smile and backs away, then turns to run after her sister.

After she is gone, I brush the tears from my face and pat Tally, who lies blinking at me with sleepy eyes. In a minute she will wail to be picked up. I steal another look ahead to my eldest, holding out her hand to help Vinnie leap a ditch. The late afternoon sun strikes red sparks in her dark hair. I think about the way her brows fly straight across her face over those somber eyes. Hers is an honest face, a strong face.

"Oh, dear daughter," I whisper, "kindness makes you prettier than you know. I hope you will always be loved. And safe."

The sun hangs low over the river now. I stand and shade my eyes, examining the line of trees that follow the water, where Redding's store is, where the doctors made their request. Can a future for my girls be so close, so simple to reach?

Maisie, 1958: Moths to the Flame

"Evie needs answers the way some people need religion. She wants me to fill in the family picture, like a puzzle with a piece shaped like her." My sisters look at me with worry carved across their foreheads.

"Go ahead if you think we can trust her. But telling Evie means telling that Tyndall girl, too. The whole town will know by Sunday." It's tempting to laugh at Tally's warning. A minute ago she was apologizing for telling Evie about Papa being a preacher. She adjusts her rhinestone glasses. "What will we do if Evie asks Lewis Allen about how he came to take over the church?" She adds this last as she reaches for an apple and begins slicing it into red-tipped moons.

"Maisie is the only one who can tell Mama's story and tell it right. It's up to her to decide when." Vinnie inserts the comment as quietly as a minnow surfacing in a creek. She's like a pendulum, always swinging back to the center.

Tally's skewed pucker makes it clear she's not convinced. "She's only thirteen. That's too young to know how to handle vicious gossip."

Vinnie is more sympathetic. "Everyone needs to know where they came from. And our mother's story might show her there's more to life than being popular."

I draw another apple from the basket. "Yes, but what if the truth drives her away? Who wants to live where you aren't accepted? Easier to go away and be whoever you want to be."

"If you can't figure it out, no one can, Maisie." That's Vinnie, giving me too much credit again. What would I have done without her? Without Tally, too. We are like three beads on the same bracelet. And Bibi Vashti clasps us to our past.

I resolve to ask Bibi what she thinks as soon as possible.

Vashti Garretson cocks her head like a listening bird. Her diklo is bright orange today. The afternoon sun slices a wedge across the table, forming a halo around her head.

I accept the delicate white cup she pushes toward me. "Evie knows things most young people don't even think about. Telling her about who we are would give her another reason to see herself as different from anyone else she knows. It would be so much easier if we lived among amari familia.... Why should she stay here? Why did we?" An old sorrow scrapes my throat. I put the cup down, the tea bittersweet on my tongue.

Vashti places the honey pot in front of me. She always knows what I need. Where would we be if she had not come to our door? "Heaven knows, she wants to get away already. She chatters all the time about what Paris must be like. She asks if she can go to New York and see the museums she's read about." I stir a spoonful of amber into my tea and taste it. Much better. The rich fluid calms me, as if my tongue, busy with sensations, can trick itself into speech. "I want her to do those things. Yet how can I take her? Even if I had the money, I would feel like a frog in a pond of sharks. No, she will have to earn it, make her way there on her own."

"A bitter bird cannot fly," Vashti murmurs.

If her words had been arrows, they couldn't have pinned me more solidly to my seat. "Mama used to say that, warning me about jealousy, and envy, and revenge." Oh, yes, bitterness came to my lips, sometimes, but I choked it back. I did what my mother wanted. "I've never struck back, Bibi, not once. Isn't it enough to omit the sin, even if you can't omit the evil in your heart?"

Vashti takes both our cups to the walnut sideboard and fills them again. "Is it evil toward others that you feel, Nepata? Or loss? It is not evil to grieve. Unless you grieve so long that life passes you by. When you have finished with your mourning, you will know what to say to your girl."

◦◦◦

Both girls are leaping outside the kitchen window, jumping and twirling, practicing splits and cart wheels. Beverly moves smoothly from one hand to the other, her legs like spokes in a wagon wheel. Evie begins well, but halfway through, the moment when she must spin herself from earthworm to sky dweller, she loses confidence and lands in a heap. Her face flames while her eyes track Beverly's every movement around the yard. Always, she measures herself against her friend.

I swirl the dishwater over my sore knuckles and worry. What makes her feel that she isn't good enough? Does my silence say something I don't mean?

I hardly had time to mourn when my sisters were little. Hard enough to keep a roof over their heads. Luckily, neither of them wanted to wander too far. I couldn't have lived with my mother's memory—or my father's—if I hadn't also seen that they married good men.

Easy with Vinnie; she saw how Art can fix a car without tracking dirt into her clean house and sit still without squirming in church on Sunday. She likes things simple and true. But Tally—she wanted to be more, have more. And she does. A big house. A big car. Milt is good to her. That's what counts. Tally wouldn't be happy if she'd married a man who shone brighter than she does. She needs to be the main attraction.

And now, my own daughter, so talented, the first one of us to make a ripple in the world, maybe. Will she give up before she can succeed? It's easier with boys. George knows what he wants and he goes after it. No second-guessing himself. Paul, too, though I wish he hadn't needed to go so far. But we women—what makes us women stop to wonder if we deserve our good fortunes?

Here is Evie, my clever, watchful Evie, growing up like a ribbon slipping between my fingers, seeing everything that goes on and understanding most of it, yet she follows Beverly, every move she makes, as if her friend had some magic formula for happiness. I guess Beverly makes her life look easy, though it's far from that. Carl doesn't understand that holding on too tightly will make her fly away at the first invitation. She's like a swallowtail skipping from plant to plant.

People are always attracted to the brightest butterfly. Even quiet girls like my Evie want to be the one that everyone notices. If you ask me, real men don't need the crowd to tell them who to want. Thank heaven Frank didn't need me to flirt with him, to move him around like a pawn with my finger.

I don't want Evie to feel that all we come down to is a pack of men on our heels. Biology isn't destiny, I heard some woman say on the news. No. But if you're female it sure can put thorns in your path.

Truth is, we're neither deserving nor undeserving, but moths dancing toward the light. Yes, moths, the homely ones like warts clinging to the kitchen screen. And others, lovely, with spans like delicate paper. Red-shouldered ones wearing capes of crimson and the dainty yellow ones they call brimstone. Plain or gorgeous, we bat our wings against anything that gets between us and the flame of our desires. Lucky if that light that so entrances us isn't an open flame.

Bibi Vashti is right, as she so often is. I can feel the words lodged tight against my breastbone. One day, they will free themselves, and, Te Del o Del, my daughter will find her role.

Evie, June, 1959: Statues in the Garden

Two years ago, Beverly and I sat in the Emily Theater and watched Debbie Reynolds hook the bachelor with a child-like personality and cute pink dresses, stiffly flounced like a ballerina's. My first year at Toccoa County High, watching boys eye girls' hips in slim skirts, had taught me that more womanly skills were needed.

This year's crop of movies upped the ante.

"Lana Turner. That's who the guys like," Beverly had said. "Jayne Mansfield. You wouldn't catch Elizabeth Taylor dead in one of those fluffy numbers." We had just sat through *Cat on a Hot Tin Roof*, Elizabeth with her full bosom and dark lipstick in a slip, tossing lines at Paul Newman like a hungry lioness. I had sighed, glad that my mom hadn't had a clue what the movie was about, or she'd never have let me see it. And because there was no way, even with my dark, curly hair, that I could come close to Taylor's sex appeal. Much less Mansfield's. It's hard to be a lioness when you're on a short leash.

This morning, Mom commanded me to try on last year's duds so some could go to her old friend, Mrs. Garretson, for alterations: skirts that could be let out in the hem and last year's coat, to be bound with new facing where it had frayed. Outgrown clothes we placed in a stack for the church yard sale. After this closet shuffle, we would have our annual foray to Pearson's department store for what I "had to have," as Mom put it. Her rules had been in place for years: two new outfits and two pairs of shoes per school year, plus new underwear and bras, if needed. And her definition of need was stringent.

I stood before my closet, thinking about asking if we could buy some of those new pencil skirts worn by all the girls on *American Bandstand*. Mom waited behind me with pencil and pad at the ready, clutching a Kleenex in her hand. Raising a sticky subject when she had a cold didn't seem like a good idea. So, instead, I focused on what was left in my closet: skirts and dresses all gathered at the waist into fluffy little silhouettes.

"So *Tammy and the Bachelor*," I sighed.

"You're pretty, like that Tammy girl in the movie, but not nearly as cheerful," Mom observed. She tapped the pad with her pencil stub. "If I don't get to work, we'll have no money for shopping."

I decided to try a new ploy. "I'm just nervous, I guess. I'll be sixteen in a couple of months, and I'm not going to school with the same old mill crowd anymore. There are kids from all over, including out by the lake and those new houses over off Toccoa Highway. Everybody's wearing whatever they see on TV." Risky. My mom believed in living up to *her* expectations more than fitting in.

"I found some lightweight navy blue and brown wool, so Mrs. Garretson can make you some of those slimmer skirts the girls wear. We'll buy the cloth today and take it over tomorrow morning." I whirled around, dumbfounded. The skin around Mom's eyes and lips crinkled. "I watch Bandstand, too, you know."

"When—" A familiar whistle trilled from the front porch, interrupting my confusion.

"George! I thought he wouldn't be here till the weekend!" Mom flew out the door in front of me. On the porch, my scrawny brother pulled off his sailor's cap, broke open his cocky grin, picked her up, and twirled her around like she was no bigger than a child. Wiry but tough, the newspaper said, when he ran the ball back for a touchdown. I stepped outside. He set my mother down and gave *me* a twirl. We all laughed and tried to talk at the same time. I ran my hand over his hair, liking the needly feel of his crew cut.

"Hold on! I need your opinions." From his back pocket, George pulled a small box with a blue ribbon on top, which he presented to my mother with a flourish.

She opened it. The diamond sparked sunlight into a little prism on our porch ceiling. I waited as long as I could stand before yelping, "Mom, let me see!" She yielded the box to me, staring up at George and rubbing her hands together, the way she had stood on the Christmas Day Dad surprised her with a small crystal clock. Only now she had tears in her eyes.

The square-cut gem rendered me speechless, too. I wanted to take it out and try it on, but I didn't dare. Instead, I threw my arms around George's neck and found my voice. "I'm getting a great sister-in-law!"

George laughed and twirled his white hat. "Oh, didn't I tell you? I met this Eskimo girl, and we're gonna live at the North Pole with Santa Claus."

Mom stepped inside the door and lifted from the table her weaver's apron, with its many tiny hooks for pulling threads. "Mary Alice will love it! When you gonna ask her?"

"First, sleep. I've been on the bus since three a.m. I'm beat. I thought I'd surprise her today after work, if I can borrow your car?" He waited, tapping his foot on the floorboards.

Mom shot a warning look at me. "We have to take Evie school shopping. But I guess we can wait till tomorrow."

I didn't mind stepping back so George could propose to Mary Alice. Pencil skirts could wait! Besides, maybe I could parlay everybody's general happiness into a Shetland sweater. I grinned at George. "I can't wait to see Beverly's face!"

He pointed a long, thin finger an inch or two from my nose. "No blabbing now, Sis! I don't want Mary Alice to hear it from anyone but me!" His lips stretched a mile wide, but his stare meant business. I promised not to tell.

Mom mumbled instructions as she tied on her apron and grabbed her keys. "Evalyn, don't forget to take Miz Garretson those two jars of honey on the table. And be quiet so George can sleep! Lord! I have to get to work." She lifted her brown paper lunch bag from the little table beside the door, blew kisses to George and me, and ran to the car.

Before George slipped into his old bedroom, he paused. "Think she'll say yes?"

I offered him the biggest grin I could summon. "Are you kidding?"

He shrugged, then smiled and shut the door behind him.

I headed inside to gather the clothes to take to Mrs. Garretson, so happy I didn't mind that chore now.

Mrs. Garretson lived in a tiny little cottage with one room for kitchen and parlor, and one more behind an old door slathered with brown stain. In all my visits to her house, which began even before I could remember, I had never been inside that back room.

Patterns and cloth were laid out in the front room on a long walnut table with two trestles. A tall hutch filled with dishes of various patterns, most of them bone china and surprisingly fine for such a little house, loomed over the table. I'd been told years earlier that her grandfather had bought the dishes for her mother on his travels as a coppersmith. Inside the lower cabinet, Mrs. Garretson kept her shears and other implements.

From around her scarf, her hair puffed, a dusky color that reminded me of sparrow's wings, no gray visible at all. When she looked directly at me, the peculiar beauty of her eyes often startled me: blue-green, like a sparkling lake, an odd copper circle running around the pupil. She tipped her head with its brightly patterned scarf and cupped her long, blue-veined fingers to one ear, to let me know she had missed something I said.

For all her kindness, there was no disagreeing with Mrs. Garretson's judgment. She had been a friend of my grandmother's. My mother considered her the queen of all disputes that could be settled with a needle and thread. She almost always inched my hems farther down than the knee-length I requested, but the clothes she made were so finely sewn that they fooled my classmates into thinking they were bought at Pearson's.

We drank tea and ate almond cookies at a small table of red enamel, near a window that over the years had been covered in tulips, roses, daisies, and various other flowers playing across soft cotton. Fiddling with those curtains, making one flower merge into another by folding the cloth, was one of my earliest memories.

I calculated. Telling Mrs. Garretson about my brother's engagement couldn't get back to Mary Alice before this afternoon, right? Mrs. Garretson rarely left home, except to go to Piggly Wiggly, and she didn't have a phone. Bursting with the news, I took a chance. "My brother's going to marry Mary Alice Burnett!"

Mrs. Garretson stopped her teacup halfway to her lips. "Mrs. Burnett's youngest? I forgot she was George's age."

She had little more to say. After a few sips, she rose, wiped crumbs from the table, and handed me one of the too-short skirts to put on. Disappointed, I buttoned it around my waist and climbed onto a rickety kitchen chair.

"Stand still, Dearie, I'm taking your measure." She mumbled, stooped, and fussed, tugging at my hem, checking and re-checking with her worn yellow tape measurer. "Sorry, Dear. The arthritis makes me snippier today."

I suppressed a laugh. "You've never said a cross word to me in my life."

Her gnarled fingers directed me to revolve slowly, and I did. "Nor would I, Dearie. Your mother means the world to me. A fair force of nature, that one is."

Mrs. Garretson approved of everyone in my family. Her chatter brimmed with "What a fine boy!" and "A smart one she is!" when my mother told news of my brother or me, and "Thank heavens for that dear man!" when she mentioned my father. But in all the years I'd known her, she'd never said more than that she knew my grandparents. So I was surprised to hear her mutter as I stood in front of the age-speckled mirror, "The very image of your grandmother! I see her in everything you do!"

I whirled. Her muddy old eyes met mine. "Really? How are we alike?"

She slapped her hand to her mouth. "Old folks should watch their tongues." From the drawer of a tiny oak curio she pulled a silver frame, pressing the cool metal into my hand. The image, a larger version of the one I'd seen long ago in my mom's locket, showed a fine profile that reminded me of an old cameo silhouette. I studied it.

Mrs. Garretson turned me back to the mirror and drew one bony finger from my eye to my chin. "Your face is heart-shaped, like hers. And your eyebrows, swooping out. Her eyes were mostly brown, though they changed color—I've seen yours do that, too—the way a creek does in the rain. A gay little thing she was, tiny."

"I'm not gay—or tiny!"

"No, I reckon you're more like your father, a bit on the serious side. But tiny—" She held the tape measure and slid its length expertly through her fingers, "—you are becoming, my dear. I have to take your dresses in at the waist."

My hands flew to my middle. "No! That can't b—" I pinched my side and realized I had only a nub of flesh in my grasp. "Well, good grief! How did that happen?"

She cackled. "At your age, fat can drop off overnight. It's those hormones they talk about. You're becoming a lady!" She unbuttoned the skirt and waited for me to step out of it before folding it and placing it on the big walnut table. "Tell your mother that, if I get the cloth by Saturday, you'll have one of those new skirts ready for your first day."

"Oh, thank you, Mrs. Garretson!" Asking more about my grandparents was impossible after the old lady tottered to the front door and held it open for me. I couldn't ignore her invitation to leave—that would be disrespectful— so I stepped through. Foiled again, I stopped on her doorstep and glanced at the faded blue-green sky. Which reminded me of my brother's worried eyes. I didn't think he had anything to worry about, but I wanted to be there to see him off to Mary Alice's place. I ran toward home.

By the time I turned the corner near the Martins' house, the mill village grapevine had filled our porch and yard. Mrs. Henkel from two doors down paused next to Mom's geraniums, chatting with two other ladies from the second block down. Aunt Tally stepped out of Uncle Milton's used Cadillac. Her two boys, Mike and Dave, poured out of the back seat and ran into the street with their balls and gloves. My uncle closed the car door behind her. She adjusted her ample bosom and the frames of her cat's-eye glasses—the ones with little rhinestones that flashed in the sun—shook out the silky folds of her dress, and patted her red curls into place. She threw a millisecond of attention my way. "You're turning out quite nicely, you know."

I lost her attention before I could respond. She headed for her favorite perch in the creaking porch swing. Uncle Milt leaned against the porch railing, an unfiltered cigarette in his right hand. The name of his appliance store, Edward's, was embroidered in blue across the white pocket of his pressed cotton shirt.

I had returned to the porch with glasses of tea for Aunt Tally and my uncle, when Mom drove into our yard with Sue Martin, who joined the group chatting on the grass. Mom waved to everybody in sight, untied her weaver's apron, opened the screen door, and tossed it onto the small table inside without spilling even one of the reed hooks from the little pockets that lined the front.

"I thought that supervisor would never shut up! What a day to call a meeting! And what did he say, besides we're lucky to have a job and he expects us to work overtime?"

Aunt Vinnie had walked over from her house down the block. She settled her broad buttocks onto the top porch step. It often occurred to me that, if you put Tally's bosom together with Vinnie's bottom, you'd have Mae West.

"I'll just go change." Mom hurried through the front door with me on her heels.

In the kitchen, George, in a tee shirt and his rumpled uniform pants, was polishing off last night's fried chicken, ignoring the ruckus outside. He wiped his mouth on a paper napkin, ruffled my hair, and went to change. Mom sent me out with tea for the front porch folks. Minutes later, George emerged in neat khakis and a white shirt.

Tom Harding pulled into his yard across the street, with Dad in the passenger seat of his rusted red Buick. Dad crossed over, climbed the steps, and clapped George on the back. They spoke briefly before Dad pulled his set of car keys from his greasy pockets. George palmed them.

Before he could reach the car, Sue Martin yelled from the curb, "Mrs. Stegall says Mary Alice knows you're here. Somebody told her at the hospital."

Mrs. Stegall straightened her blue nurse's aide cap. "She's on her way."

George frowned, then with a slow smile settled on the top step next to Aunt Vinnie. "Well," he drawled. "I reckon I better just sit tight."

Vinnie grinned. "I want to hear about those big submarines you been on." Tally sat down beside her and scooted over to make room for George between them.

"Let me tell you, it's no picnic living under the sea with hundreds of guys." The women leaned their heads together, laughing at George's wry description of the cooks' one hundred ways to serve powdered eggs.

Mom had brought out the tea pitcher and a tray of assorted cups. "Vinnie, I think I'll need some more glasses." With loud efficiency, Aunt Vinnie called to her son, my Cousin Andy. In a few minutes, he came running back from Vinnie's with a stack of multi-colored plastic, winked at his mother, stuck his tongue out at me, and ran back to toss the ball with Mike and Dave. We hadn't played together since he and my other cousins had decided when I was in fourth grade that girls couldn't do anything fun. Which meant athletic or dangerous.

When Mary Alice's blue Nash pulled up, quiet stole over the porch and the street. Even the children stopped screaming, though they continued their games of hopscotch and marbles. Nobody wanted to miss this reunion.

Mom paused on the top step, frowning. "They'll wish we all would disappear," she murmured. George ambled down the front path, his hands in his pockets, but his taut neck muscles told me he was nervous. No one else moved.

Mary Alice climbed out, her white nurse's uniform a contrast to her hair, a dark, resonant brown, lighter than her eyes, which gleamed like an animal's: black and filled with moonlight, even in the late afternoon sun. Wearing a dazzling smile, she walked like a ship gliding into dock, right into my brother's arms. George bent to kiss her. Everybody on the porch cheered. After a minute or two, the lovers straightened and separated—not by much, his arm still around her waist—so that we could see George's wide grin and tears like glitter in Mary Alice's brown eyes.

Nothing compared to what she might shed later tonight. My heart quivered, imagining. Beverly and I had only whispered about the possibility that this day would come, for fear talking out loud would jinx it. At one and the same time, I was sorry Beverly and Willeen and Granny Burnett weren't here to enjoy this moment and glad that there was one story I could tell first. I didn't want to miss a thing, settling onto a low stool that Mama used to rest her feet after work, watching and listening to the buzz of friends and family, like a hive of bees excited that the Queen had come home.

Indeed, Mary Alice held herself upright like a friendly royal. Her hand still tight in George's grip, she talked over the porch railing to Aunt Tally and the other women about the difficulty of finding a new hairdresser, now that Lula Alexander had retired. She threw a warm smile and a wink my way. I smiled back and imagined us having long sessions applying makeup and redoing my hair.

But not for long. By the time the lovers made it through the crowd gathered at the bottom of the porch, my mother was organizing supper. "Evie, come on and peel the potatoes." She leaned over the railing. "Mary Alice, will you two be here for supper?"

Mary Alice shook her head and smiled almost shyly.

Mom grinned back. "Y'all go on. Talitha, Milton, you staying?"

"Don't mind if we do, Maisie. Thanks." Aunt Tally nodded with satisfaction and went back to her beauty shop stories without another glance.

Mom turned to Vinnie, with somewhat higher expectations. "Vinnie, what about you and your'n?"

"Okay. I've got two pies at home and some tomatoes I picked fresh this morning. Andy-y-y. Come help me carry things." She lifted her bulk off the porch.

Before Mom and I got inside, we had six more guests, two cakes, and a mess of fried chicken to come. Sue Martin scurried home for a platter of baked ham. Aunt Tally jumped up and exclaimed, "I forgot the sarma!" and ran to the car.

"Did she say sarma? What's that?" Mary Alice watched my aunt's flight.

"It's a disgusting cabbage roll," I explained.

"Mom and my aunts have funny names for everything." George squeezed Mary Alice's hand and turned toward one of the men. She looked to me for an explanation.

"It's something they made up when they were kids," I said with a shrug, then added, "I think." Aunt Tally returned from the car with her dish and offered Mary Alice a peek beneath the foil. The scent of boiled cabbage wafted across the porch. Some of our neighbors sniffed with approval. Others waved their hands in disgust. We all laughed when Mary Alice faked alarm, waving the plate away.

Mom accepted Tally's gift, then turned to me. "Guess we'll just put on some potatoes and make more tea, Evie." She hurried into the kitchen, satisfied with the menu.

I turned for a last look at the happy chatterers on the porch. Most of our friends had gone, leaving a few close neighbors, the happy couple, my aunts, their husbands, and my boy cousins. With a surge of contentment, I realized that, before the night was over, I would no longer be the only "young lady" in our bunch.

I grinned as I trotted in for my date with the Idahoes.

After setting the last dish in the drainer, Mom dried her hands. "You finish drying, Evie. I'm going out on the porch to see if your Dad's still awake." She winked at me. We both knew that Dad would be either reading the day's paper by the porch light, or asleep with it falling from his hands. The kitchen clock said ten p.m., far past our bedtime, when I finished drying and putting away the dishes. I went out to settle again on the footstool. Fireflies had given way to buzzing cicadas. Dad rustled the paper.

"That Evans boy is going to run for City government," he noted to Mom. "Won't that make his papa proud." Clearly, he had not been bitten by the wedding bug, like the rest of us. Mom nodded, her crochet needle flashing. She didn't appear to be listening.

A car door slammed. My elbow slid off my knee, and my head jerked downward. Mom, Dad, and I all turned to watch George lead Mary Alice around the car, his hand on her elbow. Mary Alice shushed him. "George, there's nothing wrong with asking questions. Smart people always want to know more."

"Yeah, but she's got more questions than the ticks on an old hound." My cheeks flushed at my brother's words, but I jumped in excitement and tried to catch a glimpse of Mary Alice's ring finger. She now wore a navy blue shirtdress, her hands hidden in the pockets. They climbed the steps. George thumped my head. "My little sister is the only person who's asked me how it *smells* on a submarine with all those guys."

Dad's chest quaked with a soft chuckle. "What did you say?"

"I told her she didn't want to know, and I didn't want to think about it. I wanted to see my best girl." He squeezed Mary Alice's waist. She tilted her head to smile at him.

"What did you do tonight?" I sounded as innocent as I could manage.

"Oh, not much. We decided to elope. It's all over now." George tried to sound serious, but by the hanging bulb I could see the twinkle in his eyes.

"You did not! You wouldn't!"

Mary Alice leaned over toward me. "He's teasing. What he really wanted to say is, how would you feel about being a bridesmaid?" And she put out her hand to me.

Moonshine, flowing now from a position high in the sky, raked boldly across our wide porch, touching everyone's hair and skin with a pale glow. And in their midst, Mary Alice displayed around one slim finger a band of silken silver, flickering on top with an unsteady light. I looked from the ring to her face, dark velvet hair framing a porcelain

oval, then at George, balancing his strong body on feet placed far
apart. They looked fine and carefully placed, like grouped angel
sculptures in a garden, cast into motion by shifting shadows.

The moon withdrew behind a cloud, and suddenly everyone
became familiar again. I took Mary Alice's hand to look more closely
at her ring. George rocked from heels to toes like a quickly-discarded
rocking horse. Mom and Dad sat at ease, his hands clasped on his
knees, hers resting on top of her crocheting. Mom smiled her Cupid's
bow smile and reached over to stroke my hair. "A bridesmaid. Won't
that be fine."

Fine. Yes, everything will be fine, perfect now. A bridesmaid! My
thoughts raced with taffeta dresses, veils, and delighted laughter, so
that I heard little more before my mother roused me.

"Evie. Bed, now." Her words were sharp, but her face had
softened.

I dutifully went to bed, but sleep eluded me. Words drifting in
through the window set my imagination on fire: candlelight service,
satin tablecloths, flowers and ivory and.… My dreams were peopled,
not by quickened angels, but by still marble statues like those guarding
graves in the town's cemetery. Confused, a little frightened, I raced past
stone after stone, in a long pale dress made of clouds and starshine.

Evangeline, 1928: Remedies

Nettie's father sits quietly the afternoon the Evanses come to visit. In the parlor, she charms my husband by asking questions about the parable of loaves and fishes, which was the subject of his sermon this morning. Mr. James fusses with his unlit pipe. I think he is taken aback by Nettie—her evident beauty braced by a fine mind and frank manner—but not displeased by her. He answers her fully, then rises, knocking his pipe against his thigh, and invites the doctor to admire his new cows. They troop outside, where I hear the girls' chatter greet them.

Nettie and I move to my kitchen to examine the herbs I've collected. She asks what I use for fever. I mix a tincture of feverfew and Echinacea and hand it to her. I've been wondering if I should tell the Evanses that I am Roma, but I don't have to wonder long.

"The neighbors say you may be a Gypsy." Nettie scans the shelves above my stove, examining the label on each small jar and bottle.

"Yes," I answer. "Though we prefer "Roma," or "Romani.""

"I'm sorry," she apologizes quickly. "Roma."

"Does it matter to you?"

She turns to me, and I see her eyes are clear and steady. "Not if my patients are comfortable with you."

I turn to call out the door to my oldest, "Maisie, please take your sisters to the pump to clean up. Dinner will be ready soon." I invite Nettie to sit at the table. "After Lavinia was born, most of the ladies came around."

"What happened with Vinnie's birth?" I notice she uses my daughter's nickname.

I slip on my apron and nod toward the tiny green bottle in her hand. "I cured myself of the fever, with that same mixture you have there." While I check on the bubbling pots on the stove, I tell her the story.

"The day after Vinnie was born, Mr. Dockhart knocked on our door, looking for Mr. James. I dragged myself to greet him. His expression showed me how terrible I looked, and I'm sure he told his wife, and she told the women at church. A week later, I walked in for the sermon. The women all craned their necks to get a look at me traipsing up the aisle."

I pause for a minute and recall that long walk, holding the baby and drawing little Maisie after me, passing through the squares of light the windows make on those ancient chestnut planks, the faces of all those women who knew I was birthing, but didn't do so much as bring a casserole, turned toward me. I stir the potatoes and continue.

"Mrs. Mayhew sidled over to me as I stood listening to Mr. James greet his flock. 'I heard you took bad sick, girlie. Did you get medicine from the doctor?'"

"'No need. I made a little tea for myself,' I told her." I didn't mention that I read in Esther Mayhew's ice blue eyes that she had never considered coming to help me.

But Nettie is not fooled. "You had no one to attend you?"

I try to make my voice light. "Nella Larson, the black woman who lives at the crossroads, looked in on me. It felt good to know she was there, but, so far, nothing has gone wrong that Mama's instructions didn't cover." I open the oven to check on the biscuits. "After that day in church, a few women noticed that my girls are rarely sick and asked what I use to prevent them getting the colic or the croup. So I make blackberry syrup and vinegar gargles for their children, and special teas for their ladies' ailments. If they bring me a jar, I fill it. I am useful to them, if not their friend."

Nettie rises and shakes out her long black skirt. "Healers are rarely one of the crowd," she replies. "We all look for love, but sometimes we settle for respect. I'll call my father in for dinner."

When the doctor and Mr. James and the girls clamber through the door, Mr. James tossing Tally to make her laugh, I think I see a brief nod pass between Nettie and her father.

Before I place the roast and vegetables on the table, Nettie and James are deep in another discussion. Dr. Evans sits back with a sad smile on his face and sips his iced tea. I have a feeling he would like something stronger.

After dinner, I set some cookies out for the girls by the hearth. Over raspberry pie and coffee, Doctor Evans clears his throat and turns his attention to Mr. James. "My daughter and I, being the only two doctors in the county, are busy with all manner of cases, but the constant flow of pregnancies means we often have to go back out after a hard day traveling around the county. More and more families are moving down from the mountains to find work in the mills along the rivers, and fewer women live near mamas or aunts who can help them deliver."

Mr. James shuffles in his chair. I doubt he has given much thought to who helps women give birth. When ours were born, he hovered outside our door until I called him in to cut the cord, then cradled the baby while I slept. Dr. Evans plows on.

"Many women aren't comfortable with a male doctor. My daughter can see them, but she also helps mamas with their children's sore throats and broken bones and such and needs to be in the office most days. If we had a midwife on call, we could convince women who prefer modesty that they can see Nettie here for prenatal checks and leave the deliveries to the midwife. I would call on your wife's help only after Nettie has checked carefully to be sure there would be no complications."

Mr. James raises his head to catch my eyes. "This is something you want?"

I cock my head but do not answer, giving him time to think it through.

Dr. Evans hurries along. "She would work alone, but either I or my daughter will be available in case something goes wrong. Her pay per delivery will be two dollars and she can expect three or four deliveries a month, possibly more as the word spreads."

I think it's time I add something to the conversation. "It would help us a lot to have the income."

We all wait, our fingers slipping on icy glasses. I know my husband is thinking about buying the farm at last. He clamps his teeth on his pipe. "How will you get around the county? You cannot walk alone at night, and during the day I need the wagon."

Dr. Nettie stirs. "Evangeline can take my carriage with the gentlest mare during the day, and I will send my hired man, Sam, with her if she has to go out at night. I will still have Dad's carriage if I need it. He plans to buy a motorized car next week. Going all the way to Atlanta for it."

Mr. James holds his pipe to the side and watches our daughters with their dolls. "But what will happen to the girls when you are working, Evangeline? Sometimes I have to be out seeing to my flock."

"I will take them with me if you aren't home. Maisie will take care of her sisters, and I will be close by if they need me. They are good girls and will not be too much trouble." Everyone looks at Tally, feeding her dolly a pretend cookie. "Even Tally can play quietly." The doctor stares at our youngest as if testing this proposition.

My husband chews on his pipe stem for a moment more before removing it from between his teeth. "I think it's a fine idea." He agrees the girls will stay with him if he has no evening rounds to make.

I raise my hand to my chest and feel my heart racing. I had not realized how much I want this. Freedom to move about and work to do that truly matters outside our four walls. I'm almost dizzy with excitement. Mr. James's smile says he knows how I feel.

"It's settled." The doctor slaps the table and beams at me. "Do you suppose I could have another piece of that excellent pie of yours?"

After a second serving, Dr. Evans rises with a groan. "I have to be out at dawn tomorrow to visit a patient on the ridge. Thank you so kindly for such an excellent meal, Mrs. Grey." He bows elegantly and takes his daughter's arm. "If you are as good a midwife as you are a cook, our community will be very lucky, indeed."

Watching the Evanses drive away in their fine carriage, Mr. James's arm circles my waist. "Those two are certainly different from our other neighbors."

"Different, and interesting," I reply. "Do you think they will get on here?"

"Why not? We need a doctor badly." He shoves the door to with one hand and hugs me closer with the other.

❦

"Maisie! Vinnie! Tally! Time for school!" Ruv wakes when he hears the screen door release from its iced-over frame. He pads to my outstretched hand.

"Good boy." I put the pan of oatmeal mixed with pot likker in the corner of the porch. He waits for my nod before he limps to it. "You've grown slow, old man. I fear the rabbits are safe forever from your jaws."

This winter, I found him curled against the door each morning, instead of bounding in from the forest to my call. I took to feeding him. His right hind leg droops a bit lower than the left. A stroke, maybe? When I kneel and press my face against his wiry fur, he turns stiffly to nuzzle me. "You are all I have from home, besides the trees. Please, stay as long as you can." Released from my embrace, he hobbles back to his post.

Together, we watch a red-shouldered hawk glide from the cedar trees down slope from our hill. The sparse snow on the ground gives her enough contrast to find easily her prey. In years past, there would have been little game for her here, for Ruv laid at our door nearly every morning enough birds and small animals to keep other hunters at bay. Now Mr. James has to make time to hunt for our jogray—rabbit stew, he calls it. Through all these years, he's picked up only a word or two of my tongue. I've given over to mostly gadjikanes.

My eyes wander far over the frost-tipped evergreens to the horizon, west where my family has gone. I've had no word, though I did not really expect any. During the day, I forget. But sitting quiet by the fire at night, or on cool mornings when the girls are slow to stir, I listen for some whisper of their fate. I wonder if they have arrived, if I have nieces and nephews out there, if our vitsa—our clan—even speaks my name.

A shadow creeping around the corner of the house clears my thoughts. Slowly, a woman reveals herself, wrapped in a heavy wool coat, clutching a blanket-draped bundle I can only guess is her newest born.

"Mrs. Dockhart! What brings you here?" My surprise outstrips my manners. When she raises her eyes to mine, I see such misery that I don't wait to hear her excuses, but rush down the steps to shoo her and the baby inside. "Come in! You must be frozen. Did you walk all the way from the crossroads?" Placing my hand on her shoulder blade, I steer her toward the door.

"Maisie!" I call again. "Put on the kettle for tea!" I open the heavy door. Maisie is standing right there, on her way to answer my first call.

Mrs. Dockhart sinks slowly into the chair I pull out from our big oak table. Her bundle stirs, and one thin arm reaches out to grasp her tit. Embarrassed, she pulls the arm away and twists the blanket open, plumps one hand under the baby's bottom, and turns him to face me. His startled eyes crinkle to a whimper.

"It's all right. Go ahead and nurse him." Mrs. Dockhart looks down at her chest, brushes back her drab brown hair. "Mrs. Dockhart, I've nursed three of my own. Ignore him, next he'll be wailing."

My neighbor continues to glower at the table, but moves one hand to unbutton her top and throws the blanket over the baby's face. I can see her hands moving under the cover. She guides his mouth to the nipple and winces as he bites down.

"Amelia." She speaks in a flat tone, like an out-of-tune string plucked.

"Pardon?"

"Amelia. That's my first name."

I stand and lay my fingers lightly on the kettle. Does she think I don't know her name? We have seen each other nearly every Sunday since I came here, though usually she ignores me unless speaking is strictly necessary.

I know what brings her out. Saw it in her eyes. Her future is plain as any map. I make my voice bright like the pans shining over my stove.

"Water's warm enough. I'll pour us each a cup and you can tell me why you're visiting this cold morning." If it had been Sally Walker, I might have spared her the request, just made the mixture and given it to her casually, like I would a new plant for her garden. But Amelia Dockhart, I judge, needs to ask for herself. I'm sure it will do her soul good, and it won't hurt mine, either.

I nudge my eldest toward the loft. "Maisie, make sure Vinnie and Tally put on their wool stockings, not the cotton. It's cold this morning." I sit back down and chat easily about the church social, the children's new schoolteacher, anything to keep up a banter as Amelia finds her courage. From the way she cuts her eyes toward the loft, where my daughters chatter while they dress, I can see she counted on finding me alone.

Her hard brown eyes skim over my neat kitchen. Is she thinking, as I am, back to the first time we met? I hear the word "Heathen!" hissing in her voice, the day I confronted her at church and let her know I am Christian, too. She looks at me now, mute.

I make my voice cheerful. "Sissy Applewhite will be needing a new onslaught of casseroles about now, one week after the twins' births."

Amelia suddenly folds down the blanket, brusquely removes the nipple from the baby's mouth, and hoists him to her shoulder. He promptly lets out a loud burp, then snuggles his little head in to sleep against her chin. Around his eyes I see the wrinkles of exhaustion. He does not sleep soundly, or for very many minutes at a time, I suspect.

I watch his mother's eyes at that moment, see the flicker of satisfaction battle with fatigue and the grimmer reality that sets her jaw.

"This will be my last," she says with certainty. "I won't survive another, and neither will the babe. Jamey here may not make it another year. He's all the time whimpering. At nine months, he's barely as big as his sister's baby doll."

I measure the child with a glance and see that she speaks the truth.

"What does your husband say? Is he worried?"

She looks sharply at me, then away. "He's like most men. Perfectly content with God's will and not about to help God along by sleeping in the shed."

"Let me get you more tea." I take both our cups and turn my back so she cannot see what I select from the labeled jars above my sink. When I face her again, I place the red-rimmed set in front of her. "Could it be that your monthly is just late?"

She looks at me with those hard eyes, and for the first time I see a glimmer of hope in them. She nods. "It could be, I suppose."

I lay down in front of her the packet I made. "Make yourself a cup of tea from this morning and night for three days. Sometimes nature just needs a little help."

"Thank you." She takes a sip or two from the cup in front of her and rises, wrapping the baby tightly in the frayed blanket and placing him over her shoulder. She stops with one hand against the doorframe. Is there a softer edge to her brown eyes? "Thank you, Evangeline. I won't forget."

I shape my words slowly and completely so she understands my meaning. "For what? For a little tea? Don't be silly. It's nothing." Will that hold her tongue?

I call once more up the stairs—"Maisie! Vinnie! Tally! It's time!"— and join Ruv on the porch to watch Amelia trudge with her baby across the field. The girls scramble from the loft and clatter out the door, each in a tight woolen cap, a sturdy coat, and mittens. Maisie has wound her red scarf so tightly around her face that I can only see her olive eyes and long dark lashes. Vinnie's is neatly tucked into her collar. Tally's scarf, as usual, flies behind her. I wind it an extra turn or two, then kiss the patch of skin that shows between the gray wool and her turquoise eyes.

"Maisie, no dawdling this morning. Too cold for that." I squeeze her shoulder and bend to kiss her cheek. "Make it a good day."

The girls shrink to bird-size shadows far down the lane. Mrs. Dockhart has completely disappeared in the other direction. I look down to see my own bare hands stroking the silken oak wood of the porch banister and count my blessings.

My husband built this porch for me three years ago. I had been away a long evening and night, helping Mary Avery birth her baby, and was so tired that I nodded off on my way home. I awoke to find that Espero had ambled on her own to the barn just as dawn cracked the sky over the persimmon grove. Mr. James helped me put away the horse and wagon and followed me toward the house. And that's when I saw it: a sturdy, covered porch, posts rising to meet the overhang, with a punched floor, railing and slats framed like the elegant turn of a piano leg. Three wide steps led to the landing, where Ruv lay watching us cross the hen yard.

"What—when did you do this?" I tried to think how many hours I had been gone. Not more than twelve. "How did you do it without my hearing?" I racked my brain to think if there had been any unusual sound from the barn lately, but could think of none.

Mr. James pushed his hat back and grinned. "Knocked it together in the barn last night and set it up today. It only needs nails here and here. Happy thirteenth anniversary." Time for only a quick kiss before the girls piled out of the house, jumping with excitement about the gift.

Later that day, while he was off seeing to the fields, I took down his work jacket from the nail behind the back door. He would wear it again when he chopped wood, later. Inside the cuff of each sleeve, I sewed a message.

The little ones were in bed when he came in that night. He stood for just a minute inside the door, the jacket still hanging from his lean frame. His eyes filled with need.

"Maisie, time for bed," I reminded my eldest, reading by the hearth.

She started to protest but thought better of it. "'Night, Mama. 'Night, Papa." I heard her rustling over my head as she slipped into bed beside her sisters.

I rose from my rocking chair, tucked my knitting into the bag hanging over one point of the caned back, and, without a word, walked into our bedroom. James followed. As he gathered me to him,

I glanced inside his sleeve at the words I could embroider but had not managed to say out loud: *I love you.*

He kissed the back of my neck, and I knew he understood my throat filled with more words than my tongue could hold.

Now, stroking the sturdy oak he had hewed with his own hands, I know I am far luckier than Amelia Dockhart. If I find my own breasts filling again with mother's milk, I hope it will be the son my husband craves.

Over the river, the hawk glides, her whole body alert to the field below.

Evie, August,1959: Jezebels

In the crown of the ancient Chinaberry that stood outside the Tyndall's kitchen window, Beverly chugged the last of her Grape NeHi and tossed the bottle to the ground, where it bounced off a rock with a satisfying ping. "I've got an idea. Come on!"

She swung from the upper branch to the lower, jumped lightly to the ground, and motioned me to follow. I tucked my bottle into my armpit, shinnied down the downward-arching limb till my feet touched the ground, picked up her bottle, and tiptoed behind her into the dark house, past the rear bedroom. Carl's snores filled the hallway.

Beverly unplugged the old standing fan that stood idle outside the kitchen. "Evie, help me lift this thing." She cupped her big hands under the steel neck, dug her white Keds into the wooden hall floor, and tilted one end. I put her bottle and mine on a side table and hustled to grab the other side. Together we waddled to the doorway of her bedroom, where we set down our heavy load. When she connected the fan to the outlet behind her dresser, its motor filled the air with a steady buzz. She slapped the dust off her hands. "That should cover our talking so Dad won't wake up. And it's a lot cooler in here." She unstuck her white blouse from her sweaty chest, walked to the dresser in the corner, and flicked on the transistor radio, dialing its volume low.

I flopped onto the bed. Cedar sachet wafted over me as Beverly opened the bottom drawer and drew out two handfuls of lipstick tubes—the tiny samples they gave out at Avon parties. She spilled them onto the blue-stitched doily atop the gouged pine and chose one. I watched in the silvered glass as her mouth bloomed a deep rose.

"Beverly, where did you get those? Willeen will kill you if they're hers, and Carl will kill you if he sees you with red lips!"

Her reflected image smirked at me while she reached for a tissue to wipe the color off her mouth. "They're extras Mama threw away, and *he* won't know unless you tell him. Besides, he said I could wear make-up when I'm a junior, and I am. Or I will be, in three weeks, Headlights." She tossed the cylinder aside and picked through the jumble for another choice.

I slung a pillow at her. "Stop calling me that! Do you want every boy in high school snickering and pointing at my chest?" But I knew she wouldn't say it in front of anyone else. She never had.

She batted away the missile while imitating my pout. "At least they'll know you have a chest, instead of a set of encyclopedias."

I bit my lip to keep from smiling.

She tipped her head back to laugh, blonde hair brushing her shoulder blades, then turned suddenly and tossed me a tube: "High Beam Red."

I flipped it back with a mock-scowl. She caught it, one-handed. "Hey, when's George coming home?"

I nibbled around the edges of a secret I had promised not to tell. "He didn't say for sure when he talked to Mom on the phone last night." True enough. My brother had told Mom about his new post when he finished his advanced training—San Diego. Palm trees and sand. George wanted to surprise Mary Alice if his leave was approved around Christmas time and that meant not telling Beverly, who would blab the whole thing.

"When he marries Mary Alice, you get a sister, and I get a big brother. Wait—he'll be my uncle. But more like a brother. And we'll be aunts together!" The light in Beverly's eyes died quickly. "If Dad has his way, I'll be an old maid aunt."

Carl's rule that she couldn't date until she was seventeen in November, almost three months into her junior year, made Beverly the odd duck at school. Even I could date at sixteen, and I'd be old enough in October, but it wouldn't feel right to do it before Beverly. Not that there was much chance I was going to catch any boys' eyes.

Beverly tossed a tube into a chipped saucer, still frowning. The mopey Platters crooning on the radio didn't help. I knew how to get her back on track. "So what do you have to do to be on the varsity cheerleading squad?"

My reminder had the desired effect. Beverly twisted another tiny column of color out of its plastic case. "I need you to help me practice for the tryouts." She grinned. "Cheerleaders get more dates. You'll help me, right?"

I calculated my price. "If you'll take French so we'll have one class together. Last year we didn't have any."

Beverly pursed her lips, now flaming scarlet, and sashayed across the floor like a fashion model, her tall, angular frame well-coordinated, but definitely not twiggy. "Whatta ya say, parlez-vous?" She swished her way back and plucked another tissue out of the box. "It's still hotter than Hades in here. Is the fan on high?"

I reached over to check the setting. "Yep. High as it goes."

Beverly grabbed the front of her white blouse and fanned it back and forth across her chest, the unused tissue clutched in her fist along with the fabric. "We better go back to the Chinaberry tree. An afternoon breeze might come in. And we can—"

"A-wop-bop-a-lu-bop...." Little Richard's piano charged through the radio. Beverly and I both screamed "A-wop-bam-boom!" I leapt up so I could gyrate with her across the floor before I remembered Carl was sleeping and shushed myself with fingers to lips. Beverly ran to twist down the transistor's fat volume dial.

A second later, Carl swept through the doorway, knocking the fan on its side, its blades clacking against the hall floor, unable to fully rotate. He snatched the radio from her fingers and screamed, "Goddamn Devil's music! Can't a man sleep without having to battle sin in his own—what's that on your mouth?"

He chucked the transistor toward the wall. Beverly dodged sideways, trying to shield herself behind the door, but the sturdy Bakelite case bounced and grazed her cheek before it cracked hard against the frame. Her mouth formed a brilliant red circle. "You said I could wear make-up my junior year!"

"The school year hasn't started yet!" Carl growled, fists balled at his sides.

Beverly swiped a palm over her face, smearing blood and lipstick, and yowled like a cornered cat. Before I could react, she scrabbled toward the doorway, leaped the clacking fan, and dashed down the hall.

Carl wheeled after her. "I didn't mean to hit you, but don't ever let me see you painted up like a harlot again. And I don't want to hear that sinful music either!" I heard the front door slam and planned to escape, too, before Carl's head reappeared in the doorway. "And that goes for you, too, young lady! For all your highfalutin' ways, you're no angel, either!"

A cord of blood vessels twisted in his neck, his blue eyes almost black with fury. I dropped like a swatted fly to the floor behind the bed. How much trouble would I be in with my mom if Carl sent me home?

After a few seconds of silence, I rose. He was gone, but where? No way did I want to be in the house alone with him. The fan still beat the floor. I scrambled over the bed, picked up the machine, turned it off, and ran for the door. The only sound behind me was Willeen's walnut mantle clock ticking in the front room.

When I reached the front porch, Beverly had marched twenty yards down the brambly roadside, headed away from the blazing sun. Before I closed the metal gate behind me, I was drenched in sweat.

To our left, the railroad's wooden crossties gleamed on a sharp curve toward town. Hot wind blew dust clouds into my face. I pushed them aside with a breaststroke and ran after her. "Wait! Let's go sit in the tree. There's nothing out here but the fruit—"

"No! He hit me!" Beverly's voice echoing back sounded choked, too, though she paused. "I hate him more than anything!" she yelled. "I could spit nails into his Goddamned, rumpled-up, piss-poor— What right does *he* have to stop me listening to music? I ain't goin' back, Evie, not ever!" She strode away, arms and legs striking out from her white cotton shirt and tan shorts, beating the heavy air like sticks.

I considered pointing out that Carl had not really thrown the radio at her, but had aimed for the wall. It had bounced into Beverly's face. But I knew Beverly had to walk off anger—and he *had* lunged toward her. I hoped she'd forget I'd cowered in the corner throughout the incident.

The 12:15 to Atlanta blew its horn around the bend ahead. Glancing back to where the Tyndall's white house sat astride a yard filled with rusty dirt and crimson zinnias, I saw a furtive movement at one window: Carl, watching us. The only way out was to go forward. The train thundered around the bend toward us, its needling roar amplifying the heat.

Beverly hurried from the track's edge to cross into the persimmon orchard. I reached her as the train hurled past toward Atlanta, whirling white-hot across the burning red countryside. She turned toward me. Her right cheek was already purpling.

She plucked a wrinkled, green-stemmed orb, brought it to her lips, and stood looking at the sky, where a few clouds made relief look possible. I examined her face. Had she gotten over her anger already? I almost jerked when she changed the topic. "Where's that old house? You know, the one we tried to explore that day the wild boar chased us?"

I looked around to get my bearings. "Well, maybe it was a boar. We didn't stop to make sure. Over the hill, there. You can't see it from the road. We both screamed like Banshees, didn't we?" I might have enjoyed talking about a time when we'd both been chicken, but all I could focus on was how could she be so calm? Unless she was faking. Her face, still turned toward the hill behind me, was smooth and unlined, though her eyes crinkled to slits. Was it just the sun? I plucked a fruit and nibbled, watching her closely for a minute.

Satisfied that she was not about to melt into fury, I had a question of my own. "What did Carl mean about my 'highfalutin' ways'? I'm not stuck-up, am I?"

Beverly stared at me for a long minute. "Nah." Only a faint line flashed between her brows, so brief I almost missed it.

"Are you—" I paused, searching for words that wouldn't set her off again. Never once in all our years together had we ever really talked about why Carl was such an ass—I blocked myself from even thinking the word my parents forbade me to say. I had tried a hundred times to draw her out, but Beverly always shrugged off Carl's tirades, as if she were invincible. "Are you okay?" I ventured. I took a little bite of the fruit I had picked.

She passed her hand over the mark on her cheek and turned on her heel, striding toward the road with giant steps. "Let's go see if Mary Alice is home." Her words were muffled by an echo of thunder.

I looked up, surveying the clouds gathering over the river. She needs a little more time, I thought. So I fell in behind her, pausing only for a moment to smell a mock orange, giving the last of its summer fragrance to the hot air.

Mrs. Eugenia Beasley's white-clapboard farmhouse, with its thick gingerbread icing, squatted amid a yard bordered with lilacs on the verge of the new hospital's grounds. Mary Alice rented a room from the widow, instead of staying with her sister down the road, she said, because it was convenient if she was called into work.

I had almost caught up to Beverly when she skidded to a stop so suddenly that my head thudded into her shoulder blades. Mrs. Beasley sat on the porch, flapping a Bible story fan around her flushed face. Too late. The old lady's voice screeched like an owl hooting down a holler, "Beverly Tyndall, is that you? Y'all come on now and get out of that sun. Laws-a-mercy, child, what y'all doing out walking this time a day?" We climbed her sagging steps, circled around a vacant rocking chair, and flopped down onto the wooden floor in the corner, as far away from her as possible. A scented shrub rose shaded our nook.

The heat had made me drowsy. Beverly took two Bible fans from the lower shelf of a wicker porch table and handed one to me. We flapped them around our faces and necks in a vain attempt to move the heavy air.

"Mary Alice'll be here in a minute." Our hostess stopped abruptly, wrinkling her nose to keep her glasses on as she stared at Beverly. "Child, you sure got your mother's good looks."

Beverly and I looked at each other. You would call Mary Alice pretty, with her big eyes and soft skin. But Willeen was nearly as hard as a man. I watched Beverly partially cover her bruised cheek with a few locks of hair.

Mrs. Beasley rattled on. "A fine man, that Carl Tyndall. Kind. Took care of your mama during her trouble. 'Course, some think he caught a bargain, Willeen being such a hard worker." She fanned faster and faster. I looked again at Beverly, pondering why the landlady thought Willeen pretty and Carl, kind. Beverly shook her head. Best to avoid the explanation, which would surely have been long-winded.

"Mercy!" Mrs. Beasley cocked one overgrown eyebrow at us. "Here I've been running on, and you two young'uns thirsty as a pump in July. I'll run in yonder and get you some tea." Before she moved,

Mary Alice's car pulled into the drive. Beverly and I shouted hello and were greeted with a big smile and wave.

Once she reached the porch, dressed in her almost-crisp uniform, feet planted firmly on the floor in polished oxfords, Mary Alice pulled two big, icy bottles of Coke out of the grocery bag she clutched, handed one each to Beverly and me with a dimpled smile, and packed her landlady off to the kitchen with a pleasant, "Aren't we having your delicious salmon patties tonight, Mrs. Beasley?" Turning to me, she added, "Evalyn, it is hot enough to wilt us all out here. Why don't you run on into the bathroom and wash your face and neck to cool off? The blue washcloth on the rack is mine. Use that, wash it out, and bring it back for Beverly. What's happened to your cheek, sweetie? It looks like someone decked you." Mary Alice did not miss the swift look with which Beverly bound me to silence while mumbling something about falling. She threw a *True Romance* into her niece's outstretched hands.

I rubbed my sweaty neck as I reluctantly rose. My hand came away with a thick coating of sticky dust. Mortified, I ran to do her bidding.

By the time I got back to the porch from the bathroom, Mary Alice had changed from her uniform to a crisper green-and-white-striped seersucker shorts outfit and was curled up, legs bare, hairless, and elegantly draped, in the corner rocker. Her golden skin glowed, like she'd just stepped out of a cool bath through a cloud of White Shoulders.

Beverly bent over a white metal table by the porch swing, the magazine tucked between her two elbows, head in hands. I nudged her to take the washcloth. It didn't appear I'd missed much.

Mary Alice watched me scratch my neck. "You two look like you could use an ice rubdown."

I pondered why she scarcely resembled Willeen. Mom always said—not admiringly—that I "drew maps of folks" in my brain, to see what made them tick. I was so busy mapping out Mary Alice that I almost missed her asking me a question.

"Evalyn, dear, I asked if you've heard from your parents whether George will be home soon?" Mary Alice hunched forward, her breath escaping from between perfect lips. She wore "Decidedly Pink" lipstick. I had seen it last week on her dresser when Beverly and I visited. "I want to talk to him about some wedding plans. There's too much to put in a letter. And he keeps telling me soon, when I ask about his leave."

I tried not to scrunch my eyes suspiciously while I scrabbled for an answer. "I'm not sure. I know his training got delayed. You going with us to the fish fry tomorrow night?" That might make the church event bearable, to be with Mary Alice.

I was disappointed when she tossed her short brown waves from side to side. "Me go around with that bunch of bench-leaping hillbillies? No, thank you!" She wrinkled her dainty nose and broke into a smile. "I am going into town tomorrow, where I will luxuriate in a wash-and-set and a manicure at Lurlene's before going to meet my friend Peggy Jean at the Clocklight for hamburgers. Maybe we'll even go to a movie. How's that for sinful *in*-dulgence?" She drawled out the last two words like a drunken preacher and grinned. "Just because my man is gone doesn't mean I have to hide in the house or spend all my time at church, now, does it?"

My ears prickled. I liked her cheerful defiance of the conventional wisdom that she should stay home and pine until my brother came home for good. Still, I could never imagine my mom going out with a girlfriend if my dad were away. At best, she might visit her sisters during the day, but at night she'd be home or in church. And now I knew that Mary Alice had no use for Carl and his church.

I considered this while she directed, "Beverly, why don't you go to the kitchen and get you girls another Coke to split? I put them behind the butter on the lower shelf. And bring me one. It's so darned hot. Then I'll have to go in for dinner. You two can sit here and flag Willeen down for a ride. 'Less you just want to hit that hot clay again."

"No, *ma'am!*" Beverly headed for the kitchen.

I felt a slight thrill of anticipation at having my future sister-in-law all to myself, though I didn't know what to say to her. Mary Alice was the only woman I knew who was neither worn out nor simply silent.

I needn't have bothered wracking my brain. After Beverly vanished through the door, Mary Alice asked in a low, sober tone, "Carl hit her, didn't he? What did she do this time, forget to put starch in his shirts?"

I stumbled over my words, too surprised to lie. "Well, we made too much noise singing along to our favorite song. Carl came in and threw the radio at the wall. It hit Beverly—I mean it caught her cheek, a little. We lit out and came here."

Mary Alice rocked without a word until Beverly returned and handed her the Cokes. She took my empty bottle and poured an even amount from the other bottle into it, not spilling a drop. She handed us our drinks, sat back, and took a long pull at her own before she spoke. "So what's the best story this month, hon?"

Beverly read us two of the sillier titles: "My Sister Gave Me Away." "Short Shorts Got Me Pregnant." We hooted at that, but we sniffled over "Daddy Cries Himself to Sleep at Night." I leaned over her shoulder. Soon, we were squealing over some particularly juicy bits of descriptive melodrama in "My Teacher Proposed to Me." Beverly giggled and crowed over the ads for lacy undergarments, challenging me to pick one for my "trousseau." Through the window, the radio played, "The Glory of Love," a song from the Hit Parade. I closed my eyes and let my thoughts drift while Beverly read out loud.

After a few moments, Mary Alice's continued stillness broke into my reverie. I raised my head and saw her staring toward the road, as if she were listening for something. If lipstick made you a harlot, why weren't people shunning her, I wondered? When Willeen's car appeared around the corner, Mary Alice rose and slipped into the house.

Willeen spotted us waving to her from the front porch and pulled over. "Hey, girls, out on a lark?" Beverly and I piled into the front seat next to her. If she saw the mark on Beverly's cheek, she didn't mention it She flapped her hand through the window toward Mrs. Beasley, who had come out onto the porch. The landlady's lips moved, but nobody bothered to decipher what she said.

We drove silently, the car windows open to the breeze. My tongue buzzed with the remembered taste of persimmons.

Evangeline, 1930: Knowing Home

Spring has slowly thawed the fields. Over Dockhart's farm, the sky rises gradually from mauve to a bright blue, sparkling like the sea. A good day for berrying.

I call inside, "Maisie! Get the other girls up. We'll take the goat wagon to pick berries."

Maisie stirs in the loft and calls her sisters and her friend, Willeen. I turn back to breathe in hay from Espero's breakfast in the barn and wild roses blooming on the creek banks. Sun bakes every smell into the morning air.

Mr. James emerges from the barn with Ernie and walks across to the wagon. He slowly backs the horse toward the hitch. Espero calls from the barn, a loud whinny, which Ernie answers. My husband looks at me and shakes his head. "They hate to be separated. But there's only room for one here, Boy." When the horse is safely strapped in, Mr. James comes to the stoop and lifts one foot to the step, leaning against his bent knee with both hands. "The wagon and I barely fit on Main Street anymore. Even with the Depression, there are more cars every day. If Old Man Thompson quits blacksmithing, I don't know what we'll do. We have to think about getting a car."

"I know. I just hate to lose the horses. They're such a comfort, their smell and their sweetness. You can't pet cold metal." I hand him the list from my pocket.

"Isn't that the truth." He reads the list while Ernie waits, his massive head almost even with his hoofs, snuffling for clover in the yard. Ruv stretches out on his side, giving a loud groan that catches Mr. James's attention. "Something the matter with the old wolf?"

Ruv's tail lies now across my shoe. "He's getting old." I lift my head again to the clean air. "I promised to take the girls berry picking today, before Willeen goes. Her mother will be needing her to watch the little ones."

Mr. James is relieved. "It looks fine enough for it. I saw a mess of berries down at the ravine yesterday. I'll take this wagonload of wheat to the mill, and you'll have fresh flour for your piecrusts by sundown." He takes my hand and circles my wrist with his wide fingers. "A man has to earn his blackberry tarts." He peers inside to see that the girls are not yet downstairs, turns my hand, and kisses the spot just below the thumb. His breath tickles my skin. Then he strides to the wagon and drives Ernie away.

"Girls! Maisie!" I call back into the house. "Hurry down and have breakfast! It's a beautiful day for berry picking. If we go early, we can get them washed and boiled before I have to go check on Mrs. Applewhite." I hear scrambling from the loft, the girls rushing to get dressed. They love berries as much as squirrels love nuts. I hope Sissy Applewhite is not so far along I'll miss this whole lovely day.

I see through the screen door three sets of feet reaching for the ladder rungs. "One at a time, girls. Maisie, there's oatmeal on the stove for you all. Feed your sisters."

Maisie emerges first. "Can Willeen come, too?"

"Of course. After we pick berries, we'll walk her down to the crossroads on our way to the Applewhites. She'll be fine on her own from there." I hear Willeen's quiet voice helping Maisie direct her sisters. It's a blessing to me that Mrs. Burnett sometimes lets her stay over. Maisie is such a little mother that she deserves to have a special friend her own age.

Maisie jumps the last two rungs. Vinnie struggles to keep Tally from kicking her in the head. Tally emerges next, wrestling her clothes

into place. Willeen brings up the rear, her long legs touching the floor
from the third-to-last rung.

While the girls eat breakfast, I pack so I'll be ready when Sissy
goes into labor. Clean rags go first into the burlap cotton sack. A
selection of my special teas rests on top. Into the worn leather bag go
a sharp pair of scissors, candles for extra light, matches, and two new
blankets that I crocheted at night beside the fire. Important, I think,
for every baby to have something that has not been handed down.
Sissy is expecting her second set of twins. I expect it will go swiftly
and well.

I carry my bag out to the stoop, then check the quilt hanging over
the line. The clop-scrunch of hooves on our gravelly drive announces
a visitor, and, in a moment, a blond head bobs over the lilac bushes
on the east side of our house. I can just see Jenny, the Evans's piebald
mare, dip her muzzle to sample the watercress spilling over from the
herb garden.

"Out here, Nettie." Feet in black pumps with a bow and legs in
sheer stockings emerge from the hedge before her whole body comes
into view. She wears, not her usual simple blue or black dress, but a
silky white blouse with a bow, and a long skirt with a flounce at its
hem. A meeting in town, I guess.

"There you are." Immediately, I notice the vertical line between
her brows that means Nettie has something on her mind. "I want to
talk to you about Sissy Applewhite before I drive over to Toccoa for
some supplies. Oh, let me help you with that!"

She steps to the other side of the clothesline and lifts the edge of
the quilt, folding it over the line towards me, walks around the post
to take the lower edge, and lifts it to meet my waiting fingers. I fold it
in half again to a manageable size. All the time, she's telling me about
her plans.

"The Hospital Board is meeting about the new building, so I'll
stay over another day. You know, I think they put me on the Board

because they needed someone who can talk to nurses without scaring them." Her dimply grin almost erases the worry line.

I place the quilt in the basket at my feet. "I'll go over with the girls to the Applewhites later this morning. I checked on Sissy yesterday. She was baking meat pies for Tom and the children to eat when she's confined."

Nettie's dimples disappear. "I stopped in on my way here. The pies are done and she's starting to dilate. With twins coming, it won't be more than a few hours. I am worried that the second will be breech."

I call toward the window, "Maisie! Are you girls ready? If we're going berrying, it will have to be now!" I turn back to Nettie. "I promised the girls we'd pick berries today so we can have tarts tonight. I'll get there in about an hour and a half. Yesterday, it felt like the babies were both head down."

"Yes, but you know they can turn quickly, especially once the first is born." She smoothes her blouse down over her hips. "I'm so glad you decided to help us with the births. It's such a relief to be able to go away without worrying about the mothers and babies." Unable to stand still for long, she bends and pulls some weeds behind the alyssum.

For a minute we pull stems together. "We've paid for the orchard and the house and now we have only the price of the lower fields to earn before it's ours, pure and simple. Mr. James is ecstatic."

"That's great news. Now you'll have a living no matter what happens with the church. I hope Reverend James is not worrying about Lewis Allen and that Ducktown bunch. No one listens to them, anyway." Nettie raises her gaze from the parsley patch to see my reaction. She's come to church only a time or two, but I'm sure she hears all the gossip on her rounds. Allen and his friends have been spreading rumors that Mr. James is prospering by neglecting the congregation for his circuit riding engagements.

I step over to pull some green onions for soup. "They made quite a fuss at the monthly meeting last night, saying preachers shouldn't make money for telling the word of God. And it seems some of the women think James is too soft on sinners and backsliders. I think they believe he's married to one."

"Evangeline!" Nettie bends her head so our faces are close together. I look into her bright green eyes and see the gray bits that gather when she's concerned. "You cannot listen to those old biddies. They're envious, that's all! They would have your house, your children, your husband, and the canned goods on your shelves, if they could."

How do I explain to her my fears for my family? And with Lewis Allen and his friends stirring the flames, I am always on guard that the pot will boil over. "I know that. It's just that envy becomes hate really fast sometimes. Look what happened to that family in Hart County."

"Those people were Negro. We won't see the end of prejudice against Negroes anytime soon, thanks to the cross burners. But nothing like that has happened around here, and no one would harm you! You're the one they turn to if they can't or won't come to me. And James has been a saint, traveling all over, burying the dead, marrying folks."

I straighten and stretch my arms to re-tie my diklo. I fear that sooner or later someone will come along with tales about Gypsy thieves, how authorities know how to get rid of us in Europe. Once that happens, how far behind will the burning crosses be?

Not long ago, I heard Lewis Allen bragging on the porch at Redding's about showing a thing or two to those "uppity" Negroes and the whites who "spoil" them. "Maybe we shouldn't have let them go. We could have had us a barbecue," he laughed. I remember Uncle Pavlo saying it's dangerous to let gadje into your business, dangerous for you and for them.

I smile and pretend I'm not concerned. Nettie, as usual, isn't fooled.

"Trust in your friends, Eve." It always surprises me to hear Mr. James's pet name for me in Nettie's cool, clear voice. Both of them say it like it's a badge of honor rather than a curse. She smiles and turns to go, but returns. "Would you mind looking in on Dad, if you get away from Sissy's early this afternoon?"

Now I see the strained look about her eyes. She hasn't been getting much sleep. "Have you been filling in for him again? Is he sick?"

Nettie reaches out to the lilac bush and crushes a few leaves between her fingers. Their sticky scent fills the air. "Well, you know, he gets the blues and doesn't want to go out much. It's best he not see patients when he's like that. You have to put on a calm face when people are sick so they don't worry even more. I—" She interrupts her own thought with a glance overhead at the gleaming July sky.

"Weren't you saying something about trusting your friends?" I let it lay there on the still morning air, so quiet she can pretend not to hear it if she wishes.

Her eyes meet mine. "I worry about him. Melancholy runs in his family, on both sides. They say his mother died young in childbirth, but my aunts whisper about 'Grandma Ella's troubles.' And his father had a hunting accident." Her eyes slide away from mine, but I see the path her thoughts are traveling. "I don't know. Dad's not himself much of the time now. It's like he's a child one minute and a very old man the next." She lowers her head and brushes her skirt free of leaves. "Anyway, I've rescheduled all of our appointments for the next day. He's still good in an emergency, if you need him. I'd better go."

I watch her move away. "Baxtali thaj sastimos."

She turns, her mouth open in surprise.

"It's what my people say to a friend who's leaving. 'Good luck and health to you.' I'll look in on him. Even if Sissy goes late, they're just on the other side of your farm. It won't be any trouble to pop over there for a few minutes."

"Well, I'll stop in to check on Sissy on my way back. You know that Dad is there if you need him. A good crisis will shake him out of his mood." She already has turned to go, but reaches back and shakes my hand, the way a friend touches to reassure herself and you. "And maybe this Sunday you and James and the girls will come over and play charades. The children always cheer Dad, and he loves to talk to James about the Bible."

I tilt my chin and chuckle. "You mean, *argue* with James about the Bible. I think he likes to make my husband worry about his soul."

"It's all a good joke among friends. And if James says an extra prayer for us, it can't hurt. Thanks, Eve." She makes a crisp exit to Jenny and her carriage.

I call after her. "Why don't you take the doctor's car? You've so far to go."

"Not even I can get away with that, Eve. You know driving cars is scandalous for ladies. As if steering our way out of trouble weren't a skill we could master." Her laughter floats over the tops of the lilac crowns, followed by Jenny's hooves taking a brisk pace. I gather my baskets of herbs and laundry and call for the girls.

By the time we get to the crossroads, all the girls' lips are deep blue. Willeen takes a bucket of blackberries for her mother and starts the long walk toward her home in the foothills that guard the mountains. We watch her to the end of the Evans's fields before turning off to the Applewhite's little whitewashed house.

Sissy is sitting propped up in bed in one corner of the main room, directing her household. Her round face is reddened, but she greets me cheerfully. "Mrs. Grey! I'm right glad to see you. My water broke half an hour ago. Just got the bed cleaned. Mary, bring that chair over here for Mrs. Grey and take the little ones outside to play. Joe, you and Kenneth go find your dad in the barn and help him. I don't care if he doesn't want help. Tell him I said to find you something to do. Now git." The towheaded boys give their mama a kiss on the cheek. She winces with pain as they scoot out the door.

Redheaded Mary herds the strawberry-blonde, two-year-old twins behind them. "Susie! Teddy! Let's go now!" Maisie shoos Tally and Vinnie out, too. I hear them discussing what game to play as I draw my chair close to the iron bedstead and take Sissy's hand.

She grins. "I can't believe I'll have two more before the moon is out. If I'd known twins run in my mom's family, I'd never have married Jack. We're cousins, you know, same great-grandma. I'd have married that Episcopalian Edwards boy, instead. You ever notice Episcopalians don't have big families? What do they know that Baptists don't?"

With Sissy all you have to do is smile and nod. She carries the conversation by herself. I have only one question for her. "Sissy, did Jack strip the seat from that old cane chair, like I asked him to do?"

She laughs. "He grumbled about it, but he did it. 'What kind of Gypsy trick is that?' he said. Begging your pardon. He didn't mean nothing by it." She watches my face to see if I'm upset. I try not to let her see my concern, with some success. "The chair's over by the chiffarobe there. I told him Mary Avery swears by you, and that's good enough for me. But I don't quite understand what you want me to do?"

I show her how she can sit comfortably in the chair, her torso and legs supported by its wide arms and back slats, and still leave room for the baby to come through the missing bottom. "But first we're going to walk."

Sissy's pursed lips say she doubts that.

"Sissy, if you want water to run from a stream, how do you place the trough?"

She thinks for a minute before she smiles. "Why, downhill, of course. So you mean the babies will slide down quicker if I'm standing rather than lying down? But when do I sit?"

"Whenever you want. If your legs and hips get tired, it's even more important to give the baby—babies—a push from gravity. For delivery, you sit on the chair, and I'll catch the babies beneath. Would you like to try it?"

I move the chair nearer the bed so Sissy can sit on it. She laughs. "Well, it's more comfortable than the outhouse seat."

She chatters for the next two hours as her contractions gradually deepen and lengthen. I keep filling her cup with the raspberry leaf tea I've brewed on the old iron stove in another corner of the room. Sissy grits her teeth and moans, but keeps talking and laughing as if this is a social visit. At noon I have her sit while I feel with my fingers the bony area surrounding her vagina. A miraculous stretching of muscle and tissue has pulled her pelvis wide enough to produce the small, brown, furry head I can see in the center.

"The first one's crowning. Shouldn't be long now. Sissy, I'll hand this one to you so I can feel for the second baby. But first you have to push. Ready?"

Sissy screws up her face and pants and pushes like a trooper. Twice more and the first squirming infant slides out, his little head no bigger than my palm, his feet kicking for all he's worth. I wipe the mucous from his eyes and nose and a bit of the bloody stuff from his arms and legs before a sharp intake of breath from Sissy warns me there's no time to linger over his sweet face. I place him carefully on the clean sheet I've spread across his mother's lap.

"Hello, little fellow." She strokes his tiny hand and bears down again.

"Well, we're in luck. The second baby is head down. I can feel its hair and one little hand. It might come hand first, but at least it won't be breech, as twins often are." After the first twin's cord stops pulsing, I cut it. "There might be a second water sac to break," I warn.

Suddenly, Sissy doubles over and grips the chair's sturdy arms. I pluck the boy from his mother's lap, wrap him quickly, and settle him in the cradle. I stretch my hand beneath her and feel a tiny hand reaching for the air. "Sissy, I'm going to check to see if the other hand is wrapped somehow so the baby can't rotate its shoulders to move out." Sure enough, one arm is flung over the baby's face and tangled in the umbilical cord. With only a grunt or two from Sissy, I free the arm and the cord. Suddenly a tiny head pops out.

"Why, it's another redhead!" The second baby, a girl, has hair like fuzz on a ripe peach. She cries as I lift her from my crouch. Sissy sighs with relief.

In twenty minutes I've caught the afterbirth in an enamel dish— one fused mass for both babies—and the twins are swaddled in soft blankets in their mother's arms. Sissy looks from them to me. "They smell so good. Like earth that's just been turned over, you know?"

A knock on the door is followed in a few seconds by Jack Applewhite's bearded face. "I heard a cry. How is she?"

I wave him in and watch the couple smile over their latest offspring. Jack looks mystified when Sissy explains how the chair worked, but grins at me through missing teeth.

"Well, Jack, now you'll have another farm hand, and Sissy will get a helper, too."

Jack shakes his head vehemently. "No, my babies ain't growing up on no burnt-out cotton farm. This land's been farmed to death. I'm signing on over at the Starr mill next week. Eight dollars a week for sure, and lucky to get it, what with this Depression on. We'll move into town on the mill village and give Mr. Brown back his land."

"We'll miss you at church. What will you call the babies?"

"Aaron and Martha. For his grandpa and my grandma." Sissy smiles at her husband.

Jack wants to know if he should tell Mary to come in and get supper started.

Sissy seems willing, but I intervene. "She should have a nap at least before the children come in. Give her another hour."

A tip of his hat says he agrees. "Maybe I'll take the kids on a walk over to the ravine to look for berries. Can I take your'n, too?"

I laugh and wave my hands at him. "I doubt I could keep them here. But please don't let them eat much. They've had plenty already."

Jack grins like a genial Jack-o-lantern and shuffles to the door.

I take the babies to the cradle and lay them in, one head in each direction. By the time I've re-packed my supplies and cleaned the room, Sissy is snoring softly.

Carefully, I lift both babies and carry them to the porch, kicking the screen door open with my shoe. "It's time you met the world, Aaron and Martha." I sit on the steps, place one baby by my side and hold the other to the light. "Father Sun, greet your daughter.' I repeat the name her mother has given her, then do the same with her brother. I tell the babies how the world began with a flower blooming from the sea, how other flowers blossomed into the sky and land. How they, too, will blossom, if they keep their words gentle and sweet and learn to flow on the surface of hardships. I snuggle them close and whisper their names so they will never forget. After I return them to the cradle, I bury their afterbirth beneath the wide oak that shades the drive. "So you'll always know where home is," I whisper.

By the time my girls tumble down the hill with their friends, buckets heavy with berries banging against bare legs, the babies are asleep in their cradle, and Sissy is once more chatting happily. On cue, Mary Applewhite brings in Susie and Ted, the two-year-old twins, who swarm over their mother's bed, their pinkish hair bobbing around her like cotton candy.

"Mary, get the goo off these two, will you? Then you can set out the ice cream churn, and we'll make some berry cream." Sissy happily directs her brood.

I say goodbye and close the front door behind me. "Well, girls, it looks like we'll have tarts for days. Won't your dad be pleased!"

"Daddy loves tarts as much as me," agrees Vinnie. Maisie reaches for Tally's bucket to keep her sister from slinging berries into the trees. We head for the driveway. Jack Applewhite shakes his hands free of water at the pump, comes after me, and presses a damp dollar bill into my palm.

"I know it ought to be more," he apologizes.

"Oh, no, you've been very generous," I say, nodding toward my girls swinging their double load of berries. "Blackberries won't last forever, and we're glad to have so many."

Jack tips his hat and gathers Joe and Kenneth with one long arm. "Let's go tell Mama about the snake we saw." The boys rush through the plank door. I hear them exclaiming over their new brother and sister and describing the eight-foot rattler almost at the same time.

"I like the Applewhites." Maisie squints at me. She comes almost to my shoulders now. "They're always happy."

I agree the Applewhites are an attractive family. "It's fortunate some women have so much energy," I say to Maisie as we start home. "I think we can just manage to look in on Doc Evans on our way."

❧

While Dr. Evans watches the girls settle on the other side of his huge hearth, I watch him. He seemed fine, talking to them, but now that they're engaged with the picture books that Nettie keeps for them on a lower shelf of the library, he grows quiet, letting me carry the conversation. Maisie and Vinnie read to each other in a corner. Tally, as usual, has wandered away to stack books by herself on the rug.

"I've been thinking that Tally may not see well. Could you take a look at her?"

For a moment, I think he will ignore my request, but Dr. Evans puts down his cup of tea, hauls himself from his soft velvet armchair, and strides over to where Tally is playing. Before he gets to her, she knocks the stack with her open hand, the volumes tumbling with a clatter. I sniff his cup to confirm a considerable amount of bourbon in the amber liquid.

"Tally, can you show me your nose?" Tally looks up, clearly surprised, her vaguely blue eyes racing back and forth, searching for an answer in the air. I have seen that look many times when her sisters try to teach her words for things. The doctor slowly raises his finger to touch her nose. Tally does not focus her eyes inward on his advancing finger and seems startled at his touch. Before I can stop her, she grabs his finger and pulls it to her mouth.

"Tally, no!"

She bites down with all her strength. The doctor yelps, but stands, chuckling. "All the spirit in the world! Okay, young lady, let's play your way. Can you grab *my* nose?"

Tally frowns at him, turns her back, and hums to herself, rebuilding her tower.

The doctor walks back to where I sit in a cozy chair beneath a tall lamp and sinks into the plush surface of his favorite seat. "Congratulations, my dear. You are an excellent diagnostician. She needs glasses. Bring her to the office tomorrow, and we'll check further, but I'm sure of it. She's a bit young, but if she'll keep them on you'll see a real difference in her."

Tipping my cup to my lips hides my concern. It's good to see Robert Evans still interested in patients, but imbibing during the day worries me.

The housekeeper, Eliza Tyndall, pokes her head in from the kitchen.

"If there's nothing else, Dr. Evans? I've left a bit of dinner for you on the table. I don't think the lady and children will be staying?" Her long nose and close-set eyes always make it seem that she's looking down at you.

"No, Eliza. Thank you. Don't forget to tell your nephew to see to my new well."

"Yes sir. Carl is small, but he's a good worker. I'll send him 'round."
She lets the door swing to behind her.

Even a few months ago, the doctor would have inquired if we
could stay to dinner, though we rarely do. Does he want to be alone?
For what? To drink himself into a stupor? I try not to let him see my
suspicion. "That's right, Nettie said you had a new handyman. That
seems like a good idea."

He puts down his cup and rubs his eyes. "Well, with Nettie's
Hospital Board work, she's busier than ever, and it seems I can never
get around to anything in the house, much less the garden. I don't
know where the time goes." He seems content to let at least a few
minutes float away in silence.

"How old is this Tyndall fellow?"

He stirs himself, though with a grumpy expression that makes
me think he'll be happy to see us go. "Sixteen or so, I think. He's an
orphan, so we're going to fix a room in the basement for him. That
way he'll be here whenever I—we—need him." He leans forward to
concentrate on his cup.

I rise and shake out my skirts, having kept my promise to Nettie
and seen enough to make me think she's right to worry about him.
"Well, it's time I got the children home. Mr. James will be back from
town." The doctor does not urge me to stay.

❧

Maisie turns to me as we stride toward the sun setting behind the
hill above our farm. "What's wrong with the doctor?"

I am trying to think of a simple answer when Vinnie suddenly
shouts, "Mama, what's that in our orchard?"

A splotch of red burns through the trees. Too soon for
persimmons, and in any case this is a circular shape much larger than
a fruit. It looks like—

First I see its green canvas top, the hoop around the rear. Then its
back wheel, painted a gay scarlet, comes into shape. I stop.

"Mama, what's wrong?" Vinnie bumps into me from behind and grips my skirt.

I breathe deeply to get my heart under control and begin to walk again. Though I try to measure my pace, I cannot help speeding up until, finally, I am practically running, my skirts catching in the briars, my straw hat flying off somewhere into the thicket that rims the orchard. I hear the girls scrambling to follow. What kind of mother leaves her children in the road, no matter how excited she is? I come to a stop when we reach a place directly under the vardo, where it sits on a rise among the persimmon trees.

A figure rocks with a peculiar gait down the back steps of the wagon and walks toward me with a savage lurch in each step. His walk is all wrong, but I recognize the dusty color of his moustache and the way he wears his hat jauntily over one eye.

I scramble up the hill, one shoe flying off into the berry patch, and do not stop until my brother catches me in his arms.

Maisie, 1930: Sorrow Songs

The day our Romani relatives appeared, my mother turned into a butterfly.

She dropped the handle of Daisy's cart and skipped up the hill, dancing over violets and ladyslippers, until she reached the lame man who stepped out of the wagon. She called him a name or word I could not understand. His lips barely showed beneath a long moustache with upturned ends. He tipped his head back, laughing, then grabbed Mama's hands and spun her around.

The wagon itself looked not much different than those farmers around here use for taking crops to market, except for the canvas top held aloft by a big metal hoop. Lee's Equestrian Services, it said on the sides made of boards nailed together. What made this wagon strange was that it had red rims on the wheels. The green boards and top resembled a crown of leaves held aloft by four bright lilies.

This man was surely one of my uncles. But which one, and where were the others Mama had told us about? I wanted to see and hear better, but I meant to stay where Mama left us, till she told us to come.

She looked at the man as if he held the answer to a riddle and spoke in the tongue she uses a lot when she thinks she's alone. She taught me a few words, but when my uncle answered, I couldn't catch anything from so far away. Suddenly, Mama cried out, bowed her head, and stumbled. He caught her before she hit the ground.

I lifted Tally from the goat cart, grabbed Vinnie's hand, and ran, leaving Daisy munching clover down at the bottom. Tally squealed, reaching out for the berry buckets we left behind in the cart, but I didn't mind her. I had to get to Mama.

As I ran, two ladies climbed down the steps that seemed to fold out from the back of the wagon, placing their hands on the huge rear wheels to steady themselves, and hurried over to help settle Mama on the bottom step. By the time I made it to the top of the hill with my sisters—Tally, having wiggled her way out of my arms, digging in her heels and pulling back all the way—Mama was crying more quietly.

"Vashti Garretson!" she sobbed. "I thought never to see you again!"

I didn't want Mama to scold me for interrupting, so I stopped some distance away. Tally wiggled out of my grasp. I put my hand over her mouth to keep her from squealing again. The man swiveled his head to stare at her, and she planted her face against my skirt, pulling the cloth so tight I thought she might tear it. Vinnie clung to my other hand and chewed her thumb.

The woman called Vashti Garretson stretched tall, with a blue scarf tied around her brown hair. She had deep blue-green eyes, and skin the sun had stirred to butterscotch. The other one was small, with a nose like a bird's beak and bushels of black hair held back by a purple headscarf. She walked to the side before she stopped and ducked her head, waiting to be seen. Next to her, under a peach tree, a roan picked grass with its big slabby teeth.

Mrs. Garretson held my mama tightly. "There, now, Love. Dev arranges what we can't seem to manage, sure enough." She spied my sisters and me, standing close by, and loosened her grip on Mama to watch us.

"Did she say the Devil brought them here?" whispered Vinnie.

"It sounded more like 'Dev' to me. I don't know who that is." I answered, quietly as I could. Mrs. Garretson's eyes flashed, staring right at me like she saw everything inside. Not wanting her to think me a bad girl who had something to hide, I held my eyes steady. After a minute, she nodded. I dipped my chin.

"You've been right busy, I see." She waved her hand toward us.

The man hunkered down and waved, also. Tally clutched my hand and began to wail. Vinnie disappeared behind me. I felt afraid of him, too, a little. The few men I knew who wore moustaches trimmed them away from their lips. I held on to my sisters and looked for a signal from Mama. Though tears had made tracks on her cheeks, she smiled, so I knew it would be all right to go over to her. Tally and Vinnie skidded with me through the gravelly rocks until we landed at the man's feet.

"Girls, this is your Uncle Stephane," Mama said.

He squatted level with Vinnie's face, and looked us over carefully. I could see that his eyes were a lot like mine—green with deep chocolate swirls shooting out from the black dot in the middle. He said to my mother words that sounded like, "Shey, shey—pointing first to Tally, then Vinnie—romni." This last he said while stabbing his finger toward me. I wondered if it were some Romani version of "Eeny, meenie, mynie, moe." And had I won or lost?

Mama's lips stretched a bit more.

Uncle Stephane stood and gestured to the small woman hanging back against the wagon, letting loose a long string of words at my mother.

My mother made clear what he meant. "Mirela, murri phen, welcome." "Phen"—sister—was a word I knew. So this lady was Uncle Stephane's wife. Mama kissed her on both cheeks, turned and pointed to each of us. "Maisie, Lavinia, and Talitha."

"How old?" My new aunt, Mirela, smiled at each of us. "Bibi," she said, pointing to her own chest.

"Ten, almost eleven, Bibi." I pointed to my own chest. Bibi?

"Seven. Soon I'll be eight," piped Vinnie. "Bibi," she added, looking at me for a translation, but I had none.

Tally held out five fingers. "In August, she'll be five," Mama corrected.

Mrs. Garretson bent to look us in the eyes. "And a fair queen you will be, Maisie. Lavinia, your mami—your grandmother—would be proud you have her name. And Talitha—" She looked long at Tally. I thought maybe she had forgotten what she meant to say, but, after a minute, she straightened and added, "You are indeed a little girl." At that, they all chuckled; my Mama, too.

Mama answered a question from Uncle Stephane. "No, they do not rakh the chib. It would be a problem here." I wondered what a chib was and why we would rock it. She held his gaze for a moment before he jerked his head up and down a few times. "Vashti, your husband, is he well?"

Mrs. Garretson slowly shook her head.

Mama placed one hand on her friend's arm and looked sad. "I'm so sorry."

"There are none left in the mountains who know me. I've decided to travel out west with Stephane and Mirela and see if the kumpania will let me stay. I would not have traded my man for the world, but now I want our music and our food."

Suddenly, Mama's hands flew to her face. "Dad! Tomas! I can't believe they are gone. And Uncle Pavlo and Aunt Juba—are they all right?" Mama choked back a sob, clutching her hand to her chest to keep her breath from flying upwards to the clouds.

My uncle reached out to reassure her. "Yes, Phen, they are fine. They waited in the old Indian Territory, like we had planned. When we didn't come, they moved on to Denver and found Paolo. He has a family of his own now and a new kumpania, since our old group is mostly gone. They sent a postcard to the farm once or twice. I've sent word by a passing wagon that we are coming." He looked over the tops of our orchard that marched across the hill. "We cannot stay long. Everything is changing. The countryside, it isn't safe anymore.

We must go and find a better place, with family." He moved his feet the way grownups do when they're uncomfortable.

I could see Uncle's words worried Mama, for she clutched her arms, holding herself for comfort. Tally let out a long howl. Uncle lowered his eyes to her.

"Be still, shey. We will make some zumi by the fire. You like zumi—soup?"

Tally sobbed hysterically. Mrs. Garretson reached down and shook her, gently. "Talitha, you will make your mama feel worse. Come help me find a basket to pick some greens. Have you ever seen inside a wagon like this?" Tally stopped crying and went quietly along, Mrs. Garretson talking softly to her all the while. That made me think: this was how Mama got Tally to behave, by talking softly to her, whereas all my pulling and shoving only made her grow more stubborn. I could see how to manage her better.

Vinnie sidled up to Mama's skirt. "It's all right, Mama, don't cry." She stroked Mama's hand like a little nurse and turned her head to Uncle Stephane. "You promise you won't take my mama away?"

He nodded. "I promise, shey. I think your mama would not want to leave you, even if we tried." But the look he aimed at Mama had a question in it. I watched him closely, after that.

Mama patted Vinnie's head and wiped her own cheeks with the other hand. "I think we'd better pull the wagon closer to the house." Swiftly, Uncle Stephane turned and clucked to the horse.

Mrs. Garretson and Tally returned with a basket. Mama swung toward my other sister. "Vinnie, go show Mrs. Garretson the herb garden, please. Maisie, fetch Daisy and the cart. Gather some tinder on the way to the house. Tally and I will walk with Bibi Mirela."

After I fetched Daisy, I gathered wood and kindle in the cart. As I pulled it past the smokehouse I stopped to think. What do Roma eat? I decided most everyone liked chicken, so I unhooked a hen my father had hung the day before and shoved the door shut. I took the chicken, along with some potatoes, turnips, and beans from our cellar, to the women gathered around a fire they'd built in the old barbecue pit, between the barn and Papa's tool shed. I must have done right, for Mama nodded at me when I handed the bird over to Mrs. Garretson. Like she'd been expecting that very thing, she dipped it in an iron pot full of steaming hot water and sat down to pluck its feathers.

Uncle Stephane unlatched a copper pot from a rawhide tied to his wagon's roof. Soon the vegetables and chicken were bubbling inside it. He had pulled the wagon to the rear of the barn and left his roan munching hay inside. I looked from the path behind me to the barn: No one could see the wagon from the roads that bordered our farm.

My uncle and the women sat on little stools from the wagon. Why didn't Mama ask them to sit inside, in the parlor? Instead, she gathered Tally, Vinnie, and me on the old oak logs that Papa dragged home long ago. Often, we would sit at the campfire and roast marshmallows, while Mama told us stories about animals and Papa read Bible stories. Did Uncle Stephane know stories, too?

By the time Papa came trudging from the west fields with the horses, all of them dusty and sweaty from their day's work, we were chatting around the fire about which fruits were ripe and what game we had seen in the fields. Papa paused for a moment with his hand on Espero's bridle, then stepped closer to the pit. "Welcome," he said.

Uncle Stephane stood immediately. "Stephane Lee," he offered. "I am very pleased to meet you." About his eyes I saw an extra crinkle that made me think he did not mean what he said. If Papa noticed, he did not let on, but smiled and waited patiently to be introduced to the women. Mama spoke their names.

"So good to see you again," Papa said to Mrs. Garretson. "I'd better wash." He glanced toward his hand, moving it down by his side. Only then did I realize that Stephane had not shaken it.

When he returned from the pump, Papa sat down by Mama's side on an upturned stump. "We have waited a long time for this day." His eyes reflected only fire.

꒰ ꒱

That first night we ate stew around the campfire, my father invited the Romani relatives inside. "A picnic is mighty fine, but you must want a rest from the road."

Uncle Stephane smiled, but shook his head. "We Roma are used to the sky for a roof." Vinnie and I looked at each other. Wouldn't a house under the sky get awfully dusty?

There was much they did that I did not understand.

My mother had sent me back with the cart to bring back dishes, forks, knives, spoons, and cups, along with a jug of whiskey from Papa's cabinet. I had seen mugs and plates hanging in nets from inside Uncle Stephane's wagon, but I thought perhaps Mama wanted ours for our guests because they were finer. Instead, my uncle and the ladies used the dishes and utensils from the wagon, while we ate on our own plates.

After dinner, my uncle pulled out a pipe at the same time Papa reached inside his pocket for the little Meerschaum he favored. Everyone settled down to watch the flames. Daddy poured some whiskey into one of our cups, intending to pass it across the fire, but Uncle shook his head, tossed the coffee he'd been drinking out of his own cup, and passed it to my dad. My father shrugged, filled the cup, passed it back, then lit his pipe from a stick he thrust into the campfire's glow.

Tally loved nothing so much as smoke. She wandered over and reached her hand out to trail in the vapors from Uncle's pipe. Soon Vinnie, too, twirled in the billowing fumes. Uncle Stephane watched them, his pipe clamped in his teeth. His eyes snapped and tickled you, even with his mouth busy doing something else.

Still, it surprised me when his arm suddenly swept out and pulled Vinnie and Tally to him. Tally climbed onto his knee. Vinnie leaned against his leg—the good one. He patted Tally's hand to stop her from snatching the hot pipe bowl. I moved to put my arm around Vinnie. He reached out, his palm held stiff against my shoulder. "No!" he said, firmly.

I was too old to throw myself into Mama's lap, so I ran behind her and buried my head against her shoulder, not wanting anyone to see me cry. She patted my arm.

"Stephane! She did not mean to come so close." Mama and Stephane stared at each other. Daddy frowned.

Mrs. Garretson walked around the firepit to crouch beside me. "You are a big girl, now. Come sit with Mirela and me. I'll show you how to weave a basket."

She led me toward the stool where she'd been sitting. I sat beside her on its wide seat as she lifted reeds from the stack she'd brought from the wagon, and tucked one under another. She handed two to me and slowly repeated the movement of one over and around the other. It did not take me long to get the hang of it. I watched Uncle Stephane for clues to why he didn't like me as much as he did Tally and Vinnie.

Mama seemed to forget me. "Tell me now, Stephane," she said. I saw her swallow twice like something was caught in her throat.

Uncle Stephane began his story. "When they couldn't get Papa out of jail right away, Bibi Juba and Kako Pavlo struck off for Oklahoma on their own, telling Tomas to wait for word on Papa's case and they would come back if they could help. You know, Kako thought the Indians might be nicer to us than the gadje. Begging your pardon." He ducked his head at my father. "Can you rakh the chib?" Uncle Stephane hooked his thumbs in the pockets of his vest.

My father crossed his arms and shook his head.

"James understands a word or two of Romanes." Mama's voice sounded like a warning.

"You know about Roma?" Uncle raised his brows to make it a question to Papa.

Papa's words came out with a fog of smoke from his pipe. "I met some Gypsies—Roma—in Belgium during the war." I dropped my braid of reeds. My papa never talked about the war. But he must have done so with Mama, for she didn't look surprised. I reached down to pick up my work and waited to hear more, but Papa clamped his teeth around his pipe and fell silent.

Uncle spoke directly to Mama. "It is not a pretty tale." He jerked his eyes at Tally and Vinnie, who were still playing with his beard and the bright buttons on his vest.

My mother called to my sisters. "Tally, Vinnie, come here." She told Vinnie to help Tally put on her pajamas and go to bed. Tally at first shook her head. My mother and father both simply looked at her. She took Vinnie's hand.

"What about Maisie?" Vinnie asked.

I half rose to go along, but Mama said, "Vinnie, you're eight, old enough to be the big sister for a while and give Maisie a break." I watched Vinnie nudge Tally toward the house and gazed around the circle of adults. Why was I being allowed to stay?

I settled back down by Mrs. Garretson. Mother's eyes were glued to Uncle Stephane. "Go on," she urged.

He watched the fire and continued his tale. "When I arrived, Tomas and I went to the jail and asked to see Father. We found him feverish: his eyes were too bright, and his skin felt like a fish just pulled from the stream. Tomas talked with a tall guard he'd met before. Next day when we came back, Papa showed us the extra bread he'd stashed in his inner coat pocket. As we left, Tomas went to speak again to the guard, but the man began yelling at Tomas. Before I could understand what they were saying, two other guards came and grabbed Tomas's arms and legs and hauled him away. I screamed, but one of them turned and showed his gun. I watched them disappear through a steel door."

My uncle raked his black hair back from his forehead and cradled his head in his hands. Night had fallen and the air had grown damp with dew, yet no one moved. When he lifted his head, we all leaned forward to hear him better.

He explained how he gathered his courage and returned the next day to the jail. A sloppily dressed officer at the desk claimed not to know where his brother had been taken, but leaned over and muttered, "One or two pieces of gold might buy a New Orleans copper, but it takes more than that to keep him. And more than one cop to hide a secret."

Uncle's eyes burned with so much pain that I watched my fingers moving among the reeds rather than look at him while he continued. "What could I do? Tomas held almost all our gold, and I didn't know if I'd ever see him or it again. I didn't have enough money to bribe the guards." Mama's eyes never moved from him as he explained how he tried to get a doctor to come into the jail, but none would come, no matter what he offered. He tried to smuggle in a little extra food and clean clothes for my grandpa, but uncle was searched and everything he brought, stolen.

"They took away everything except the locket with Mama's hair in it. Remember, she sent it along for Papa, in case we couldn't bring him out right away? I had sewn it into my coat, and I ripped it out to give to Papa. Every time I saw him after that, he held it tight in his fist. When the cops came by, he hid it in his mouth. Then one day he handed it back to me.

"'Not even her image should see what happens in here,' Papa said. The next day I came and his cell was empty. 'Gone,' they said. 'Probably buried in Potter's Field.'"

Mama softly sobbed, and Papa put his arm around her. Uncle Stephane talked of wandering the streets for days after their father's death, trying to think of a way to find where his body and their brother had been taken. Until, one evening, he found himself standing on the corner of Canal and Grand Boulevard.

Stephane's voice filled with wonder. "The sky poured rain. Someone brushed against my hand, and I heard these words: 'Sar san, phral?'"

Uncle paused to explain: "'How are you, Brother?' The man whispered, 'If you need help, find Papa Louie on Iberville down by the river. He knows people.'"

We traveled through Uncle Stephane's story into the streets of the warehouse district, saw the skiffs hauling fish from the big trawlers in the sound, smelled fish guts rotting on the piers. Out of the tangle of men loading, dragging, twisting ropes along the waterfront, somehow he picked out Papa Louie.

"He was much smaller than you would think, a little man watching workers unloading the skiffs. I knew it must be him, because his clothes were clean. Also, he seemed to be in charge of keeping the cops happy. Two of them walked away with big smiles on their faces when he handed them packages wrapped in string."

He described how everything just came tumbling out of him, the whole story dumped in the lap of this stranger. "Papa would have done it slower, maybe brought some ale or some wine, played a little checkers or something before asking his favors. But me—I let it all spill out. Louie listened to me, his eyes glittering like fish scales. He said, 'Go back to your hotel. Wait.' And turned his back."

Uncle did as he was told. "I wanted to write to you, Phen, but I hoped to do so with good news after a day or so. If I had known what would happen next, I would have written that night." He had paced his tiny room till midnight, listening, waiting for the message that came slipping under his door in a big scrawl: "Come to the warehouse before dawn. Bring what you can."

The next morning, happy to be making some headway at last, sewn into his coat every penny he could find, every gold button hidden in his and Tomas's luggage, he got to the corner before two men in suits came from behind and dragged him into an alley.

I could not follow much of what he said after that, half in Romanes. Mama whispered the English to Papa. I think they did not want me to hear some parts. But what I did understand set a story dancing before my eyes: Uncle Stephane made to work from sunup to sundown, crushing rock for new roads all across Louisiana, sleeping in tents on the roadsides, guarded by big men with dogs and shotguns. Thirst. Hunger. Skin so burnt it peeled in strips from his back when he took off his clothes to bathe.

"Marimé. Marimé. Everything marimé." He wrung his hands and muttered into the fire as if watching the pain charred into sticks. Marimé must be very bad, I thought.

"Louie must have sold me out, told the cops I had gold, I figured. They took every dollar from me, of course, before they threw me on the chain gang. Still, I had hope. Hope that Tomas survived and would find me. Hope I would see you again, dear phen." Uncle Stephane raised his hands and moved them toward my mother as if offering her a platter. "Until, after many years, there was no more hope left."

Uncle paused and his voice became a quiet stream, telling how he made a friend, a Negro man who shared his food and water and passed the word out: had the other gangs they passed on the road seen a Gypsy named Tomas? It took almost two years, but one day word came back: A foreman didn't take kindly to Tomas's defense of a teenaged boy he'd sent for lashing. Uncle Tomas took the boy's beating and his own.

Uncle Stephane lifted his face to the moon, tears like silver streams coursing across his face. "Our brother is buried at the foot of a gravel hill somewhere along the road from New Orleans to Baton Rouge."

A light breeze ruffled my mother's hair. She slumped against my father's chest and the night air carried her sobs away.

Uncle had wailed when he heard the news. His tears were met with blows from the boss and a stomp to his hip that fractured the pelvic bone. He tried to work, anyway, dragging his wounded side until he collapsed. After he spent three months in a bed among a row of desperate, dying men, a doctor said, "If you aren't dead, you can work," and sent him back to the road gang.

"After that, there is little more to tell. I couldn't work at that pace anymore, no matter how much they poked and punched me." Uncle shrugged. There were no words for the insanity of the gadje bosses. "One day they handed me a set of mismatched clothes and some coins and told me to walk away and never come back. I thought they might shoot me in the back and say I tried to escape, but by then. ... Well, I left, anyway." His voice reached out across the fire to my mother. "The first thing I did was send a letter to the farm. Later, I found out Mrs. Garretson never received it!"

Mama stirred to look at her friend. Mrs. Garretson stopped weaving and raised her head. "I caught some of the young men thereabouts checking the mailbox. They must have taken Stephane's card. Probably thought it might have money in it. I don't even know if I got all your letters—maybe four in all these years."

Mama shook her head. "Now I see why you wrote back so rarely."

Uncle Stephane resumed his tale. "I walked every step to Baton Rouge, after they let me go. There were many small hills, and I could not dig each one. Though I tried." He wagged his head. "I went back to New Orleans to look for Papa Louie, intending to kill him, if he'd turned me in. Or to get his help, if his eyes were honest." Uncle's own eyes glittered like stars between his collar and hat. "At the docks, Louie listened to my story and called another man in to tell how he'd been just one block away from meeting me with a note from Louie to a friendly cop, when he saw the officers pass in an old trash wagon, me lying, limp, in the bed."

"'We thought you were dead,'" Louie said. He invited me home with him to rest while he tried to locate Papa's grave. "I tried to get his help looking for Tomas, but he shook his head. No way to trace him anymore."

Louie paid for the gravestone erected over my grandfather's grave. He sent his own daughter to tend Uncle's wounds—cuts so deep they were infected, the hip inflamed. Mirela spent a year nursing him before they both stood before the elders and made their promises to each other. She set out with Stephane to gather his family.

I stole a glance at Mirela. Her plain face lit with a blush.

They'd found Mrs. Garretson living alone, her young husband under another mound behind my grandfather's blacksmith shop. Was it all right, Mrs. Garretson wanted to know, to bury him there? Mama nodded, her face a long spool of sorrow.

Uncle reached behind him and pulled a violin from a case.

"Grandpa's fiddle!" Mama exclaimed.

"I cannot do what he did with these strings, though I am trying to learn." Lifting it to his chin, he pulled the bow across once, a long moaning sound like cats wailing in the night. He bowed his head over the instrument in his lap and cried.

I went to sit on a low stump at my father's side, vowing to remain awake for every word. When my eyelids grew heavy, I leaned on Papa's shoulder, fixing my eyes on the fire to help me concentrate on what the grownups said. A song wove its way into the flames, a sound that almost pierced the sky and then plunged low into some depth where I could not follow. I wandered among clouds and climbed between molten pillars, seeking its source.

Mama whispered in my ear, "Time for bed." We walked from the fire to our porch. Questions bloomed in my head, but I was too sleepy to shape them on my tongue. Mama called my name as I began to climb the ladder to the loft.

"Maisie, tomorrow, when you are less sleepy, we will talk." She stood in the little hallway that led to her room, my father behind her, a kerosene lamp in his hand. Her long dark hair sparked red in the light. She pulled her shawl tighter around her shoulders, then turned and followed my father to bed.

I don't know if it was in my dreams or through the floor of the loft that I heard her saying, over and over, "I will never leave you or the girls." I couldn't understand what Papa replied, but his tone sounded unconvinced.

The next morning, I crept downstairs as Vinnie and Tally lay snoring in their beds. Mama sat down at the kitchen table and pointed at the chair across from her. "Here are eggs ready for you. Your papa has gone to plow already." She watched me chew for a long time before she spoke more. "You are a big girl and it is time you knew more about what happens in the world. I cannot explain to you all the Romani ways now, but you must know that your Uncle Stephane didn't mean to hurt you. He thought he was teaching you the right way to behave." She looked down at her long fingers spread on the polished wood. "He thought that *I* would have taught you the right way."

"The right way to do what? Did I do something wrong?"

"No. No, daughter, you did nothing wrong. It is hard to explain." Mama's eyes sought the window that faced the barnyard. Shapes moved about near the wagon. She seemed to see the answer there.

"Roma like to live all together—brothers, sisters, uncles, aunts, cousins. That way we can come to each other's aid, if necessary. Even those who settle, like my parents, those who no longer live on the road, have many friends and family who come to visit, so the house is always full. We have had to make rules about how to behave, how to remain pure under such circumstances, on the road, or in crowded quarters. Some of those rules may seem harsh to us, but they were needed to keep people safe and help them get along." I stopped eating to show I was paying attention.

"One of the rules is about how women are treated once they have their periods."

Good thing my father had already gone to do his chores. He would have fiddled with his pipe, or disappeared after a few minutes, like he usually did when Mama talked about "lady things."

"Once you have your period, you are a woman, no matter how young you are. In my family, girls get their periods young, and Stephane knows this. He assumes you bleed every month, as I did at your age. As you do. So he applied the rule to you. He should have been less abrupt, but he did not mean to wound your feelings, just to warn you."

"What rule?" I felt confused and curious at the same time. Why would you need a rule about periods? "Warn me about what?"

"The rule that says women should not come near men if they have their periods and must not let their skirts brush against them at any time."

I felt my forehead pucker. "But I don't have my period right now. And why?"

"Menstrual blood is marimé. In fact, according to the old people, the whole lower half of our bodies is marimé—men and women— but especially women who bleed." Mama sat back, her hands in her lap, and watched my face. "It seems strange, I know. But, really, it's not that different from what people here believe. Most of the things that come from the lower half of our bodies are considered unclean by everyone. Our county just built sewers in town so they could take the toilet waste away, because they found that manure—human, animal, all of it—causes illness. The Roma have known this for years. So, in tight quarters, they had to be extra careful to keep rules of cleanliness. But menstrual blood is also to be handled with care because it comes from the womb, which gives life, and makes women powerful. It is part of our bodies and carries who we are. So it must be handled carefully, not spread around, disposed of at once."

I nodded. It made a little sense to me. I had watched my mother handle the placenta at births, carefully wrapping it in clean cloths and burying it. "To mark a person's home," she always said. But the blood that came out of my body every month? Mama made me wrap my bloody rags in a clean piece of cloth and burn it immediately.

"It sounds like having your period is both good and bad."

Mama smiled and grasped my fingers. "Mostly good, because it helps you have babies of your own."

"I thought I had made him mad, somehow."

My mother cocked her head and eyed me for a moment, deciding whether to speak. "Well, Maisie Grey, not only was your uncle not mad at you, but he said something very nice about you, and I will tell you if you promise not to tell your sisters. And perhaps your father would not be so pleased to hear it."

I did not have to think long before nodding my head. It isn't lying not to tell everything you know. "What did he say?"

Mama leaned close so that I could see the gray and amber bits that floated in her brown eyes. "When he met you three girls, he commented that Tally and Vinnie are girls, but you are a romni—a full Romani woman."

It took me a minute to remember that my Papa did not like us to be proud. "But why does he think I'm a romni?"

Mama cocked her head in the other direction for a moment. She jumped to her feet and pulled me over to the window. "Look at Mrs. Garretson and Mirela making breakfast over the fire." I looked and saw the women moving about for just an instant before Mama spun me around. "Now, what are they wearing?"

I concentrated on answering her question. "Mrs. Garretson is in a long purple skirt and a blue top, with a black lacy shawl. And Mirela is wearing a pink blouse and a skirt with a red design sewn in. She isn't wearing a shawl. Her scarf is yellow. Mrs. Garretson's is red. Why?"

Mama nodded. "And what else?"

I started to turn, but Mama spun me away. So I closed my eyes and tried to remember the women moving about. "Oh! Mrs. Garretson has on gold earrings, a long loop, and Mirela's have two loops, I think. There's something made of gold at her waist, maybe a belt or a brooch tied around on a ribbon. Shiny, not dull like the cooking pot."

I looked at Mama to see if I got it right. She beamed approval. "And what color bird was singing on the elm tree by the barn?"

"A scarlet tanager. But what—"

My mother put her hand on my shoulder and squeezed. "Roma notice everything. Our survival depends on it. We know the difference between a tanager and a cardinal, and between brass and gold. We know how many petals are on a daisy, and the difference between baneberry and poison ivy, too. Women must know all this and more." She looked past my shoulder. "Including the difference between Vinnie's step and Tally's."

My youngest sister struggled down the ladder in her nightgown. She ran to Mama and tugged on her skirt. "Are Bibi Mirela and Kako Stephane still here?"

For a second, Mama held my gaze. She reached down to stroke Tally's red hair. "For the moment, yes," she replied.

"When they go, can I go, too? I want to cook around a fire every night. It's fun!"

"Well, you must enjoy them while they're here, for I can't do without my Tally." Mama pushed my sister to the table. "How about breakfast inside and dinner by the fire?"

Vinnie skipped steps on the ladder to get down faster. "Mama, Bibi Mirela said she would teach me a dance today! Can I go see if she's ready? I could take them some biscuits." Vinnie pushed her hair behind her ears and smoothed her skirt. She had skipped a button in front so the cloth hung crooked.

"Well, first let's get that hair brushed and your clothes on straight." Mama re-buttoned Vinnie's skirt and sent her to sit with Tally. "I bet our visitors would like some biscuits. What a good idea, Vinnie."

Mama smoothed wisps that had flown from my braid and whispered in my ear. "Remember—being Roma means never telling everything you know!"

On the third day since we'd found the vardo in the orchard, I awoke to an empty kitchen. Tally and Vinnie were still asleep. I made some cinnamon toast, ate mine, left theirs covered on the table, and headed for the chicken coop to feed the hens. I had unclasped the sliding lock before I heard Uncle Stephane's voice around the back.

"But, Phen, how do your neighbors treat you? How do they treat your girls? What will it be like when they are ready to marry?

Peering around the coop, I could see a bit of my mama's face, none of my uncle's.

"They are not as kind as I'd like, many of them, but some have become friends. No one has tried to harm us. I have good work, Stephane."

"Handling the kul of gadje! What would our father say, to see you living so close amongst them?"

"What choice did I have? And now that I know them, I see gadje are like Roma—some good, some bad, most in-between. Does my husband seem bad to you?"

Uncle Stephane's voice pleaded. "Bad, no. But can he understand you as your own kind do? And how can you live with people who mix freely, men and women, and keep their dogs inside with their chavvies?"

"Women everywhere have babies the same way, Stephane. If we mix at night, why can't we mix during the day? It never made sense to me." My mama's tone meant she was vexed. "Neither does your insistence on sleeping and eating out here. I keep a Romani household, very clean."

"If you are Roma, you follow Romnipen as we have done for hundreds of years, Evangeline. You will feel differently, surrounded by your own people."

Mama interrupted. "Times have changed, Brother. Roma must change, too."

"You say 'change' as if it were a good thing. If you come with us now, I may be able to get you and the girls into the kumpania. Paolo is baro rom now, he will understand how you had no choice but to marry the gadjo. Our mother must have been frantic when Papa did not return. She—you—did the best you could. But now we have our kumpania back together, Phen, we can be a family again. Your girls can learn to be strong romnya."

"I would like my girls to know their family. But I cannot just leave my husband. Or take his girls away from him." Mama's voice snapped, but Uncle Stephane's grew more fierce.

"But you must come now! If you wait and Paolo knows you have chosen to stay, after I came for you, he will not be able to speak for you. Most probably there will be a kris before they will let you in, anyway. Maybe they accept your husband, maybe not, but you must come now, Phen!"

My mother muttered something so low I could not hear, but it ended in a sob.

"I will not be able to see you again. You know that, don't you? You will be gadje now, you and your girls, too!" My uncle's footsteps turned away. I had gathered myself to rush out to my mother, but I heard his boots scratching once more on the graveled yard. I peeked farther around the corner.

"Here, Phen. Keep this for your girls to have one day." He handed my mother a long chain. "No!" My mother had been about to throw her arms around his neck, but he caught her by the elbows and held her away. "You may stay with them, but you will never be one of them." He shook her a little, or perhaps he could not make his hands let go for a moment. His arms fell to his sides, he turned his back, and left.

I did not rush to my mother. She never liked to cry in front of us. Later, at dinner, she fingered the chain around her neck. Maybe one day she would show me what it contained.

I gave Tally my cake to keep her from blubbering because the Roma had gone without saying goodbye.

Evie, August, 1959: The River

Carl's truck was gone when we arrived back at the Tyndall's house after visiting Mary Alice. An unspoken message of relief passed in a sidelong glance between Beverly and me. She followed directions to chop vegetables for salad while Willeen put last night's casserole into the oven. I offered to make biscuits so Willeen could get out of her work clothes. Cutting the flour into perfect circles allowed me time to daydream, staring out at the front yard. No way the peace would hold. I knew that.

Returning from the bedroom, Willeen fixed Beverly and me with a long stare and brought a bottle of peroxide out of the pocket of her housedress. "What happened to your cheek?" Her eyes flicked from one to the other of us.

Beverly squared her shoulders. "We were singing to the radio. Dad yelled at us for being too loud. I got startled and fell against the door." Her words rushed to a stop. I tried not to raise my eyebrows at this sanitized version as I put the salad bowl on the table.

Willeen daubed Beverly's wound with the medicine, waiting patiently when Beverly winced and pulled away. "That's all? How did the radio get cracked?" I couldn't help but cut my eyes at my friend. We'd forgotten to pick the pieces off the floor.

Beverly shrugged, her hands casually crossed on the table now. "Dad threw it against the wall. He was pretty mad." Close to the truth. No mention of the lipstick. I sat still enough to be ignored.

Willeen wagged her head. Then without another word, she turned and opened the oven to lift out the biscuits. Their warm aroma filled the air as she raked them into the checkered-cloth breadbasket, which she placed on the table next to the butter dish. She sat down and took a paper napkin from the pinewood holder incised with an image of praying hands. "I have to work tomorrow, but your dad doesn't. He'll be helping Preacher Allen get ready for the fish fry all day. You girls iron your clothes while I'm at work so you'll be ready to go soon as I get home. Do you want any tomatoes, Evie?"

Over Willeen's shoulder, I could see Beverly's face. A tic in her cheek jumped like a frog after a fly while she sat down at the table and passed the bread to her mother. We ate quickly and asked to be excused.

On our way back to Beverly's room, I whispered, "Why didn't you tell her the truth about your cheek? You were so mad!"

Beverly shrugged. "What good would that have done? He'd say it was an accident. Which it was, kinda. This way, they won't fight, and we'll get some sleep."

We were sitting on the bed in our pajamas, debating whether to take French or German, when we heard the front door slam. Beverly reached over and clicked off the light. Thirty seconds later, Willeen and Carl were yelling in their bedroom. Though I pressed my ear to the door, the fan buzzing in the hall muffled their voices so much that I couldn't hear.

Beverly tossed a pillow over her head as I slid into bed beside her. "Well, that worked out well," she muttered before I drifted off to sleep.

We were not permitted to have bare arms, much less a low-cut bodice or a plunging back, when we went to Beverly's church affairs, so both our dresses sported little semicircles of fabric sewn across the tops of our shoulders, enough to hide the rounded curves without defeating the purpose of a hot-weather dress. Beverly kept tugging hers—a muted pink, apricot, and aqua plaid—away from her armpits. I wore a blue gingham check that my mother called "sweet." My bushy ponytail defied my attempts to tame it with chipped gold barrettes.

Poking through the items on her dresser, Beverly named the kids we might see at the fish fry. "You like Sandy. We'll avoid that nasty Rena—you don't know her 'cause she never comes to Bible school. There's a new boy I saw at prayer meeting week before last. I haven't met him yet. Name's Tommy. He has brown eyes like Bobby Darin!" She flipped some hair over the bruise, now a thin purple border surrounding a greenish crescent about an inch long on the brim of her cheek.

I brushed my hair all over again to make it lie flat and voiced a question I'd been pondering since our chat with Mrs. Beasley. "Do you have any pictures from when Willeen was young?"

Beverly stopped rummaging and drummed her fingers on the dresser. Then she whirled. "I know! I found a picture album hidden in her drawer one day when I went in to borrow a half-slip. I forgot all about it. Maybe there's a picture in there. We can at least see if Mrs. Beasley was right about her being good-looking."

She disappeared in a flash and came back with the album before I had finished protesting. "I don't want to get in trouble. Things are hidden for a reason, my mom says."

Beverly checked the wind-up alarm clock on her dresser. "Mama won't be home for thirty minutes. I'll get it back into her room before then." She opened the velvet cover with a painted-on palm tree. I sat beside her, careful not to muss my dress.

The first snapshots of Willeen and Mary Alice as babies drew me in. Snugged into the black paper corners, photographs of the girls, and of Granny Burnett and her husband, showed how the tall father had the pretty bow-shaped mouth that lent sweetness to Mary Alice's face, and the short, almond-eyed mother contributed Willeen's severe jaw line.

Beverly kept fanning the pages till she came to several that showed an older Willeen. In one, about four inches wide, I recognized her angular face turned partly away from the camera. She sat on a garden swing with two girlfriends, all of them squeezed together in layers of frothy dresses. With a shock, I realized the middle one was my mother: dark eyes glinting, painted lips curved, teeth showing in a laugh. I had never seen her look so pretty, even with her hair simply pulled back in a close crop, no effort made to gild the lily, other than the modest attention to lips. Her dress, too, appeared plain, only a row of buttons marching down the front for adornment.

The third girl with them was the main attraction: Obviously blond curls caressed her high cheekbones, accompanied by a dimpled smile. Wide eyes of some light color, perhaps blue or green, flashed a frank gaze at the camera. "Is she related to you?" I stared at Beverly's cheekbones. Yep. Same sharp angle.

Beverly peered at the photograph. "Hm. We don't have any blondes in the family but me, that I know of." She bent closer to examine it. "She's older than they are, don't you think? Maybe she's their teacher."

She turned the page and caught her breath at a photo of a woman who laughed at the camera with a smile made dazzling by lipstick that must have been crimson. She wore an elegant ivory dress. Her eyes sparkled. The curly hairstyle softened her strong jaw. Willeen. Unmistakable, but so different from the mother who fried potatoes over the old metal stove.

"Ma never curls her hair now," Beverly murmured, touching the photograph gently, as if she were afraid the makeup would rub off on her hands. "Mrs. Beasley is right. She was pretty. But why does she look so plain now?"

At that moment, we heard Willeen's car crunch into the drive. With a snap, Beverly closed the album and scrambled off the bed. She was innocently brushing her already-smooth hair before the mirror by the time Willeen peered in the doorway at us.

Willeen went away and came back with a box of face powder in her hand. "How's your cheek?" Beverly patted the bruise as her mother stood beside her at the mirror, opened the box of powder, and dipped the brush into it. "Hold still."

Beverly's stare widened, but she obeyed. The powder blended the purple bruise with her tanned cheeks. Willeen stepped back to survey its effect. Beverly blurted, "But Dad says I can't wear face powder!"

"He's making an exception. He told me how he threw the radio and hit you by accident. Lucky it didn't break a bone." If Willeen knew about the lipstick, she didn't say.

Relief poured over Beverly's face. Willeen took the powder box, walked toward the door, opened it, and looked back around its edge. "No more music 'less your father is out of the house. How 'bout that?" She closed the door behind herself.

Beverly bent to retrieve an overlooked piece of lavender plastic that had flown into the groove of the baseboard. She tossed it into the metal wastebasket next to the dresser. "Well, not with this radio, that's for sure."

Carl and the other men from Greater Grace Holiness Church had made tables of planks laid across sawhorses in the old campground by the river. Lights winked along the low-hanging branches, cords leading back to some complaining machine that hummed fitfully in the looming dark. As we arrived, they were building fires in the charred brick barbecue pits at the edge of the clearing. A few women had buried their hands in a great mass of bass and catfish, slim filet knives flashing occasionally in the glow of the big round floodlights. Preacher Allen supervised them all. Shirtsleeves rolled past his elbows, the metal clasps on his red suspenders gleaming in the lantern light, he waved his arms and joked with the men, but I didn't see him lift a stick of wood.

Willeen dug the bucket of coleslaw out of the back floorboard and carried it to a table covered by other dishes with upturned plates for lids. Beverly and I followed, carrying pies. The smell of frying fish drifted toward the darkness beyond the lights, where children fumbled at hide-and-seek. I reached out to tag a child of about six who ran shrieking through the bushes. Beverly grabbed my shoulder and wrenched me back.

"What are you doing, Evie? We're too old for hide-and-seek. Honestly, do you want the high school kids to call you a baby?"

I scanned the jumble of kids and parents. "I don't see anybody our age."

Beverly pointed toward the river. By squinting, I could make out a knot of teenaged girls under a gigantic willow tree. Beverly sauntered over and stood listening to their running commentary on the boys who were jostling and joking in a separate group by the riverbank.

Black-haired Sandy waved at me and reached out to pull us into the circle. A busty blonde with a white kerchief tied around her long ponytail frowned, stopped in mid-sentence, and nodded at us. Rena, I presumed. I realized I'd seen her cheer alongside Sandy at football games. We greeted a couple of other kids we knew from camp.

"Varsity tryouts are coming up, Beverly. Are you thinking about that?" Sandy encouraged Beverly with a smile. When Beverly replied with an enthusiastic "Yes!" Rena turned away. Not fond of competition, I guessed.

Sandy turned her soft blue eyes to me. "You're a freshman, right, Evie? Isn't your brother George Gates?" She had covered her widow's peak—which I thought made her look exotic—with a polka dot headband.

I shook my head. "Sophomore. Yeah, George is my brother. Do you know him?"

"My older brother, Jeff, played football with him." She said this to the rest of the group as if it made me one of them.

I relaxed a little. The girls' talk was similar to reading *True Romance* stories: you didn't necessarily believe every word of it, but you needed the information. I could sort out the useable from the dumb stuff.

Rena pointed toward the boys, now chucking stones at the water in a contest of their own. "What do you think of Ted? He stares at me in school. If Joe weren't such a catch—honestly, I'm so mad he had to work tonight. That's Ted's older brother, Jack, in the yellow shirt. He plays football at Tech. Ugh! That old Jim Marshall's had a crush on me since we were in fifth grade, but he smells too much like trout. There's the new boy, Tommy Turner—he's not bad, but he blinks too much." It wasn't hard to figure that getting along with Rena meant assuming that every boy either was already, or was about to be, her boyfriend.

Beverly grabbed a plate of pickles. "Like this?" She stumbled around with the platter, batting her eyelids and grinning goofily, until they all collapsed in giggles.

I was so entranced by the other girls' stories that I didn't notice Rena was gone until she reappeared, holding a long strip of cloth. She held out one end and called, "Beverly, you're tall. Come and pin this banner, will you? Preacher wants everyone to see it all week as they drive by."

Beverly climbed onto one of the creaky benches, struggling to keep her balance, and stabbed with the clothespins Sandy had handed her at the wire strung between trees.

Out of the corner of my eye, I caught Rena gesturing. A taller figure stepped onto the bench beside my friend, a figure wearing pants and polished shoes. I couldn't see Beverly's face, but she stumbled in surprise. Tommy Turner reached out a hand and touched her waist gently, steadying her. My own waist felt warm and quivery where he touched hers. A sly smile played across Rena's face.

I could tell by the taut muscles in Beverly's neck that she was determined not to be shaken. They got one edge of the banner pinned. She thanked him and said, "Let's get the other end," like it was a chore she performed for every sock hop just before being crowned queen. Tommy laughed at something she said that I couldn't hear. As she hopped down, he stretched out his hand to steady her and whispered in her ear. She gave a short nod. I glanced at Rena again. She didn't look nearly as happy as Beverly.

I could hardly contain myself till Beverly reached my side. "What did you say to him? You actually made him laugh!" We huddled together behind the trash cans, outside the lighted circle where the other girls were now helping the women load the tables with bowls piled with everything from butter beans to collard greens. The boys had sauntered down to the willows, where I heard them chucking stones into the water, again.

Beverly hitched one shoulder to her ear. "Oh, he asked me if I learned decorating for Pep Club, and I told him, 'No, I learned hanging out Mama's wash. Where did you learn?' He thought I was kidding. They just moved here from Augusta. His dad bought Clark's hardware store. They probably have a maid."

"A maid? Really? And what did he whisper to you?"

She examined her fingernails. "He wanted to know if I'm coming down by the river to watch the Marshall boys set the traps for tomorrow morning. I don't even know what they set traps for."

"Fish, silly. This is a fish camp *and* a campground. Remember?" Beverly shrugged, unconcerned about how the fish got onto her plate. "What did you say?" I watched her gingerly tug at a hangnail.

"I didn't say anything. You saw me."

"But you nodded. That means yes, last time I checked."

One corner of her mouth tilted in a grin. "We can wander off after supper like we're playing with the little kids, and no one will even know we're gone. Wanna come? He has friends." I gaped, thunderstruck. How could she even consider this, after what Carl had said and done yesterday? "Come on, Evie. It'll be fun. And we're not going for a 'walk.' We're going to watch the guys set traps."

"Yeah, you and I both know that's *not* why he wants you to come. Are the big girls coming, too?"

Beverly paused as if the idea had never occurred to her. "I don't know."

A gray-haired woman with netted hair spied us behind the cans. By the time we'd finished helping with the plates, mothers were calling children for supper. The older boys, too, straggled back into the clearing, pushing each other, horsing around.

Though I'd never seen him lift a finger in the kitchen before, Carl pushed fish fillets around on the grill. He motioned to us, and I froze, remembering the last time he'd paid attention to me. But he grunted, "Y'all come and get some before it gets too done." For a change, he looked almost happy. Beverly pushed me toward the stack of plates and sauntered over to her dad with innocent eyes.

We ate with the older girls, crinoline to crinoline at two tables pushed together to form one long line under the Revival banner. After the preacher's blessing, Beverly sat with a half smile on her face, listening to their talk about who was going with whom, who had a ring or school sweater—or would be sure to get one in the fall—and what they were going to wear, smell like, or say at the next event. I devoured the fish, so flaky a single poke scattered it into bite-size pieces. From the girls' soft chatter I gathered that Holiness girls on dates went to church socials or visited friends, instead of going to movies or community swimming pools, like Methodist girls.

After dinner, the smaller kids ran off to play in the mist under the trees, while the men gathered along the river bank and the women cleared the tables, humming and tinkling with laughter over their own gossip. Willeen snagged us to help divvy leftovers and wrap them in wax paper for various "shut-ins." Impatiently, Beverly dumped all the beans onto one plate, so that her mom took the bowl from her and dismissed us with a command to "go play."

By the time I turned around, Beverly's plaid skirt had almost disappeared into the woods. I ran to catch her, keeping the river's chattering voice on my left as I hunted for her blonde hair in the slivers of moonlight slanting through the pines.

Big rocks bounded the narrow river on both sides, creating shoals that sang like a rushing chorus. Following their song underneath cedars mixed with pines, I caught up to Beverly as she came out into an open area on the nearest bank, where boys watched Jim Marshall and his older brother drop funny-looking contraptions with sturdy nets into shallow pools created by the circling rocks.

Beverly threw me a puzzled look as we hesitated by a cluster of berry bushes. I peered closer at the wooden boxes. "Fish traps, I imagine." Why would a fish swim into something so obvious-looking, I wondered? Then I saw Jim's brother toss a carton of shining commas into the water around the traps. Minnows.

Some of the older girls, led by Rena, ambled into the clearing. They feigned surprise on seeing the boys, as if they'd come out at that exact spot by accident. Judy gave away the hoax by asking, "How is Jim going to play a radio way out here?"

Beverly's eyes widened. This was news to her, too.

The boys smiled with secret knowledge, and the Marshall brothers stepped away into the tree line. After a short wait, two yellow eyes crept out of the woods, accompanied by the sound of twigs and grass surrendering to some heavy weight. Jim Marshall drove his dad's pickup, "Marshall's Fish Camp" lettered on the side, his hair flaming under the moon's spotlight. He clicked on the radio. Elvis's voice spilled toward us, pleading, "Don't be cruel." The girls made a low, crooning sound in their throats to show they adored the King.

Rena warned, "Turn it down! Do you want to spend the whole summer in the house?" Jim edged the volume lower, slid off the seat, and took his place beside the truck. Some kids twisted their shoulders back and forth. Others snapped their fingers. All their lower limbs appeared locked.

"Why isn't anyone dancing?" I asked, watching the waist-up-only action.

Beverly laughed. "No one wants to get caught, I guess."

I looked down. My own right foot tapped steadily, though my hands stayed neatly folded across my skirt. Methodist or not, I didn't need Carl or the preacher on my case.

Tommy Turner spotted us and hurried across the open space to grab Beverly's hand. Her back stiffened as she pulled away. "I can't leave the clearing," she protested. The backbeat melted away to silence.

"Why not?" Tommy's brown eyes radiated sympathy, like he would fix any problem she could name.

Beverly replied, simply, "My dad."

Let's see you fix that problem, I thought. I hadn't decided yet if I liked this shiny-eyed guy with the almost-ducktail.

Tommy sighed. "I know. My dad's strict, too." He grinned. "How about a dance, then? We can stop if anyone comes spying."

A flourish of strings trembled on the air. "Oh! The Platters!" someone exclaimed. The violins shrilled in crescendo.

"What about my friend, Evie? I can't leave her standing here. She doesn't know anyone." Instantly, I understood she'd intended all along to use me as an excuse.

Tommy wasn't defeated. "Give me a minute, okay?" He jogged back across the clearing to talk with a crew-cut guy, who twisted so he could look at me. I blushed and pinned my gaze on my right shoe, now motionless. What if Tommy came back and said, "Sorry, my friends can't be hanging around with runty little fat girls"? But the worst thing I could imagine was that the other boy would go along. Fear pounded in my veins, faster than the slow ballad on the radio, when I saw him fall in beside Tommy. They walked back toward us. The friend had a dimple in one cheek. Cute, sort of.

"Beverly," I moaned. "What can I talk to him about? What do I do if he tries—you know."

Beverly shook her head, in a trance. I hadn't even the faintest idea what he might try, but I could feel uncharted territory opening around me.

Both boys came to a stop squarely in front of us.

"Evie," Tommy said gravely, "my friend Bob Baker's been dying to meet you."

I looked around in panic. Bob coughed and found his voice. "Yeah, Evie, uh, have you seen the falls over yonder?"

I had to admit that I had never seen the falls. Bob took my elbow and guided me away while another slow song flowed into the clearing. Tommy put one arm around Beverly, grabbed her free hand with his, and pulled her to him.

Bob and I walked six or seven yards past the pickup. The music faded, the sound of rushing water replacing it among the thoughts tumbling around in my head. I hadn't discussed with my mother whether a "walk" in plain sight of others counted as a forbidden "date." About one thing I was sure: if Carl and Willeen found out, Beverly and I would be in disgrace, at least in the Tyndall house.

Bob stopped alongside a huge boulder and leaned against its level top. I flinched when he spoke. "Why don't we sit here?"

Looking back, I could still see Beverly swirling around Tommy in the clearing, maybe twenty feet away, but Bob and I were secluded underneath a huge tree that arched over our heads. I sank down, aware of my crinoline scraping my thighs when I pressed against the rock, careful not to get too near my "date." Bob picked out a stick from the ground and took a knife from his pocket, his teeth whistling that peculiar sound that whittlers use to hone their concentration. When he spoke again, I jumped. "You're George's sister? How old are you?"

Stammering, I told him my age and admitted to being George's sister.

Bob looked at me for a moment, put away his knife, and threw the stick out of sight. "Look, you don't have to be nervous. I won't touch you or anything. I don't date fifteen-year-olds." I knew I should probably feel insulted, but he made it sound like a point of honor rather than a rejection.

Somehow, I found my voice. "I'll be sixteen in October." I stopped, panicked. Did I sound desperate? I settled on honesty. "I know you're helping Tommy out. So he can go with Beverly. I mean, we're just chaperones, right?'

His face relaxed. "Chaperones, yeah. Gotta help a buddy out if he needs it. Or *her*, right?" Maybe it occurred to him that my feelings might be hurt, because his next words rushed out. "Not that I wouldn't want to try nothin', you being so cute and all."

Too incredulous to control myself, I stammered, "Me? Cute?" I could have chewed off my tongue the minute I heard myself. Bob laughed.

A faster song pounded from the speakers. I looked to see how Beverly would adjust her steps. Across the clearing, a thickset figure moved into the circle of light. The buckles on his suspenders flashed in the headlights—the preacher! Desperate, I ran toward the clearing, trying to stay in the darkness and to get Beverly's attention while she pirouetted in the moonlight.

Finally, she looked my way. Something in my face must have made clear the danger, because she broke away from Tommy and sprinted toward me. The music broke off in the middle of a song.

Over my shoulder, I saw the chunky figure lean backward out of the cab. He must have flicked the radio switch. A few kids on the other side of the truck bed froze. The preacher half-turned from us, focused on the gaping faces before him. Beverly urged me on toward the cover of the woods. We galloped at breakneck speed until Beverly skidded to a stop and I almost piled into her. A figure crouched on the ground before us.

"Mrs. Watson! What are you doing out here?" Beverly's eyes bugged out as her Sunday School teacher struggled to her feet, swiftly snapping her garter belt and brushing leaves off her plain blue dress. Her hair glittered in the thin light, trailing down in one long, thick, golden coil beneath a half-untied ribbon at her nape.

"Oh, well … I …" For a moment there was only the sound of the three of us gasping for breath. Mrs. Watson tightened the ribbon and tucked straggling tendrils behind each ear. "I came out looking for Jimmy and Ellen and, well, I guess somehow I got a rock under my hose, these thin sandal soles, you know. …" She picked up her dainty foot to show how thin were the soles on her white braided sandals. "Well, I just had to get it out and you know how you have to take everything off to get to one thing. My garter belt got all twisted. Did you see my two hooligans out here?" She lowered her chin. Embarrassed? Intent on figuring out an alternative explanation, I missed her conclusion about what Beverly and I were doing.

Beverly missed nothing. She moved swiftly to her teacher's rescue, helping her brush off the leaves. "Oh, yeah, my ma complains about wearing hose, too." Her voice steadied into earnest concern. "Would you like for us to go find Jimmy and Ellen for you? I think I saw them earlier over by the cars."

Mrs. Watson heaved a huge sigh. "Thank you. I'll just go back and tell Mr. Watson to get the truck ready. Really, that's awfully kind—" She wandered away, still murmuring vaguely, the seams of her hose crooked as snakes.

I grabbed Beverly's arm and twirled her around. "Beverly, are you out of your mind? We don't have time to look for lost kids—the preacher caught you dancing! We've got to think of something to tell your dad."

Beverly smiled, her hair and teeth gleaming. "That will be our excuse, silly. We were playing with the children and ran into Mrs. Watson, who asked us to catch Ellen and Jimmy and bring 'em back to the camp. The preacher got confused, with so many teenagers around, that's all."

"Beverly! You're gonna *lie*?"

"Well, gosh darnit, Evie, were you gonna tell 'em the truth and have us both tarred within a lick of our lives?"

I shut my gaping mouth. No. I would not chance Carl's wrath again. What else could we do? Suddenly, lying seemed the simple way out.

❦

Finding Jimmy and Ellen hiding behind a tree took less than five minutes. We scurried them back to their mother, who herded them toward a truck with one open door.

"Wonder what on earth the preacher is saying?" I peered around. No one older than twelve in sight.

"I wonder what my Sunday School teacher was doing in the woods *with her hose down*." Beverly arched her eyebrows at me. "Bet she tells everyone she fell."

"She did have dirt on her backside, but she didn't say she fell, did she?" I parsed my memory like Perry Mason addressing a witness.

We stared at each other. "If she was sitting on the ground, what was she doing, looking at the stars?" Beverly snickered. "And with who? Mr. Watson is right over there. He doesn't look like he's budged." Indeed, Mr. Watson was ensconced on a rock, the baby wiggling in his arms as he talked to two other men.

I tried to reason it out. "Well, she could have been with someone we passed in the woods, or someone who slipped back here without anyone seeing."

"Evie! You're saying my Sunday School teacher messed around with a man who wasn't her husband!" Beverly's mouth formed an exaggerated circle of surprise.

"Well, yes," I said, defensively.

She giggled. "But, but, she's got *religion*!" We both doubled over with laughter. Willeen looked our way. We straightened up a little but kept giggling.

Jim Marshall appeared over Beverly's shoulder. He leaned against a tree, smoothed his hair with one hand, and looked at each of us like I should know what he had to say. How much had he seen?

I turned my back on him in panic as the preacher stomped into the floodlights, a dozen embarrassed teenagers in tow. He shouted to their surprised parents his outrage at what their children had done. "We'll deal with this in service tomorrow!" he promised.

Parents pushed reluctant teenagers into cars and pickups. Rena, pouting, waved at her friends as her father snapped, "Don't think you'll be sparking with your fella on the front porch anytime soon."

Next the preacher pointed to us. Beverly looked her father right in the eye and told him the preacher must be mistaken if he claimed to have seen her dancing. She turned to Preacher Allen. "Ask Mrs. Watson! We found Jimmy and Ellen for her." I held my breath.

Preacher Allen hurried off to hail the Sunday School teacher as she bent to climb into the car with her baby. He drew her aside. They whispered. Then he stalked back.

"Well, I guess I saw things wrong." His downturned mouth read disappointment. "But don't forget, young ladies—" He raised one tobacco-stained finger in our direction. "—God has a punishment for Jezebels who go teasing boys by swinging their hips. You stay in the right path, like your Pappy done taught you." He glared at us for a long moment before he whirled to march away.

As we watched him go, I finally let air rush in to my lungs.

My suitcase was packed fifteen minutes after we returned from the river. I sat beside it on Beverly's bed, waiting for my mom to pick me up. The phone rang. Willeen stuck her head into Beverly's room to deliver the message: Mom wasn't feeling well. She would pick me up after service on Sunday.

Beverly guffawed. "You're in for some more holy-rolling, Baby Wet-tears. The preacher was plenty wound up tonight. Tomorrow should be wild."

I sniffed and pretended not to care. "It was almost ten years ago, that time I got scared, when the man jumping over the pew practically fell on me." I slowly unpacked my pajamas and toothbrush.

"The trick is to look at it like television." Beverly slipped her nightgown over her bare breasts and let it fall to her knees. "Hurry, so we can talk before Mom comes in."

In bed, I told Beverly about Jim Marshall trying to get our attention, before the preacher took center stage.

"Creep," she whispered. "He's so ugly, with those glittery eyes and those pock marks and that orange hair. He'll tell whatever he saw if he gets a chance."

"Why isn't he in trouble? He was the one who played the music."

Beverly shrugged. "They don't go to our church. I don't know if they go to services at all."

Willeen glared around the door, putting an end to our whispering. Thinking about church the next day kept me tossing long after Beverly began to snore.

Sunshine streaming through the windows cast lots among the worshippers: those who sat on the window sides of the two columns were bathed in golden light; those on the aisle sides were as ordinary as Sunday clothes could make them. Suspended in stained glass above the choir, Jesus Christ raised one hand politely for attention and cuddled in the other, close to his flowing pink robes, two small lambs. He surely had saved us last night. But would our good luck continue?

I scanned the people in the pews. Bob and Tommy had not come clattering down the stairs with the other kids to the Sunday School room. Sandy had reported that Rena had a headache. Did the boys have headaches, too? No, there they were, in the fourth row, grinning a little sheepishly.

Carl directed us to the second row on the right side of the sanctuary. I slid in next to a lady with white hair that shone against the blazing window. I liked her smell, like rosewater. Beverly, Willeen, and Carl slid in after me. Directly in front of us, Mrs. Watson had put on a hat so wide I could see only one half of the burgundy-robed choir, until they rose for a hymn. As they sang, she rocked to comfort her baby, snuggled in a yellow-flowered blanket in her arms. Her husband kept his arms outstretched around Jimmy and Ellen, who occasionally looked at each other and made silly faces, collapsing into giggles that their father swiftly hushed.

An hour later, after two deacons testified at length about how faith had changed their lives and one read a long list of announcements, the choir rose for another hymn. I stole a glimpse of the rosewater lady's watch and yawned. At my church they'd be eating Mom's hamburger casserole by now. Beverly fidgeted, impatient, too. She clicked the toes of her patent leather pumps against the polished wood floor.

"Be still!" I heard Willeen hiss, twice. The last time, Carl leaned over and glared. Beverly sat ramrod straight and stared out the window.

The choir finished another selection, settling down with muffled coughs and a slight rustle here and there. A stir went through the congregation when Preacher Allen stalked to the pulpit. He drew out his glasses, which he slowly settled on his nose, and fixed us all with a steady glare. Even Ellen sat motionless while he read the scripture on Sodom and Gomorrah. Then he rasped, "Deacon Tyndall, please lead us in prayer."

As Carl pulled himself upright, our whole pew trembled. He sprinkled our bowed heads with references to grievous sins and "the sacrifices of our Lord Jesus Christ." It amazed me that a man so silent at home could pray out loud in a group like that.

Finally, he thanked the Lord for showing his daughter and her friend the right way, when others lost their heads and succumbed to vile music, sexual temptation, and drink.

I could feel Beverly stiffen beside me.

Carl had no more muttered "Amen" than the preacher raised his voice in a great shout, "The angels said to Lot, we will *destroy* this place, because the cry of them is waxen great before the face of the Lord; and the Lord hath sent us to *destroy* it'! To *destroy* it, children! The Lord God could not *abide* the great hue and cry raised by the *wicked* children of Sodom and Gomorrah, just as all *righteousness* cannot *abide* the sight of *sin* before our Lord Jesus Christ!"

A chorus of "amens" after nearly every sentence rattled me. The "amens" soon progressed to louder cries of "Praise the Lord!" The preacher settled into a rhythmic cadence. In my head, I heard Elvis drawling, "Lawdy, Lawdy, Lawdy, Miss Claudy," while the preacher rocked on his heels, swung his arms above his head, and delivered the word to his chorus of listeners.

He mopped his brow with a snow-white handkerchief, and his voice sank to a near-whisper. "What did they *do* in those ancient cities, that *you* and *you* and *you*, my friends, have *not* done?" With each "you," his finger pointed to a shame-faced teenager. I didn't dare do more than look briefly around. Beverly's head turned back and forth, from one embarrassed teen to another. Her wild-eyed look said she wanted to flee.

The preacher stretched himself taller and taller, like a black cloud gathers in height, as his voice lashed the air around us. In front of us, Mrs. Watson rocked back and forth, comforting the infant she cuddled close to her chest, crooning steadily as the baby whimpered. The air filled with expectation.

A voice behind me suddenly declared, "Praise the Lord Jesus! Praise Jesus!" I jumped. The rosewater lady jerked upright. "Amen!" she yelled, right on cue.

"Yes, *praise* the Lord *Jesus*, brothers and sisters, but *praise* him with *hymns* and *psalms* to the *Almighty*, not with the *Devil's* music, not with *rock* and *roll*, which *offends* the *ears* of the *Almighty*." Preacher Allen roared, "This wicked music was sent by the *Devil* to make *harlots* of your *daughters* and *adulterers* of your *sons*. And it will *kill you*, brothers and sisters, just as *surely* as Lot's *wife* turned into a *pillar* of *salt*, because the Lord God *despises wickedness* and will *stamp it out wherever* it is found!"

A sudden movement in the pew in front of me drew my attention.

Without a sound, Mrs. Watson stood, threw her baby into the air, and leapt into the puddle of light before the altar. I watched the baby catapult toward the ceiling, the yellow-flowered quilt falling away. He began to swiftly descend, arms and legs jerking in an attempt to find balance. His mother writhed on her knees, waved her arms toward heaven, and spoke in a babble that contained no words.

Mr. Watson stood, caught the baby four feet before he hit the floor, and resumed his place on the bench. The baby made no cry, perhaps stunned. The husband put one arm around his other two children, who gaped with open mouths at their mother. Ellen steadily bounced her foot in the air, where it dangled over the edge of the pew, as if she were waiting for her favorite cartoon to come on TV.

Men began to leap over pews and women to dance down the aisles, all speaking in a strange tongue that sounded like gibberish to me. My memory from long ago did not do the reality justice. Why, I wondered, did the Holiness dance *in* their church, but not outside it, while we Methodists danced outside the church, but not *in* it?

Beverly leaned toward me and whispered, "They're speaking in the Unknown Tongue. Only the righteous can understand it." I remembered her saying, last night, "The trick is to look at it like television." My mind kept replaying the sight of the baby falling through the dust motes. When we finally stood for the closing hymn, I couldn't wait to be delivered into fresh air.

"Look! Granny's here!" Beverly flew out the back door and around the house, barreling into her grandmother, wrapping that small woman in a hug. I ran behind her.

"Does Carl know you're in shorts on a Sunday?" Granny's tone was mock-stern.

"Nope. And if you come in with me, he won't say anything, either, 'cause he won't want to start one of your Bible arguments."

Granny laughed, throwing her head back to reveal strong white teeth. "Well, let's go in and face the music," she chirped. "Evie, good to see you, honey. You two get those icebox cookies and coconut pie out of the back seat for me. There's a jar of Brunswick stew in the front floorboard, too. That ought to buy some good will from your papa."

We marched in triumphantly, cookies, pie, stew, and one tiny elfish woman in tow. Carl looked up and grunted. Granny smiled at Carl. He grunted again and raised the paper over his face. Apparently, he didn't feel like making a fuss in front of Granny. She could quote scripture like he could, and she never seemed daunted by his glares.

After fifteen minutes, we had told Granny all the new jokes we'd heard and eaten two each of her cookies. Already, the smell of ham and green beans crowded the kitchen. "You'll just get in my way. Go on!" Willeen shook her apron at us, pointedly ignoring our wardrobe choices. Granny grinned, peering over her glasses, and plopped peeled potatoes into a bowl.

We ran out the door to our sanctuary. Beverly settled into the crotch of three branches, wrapping her arms around her knees. I found my own niche. The question I'd been waiting to ask burst out. "What was Mrs. Watson thinking, throwing her baby like that?" I had thought all the way home about the infant's short arms, gracefully stretched like angel's wings. "Do they do that a lot?"

Beverly sniffed the air at the same moment it occurred to me the sky had darkened. "Nope. Sometimes they throw the Bible, or their clothes, but I've never seen a bab—"

"Their *clothes*? You mean like the coat they wore in, or a scarf—"

"No." Beverly grinned. "I mean their *clothes*. Once, old Miz Benson ripped open her blouse. And Mr. Hadley tore off his shirt and slung it over his head. It landed right next to Rena. She said didn't the Hadleys know to take a shower 'fore putting on their Sunday best?"

"Hm. Do you really think they don't know what they're doing? I mean, how could you get so carried away you'd undress in public? Are they unconscious?"

Beverly picked a sprig of berries and slowly squashed them between her fingers, popping out the seeds. "Not unconscious, exactly. They run around without bumping into things, so they can see. Dad says they're 'transported by faith,' taken with the Holy Spirit. Like they've been chosen." She laid a pile of sticky seeds on a leaf balanced on her leg.

"Yeah, but do you *believe*—?" I reached over, grabbed some berries, and helped her add to the pile. We had long ago learned the seeds were poisonous to eat.

"I guess I do, a little. I mean, sometimes I get so entranced with the moon and the smell of the night air that I circle around and around until I fall down. 'Night frenzy,' Ma calls it. Isn't that like what they do? Lift their heads and shout whatever comes?"

"Yes, but isn't it supposed to mean something? That's what the preacher said." I imitated. "Miz Watson is talking with Jesus, friends, talking with Jesus.'"

"Yeah, maybe it means something to Jesus, I reckon. To us, it's like night frenzy."

"But if you want to talk to Jesus, why do you have to speak a strange tongue? I mean, wouldn't God understand every language?"

She frowned down at the berry seeds. "I said I believed they were taken by faith. I didn't say I believed God wants us to speak in tongues." Her eyes drifted to the house. "I think people need to jump and shout to feel alive. If they can't dance to rock 'n' roll, they dance to hymns and make excuses for it."

"But if God loves all of us, why do they have to work so hard to get his attention?"

Beverly brushed the leaf and the berries from her leg and watched them fall into the dust. She turned her palms up. "I don't know, Evie. Maybe we want everybody else to think God chose us."

"Seems like a lot of trouble to go to. Why do people make so many rules?"

Her mouth flipped into a smile. "God, Evie, so other people have to follow them. Don't you understand anything?"

I didn't understand, but a tickle on my cheek diverted my attention. "It's raining."

Beverly drew her knees to her chin. "It might blow over. They'll be talking church gossip and if we're not there they can't ask us about last night."

I changed the topic. "Well, Tommy likes you. He practically fell over his own feet looking back at you when his dad drove up!"

Her smile remained hidden behind her kneecaps, but I could hear it in her voice. "Yeah, well, let's hope Jim Marshall and the kids at church keep their mouths shut so I can get to know him better. If Dad finds out about last night, I'm cooked."

I wanted to ask if she thought Bob liked me, but I was afraid to hear the answer. Suddenly lightning buzzed right over our heads. The drip became a pour. Granny shouted over the thunder, "You two come in now and get on some dry clothes. Run!" She struggled in the high wind to keep open the flapping screen door.

The storm chased us to the door, instant puddles splashing mud on our legs.

Evie, August, 1959: Grafts

After we washed up, Beverly smoothed my frizzy hair with one hand and sprayed sticky mist with the other. "I don't see why you can't stay this whole weekend. It's our last chance before school begins. I need you to help me practice cheers."

I twisted the rubber band another loop around my ponytail. "Mom says we need to spend a few days apart, reviewing work before the school year starts."

"Honestly, who but you—"

"Oh, Lordy!" Granny exclaimed. Beverly and I ran toward the kitchen.

Her grandmother stood with hands on her wide hips, gray hair straggling over her nose, flour dusting her chin, staring at an iced cake that had caved in at the middle. The sky roared, as if to emphasize the disaster. Rain pelted the window. "Now isn't that the worst gol-durned mess you ever saw," Granny said, with satisfaction. "You all will have to help Willeen with the rest of dinner while I start this over again. I promised her I'd make this Turner wedding cake for that shower she's going to tomorrow night."

Beverly combed her heavy bronze hair in the doorway. "What's a Turner wedding cake?" She rolled her eyes at me. I had forgotten that Granny was a Turner before she married, like Tommy.

"Yeah, I thought you had wedding cake for a wedding. Not for a shower." I waved my hand, dismissing Beverly when she mimed lifting a veil from her face.

"Oh, that's just what they call a white cake in the mountains, honey." Granny busied herself with measuring flour and baking powder. "My grandmother created this recipe, and it's tricky. Don't talk to me so I can count my strokes." And she bent over her bowl and spoon, her back to the rest of us.

Beverly put her comb away and sidled over to Willeen at the stove. "I don't think I ever heard much about the Turner side of our family. Where are they from?"

Willeen handed a bowl of steaming potatoes to Beverly. "Mash these for me." She handed me a bowl of biscuit dough to roll out on the wooden washstand she used for a baking area. "Evie, the rolling pin and biscuit cutter are in the drawer there." Finally, she looked at Beverly. "Why are you so stuck on learning about family all of a sudden? Couldn't have anything to do with that new boy I saw you with—Tommy Turner, I think his name is—now would it?" Beverly's cheeks turned scarlet. Willeen didn't need any more information. "We're not related. But do not get ideas, young lady, about going out on dates until after your birthday."

Beverly muttered, "Think I'm going to get a lot wiser in nine weeks?"

Willeen packed wings and legs into the frying pan like she didn't hear.

I asked a question to give Beverly time to recover from her mom's correction. "Well, how did you meet Grampa Turner? Is he from the mountains, too?" Granny made a sound like "Pffft." I'd forgotten we weren't supposed to disturb her while she stirred.

A mischievous smile came over Willeen's gaunt face. "Well, Daddy used to say he found Mama in a gunny sack." She laughed as a sound like an explosion came from her mother's end of the kitchen.

Granny slapped the bowl down. "Three hundred and fifty-nine strokes! Forty-one more to go. We met at Tallulah Falls, where I went visiting my cousin, Edna Davis—she's a McCall now. Your dad and

a cousin went on a picnic to the falls, same day as me and Edna."
She smiled, scraping the bowl's rim. "I was right smitten. I didn't
let him know that right away, of course. Daddy wouldn't even hear
of us marrying for two years, till I turned sixteen. But that's how it
happened."

Beverly could not contain herself. "You started courting at
fourteen? Dad won't let me even look at a boy straight, and I'm sixteen
already. That's not fair!" And she jammed the old iron potato masher
down with all her might.

"We'll have mighty smooth potatoes tonight." Willeen chuckled.

Granny stopped scraping and glowered at her granddaughter.
"Now wait a minute, young'un. Being married at sixteen was no party,
I got to tell you. My Grammaw Turner and two of her daughters all
died before they reached thirty, from having too many babies too fast.
My daddy said, 'Lydia, I lost my baby sisters and my maw before I was
five. I don't want to lose you, too. It'll keep, daughter. You just wait.'
Well, I couldn't bear to hurt him after that, so we waited. Then the
babies came real quick, you know."

"I ain't gonna get pregnant just 'cause I look at a boy," Beverly
grumbled.

"Hand me that other cake pan, will you, Evie?" Granny sat the
batter bowl down. I reached to the top shelf of the cupboard behind
me and handed over the tin.

Beverly's face lit as if she'd suddenly remembered something. She
set down the potatoes and looked at her mom. "Evie's mom was only
fifteen when she married, younger than Granny, even. Why'd you and
Dad get married so late? Weren't you about twenty?"

Willeen wiped her hands on her apron and stared out the window
at the front yard, where harsh sunlight after the storm gleamed on the
silver grate of her car. "Twenty-three."

Beverly spooled some potatoes off the masher with her finger
and tasted. Willeen chopped a squash into chunks, her square back

still turned. The biscuit cutter made a soft plunking sound against the wooden board as I twisted out rounds of dough. The silence ticked on. Beverly and I looked at each other. What big deal was this?

Granny murmured, "I reckon there's a cat clawing its way out of that bag, ain't there? She's old enough to hear, now, don't you think, daughter?"

"Hear about what?" Beverly watched the nape of her mother's print dress. "What's going on, for Pete's sake?"

Granny raked her batter into the cake pans with a spoon. "Beverly, don't yawp at your mother. Everybody's got some explaining to do sometime. It's not that big a deal."

A look of satisfaction crept onto Beverly's face. She'd finally hit the jackpot. She wriggled onto the wooden stool in the corner, settling in for a tale, on her face the same expression she'd worn when people leapt around her church.

Willeen turned around with tears on her face. Beverly and I glanced at each other. Her mouth was a big "o." I tried to place the dough circles onto the baking sheet without making a sound. Granny moved toward her daughter and touched her arm. Willeen shrugged her away, not angrily, but straightening her shoulders, being brave. "I was married to someone else before your dad. We had the marriage annulled. I didn't tell you before because I thought you were too young to understand."

The stool teetered against the wall as Beverly stood, her mouth still open and her hands hanging at her sides. "What does that mean, annulled?"

Willeen's mouth worked, but no words accompanied the movement.

Granny asked, "Want me to tell them?' At Willeen's nod, Granny sat down and folded her hands. "Willeen's first husband didn't tell her he'd been married before. Everything seemed fine for a few years, except he had to go away to war. It must have been 1942, about

Christmas, a letter come in the mail from his ex-wife. He hadn't informed her of the divorce he got in Mexico, like the law said he had to, so they was still married. That made his marriage to Willeen illegal."

"What a bastard!" Beverly crossed her arms and looked sorry she had asked.

Willeen cleared her throat. She didn't even blink at Beverly's curse, just took over the story. "He'd been posted to a boat in the Pacific. Took months to find him, then we had to get the papers to him—" She put her hand to her face, shoulders shaking.

Beverly went over and rubbed her mother's back. "So you could divorce him, right? Or—no, his other wife was his legal wife. What did that make you, Mom?"

Granny huffed. "It made her unable to marry again, but not quite married legally, either. So we had to get the papers for an annulment, on the basis of fraud. Took some time." She shook her head with a sad expression. "The very next week after he signed the papers, he got killed out in the Pacific."

"Oh!" Beverly stopped rubbing for a second, then patted her mom's shoulder. "Well … when did you and Dad meet?"

Willeen wiped her eyes and hurried to take the frying pan off the stove. She looked down at the burnt chicken as if figuring how to resurrect it. "We knew each other already. We used to work for the same lady, doing odd jobs, while we were still in school. We met again after I went back to work for her, during the annulment. We decided to get married after that."

"So that's why Miz Beasley said you were in trouble and Dad took care of you."

There was a beat when everything seemed all right, the sun shining through the windows, the smell of dinner all around us while we worked together. Then everything changed.

"Wait a minute." Beverly whirled to face Willeen. Something—
not anger, but kin to it—knotted her brow. "Granny said that you
didn't get word about his other wife until Christmas, 1942, and after
that it took months to get the papers done. I was born in November,
1943. Mom, were you pregnant with me before you married Dad?"

Willeen twisted away from Beverly, but Beverly wouldn't let go.
"Well?"

Granny shook her head at Willeen. "I told you, you needed to tell
her everything."

The air grew heavier every second Willeen remained silent. My
mother's voice calling out from the front room brought relief. She
would know what to do. "Willeen, sorry I'm late. We had a time,
sorting out all the potluck dishes." She hurried into the kitchen. One
look around switched on her take-charge voice. "What's going on?
Are you all right, Evie? Did you two make trouble?"

"She's all right." Willeen lifted her head and let her hands fall to
her sides. "We need to tell Beverly about her mother."

Beverly's gasp snapped my head around, but her words ripped
my heart out. She yelled at Willeen, "What—you're not my mother?"

Willeen seemed to shrink a couple of inches. She did not look
away from Beverly, or attempt to cross the room to her.

The fear in my mother's face shocked me. Not whoops-there's-
a-snake-fear, but downright, too-scared-to-breathe panic. Her heavy
eyelids flew open so far I could see whites rimming the iris. She
gestured to me and said, "Maybe we should go."

Beverly and I locked gazes. "No." I didn't know for a moment if
the voice was mine or Beverly's. She shook her head. "I want Evie to
hear it, too." And she marched across the room and stood next to me.
I set my feet wide on the floor and didn't budge.

Mom lowered herself onto a chair next to Granny's at the table.
She placed her hands flat on the oilcloth and sighed before she said to

Willeen, "Evie may as well hear it from you. Otherwise, she'll pester me with questions, later."

Feeling a surge of power, I dragged a chair over near Beverly's stool. We both sat down. For once, we wouldn't have to beg the grownups for what we wanted to know.

The three women looked at each other, choosing who should start. Willeen remained standing, holding onto the counter for dear life. Mom peered into Willeen's face. "Are you okay? If not, I reckon I can tell some of it." She jerked her head toward the living room. "But shouldn't Carl know about it, first?"

Willeen scraped her hands together as if wiping mud from her fingers. "I'll tell him." She walked to the living room. We heard Carl's voice rumbling like gravel hitting a creek bed, and Willeen responding with a firm, sharp, "Yes. We have to."

The front screen door slammed and Willeen reappeared in the doorway. "I don't know if we'll see him more tonight." She shrugged like she didn't care. Bewilderment clogged my thoughts, like I was looking into a room full of strangers.

Willeen folded her arms and leaned again on the counter. "I've spent so long thinking how to tell you this. Can't find a good place to start, so I'll begin with her name. Antoinette Evans. We called her Dr. Nettie. I used to work for her in her office after school and on weekends. We were good friends."

Beverly sucked in a huge gulp of air. "You mean—a medical doctor?" Willeen nodded. I searched my memory for female doctors and found none, but the photo of three girls in a swing flashed into my mind. Nettie—the blonde. I was sure of it. How could I have missed Beverly's face in hers?

"Her father was a doctor, too, but he was sick." Willeen tapped the side of her head. "Sometimes he would be working and acting cheerful and right on top of things, and then in a couple of hours he would be distraught and throwing things, before he'd go drink till he passed out."

"Manic depressive. That's the name of the disease." My mother said it quietly, quickly. Granny nodded, as if agreeing on the color of the curtains.

"Nettie had quite a time managing him. She had to take over the practice completely—a lot for a young woman. She had Carl move in with her and her dad, to help with the upkeep and to look after old Doc Evans. Carl slept down in that cold basement." Willeen's eyes dropped to her feet.

Mom whispered, "My mama worked for her, too, before she died. I tried to help her as much as I could, after that. But I had the little ones."

"We all helped her all we could, because she helped us, she—" My mother grabbed Willeen's hand as if she were saving her, or drowning herself. Granny walked over and put her arms around her daughter. "You tell it for a bit, Maisie."

My mother seemed to gather herself, folding her hands, drawing herself taller. Her jaw clenched, then relaxed. "We didn't notice anything unusual about Nettie, at first. Like her dad, she'd keep long hours. Sometimes I'd look over and see her lights on in the early morning hours, when Paul kept me awake."

I jerked at the familiar name: My Uncle Paul, still a mystery to me. Mom saw my reaction and explained, "The doctors' house was across the road and one field from Papa's and Mama's farmhouse. Your Uncle Paul had colic, even after he started school, so I stayed awake with him a lot of nights. Some nights, after George was born, I went from one of the boys' beds to the other, reading them stories, singing songs." She parted her lips, but checked her words for a moment, deciding what to say.

"Then came that terrible evening," Willeen struggled to get words out.

Beverly leaned forward. "What happened?"

To my amazement, Mom wiped tears from her own cheeks as she choked out her words. "We were out bringing the cows in—me and Tally—it was before she married—and your dad was chopping wood." She rolled her eyes in my direction. "George had just begun first grade. It was fall, cold. A little bit of frost in the air." Her next words exploded a moment of silence. "Loud over the meadow in their front yard, across our ditch and into our back lot—one shot. Clear as a bell. Shotgun." She rested her elbows on the table and covered her nose and lips with her hands. Several long breaths gusted through the room before she continued. "Frank ran over there. I was pregnant, and he didn't want me to go." She paused to twist her head toward me. "I never told you I lost two babies between you and George, did I? Both little boys."

All the stories pouring out of my mother felt like waters rising over me. I blinked to keep from floating away.

Mom covered her eyes again. "I'm glad I didn't see it—"

"I did," Willeen said in a flat tone, maybe the only way she could make the words hurt less. She battled on, choking, it seemed, on every other word. "Doc Evans shot himself in the head. Carl got to him first and wouldn't let Nettie in the room. I was working on their records right next door and I went in behind him. Then I threw up." Her mouth now formed a straight line. The sound of her lips unlocking made a sucking sound. "They spent days cleaning that room. Nettie took it hard, real hard."

Granny rubbed Willeen's back with her big, calloused hands. "Poor soul. Imagine how hard it must have been, him a doctor, knowing what he had, how bad it would get."

Listening to them was like finding a part of my life I'd missed. My mama and Willeen young and trying to start their lives, the baby brothers I never knew, and Carl—Carl helping out and taking care of someone else! People I knew, before I knew them. I kept shaking my head to clear my vision, as if that could make it all come together better. Beverly locked and unlocked her fingers, and I could see she felt the same way. All those questions, all these years. Now, more answers than we could absorb.

My mother sighed. "There came a time, a year or two later, when I looked over there and there were no lights on at all for days at a time, not even in the early evening. Carl said Nettie had taken to going away a lot. Not just to hospital board meetings in Toccoa, but to Athens, even Atlanta, at first for a day or two, then a week at a time, and Willeen had to cancel all Nettie's appointments. She'd come back and say, 'We needed more supplies,' or, 'I had to consult a specialist about a patient.' She wasn't quite herself for a few days after each trip. We didn't know what to think." Mom looked down at her hands.

Willeen took the story again. "Gradually, some patients stopped coming, because they couldn't rely on her, but it didn't seem to bother her. She gained weight, though she barely stopped to eat—folks still came to her for emergencies, rather than go all the way into Toccoa to the hospital, and there are always plenty of accidents in a farm area. I was working on getting my annulment, so I might not have paid enough attention to her."

Tears reappeared on her narrow face. "Then Mary Avery said Nettie snapped at her, told her she had enough babies to worry about, she should make sure she put a stop to her yearly pregnancies— mighta been true, but Nettie didn't usually snap at anyone. She started staying away longer and longer."

"And then she didn't come home at all." None of us had heard Carl come in. He stood in the doorway, his hands shoved deep in his pockets, chin almost to his chest, his blue eyes stabbing at us from beneath his heavy brows. None of the women stirred, but it felt like they moved over to make room for him to tell part of the tale. He didn't even acknowledge them, but directed his words at Beverly. "I found her in an old, ratty hotel on the south side of Atlanta. She was sick, puking, her hair—She had such pretty hair." He pointed to the stamen inside one trumpet-shaped day lily in a jar of blooms that stood on the table. "Like that, just that color."

At that moment, I felt how much he loved Nettie, and the thought shook my insides. Beverly's hand stole into mine. Willeen did not flinch, did not seem particularly concerned. This must have been something she'd known for many years.

Carl's voice sounded softer than I'd ever heard it. "She wanted to see a doctor she knew at Milledgeville."

Beverly's grip on my hand tightened at the word, Milledgeville— where you took crazy people, where patients sat in padded cells and were locked into their rooms every night, where they gave people so much medicine they drooled like babies. Every school child in Georgia knew about it. How many times we'd yelled at each other, "You're crazy! They're gonna lock you up down in Milledgeville."

Carl moved his eyes to Beverly. For the first time, I saw something like love in them. "She had you in her belly, and she didn't want to hurt you. Didn't want to be alone, not even for a minute." He let the words lay there. For a moment the air had a sweet scent, maybe from the lilies, or from some thought that everybody shared.

"You're really not my mama?" Beverly whispered it this time. Willeen clamped her hand over her mouth and shook her head. A long sob tore through us, a sound that came from Beverly but felt like it ricocheted around each of us. "No!" she cried. "My mama didn't lose her mind."

Willeen reached her in two quick strides. She folded Beverly into her arms and pulled her to her feet. "I think she's had enough. That's a lot to hear in one day."

"No!" Beverly pushed Willeen away. "No, I want to hear it all. Who is my father? Is it you?" She turned to Carl, her eyes burning like twin suns. "Did you get her to have sex with you? Did you?" It was hard to tell if she pleaded for him to say yes or no.

Carl wagged his head.

"Sweetie." Willeen spoke just loud enough for me to hear. "Sweetie, we don't know. Someone she met when she went away— she couldn't tell us who. I don't think she knew." Even with Willeen holding on to her, Beverly sank to the floor as fast as a stone thrown into a pond disappears from view.

Mom and I rushed to help lift her. We walked her into the bedroom and helped her onto the bed. Willeen whispered in her ear, "We'll talk more later, after you've had some rest."

Mom turned to me. "Let's go, Evie. Grab your things. Willeen, I'll call you later." Her hand rested lightly on my arm, steering me toward the door. My tongue felt unglued. I couldn't form words, not even "good-bye."

◦≪⟨≫◦

My mother's tight grip on the steering wheel told me she was tired. And probably snappish. My palm radiated the warmth of Beverly's hand where she'd gripped mine. I knew that as soon as she recovered a bit, she'd be demanding answers, but my head was full of questions *now*. The shape of Mom's mouth set me between the lion and the serpent. Maybe if I began with something that would not sound like meddling?

I looked out the window at the pines passing beneath the moon, took a breath, and said, "Why don't we have any pictures from Grampa's farm?"

Mom readjusted her hands on the wheel and cocked her head to the side, so I knew she would answer. "We didn't have a camera. Only a few people did in those days. Carl sent one to Nettie from Japan— he was stationed there, before she went away—and we took some photos on her lawn. I'm not sure—maybe Willeen has some."

The picture of three young women in a swing drifted into my mind like a flurry of cherry blossoms. Japan? "Carl—in the war? How was he home when Nettie—when Beverly's mother got sick? And when her grandfather died?"

"Oh, I can't remember now exactly. I think they sent him overseas after we buried Doc Evans. And he came home to recuperate from an injury about the time Nettie went missing. Rode the bus from his base and took Doc's car to look for her. He has shrapnel in his leg, you know."

I drew my head back. "Really? I never noticed him limping."

Mom shrugged. "It bothered him for a long time, but he's pretty tough. Yep, he was quite the hero. He saved some guys on a boat. Like that young senator you hear about running for president— what's his name? Kennedy. Well, Carl got a medal, too."

I could have floated to the car's roof. "No! Carl—a hero?"

Her voice dropped lower. "Tell you the truth, I think he tried to get killed. He was desperately in love with Nettie, but she didn't love him back. They were too different. He couldn't see that."

Confidential information from my mother was a rarity. An opinion about someone else? Unheard of. I pushed my luck. "How did Carl and Willeen get Beverly?"

"That's a long story."

I sighed with all the drama I could muster.

"Don't pout. I'll tell you what I know." She sat up straighter. "A doctor said someone needed to be the baby's legal guardian, since Nettie wasn't mentally competent. The state wouldn't give the child to Willeen because she wasn't married. After Carl got well, he came to visit and the social worker asked if he was the father. He said yes, thinking the social worker didn't know better and he'd get custody, then Willeen would care for her while he shipped overseas again."

"Did they fall in love?"

Mom wagged her head with a wry smile. "Daughter, you read too much *True Romance*. Not every marriage is about falling in love."

"So, why did they get married? Were you there when that happened?"

"Yes. The social worker wanted to know what would happen to the baby if Carl died in the war. They decided to marry so Willeen would have a right to her if anything happened to Carl." A deer bounded into our headlights and disappeared like a ghost. Mom flicked the lights to high beam, then settled back. "Your dad and I stood up for them down at the courthouse."

A strange feeling rose in my chest like a fish bobbing in dark water: Carl wanting to take care of Beverly, me wishing he would get the chance. I began to see what grownups talked about as regret: seeing how something could have worked out, and knowing how it did. "What happened after that? They didn't move here till Beverly was four or so, right?"

"Yes. Carl shipped out for the Pacific a couple of months after Nettie delivered Beverly, a week or two after he married Willeen. Willeen took the baby to her sister's house near Milledgeville. Carl wasn't discharged till Beverly was past four."

Four. That one word revived my memory of the sprite with bright green eyes and sunlight in her hair. When we met, Beverly had not yet known her dad and his fearful ways. "So they married for Beverly's sake?" It made perfect sense to me, now. Willeen and Carl didn't care much for each other. All along, it had been about Beverly.

My mother squirmed in the seat, uncomfortable to be talking about this. "Tell you the truth, I don't think they ever intended to live together. You have to understand how people thought in wartime. No one could see very far ahead. Willeen and Carl thought things would work out, and they did, I guess. At least, until now."

"Humph." My new compassion for Carl couldn't cross that line. "You call that working out—Carl stays on Beverly like an old hound all the time, and she hates his guts? I don't understand why he wanted her, he's so mean to her."

Mom's voice went from patient to stern in an instant. "Evie, did it ever occur to you that he worries she'll get in trouble, like her mother? That he's trying to look out for her? He goes overboard, but he loves her, because he loves her mother."

"*Loves* her? You make it sound like Nettie is still alive!"

Mom nodded, which sent me stumbling willy-nilly through my rushing thoughts. I gasped, "Then why doesn't Carl take Beverly to see her?"

Mom grimaced and gripped the wheel again. "Beverly doesn't need to see her."

"Why?" Seconds ticked by. "Why, Mama?" I hadn't called her that in years.

Something terrible weighed in the air. Mom covered her mouth. Her voice came muffled through her fingers. "There's an operation they do on people's brains, if they get depressed and can't shake out of it, or if they just get out of control, the way Nettie did —well, we don't know what she did, exactly, but Beverly was the result. In the asylum, they called her 'promiscuous.'"

"What does that mean?"

Mom wiggled into a new position. "It means she had sex with lots of men."

In my head, the preacher shouted "Jezebel!" and Carl screamed, "Don't ever let me see you painted up like a harlot again!" My blood boiled. "So Carl thinks Beverly will do that? But she isn't bad. I know she isn't!"

Mom's sigh seemed freighted with resignation. "I know. It's normal for girls to want to talk to boys, go out with them, kiss them." She took a deep breath and added, "But Carl is afraid she'll go too far. It's *not* a good idea to have sex until you're married. Especially not the way Nettie did, going off with strange men."

This was unfamiliar territory with my mother. My head began to swim. "But can't doctors do something about it—I mean, so they don't get pregnant?"

"Well, there's a few things women can try, but nothing that's surefire, unless they have their tubes tied, and that's … final. And, if you're in a manic phase, like Nettie, you're not going to make sure you don't have sex at the wrong time, or make a special tea to drink, or anything like that. Manic means uncontrolled and that's why the doctors wanted to do the surgery."

I imagined a surgeon cutting into someone's brain and flipping a switch to make her stop wanting sex. "How does the surgery work? Did it help?"

Mom sat silent so long I turned. Tears pulsed down her cheeks. I pulled the spare handkerchief from her purse and handed it to her. She wiped her nose and crushed the cloth in her fist. "The surgery stopped most of her wildness, but it made her simple, like a child. She doesn't remember anything for long. She can't hold a conversation. She mostly watches the curtains blowing in the breeze, or water in the fountains on the grounds. Sometimes, she gets very upset for no apparent reason, and they have to strap her down. Nettie isn't really there anymore."

"You've seen her?" One surprise after another made my stomach lurch.

"Willeen and I went down there once or twice when you were small, and later I went a couple of times when you were at Beverly's. It's terrible. Nettie was so smart, so wise, so beautiful. And now she's more like a puppy that does naughty things and can't understand why people get upset." I could hear her intake of breath that meant what was coming would be the worst. "Once, when Willeen and I were there, she took off her clothes, saying her nipples were dripping, she needed to feed her baby."

I stammered, "So she knows she had Beverly? Does she miss her?"

Mom hesitated. "I think she associates Willeen with some vague memory of Beverly as a baby. If she remembers, the orderlies said, they have to sedate her for days."

A lump collected between my throat and chest. "So seeing Beverly might send her off like that. What is that operation called?"

Mom sounded out the word as if it were ashes in her mouth. "Lobotomy."

"Oh." My quill of questions had temporarily run out. I curled against my mother's shoulder and listened to the car wheels until they came to rest in our driveway. Dad came down off our porch to help me inside.

Instead of drifting off to sleep, I watched the strange word swirl around my ceiling until I couldn't stand lying still any longer. I crept to my desk and opened the big dictionary Dad had given me last Christmas. I couldn't believe what I read. One description of lobotomy included drilling two holes in the patient's head and injecting alcohol to "disrupt the areas that were believed to give rise to and reinforce recurrent patterns of thought." Farther down the page I found another: driving a sharp instrument into a person's eye socket to sever one part of the brain from another. My mind built an image of a knife slicing down into a beautiful, green-eyed stare.

When I threw up in the hall on my way to the bathroom, Mom appeared, pulling my hair back from my face and wiping my mouth with a handkerchief. She and Dad helped me back to my room. Dad patted me and left us alone.

"Okay now?"

I nodded, but it was a lie. Mom padded in her slippers to turn the light out on my desk. She must have looked down at the dictionary, still open to that awful definition, for she came back and sat on the edge of my bed. "You see, now, why we didn't tell you or Beverly? There's no way to tell it without hurting her. Her mother wouldn't even know who she is. I don't know how Willeen is going to do it."

"But why, why do they do such things?" I didn't really expect an answer and Mom didn't offer one. Instead, she lay down beside me and put her arms around me. "I hope Willeen doesn't let Beverly know about that operation. It will kill her." Another thought bolted me upright. "So I have to lie to her, too?"

I watched the pupils of Mom's eyes grow wide and deep. She didn't answer. Floating on the air came Tally's long-ago comment: *Not telling everything you know is not the same as telling a lie.* Grudgingly, I admitted the distinction. "The good kind of lie, I know," I lay back down.

My mother nestled my head under her chin. "There's only one kind of lie, Evie, but many kinds of liars."

I wanted to reach for an explanation, but exhaustion swept me into oblivion. I dreamed of dangling at the end of a long rope over a valley of sharp spikes. As the rope began to fail, I was suddenly snatched to safety. My savior was neither of my parents, but a large bird that shouldered me onto her wings and flew me away.

Opening my eyes sent a hundred metal stakes pounding through my sockets. Slowly, the images that had spoiled my dreams returned, centered in my mind like a kaleidoscope shaping a pattern: *My best friend found out she's adopted and her mother is insane. And that everybody's been lying to her for years. And I can't tell her the whole truth, either.* I shook my head to clear away the images. My insides felt off-kilter, as if the world would never be in focus again.

Clanging pots announced Mom making breakfast. If I got out of bed right away, I could catch her before she left for work.

She gave me the once-over as I walked to the table in my nightgown and sat down in my usual chair. "Feeling better?"

"Yes." I hesitated to share my dreams. "Can I call to see if Beverly's okay?"

Mom looked thoughtful as she took off her apron. "Maybe you should let her sleep for a while. She had a big shock. And I don't know what Willeen told her about the operation, so don't mention it unless she does." She stopped in the act of hanging her apron on the hook by the back door and pointed at me. "And you know you can't tell anyone else about any of this, either. When Willeen and Carl moved back here, they brought Beverly and said she'd been born after Carl went overseas, and that was that."

"Does Dad know?"

"Of course."

"Mary Alice?"

"Yes, surely. She'd have been old enough to know Willeen wasn't pregnant."

"George?"

Mama shook her head. "Not unless Mary Alice told him."

We were still discussing what I should and should not mention when a knock at the door was succeeded quickly by the screen door slamming.

We jumped when Beverly's tousled head appeared around the doorframe. "Scared you, huh? Is it all right if I spend the day with Evie? I want her to help me practice cheers. And Mama says she'll give you a ride to work if you want." I scanned Beverly's face and saw only eagerness. She bounced on the balls of her feet while she crossed the kitchen and sniffed at the frying pan with the downturned plate on top. "Mmm. Bacon. Okay if I have a slice?"

My stomach turned over at the thought of food. I turned to Mom and watched her own surprise grow into calculation. Maybe this is a good idea, her glance said.

"Sure, help yourself. Evie, there's tuna in the cupboard for lunch." She gave Beverly one more searching look before heading for the front door. She called to Willeen, "Coming!" and yelled to our next door neighbor, "Willeen's driving today. Come on!"

Beverly assembled two plates of eggs, bacon, and toast. She set one at my usual spot. "C'mon, Headlights, get a move on. I have to learn three cheers today."

I slipped into my chair. "Glad to see you so chipper. I was afraid—"

"What? That I'd be upset Carl's not my dad? Look at it this way, now I don't have to listen to him as much. And Willeen feels so bad for lying to me about being my mom that she won't ride me so much, either." She shrugged like she had no cares at all.

After three bites, my stomach lurched like a Tilt a whirl. I pushed the plate away. "Aren't you upset that your mom's—" I stopped, confused. I'd started to say *down there with her brain cut to pieces*, but then I wondered—did Willeen tell Beverly that her mom is still alive? "I mean, all these years we thought Willeen was your mom."

Beverly stood and took her plate to the sink. "She is my mom. I don't know that woman in the hospital. Are you coming?" She wheeled toward the back door, ignoring my gasp. She knew her mom was shut away, and where.

The floor tilted, but Beverly somehow remained still, upright, as if everything around her were nailed down. But not out in the open. I picked my words carefully. "Did Willeen tell you anything more?"

She paused, hand on the screen. "Nope. Don't want to know more. Really, Evie, you should worry about your own family. Why doesn't your horse trainer uncle visit?"

The slap of the screen door underscored her comment's sting. *There's no way to tell it without hurting her*, my mother's voice said. After a minute of struggling to give Beverly leeway, I got up from my chair and called behind her, "Okay. But I'm not jumping. Let me get some clothes on." I stumbled through dressing, grabbed a book, and returned to the kitchen. Through the window, I watched Beverly leaping in the back yard for a minute before I slammed through the door. Who knew that truth was such a burden?

From the metal patio chair by the shed, in the deep shade, I read *Marjorie Morningstar*. I looked up now and then to see Beverly practicing under the outer edges of our big oak's reach. Later, we stopped for a quick lunch, then Beverly sprang into action again, matching motions to words. *Go!* Stomp. *Fight!* Clap. *Score!* Turn. *Go!* Clap. *Fight!* Stomp. *Score!* Turn. *Go for six more!* I had read halfway through the book when she insisted that I try a move with her.

My head still felt like a bell that had been rung, but I decided to humor her. We had paused from the endless repetitions for a water break when Mom appeared at the back door, untying her weaving apron. "You girls look good. Want some cookies?"

"You can't feed me enough cookies to make me tall and graceful." I dragged myself into the kitchen. "I'm not going to try out. I'm just helping Beverly. "

Mom took a packet of cookies out of the cupboard and arranged some on a plate. "Beverly, Willeen is dropping off Carl's suit at the drycleaners and will be back to get you in a minute." She put the plate halfway between us, and gave my ponytail a playful slap to make it swing. "What will you do, if not cheering? You can't study all the time."

"Well, I'm thinking about joining the school paper."

Beverly grabbed an oatmeal cookie. "That's for nerds! No need for cool clothes if you're reporting on the new teacher in the math department." She swallowed, beaming at me.

I tossed a half-eaten cookie onto my plate. Enough of being bossed around. "What's cool about long skirts and bulky sweaters?"

Beverly's smile grew wider. Everybody knew cheerleaders were by definition "cool." "Say, I think Howard Pearson's on the paper. He's cute!"

"So?" I lowered my eyes and picked up the cookie.

"So—he's cute. You know who he is, right?"

Mom leaned over to plunk some more cookies onto the plate. "Oh, Mr. Pearson's son, from the department store? His father's a nice man. He offered me credit when we bought the new sofa. But we didn't need it, thank God."

Vaguely, I remembered a brown-haired kid tossing a ball against the stairs when we went to put school clothes on lay-away. "Yeah. Guess so."

"Howard's on the baseball team, too. Made All-State last year. Not as cool as football, but he's a senior!" Beverly's face wrinkled so suddenly that it chilled the room like an instant thunderstorm. "I'll never make it." She buried her head between her folded arms.

I blinked at her sudden lack of confidence. "Why not? You're as blonde as the others." The sharpness in my tone surprised even me. I bit my lips. Beverly lifted her head, and I saw that my comment had stung more than I'd intended.

She leaped off the chair and grabbed her book bag from the table. "You know, Evie, you've got those big eyes. Your figure's not bad. Why, if you cut your hair right, you'd be cuter than anybody in school. You just won't give up your precious books long enough to learn something new. I'm going to see if Mama's here yet." She pranced off, grimacing at me over her shoulder, glad she got the last word.

Mom thrust her hands into the pockets of her dress and watched Beverly disappear. "You could have been kinder, Evie."

I cupped my chin in my hands, leaned my elbows on the table, and closed my eyes to stop the whirling. "I know. It's just that all day I didn't know what to say. She didn't want to talk about yesterday at all."

"Not a word?" Mom's voice knifed through my headache.

"She said she doesn't have to listen to Carl anymore because he's not her father, but Willeen is still her mother because she doesn't know that woman in the hospital."

"I don't like the sound of that." Mom's hands dug deeper into her pockets.

"Me, neither. But what can we do?" There was something wrong about the way Beverly acted, as if she were playing a part. "Maybe she needs to think about things and wants to be left alone. Do you think I should let it go?"

My mother puckered her lips and moved her head from side to side. "Sometimes there's nothing you can do but catch someone when she falls."

That snapped my head up. "Why? What do you think will happen?"

Mom lifted her cooking apron from the hook by the back door and tied it around her waist. The kitchen filled with the sound of the clothesline snapping in the breeze. "I don't know. But things that fester tend to smell rotten sooner or later."

It occurred to me that, for the first time, my mother hadn't told me the Tyndalls' affairs were none of my business.

I rose, wearily. "I'm gonna go review my school supplies."

She twisted her head around to half-smile at me. "Okay. Dinner will be ready shortly."

I traipsed down the hall toward my room, feeling a mite older and dizzy with worry.

Fruit

Evie, August-October 1959: High School

My night with the kids at the shoals had enlightened me that, since I could never be a cheerleader, there was one remaining quick route out of Nerdom, and that was to be the girlfriend of someone reasonably cool. Until then, I hadn't realized how much I never wanted to hear the words "Professor Know-it-All" again.

And Bob Baker seemed to at least find me tolerable.

So the opening day flutter in my stomach was worse than ever before. What would I say to him if I saw him? *When* I saw him. Tallulah High was not big enough to get lost in. The corner of my mind that wasn't occupied by what Bob had said—"You being so cute and all"—was stuck on the other problem that bamfoozled me: Why was Beverly acting so strange, as if nothing had happened?

I glued my eyes to the sidewalk to minimize distraction while I thought. It took a loud "Hey, Girl!" to jolt me awake.

Jim Marshall stuck his head over the roof of an old navy sedan parked in front of the tire shop and grinned at me. A lightning bolt snapped along my spine. I remembered his bold look the last time I'd seen him at the shoals. Had he told anyone what we'd done?

He leaned on the top of the car and watched me walk toward him. "Evie, ain't it?"

I mumbled, "Yeah."

"Oh, you ain't going to be stuck up, like your friend, are you?" His eyes flicked like a blue marble running in a fast game over my breasts and hips. Bob had not made me feel this way, like my body was one big billboard to be read.

I disliked Jim so fervently that I didn't even try to find the right words. "You mean Beverly? She's not stuck up, and neither am I."

He slipped a wrench into his back pocket and grinned at a guy inside the car, a towhead who popped out from whatever he'd been doing beneath the wheel, turned, and flashed a grin. His hair was whiter than his teeth. I pushed that thought aside to listen to what Jim repeated, which turned out to be something I didn't want to hear.

"I said, so why don't you come to the movies with me Friday?"

Shit! That word came bubbling from my chest and almost passed my lips. I scrambled frantically for a substitute. "Well … I can't. I ain't old enough to date." Grammar slipped along with my composure. Are you ever gonna learn to sass back at boys? I chided myself. About the time I learn to juggle glassware on stilts, I guessed.

"That's okay. We can just talk. What's your phone number?" From his jeans pocket, he pulled a little book and a pen that glinted silver in the sunlight.

"Uh. We just got a new one. I can't remember it." Half true. I could not remember my phone number at that moment, even though we'd had it since George went into the Navy four years ago.

Jim looked at me, his lips twisted into a sneer, and tossed the book inside the car. "Sure!" he said, and dove in after it, leaning over to say something to the blonde-headed boy. They sped off while I tried to get my bearings.

Suddenly, the car turned and screamed straight at me. I skipped backwards onto the grass to avoid being hit. Their laughter echoed as I flew toward the first bell, which was ringing a few blocks ahead.

☙❦❧

The big brick building with its wide columns appeared. I tried to slow my breathing and put Jim Marshall's game of chicken out of my mind. Last year, I'd half-expected something like a commercial for

American Bandstand: jolly groups of boys and girls trying out the latest dance steps across the wide lawn. This year, I knew better. Countless kids screeched names and insults, some jumping to swipe each other's hats or notebooks. Couples leaned against the towering oaks, a few kissing right out in public.

I passed four boys in white tees slouched against a side wall, smoking cigarettes with their fingers bunched around the glowing tips. Unfamiliar words popped out of the din.

"Hey, man, I heard you blew off that Bent Eight last night!"

"Oh, man, it was fried!"

I needed someone to translate, or at least to check my backside for a hanging slip. Teetering on the curb, I mentally reviewed my outfit—brown pencil skirt, beige blouse, cordovan penny loafers—and drew several deep breaths. Suddenly, from somewhere near the school's concrete steps, my name rose over the shredded conversations.

Tommy Turner stood on the highest level, Beverly next to him, waving both arms in her white and red junior varsity cheerleader sweater. Tommy brought his hands to his mouth and hollered "Evie!" again. Everybody near them turned around to see who would answer. Bob Baker was one of them. A blush started at my neck and curled upward to my cheeks. He followed Beverly's pointing finger and smiled.

Here goes. I stepped into the street, angling my shoulders to cut through kids gyrating around their friends. The crowd swept me this way and that, till I finally managed to break free of the crush and reach the bottom step at the same time as a boy I didn't know. He wore a letter sweater like Tommy and Bobby, with a big red "T" for Tallulah High.

Rena and Sandy stood one step above him. A red scarf encircled Rena's blonde ponytail and looped down to the shoulders of her maroon varsity sweater. Sandy wore her hair neatly bobbed, held back over one eye by a pristine silver barrette. The gold ribbon I had tied that morning around my hair felt suddenly like a wretched choice. Rena's voice knifed through the shouts and calls as I began the ascent. She addressed the boy below and she didn't sound pleased.

"Mike Bailey, I don't want to hear about that. Joe can do what he wants. Besides, that girl is so dumb she wouldn't even know if the movie played or not." Without missing a beat, she called to the top, "Oh, Beverly, here's your friend, Libby. Sandy, you remember Libby from the fish fry." Rena seemed happy enough to drop the subject of Joe.

Sandy swiveled and waved a welcome to me. "*Evie.* Her name's Evie, Rena."

Beverly grinned and called, "How does it feel to be a sophomore?"

From somewhere behind me, someone whistled through sharp teeth. "Sophomore?" Mike repeated, looking me up and down. "She *must* be a senior."

Rena smirked. "Sure. And she has a movie contract, like Lana Turner."

"Easy, Boy." Bob's gaze held a warning. My spine tingled. Was he claiming me?

I tried to swallow my fear and smile at the same time. All I could think to say was "Hi." So I shifted my feet and assumed a shoulders-back, confident pose. The bell rang at almost the same moment that two books slid off my notebook like butter off a plate.

Nearly everyone raced away. Bob raced down to retrieve my books and tossed them in my direction. Tommy yelled at Beverly while he jogged backward. "After school?"

Beverly shook her head. "Can't miss the bus."

"Bob's got a car. Meet us right here."

"Not today." Beverly shrugged and turned her back with a wicked smile. "Never let 'em see you care. Know where your classes are?"

"Yeah." I stammered, still juggling books. "I think so."

"When's your study hall?"

"Sixth."

"Good. Meet me in the third floor bathroom. I can get out of Health, but it might take me a few minutes."

"Okay. We need to talk about the wedding. Mom has the pattern for our bridesmaids' dresses."

Beverly flapped her hand and climbed the steps.

The bathroom's big heavy door creaked like a vault as I slipped in. Light blazing through the tall windows over the line of porcelain sinks almost penetrated to the interior wall, where the toilets were hidden behind big walnut panels. At the far end, just beyond the last stall, another set of windows were tilted open to the crisp air, and overlooked a little alcove with a full-length mirror. Beverly wasn't there.

I was exiting a stall when I heard the big door clack. Beverly stood just inside the doorway, lighting a cigarette. She had tied her sweater around her hips, revealing a white blouse underneath.

"Beverly!" I clapped my hand over my mouth. "What are you doing?" I mumbled through my fingers. "If you get caught—if *we* get caught—" I imagined being expelled the first day of school. Mom's disappointed face floated above the sinks.

Beverly grabbed my arm and pulled me toward the alcove. "They won't catch us if you get over here by the window. By the time someone gets around the corner—" She made a gesture like pitching the cigarette over the windowsill, but brought it to her lips and took a deep drag, instead.

"Since when do you smoke? And why? "It *smells*." I wrinkled my nose.

Beverly grinned and took another pull. "Since Tommy taught me how to inhale last week at the Clocklight."

"Tommy taught you! At the Clocklight? You've been *out* with him?"

Her green eyes relished my amazement. Had it been just a few
weeks since Carl had thrown the radio? A week since she'd learned
Willeen and Carl weren't really her parents? "Well, not exactly on a
date. I walked to the crossroads one afternoon to get my shoes from
the shoe shop." She picked up one heel to show the new sole. "He
came by in a car with one of his buddies and invited me to have a
Coke." She laughed at my expression.

"Weren't you late getting home? The Clocklight is a long way. Did
Carl—"

"No, Dad didn't catch me. He sleeps during the day, remember?"

"What if he'd waked early?"

"What if, what if—Evie, you're such a worry wart." She sneered
and took a drag.

Bile rose in my throat. "Since when are you so brave?" I sniffed.
And immediately felt sorry. *You should be nicer to her, she's had a shock,* my
better self said.

"Since I don't give a shit." Beverly ground the butt into the big
white tiles, then picked it up, flipped it into the nearest toilet, and
flushed.

"You don't give a—" I let my voice trail off. Smoking, cursing,
hanging out with football players—what had happened to her? Could
shock make you reckless?

"C'mon, Evie, say it. Let a dirty word come out of your mouth.
Please." Beverly smiled and boosted herself to sit on the low sill.

"Cursing and smoking are cool, I guess. All the in-crowd do
it. And you're in the in-crowd." Anger constricted my throat, but I
fought it, not wanting to start off the year with a quarrel. I smiled to
defang my words and raked a comb through my hair.

"No. But I'm *going* to be in." Beverly pinned me with a steady
gaze. "I'm going to be a varsity cheerleader. Tryouts are the end of the
week." She slipped down from the sill. "You'll come, won't you?" If
she noticed my unenthusiastic nod, she didn't let on. "I gotta go. You
better go, too. Old Miz Haley will come looking for you."

"We haven't talked about our dresses! We're gonna be bridesmaids together. That'll be a lot more exciting than cheerleading." I shoved my comb back in my purse.

Beverly's look labeled me hopeless. "That's easy. You get a dress fitted, you get your hair done, you walk down the aisle, and that's it. I get to be a cheerleader all year long." She held the door open for me, grinning.

That Friday, I scrambled to find a place at the stadium fence to watch Beverly. I spotted her, wearing the number twelve pinned to her chest and struggling with a group of fifteen or so girls to do everything the varsity cheerleaders demonstrated. Miss Addison, the gym teacher, and Mr. Simmons, the band director, sat in the stands behind the locked gates and judged the candidates.

I never had any doubt Beverly would make it. Not even during the second cheer, when she wobbled a little coming down from a jump—no worse than the stumble with which Number Nine ended. Not even when Miss Addison announced Beverly was in a three-way tie, to be decided by a final routine. Or when I heard the sound of ripping cloth.

Beverly's hand flew to her rear, and her face turned crimson. I wanted to rush over to comfort her, but then she broke into a determined smile, spun into the air, and came down in a perfect split, arms raised triumphantly.

Everyone by the gate cheered. Even Miss Addison grinned broadly. "I guess that's about it." She huddled with Mr. Simmons, then turned to face the group. "The winners are four, ten, and twelve. Tyndall, maybe you can find shorts a little looser for practice."

When they unlocked the gates and let us well-wishers in, Beverly bounced with excitement as she reached out to hug me. "Evie, did you see? I figured my shorts were already ruined, so what the hel—heck."

Rena sauntered over. "Congratulations," she said, coolly. "It's not often that someone so tall makes the squad. You're very … enthusiastic."

"Isn't it great! We'll get to go on road trips together." Beverly moved to give Rena a hug, too, but Rena smiled icily and wiggled away. Beverly returned to her admirers.

Tommy Turner crossed the field toward us, his dark hair damp from his after-practice shower. Rena's voice dripped honey. "Oh, Tommy, Beverly made the squad! I'm so glad I could show her how to do it."

Tommy mumbled, "Good job," and made a beeline for Beverly. Behind his back, Rena's eyes narrowed. She turned and flounced away.

After Beverly had crowed the story of her triumph, she bobbed like a balloon several times, tied her sweater around her waist to cover her torn shorts, and dashed away. "I've got to go find out about my uniform!"

Tommy, towering at my shoulder, shook his head. "She's really something."

"Yeah. She is." I tamped down the me that wanted to change places with her.

Mom sat shelling peas on the porch, wearing a sleeveless shift with purple flowers and red pockets. I dropped onto the top step. She let me settle before she spoke. "How did it go?"

I leaned back and let the porch's wooden pillar support my back. "She made it. I felt like—What does Dad say? A rooster in a hen house."

Mom's chin tucked into a challenging position. "How many of the girls who did make it can get A's in Science and English *and* History? Maybe you're expecting too much in the way of gifts from above."

"Well, why can't you have more than one gift? Good looks, good grades and, and—"

"And lots of boyfriends?" Now her voice filled with soft chuckles.
"Mary Alice is beautiful, she *had* lots of boyfriends, and her grades
were good enough to go to nursing school. Why can't I have more?"
Mom held out her arm to make a circle for me. I drifted into the
swing beside her, letting her rub my shoulder. "Sometimes, daughter,
we have to work for what we get, so we can appreciate it, I guess." She
stroked my hair. "Besides, you are pretty and you will get a boyfriend
and good grades, too, I bet."

I snorted. "Right! And what good will it do me if I do? Who
on this street"—I swept the whole block into an imaginary rubbish
heap—"ever went to college? And I am not pretty. I have messy hair
and bulging eyes and a sharp chin and—"

"And a big inferiority complex. Didn't think I knew big words,
too, did you?" Now she was laughing at me. "A sharp chin and bulging
eyes, hm? They're like mine, so I guess I'm pretty ugly. And your hair
isn't messy. It's wavy. There's a difference."

It was true. I did have Mom's chin and eye shape, if not her thick,
glossy hair that stayed in place. I sighed deeply. "Yeah, but on you they
look good. I guess I'll just be *Professor Know-it-all* the rest of my life."

"You can't be a professor unless you go to college. Even I know
that."

I gave her an evil look for making me laugh when I wanted to
sulk.

She patted my shoulder. "Besides, Beverly needs to be good at
something, too."

"Yeah, well, it's sure not French. She got a 67 on her quiz. I saw it."
I smiled with satisfaction, but Mom stayed silent. Had I overstepped
her bounds of humility?

She scooped a handful of unshelled pods and stared over the
porch railing as if scanning for a sign in the trees. "How is she this
week?"

I bent over to retrieve my books and stowed my disappointment in our too-short focus on my talents. "Well, happy, today. She seems—" I stopped to think, but I couldn't put my finger on what was different about her. "I dunno. I guess she's okay."

My mother's eyes moved back to me. "Reckon we better talk to your counselor about scholarships?"

Something in my chest pecked like a bird almost out of its shell. "Yeah. Guess so." As the screen door slammed behind me, college seemed a million years and lots of maybes away.

༕⊰◦⊱༖

A week later, Beverly hooked her arm into mine as we left the pep rally, dragging me toward the parking lot. "Come on. Bobby's going to give us a ride home in his car."

"What? Are you kidding? We can't do that—I mean, our birthdays are still a ways away. How am I going to explain—"

She gave me a shove toward Bob, standing alongside a shiny green sedan waxed to a high gloss. "Are you coming?"

I squelched my doubts and followed. "He likes to be called Bob."

As Bob held the door open, I climbed into the front seat and watched in the mirror while Beverly got into the rear. Tommy tossed her books to the side, so they rested on top of his, scooted over, and draped his arm behind her on the seat's back. Beverly playfully slapped him on the arm. He didn't budge.

Bob moved around the car to climb into the seat next to me. "Where to?"

"Know where the old granary is? You turn there and then onto our street, Sumter."

"Yeah. Over by the tire store. Sure." Bob cranked the engine and pulled the car away from the curb. I settled back until I realized what he'd said. The tire store! I scanned ahead to see if Jim Marshall and his tow-headed friend appeared on the way. But mostly I concentrated on finding something to say.

I learned that Bob was a halfback, his best class was probably math, and he didn't think much of Elvis. I told him about the book I was reading, my French class, and my love for Little Richard. He nodded at the first two items, frowned at the last. We said nothing for the last two blocks.

When we stopped at my house, Bob reached across me to open the door from inside. A whiff of something spicy, but not Old Spice, tickled my nostrils, and my thigh tingled where his arm grazed my skirt. I was surprised when he jogged around the car, closed the door, and fell in beside me while I climbed the crumbling concrete steps that led to our porch. Two squeaks on the floorboards, and we stood at the front door. My mind went blank.

Bob found his voice first. "Say, Evalyn, would you want to go with me to the drive-in, after our game tomorrow night? We could take Beverly and Tommy, too." His words were still streaming through my head when the screen opened.

Mom looked first at me, then at Bob. "I got off early. Who's this?"

Bob cleared his throat and spoke quickly. "Mrs. Gates, I'm Bob Baker. I drove Evalyn home. I was just asking—"

Mom watched his mouth as if she weren't sure she could trust her ears before she interrupted. My mom never interrupted. "Is that Beverly out in the car? And who's that with her? Evie, why don't you ask them to get out? I'll bring some Cokes." She disappeared before I could stutter a sentence.

I waved for Beverly and Tommy to join us. Tommy and Bob flopped into the swing.

Beverly grabbed my arm and whispered in my ear, "Is she mad?" at the same time Mom's head reappeared around the door. "Evie, come help me carry these glasses." Walking into the dim house felt like crossing the threshold to doom. Mom's face shut clam-tight when I reached the kitchen.

"Mom, I didn't mean to do anything wrong. Bob offered to take me home, and—"

"Did you go anywhere else with him?"

"No, ma'am."

"I see. Well, we can talk about this later. Right now, you'd better tend to your guests."

She hustled four glasses onto a tray, popped ice cubes into each one, and pointed to two Cokes sweating on the counter. "Pour these and take them to your friends. I'm going to change clothes." She stepped toward her bedroom, already unzipping her work dress.

I had settled on honesty as the best policy by the time I reached the swing, where Beverly sat between the two boys. She tinkled ice in her glass and watched Tommy. He and Bob drank half their cokes in two gulps.

I sat in Dad's rocker. "My parents are fairly strict," I began, trying to read in Bob's eyes whether he thought me a dork. He nodded briskly.

"Beverly told us about them," Tommy interjected. "She said we're lucky your dad's not here with a shotgun." The sparkle in Beverly's green eyes proclaimed a joke.

I relaxed a little. "Well, not that bad. But I can only double date when I'm sixteen."

"And if she can only double, I have to go with her." Beverly dug into Tommy with her elbow, her glass clinking against his.

"You'll be sixteen soon, right?" Bobby's question surprised me till I remembered our chat at the shoals.

"Yeah. October 21st."

The boys exchanged a look. Bob nodded. "Not too bad. Just a month."

"Almost two months! What is this, the Sisters of No Mercy?" Tommy sounded pissed. Beverly flicked a melted ice cube at him, creating a tussle long enough for me to wipe sweat trails off my glass and wonder, what now? She didn't mention her birthday, November third.

Bob thought of a solution first. "No sweat. We'll all meet at games, for now. And maybe you can get a lift to the drive-in to meet us. Think that's a good idea, Evie?" He bobbed his head with satisfaction at finding a solution.

"Sure! Great idea!" Beverly chortled before I could even form an opinion.

"I'll check with my folks. To make sure." I swirled my glass to hear the cubes jingle.

Willeen's car pulled into our drive. She stalked up the steps, stopping to take in Tommy's arm thrown casually around Beverly. Then she switched her glare to Bob, sitting with hands clasped between his knees. Beverly and I were the last to catch her eye, but clearly we were the targets of her thoughts. She spoke as if she considered each word. "I came to borrow some shears from your mom, Evie. Is she home?"

I hadn't even seen that Beverly had brought her books out of the car, but now she waved them. "Mom, this is Tommy Turner and Bobby Baker. They gave us a ride home so I could visit with Evie. Thanks, you two. See you at the game tomorrow."

While she spoke, the boys nodded to Willeen, waved goodbye to Beverly and me, and hurried to Bob's car. Willeen's eyes stayed fixed on Beverly. Beverly scowled right back.

When Willeen stepped inside to talk to Mom, Beverly shrugged. "What did we really do wrong? You saw all the other kids catching rides home. It's not like we went necking in the woods with them."

I caught my breath, but part of me agreed with her. Why the big deal? It was only a white lie. I slumped on the swing. Beverly sat next to me and pushed off against the floor, so that we flew to the end of the chain in a rush.

After dinner, I cleared the dishes, then sat next to Dad at our blue dinette table.

Dad took off his glasses, rubbed his eyes, and peppered me with questions while he polished the lenses with his handkerchief. Who were their parents? How had I met them? And when? At the sink, Mom cut dead leaves from her plants and focused on when I had gotten permission to accept rides home and how I had decided it would be okay.

"Well, this wasn't a date, just a ride home. So I thought it would be okay." I knew this tactic stood a prayer's chance of working, but I couldn't muster any other defense. I mouthed my mother's next words to myself as she said them.

"You can't do what you haven't gotten permission to do. If you have any doubt, you ask first. Isn't that what I've always told you?" She cocked her head as if listening for me to deny it, while she passed the flowerpots underneath running water.

Dad reached into his pocket for a cigarette, twirling it between his fingers. Mom didn't like him to smoke inside. "Going out with boys is serious business, honey. That's why we have to ask a lot of questions before you go around with anyone."

"I know. I just didn't think a ride would be a big deal. I didn't feel well, and—"

"She sick?" Dad swung his head to Mom, who pursed her lips. I hoped they hadn't counted the days of sanitary napkins in the trash. "Oh. Well, hon, we got to have an understanding about this, because I don't want you getting stuck with some character who don't know how to act." He sat back and waved one white-socked foot over his knee.

Finally, an opening I could exploit. "Bob is a real gentleman. Isn't he, Mom?"

Mom acknowledged that he seemed polite enough. "But that's not all there is to it. We have to trust you to tell us before you decide to go with someone." She pointed the scissors at me before snipping a dead chunk from her potted mint.

"It was just a ride home, not a date!" I tried not to whine, but Mom did not miss it.

Her words snapped on the heels of mine. "I know exactly what a ride home means and so do you, Missy!"

Dad leaned forward. "Your mom's right, honey. This guy drove you home and now he wants to take you out. You see how one thing leads to another?"

I had to admit, I did. I sat back and crossed my hands in front of me. Fine. I hoped that Bob would wait until I could date in a few weeks. "Okay. So what's my punishment?"

Dad looked at Mom, who looked at me with surprise. "Do we need to punish you?"

A tiny glimmer of hope sprouted in my chest. "I'm not in trouble?"

Another look passed between them. Dad shook his head slightly at Mom.

Mom ticked off the points on her fingers while dangling the scissors from her thumb. "We want you to be clear: You're almost sixteen, no sense in counting a few weeks against you, but double dating only. We have to meet any boy you date before you go out with him. If you follow the rules and stay out of trouble, you can stay out till ten o'clock, and we'll consider letting you date by yourself in six months."

Ten o'clock! Mom's face said no messing with the rules. Dad wanted to be sure I understood them. "It's good judgment we're looking for, Evie. We want you to follow our rules till you know enough about dating to make a few of your own. We trust you, sweetheart. But we raised a boy—"

"Two." Mom corrected him. It took Dad and me a minute to realize she counted Uncle Paul, too, though he left school early to go out on his own.

"Two," Dad repeated. "And we know boys are a cantankerous bunch with minds of their own. They don't get from dating to marriage without a detour or two." I tried not to sigh at another of Dad's roundabout ways of making a point.

"Yeah. Wild oats." I had heard about wild oats the last time we talked about dating, because our church had a hayride for my class, and my parents thought I should be prepared for boys to "get fresh." It seemed like a century ago.

Mom wiped her hands on the dishtowel, walked over and slipped her chair under the table, a sure sign the discussion was over. "We want to be sure none of those wild oats are planted in your field." My head snapped up.

Dad swiveled around to laugh at her. "Maisie Gates! Are you making off-color jokes in front of our young 'un?" While they were laughing, I remembered what would be Beverly's first question tomorrow at school.

"So, umm, let me see if I understand the rules. I can double date now and maybe single date in six months. And you've met Bob. At least, Mom has. So tomorrow I can go to the drive-in after the game with him, if Beverly goes, too. Right?"

Mom looked at Dad, then at me, her eyes narrowing. "Your dad has to meet him first."

"Well, if Bob comes by to meet Dad first?"

Mom paused. "Are you sure Beverly has permission to go with you?"

I didn't, but I reassured her that Beverly would be speaking to her mom and dad even as we spoke. If she could wave away the last few weeks of our prohibition, why shouldn't Carl and Willeen? And, if they wouldn't, well, I only had to wait till Beverly's birthday. For a change, I might be ahead of her with one milestone.

Dad chuckled. "Well, Maisie, I guess we're going to bed late tomorrow night. Gotta wait up for our girl after her first date."

I hopped out of the chair, suddenly full of energy. "Thanks, Dad!"

Mom shook her head. "Don't go bleating like a silly sheep! And be home by ten!"

I paused and decided to forego the fight. "Okay! Ten!" I waited till I got to the door of my room, before I whispered, "All right!"

Lying in bed with my yellow-and-green-flowered bedspread tucked around me, I tried to remember every word Bob had said. Had my mom scared him away? He'd said he would call tomorrow before he left for the pre-game practice. What if he didn't? What if he did! And would he come to meet my dad?

Beverly and I primped in the mirror before class the next morning. "How did you get Willeen and Carl to let you date before your birthday?"

She laughed, tugging to straighten her new blue sweater. "I told Carl you were too snooty to get in trouble. He feels better when Little Miss Goody Two-Shoes is with me."

"Seriously." I turned to her with wet hands.

"Seriously." Beverly handed me a towel. "I told him I'd double with you until I'm seventeen. He bought it." I doubted Carl's swift agreement, but my excitement prevailed.

"Now, if Tommy could just get his own car, life would be perfect." Her eyes shone while she held the door for me.

Faster than Beverly could pull off a cartwheel, my life changed. Every day before school, Tommy and Bob met Beverly and me by the flagpole and escorted us to class. After school we reversed our routine, meeting by the front doors and walking out together. Bob and I dropped off Beverly and Tommy by the auditorium, where they clung to each other, whispering and smooching. Bobby and I continued on till we reached the field house.

"Gotta go hit some guys," he'd joke almost every day, and leave me with a kiss on the cheek. As I headed home, I'd watch as Beverly descended the steps to the cheerleaders' room and Tommy ran at top speed to make practice.

By the end of the second week, I was calling him Bobby, like Beverly, and getting used to his arm around my waist. Beverly and Tommy, Bobby and Evie. We end-rhymed.

I rushed to the fence after games to receive another peck on the cheek from my hero. Whispers swirled around me in the halls. Kids who knew me in grade school called me Evie, not "Professor-Know-it-All." Older girls threw me envious looks.

"Cradle robber," Rena murmured, shouldering past Bobby and me one afternoon.

"Don't mind her. She's jealous." Bobby reassured me, handing off my books in front of my classroom. Then he patted me on the back and turned to his friends waiting at the end of the upper class hall.

People spoke to me who never noticed me before. In French class, a girl with jet-black hair and twinkling bracelets leaned over to show me a copy of Elle, which our teacher kept so we could practice our vocabulary. She pointed to a photograph of Audrey Hepburn portraying Holly Golightly. "I could do your hair like that. You have the neck for it. You should come over after school some time."

I murmured a vague answer. "Sure. Sometime."

After class, I quizzed Beverly about her. "That's Veronica Wheeler. Her dad is the new superintendent at the mill. Way to go, Headlights. She's rich. And snooty, I hear."

Every Friday night, after home games, the four of us would drive to the Clocklight Drive-In. We drank Cokes or milkshakes, Bobby and I sitting sideways so we could see Tommy and Beverly over the back of the front seat. Eventually, Beverly and I would retire to the ladies room to compare notes. By the time cheesy pumpkin decorations appeared in the drive-in's windows, the routine felt comfortable. Safe.

"I'm glad Bobby's not pushy about—well, you know." Odors of grease, meat, and fried potatoes wafted through the room's vents. I tossed my blue plastic comb into my purse.

Beverly turned to look at me in the mirror, scarlet lipstick in mid-air. "I like pushy. Tommy is a great kisser. Maybe you should give Bobby a little push."

I pretended I had considered the matter carefully, instead of shoving it out of my mind. "I think I'll just let events take their course."

"Suit yourself. Just keep him busy while events take their course in the back seat." She put her hand on my back and propelled me out of the restroom.

Occasionally, Tommy would lean over to whisper to Bobby, and Bobby would turn to me. "Let's give them some privacy." We'd wander off, holding hands, and find other friends to talk to while Beverly and Tommy cuddled in the backseat.

Afterward, Beverly and I would usually spend the night at my house, because Willeen didn't want us riding on the country roads late at night. We were too tired after a game and the date to chatter the way we used to. I missed our long conversations in the dark. Could anticipation be more fun than actually dating? Not possible. Was it?

On our third date, I got my first real kiss. Bobby and I stood behind his car in the Clocklight lot at half past nine. Beverly and Tommy still huddled in the back seat. Suddenly, Bobby put his arm around my shoulder and pulled me close. "Evie, you're a good sport," he said, and bent down, his mouth close to mine. Suddenly, my nose itched. "No rush," he said, waiting for me to bring down my hand. A feather brushed my lips.

"No rush." He repeated that whenever I fidgeted in his embrace. I learned to pucker whenever he bent his head close to mine. Smack! That was all there was to it. I told myself Bobby was more of a gentleman than Tommy Turner, and that's why our kisses weren't the lip crushers Tommy gave Beverly. Some part of me wondered how I ever thought kissing would be such a big deal. The other part of me wondered why it wasn't.

Bobby seemed excited after Career Day assembly, when the counselors told us about the choices ahead of us. Mrs. Center, the head girls' advisor, had kept it simple: teacher, nurse, secretary. Until motherhood, of course. I couldn't imagine raising my voice to ask her about literature programs in the still auditorium, where girls filed their nails and yawned as they listened to her drone. The boys piled out of the room, chattering loudly, after Mr. White gave them his pep talk on possible college majors. Football practice was called off that afternoon. Beverly and Tommy and Bobby and I headed for the Clocklight.

"I'm going to be an accountant." Bobby dangled his head over his fries as if he were counting them. "Do you know what those guys make?"

Tommy barked. "No bean-counting for me! I'm going into the Air Force. I want one of those jets humming under me. How about that, Bev? You wanna be an Air Force wife?"

"Long as I get to see the world and drink martinis by the pool." Beverly had taken on new moods since she'd been going with Tommy—calmer, sometimes even placid. Whenever they weren't snuggling, she acted just a little bored, like a movie star trying to fit into a small town. I watched bubblegum pop around her scarlet lips.

"And what about you, Evie? You wanna be Marilyn Monroe or Jayne Mansfield?" Bobby passed a Coke bottle over the seat to Tommy. I had figured out its real contents and tried not to count the swigs they took.

"Neither." I shook my head when Tommy offered the booze to me. Beverly snatched the bottle and took a sip. The boys guffawed. After a couple seconds of silence, I realized they were all waiting for me to answer. "I want to write book reviews for The *New York Times*."

Tommy stage-whispered, "Your friend scares me." Beverly straightened her skirt and avoided looking at me.

Bobby patted the steering wheel with both hands. "That's nice, Evie." He switched the key so he could turn the radio on.

A week before my birthday, Bobby and I ran out of things to say while listening to the lip-locks going on in the backseat. I got out of the car and followed him to the spot under an overhead light where Sandy showed off the class ring Mike had given her. Girls had gathered around to hear how Mike had hidden the ring in a box of popcorn and how Sandy felt when she found it.

"Good thing you didn't swallow it." Rena waltzed toward us with a boy I'd never seen before. It took me a second to realize that the red letter on his sweater was a "G" and not a "T." A Georgia college student. I recognized him from the fish fry an instant before Rena introduced him. "Everybody, this is Jack. Jack, this is Sandy, Judy, Brenda, and—um, Evie." While the other girls were asking Jack a hundred questions about how a Georgia player had met little ole Rena, she glanced around. "Beverly's not with you?"

"She and Tommy are in the car."

She looked at me like she'd never seen me before. Her pink sweater glistened with fake pearls around the collar. "Question is, why aren't *you*? Hey, Bobby, is your hot romance cooling off?" She smirked, pleased that everyone else chuckled at her comment.

All of a sudden I felt naked. I looked to Bobby for help and saw his eyes locked on the steamed-over windows of his car. Rena smiled triumphantly while she slipped her hand into the pocket of Jack's coat. I barely listened to the chatter, after that. Rena's taunt played over and over in my head.

Bobby didn't seem to notice my silence as he drove to my house. I muttered that I had a headache, shoved the car door open, and ran for our porch.

"That you, Evie?" I mumbled a hello toward Mom and Dad's room as I headed for my bedroom. It looked smaller than it had when

I left. I threw off my clothes, pulled on a nightgown, and slipped under the sheets. Every scene I could remember from the past few weeks played in my head.

❧

Sunday morning I pleaded a headache and stayed home from church to lie in bed and pour over every memory again. I needed to talk with someone, but the only person I could talk to about boys figured in my humiliation. By the time I'd scalded my tongue with the bitter grounds of my second cup of coffee, one clear thought had bubbled to the surface: maybe it wasn't all that hot a romance to begin with.

Not one argument had passed between Bobby and me. In a few weeks, Beverly had slammed out of the car or turned her back on Tommy half a dozen times, and he'd chased after her and even brought her flowers to class. Each time they made up, they spent less time talking to us and more time throwing Tommy's coat over their heads while they made out. Bobby and I went car-hopping with friends, instead of finding a quiet place of our own. But the memories that stuck like golf balls in my throat were images of where Bobby's eyes were aimed more often than not: into the rearview mirror as Beverly chatted in the back seat.

"My boyfriend is in love with Beverly." Once I said it out loud to myself, I could breathe better. I decided to wait until the right time to confront Bobby. I washed my face, combed my hair, and sat down at my desk to write a report on *Wuthering Heights*.

❧

By Thursday night, I was irritable as a bear with an itch. We were allowed out on a school night because we had practice for the homecoming ceremony. The "sponsors" of football players would meet our dates at center field and march to the sidelines, wearing the new suits Miss Addison had demanded. Then, the homecoming queen and king would be announced before the girls scurried off to zip ourselves into frothy dresses, while the boys finished the game and changed into coats and ties.

"Carl complained about having to buy me a suit—where am I going to wear it afterwards?—but Willeen got him to spring for that and a new dress for the dance." Beverly paused at the door to the gym and peered at me. "What's the matter? Don't you feel well? No? Well, we just have time to grab a burger at the Clocklight before we have to be home." I swallowed bile and followed her to Bobby's sedan.

The boys were too busy talking about running up the score against Athens to wonder about my silence. We followed the usual pattern: Bobby and I got out and sat on the hood of his car, leaving the inside to Tommy and Beverly.

As soon as we parked our behinds against the grille, Bobby touched my shoulder. "Don't you feel well, Evie?" How do you break up with a guy who is unfailingly polite?

I couldn't look at him. "No, not really." I examined my fingernails, waiting for him to ask why. Instead, he offered me his coat, with its big red "T" across the back. I shook my head. Last week, I would have died to try it on. Now I wanted him to put his arm around me and demand to know what was eating at me. Instead, he leaned back on the warm metal hood and took out his knife, opening and closing it against his thigh.

"You aren't still worried about what Rena said, are you?" How long had he known what was bothering me? And why wasn't he mad, too?

I took the opening. "How long have you been in love with Beverly?"

"What?" Bobby's pale blue eyes were wide open now.

"You follow her with your eyes like she's your favorite flavor of ice cream. And you haven't tried to get fresh with me, not once. You're the perfect gentleman." I snuggled my chilly fingers inside the cuffs of my corduroy jacket.

"I, I don't know what you mean. You can't hold a fellow accountable for where his eyes go. I mean—" Now he put his knife back in his pocket. "Evie, we haven't been together that long. I didn't know you wanted me to—I mean, I try to be a gentleman."

I turned to face him, huddling deeper into my coat. "I've tried to be interested in football, but, let's face it, I don't know one down from another and I couldn't care less. And you sure aren't interested in poetry." He wanted to be an accountant—that alone should have opened my eyes. "And as for being a gentleman, you could at least try to put your tongue in my mouth!" I couldn't believe I'd said such a thing.

Neither could Bob. "My tongue—" He gaped at me for twenty seconds or so, before anger ignited in his eyes. "Well, I sure never knew you were that kind of girl."

"What kind of girl is that? The kind you don't want to French kiss?" That moment, I realized I didn't care where his tongue went. I cared where it wasn't. I shot to my feet.

Bobby glanced around for eavesdroppers. No sound at all came from the back seat. "Evie, you're talking crazy. Come on! Homecoming is tomorrow. Don't you want to go to the dance?" His tone turned to pleading. His hands clenched helplessly.

"Sure—if I want to watch you watching Beverly all night." I bit the inside of my cheek. Mrs. Garretson had found some deep green wool for my suit, and she'd made a buttery sateen with embroidery around the bodice that I'd planned to wear for the dance. Bobby had bought my corsage already. Yet all I felt was disgust. "I deserve better than that."

Car wheels spinning over gravel distracted us. Mike pulled in two spaces over in his Daddy's T-bird, Sandy bundled close to him. They'd been dating since last year and somehow that fact made me mad, like I'd been denied something. And being mad made me brave. "You don't really care about me at all, do you? You're dating me so you can be close to Beverly." I saw Sandy's head snap our way. I wasn't shouting, but I wasn't quiet, either.

Bobby grabbed my sleeve, nudging me toward the rear of the lot. "For God's sake, Evie, what's gotten into you? Keep your voice down!"

Suddenly, I wanted to hurt him. "What's the matter? Do you think she doesn't know? Think Tommy doesn't know? Think anyone in this whole damn school missed it?" I set off across the asphalt, shouting back, "I was the only one too stupid to see what's going on."

"Where are you going?" Bobby threw his arms out like Jesus on the cross, totally innocent. Rain began to fall, lightly. A peal of thunder announced more to come.

"Evie, what's wrong?" Beverly poked her head out the back window, then struggled to lift the latch that flipped down the front seat. Tommy scrambled out after her.

"I'm going home," I announced. "To study!" Probably the lamest thing I had ever said, yet I didn't care how cool I looked. I marched toward Mike and Sandy, who were watching out the T-bird's windows. "I need to go home. Now!" I sobbed. Mike looked at Sandy, then scrabbled out to open the back door for me.

"Evie," Beverly yelled. "Why are you upset?" She was wearing Tommy's letter jacket. Any sympathy I had for her swished down the storm drain at my feet. Beverly always took all the attention. Why couldn't I have this little bit, my own boyfriend, to myself? I turned away and climbed into Mike's car.

"You all right?" Sandy's face flushed with concern. I nodded, once.

Beverly shouted, "I'll call you later!"

Mike spread his hands in a "What can you do?" gesture toward Bobby and crawled into the front seat. "Where to, Madame?" He raised his eyes to look at me in the mirror. I gave him my address. Neither he nor Sandy asked me any more questions. So they knew. Everybody knew, I'd bet. Except foolish Evie, the queen nerd.

All the way home, I bit my lip to keep tears from spilling down my face. Bushes smeared like green finger paint and cars like blobs of melted light. Before I knew it, I stood on my front porch, not remembering if I had thanked Mike, whose car had zoomed out of sight.

The door opened. Mom tried to shake the sleep out of her eyes. "I thought you two were going to have a sleep-over?" She peered at the empty drive. "Where's Beverly?"

Thankful for the shadows on the porch that hid my tear-stained cheeks, I said no more than necessary. "Bobby drove her home. I don't feel well and Mike and Sandy were coming this way, so I caught a ride." Mom's curlers bit into my cheek when I gave her a quick hug. If she doubted my words, she didn't make me explain. "I need some sleep. I'll be fine."

I took care not to slam the door to my room and flung myself toward the bed. I'd gone from being the envy of every sophomore girl to having no friends left in the world.

❧

The next morning, I explained to Mom that I didn't like Bobby enough to go to Homecoming with him. She didn't seem surprised, tying on her work apron without taking her eyes off me. "I guess you can use your suit next year."

I followed her out the door, grateful that she didn't make me feel guilty for wasting money on clothes, and wondered if kids at school would ignore me, now that I wasn't a halfback's girlfriend. I dawdled so that I would get to class a few seconds before the bell and almost made it to my homeroom door before Beverly shoved me from behind into the bathroom. Our footsteps echoed on the tile.

"Wait for the bell to ring." Her eyes were nearly emerald with anger. She faced the mirror, lifted a strand of hair, and began to tease it with a rattail comb.

Why should I care if she was mad? I settled against a sink. "How do we get back into class?"

She pulled two pink slips from her purse. "You can buy these in the cafeteria for a dime. *If* you ever need one." Her tone accused me of being too boring to need a fake excuse.

The bell clanged. Another girl sidled out the door, watching us from the corner of her eyes. If I thought we'd ease into it, I was off base by a mile.

Beverly threw down her comb and crossed her arms. "One day before homecoming, and you're a shrinking violet? Why the hell did you break up with Bobby? Tommy's dad's too cheap to buy him a car. We can't go to the dance if we don't go with you and Bobby."

"What does that mean? Shrinking from what?"

Beverly did a pretty good imitation of me at the fish fry. "'What'll I do if he kisses me? Ooh, what if he wants to walk in the dark? I'm afraid he might touch me *there*.'"

It all seemed so long ago. "You think I broke up with him for *that*? I got tired of watching him moon after you, that's why I ditched him!"

"*Duh*, Evie. Why d'ya think he'd pick a sophomore? When he could have any girl?"

Stunned, I struggled to make sense of it: She knew he had a crush on her, but expected me to keep dating him? Suddenly my own temper blazed. "So this is all about *you*? How are *you* getting to the dance? I don't give a shit! What about how I feel going around with a guy everyone knows is pining for *you*?"

We glared at each other for a long moment before Beverly's grin erupted. "Did you say—Who's the bad girl now!"

A skinny kid with a yellow sash across her chest stuck her head in the door. "What are ya'll doing?"

Beverly spun around and showed the passes. "My friend threw up. We're just going back to class." The hall monitor squinted at the scribbling on the pink papers and reached out to take them for a closer look. "Oh, good grief! Leave us alone, will you?" Beverly snatched the passes away from the girl's face and scowled at her as the door slammed shut.

A few days ago, I would have been amused at how Beverly took charge. Now, tears welled. "Beverly, why didn't you tell me Bobby wasn't interested in me?" I said it carefully, quietly, so my eyes wouldn't overflow.

I listened to her explanation about how she'd hoped she'd been wrong, until she saw Bobby seemed miffed, but not upset, when I left. Her eyes held a sort of apology. "All the guys think you're cute. They just think you're not likely to give 'em what they want."

"And how much are you planning to give them?" I dried my eyes with a paper towel.

She made a face at me in the mirror as she finished teasing her hair. "Evie, I'm not gonna give anyone anything I don't want to give."

I thought about her chasing the bull, me running away from it. But today it felt more like we were on separate roller coasters, Beverly careening someplace I didn't want to go. With sudden clarity, I knew things would never be the same. I opened my handbag. "Things weren't working out with Bobby. He's boring. He wants to be an accountant, for Christ's sake." With a grace I didn't know I had, I reached for a peace offering. "Mom got me a new lipstick for the dance. What do you think?" I offered her the golden tube.

Beverly snorted, her eyes a shade lighter. "Yeah, maybe he's too tame even for you." She took the tube, spreading some on her upper lip and pressing both edges of her mouth together. The brownish red didn't look bad on her, but I noted that it looked much better on me.

She handed it back and turned to face me. "Evie, I'm sorry about Bobby, okay? I'm just so crazy about Tommy that I guess I didn't put two and two together."

A minute ago I'd been furious. Now I was—what? Indifferent? No. But something less than satisfied. I considered my own reflection in the mirror and let her blur into the background. "Well, be careful tomorrow night, okay?"

Beverly fluffed her hair with her hands and handed me one pink slip with a twisted grin. "I won't have a choice, with my mom driving."

I felt a twinge of guilt about creating such a fuss, but also a little freer. And scared to be completely on my own.

Evangeline, 1933: Stargazer

Mid-April, it should be brightening, but we've seen nothing except rain for nearly a week. Mr. James hesitates just inside the door, his brimmed hat tipped low to keep the water out of his eyes.

"You're sure you'll be all right?" He searches for any hesitation in my face. I know he's thinking of the baby I lost a year ago.

I'm determined to reassure him. "Of course. Nettie should be home from Toccoa later today. And the baby hasn't turned yet. He's still bumping his head on my rib cage. I'm more worried about you. Can't that congregation wait another week for a wedding?"

Mr. James smiles, probably because I said "he." He settles his hat again with one hand, bends, and kisses my cheek. "Good thing we bought the truck. Espero could pick her way through a stream, but that pickup might float a little better than her in a flood. Don't know how good a wedding day it'll be, but the preacher had better be there with bells on."

I smile, too, thinking of our own wedding, me grasping a bouquet of daisies from the meadow, Mr. James dripping creek water on Mrs. Garretson's rug from his climb to get them. "Practically any day is good for a wedding if the couple is willing."

My husband pecks my cheek again and steps onto the porch. One look at the water pouring off the roof, and he's sprinting to the barn.

A clatter spins me around. Maisie thumps down the ladder from the girls' room. She is so tall now, at thirteen, that her feet reach the floor while her hands cling to the top rung. She swings her book bag and her thick, dark hair over her shoulder, then calls to her sisters. "Vinnie! Tally! Don't make Dad wait." She wags her head at me. "I am tired of missing the first bell because Tally can't find her shoes and Vinnie can't decide what to wear."

I wave her to me. She plods, reluctant. Her smile says she is faking. I cover her ears with my hands and tilt her head back. She is so pretty, long-lashed and golden-skinned, like my mother. I tip her face down and kiss her forehead, which is even with my lips. "Be patient with your sisters. You have a head start on them. They will keep you company in dark times to come."

"You mean like if Georgie Applewhite holds her down and tries to kiss her in the school yard?" Vinnie jumps down the last few feet, her skirt flying up to show her solid thighs in black knit stockings. She is wearing a yellow sweater over her red jumper.

"Interesting choices," Maisie observes. She reaches out to slap the tassel on Vinnie's green cap. "And where were you when I was trying to fight George off?"

Vinnie grins at me, reaching for a hug. "Cleaning blackboards for Mr. Ames and getting an 'A' for the week."

"I helped you, Maisie. I socked him in the eye." Tally half-falls down the ladder, waddles over and holds out one foot for me to snap her galoshes.

"Yes, you were a big help, Tally." Maisie rolls her eyes and bends over to snap Tally's other overshoe.

"Is this thing with Georgie serious?" I ask. Maisie shrugs as the truck's horn blasts outside the door.

"Ah-oo-ga!" mimics Vinnie.

"He better not mess any more with my big sister." Tally grimaces fiercely, rises on her tiptoes to kiss my cheek.

"Come on, Tiger. You, too, Fannie."

Vinnie laughs like she always does when her big sister calls her by that silly name and skips down the steps with Tally to the truck. Maisie smiles over her shoulder at me as she follows.

Mr. James has pulled the car close to the door so they won't have to jump over the puddle brimming the lower step. Vinnie settles next to her father, and Tally scrambles onto Maisie's lap. I blow them a kiss and wave till the truck disappears behind the lilacs bordering the drive.

A splash of yellow from the forsythias on the other side of the path draws my eyes to the cleft in the greenery where we buried Ruv last fall. "Rest easy, dear friend," I whisper to that good dog, as I often do. I turn to savor the silence in the house.

The best thing about having the truck is that Mr. James can drive the girls to school in bad weather: I don't have to keep them busy in the house on "mud days." I consider the basket of herbs and the fabric lying folded on the kitchen table. First, I think I'll have another cup of tea, rest a bit before I wash the herbs and hang them to dry and cut out the girls' summer dresses.

After steeping some peppermint leaves in my cup, I settle into the rocking chair to rest and dream. I'm more tired with this baby than with the others. Being almost thirty makes a difference. I gave birth to Vinnie and canned fruit on the same day. Now I have to slow down and bide my time, or else my limbs feel like they're made of stone.

The calendar over the stove shows I'm two weeks short of nine months. Baby should be turning by now. I sip my tea, watch the low-banked fire, and stroke his little head, now lodged under my left breast. "Easy, fellow. Time to move down and think about your debut." I feel him stretch a little toward my toes, so I keep stroking after I close my eyes. Why am I so tired?

When I wake, the rain has risen to a storm, darkening the panes. The mantel clock chimes over and over. Noon already, and I haven't made a start. The girls will be home in three hours.

Reaching to tie herbs onto the drying rack near the stove makes my back ache, but I manage to get through all the mint bundles before I stop for another rest before the fire.

I wake again to the clock chiming. Just once, I think. That means another two hours to cut out the fabric before the girls get home. I rise to my feet. At the first step, liquid crashes to the floor beneath me. I stare down at my soaked slippers and feel a kick of sharp pain in my lower belly.

This can't be! I think. But it is. I breathe through another pang and start for the door. Before I get there, a blow doubles me over. No time to get Nettie. I reverse course and hobble to my bedroom, grabbing my bag from the hooks by the door.

It's even darker in the bedroom, but I can't catch my breath long enough to fetch the lamp and trim the wick. I lie down on the soft cotton coverlet, planning to get up in a minute and fold it back, so I won't stain it. But the pains keep coursing through my body.

With my other babies, I could ride the spasms in waves, like a ship, floating over the silence between agonies long enough to find some air. These billows keep crashing. I feel carefully around my belly. There is the head, a little lower now, its chin even with my belly button. Feels like a heel pressed against the pubic bone. The baby hasn't turned. It will be a breech birth.

I grit my teeth and focus on holding on till Maisie comes home. I will send her for Nettie. Then I remember: the girls will have to wait at school until their dad gets back from the mountain wedding. The rain will surely delay Mr. James. Perhaps they'll catch a ride with someone else. I listen to the thunder, watch the crackling light, and try to find a way to lift my body above the torrent.

Sparks of lightning reveal the darkness gathering outside. A faint knocking in my head becomes the slam of the door. Maisie's voice calls. "In here," I gasp.

Her serious face peers down at me. "Mama?" Her eyes flick from my sweating face to my twisting torso. I cannot keep my body from writhing like a snake caught by a pitchfork. I bite my lips against the urge to cry out.

"Your father?" I croak from between clenched teeth.

Maisie wags her head, sending drops of water spraying. "He didn't come. Mr. Redding dropped us at the mailbox. He says the bridges are awash in floodwater." Her eyes widen as I jackknife away from her. "What can I do, Mama?"

I touch my lips with my tongue, but my mouth is too dry to produce spit. Maisie disappears, returns with a wet cloth. My good little nurse. She puts it between my lips so I can suck its moisture. I swallow the trickle and manage to speak.

"Go for Nettie. Wait!" I reach out, struggling to keep control of my breath. "Give the girls something to eat, first. Tell them to start their homework. Not to come in here."

She leaves, and I am alone with the hammering cramps that threaten to wring me inside out. *Why, Baby, why such a hurry? You're— I'm—not ready.* It takes a moment to realize the words are in my mind, not on my lips.

I hear the door creak and turn my head. Tally scampers in and stands over me, a crayon in one hand, a cookie in the other. I swallow again, feeling my dry throat chafe, and smooth out my forehead. "Give Mama a kiss and go back to your work, Tally. Get it done before Papa comes home." Each word comes slowly, so slowly I gasp through three waves of pain before I've finished. But Tally seems not to notice. She kisses my cheek and runs away, closing the door softly behind her. She needs to see I am available. I grip the sides of the mattress and hold on. The sea washes me away.

꧁꧂

The early-rising moon makes a path through my window. My swollen feet hurt from bracing on the iron rungs. I don't know why this babe won't come. It feels hot, low in my belly, like he's pushing as hard as I am.

"Mama?" Maisie again. Must have dozed off. She looks far away, like another room was added between us.

"Yes." I concentrate on forming the word. So tired.

"Nettie isn't home. That Tyndall fellow says she went to town and can't drive back since the bridge is out. He says he'll take the horse to ford the stream, if you want."

"Doc Evans?" I have to spit words out between gritted teeth.

"He's—he isn't well enough to come."

You mean he's too drunk to come, I think. No help there.

I draw a map in my mind of our neighbors' farms in relation to the water. The Reddings are on the other side of the raging creek. The Applewhites have moved to town. Their farm lies vacant. The Burnetts' place lies on the other side of Doc Evans's pastures, too far for Maisie to walk in this storm. My mind pushes an image to the top of its seething nerve ends: Amelia Dockhart trudging through snow across our cornfield.

"Get Mrs. Dockhart. And tell Carl to cross the creek to get Nettie, if … if he can." Getting those sentences out feels like a trip across a dangerous void.

"Wait!" I call her back and gesture to the chest at the foot of the bed. "Tie a sheet around … bed post." Each word costs a fortune in pain. I don't have the strength yet to pull on the sheet ends that Maisie hands to me, so she lays them at my side.

"I'll hurry, Mama." I hear the tears in her voice.

"Good girl."

It seems like only minutes before she returns this time. I lost consciousness. Waves of anguish are still roiling inside me, but they feel somehow far away now. I look at Maisie, then behind her, expecting to see Mrs. Dockhart. Then back to Maisie's face. She shakes her head, tears streaming now down her chin. I close my eyes to avoid seeing her fear.

I am her mother. I have to get her through this.

A while later—how long?—I wake again and see Maisie holding a steaming bowl. No, it's Vinnie, tears flowing as if her turquoise eyes are running down her face. She has made gruel and now she's offering me some. I weakly wave my hand toward the nightstand. She puts the bowl down, kisses my cheek swiftly, and backs away.

It's Maisie again, shaking my shoulder. "Mama, why are you bleeding so much?"

I try to raise my shoulders, but I'm so tired. Maisie reaches around my back and gives me her thin little shoulder to push against. I manage to rise an inch or two. Oh, God. The bed is wet, red with blood, from my hips to my toes. Where is it coming from? I shift my hips. I feel pressure, but no feeling like the baby's crowning.

I gather all my strength. I have to feel down there and see what's wrong. Pushing against my girl, I make it far enough that I can touch between my legs. I feel globs of blood, push them aside. A small smooth arch.

"Footling!" I gasp and fall back with a ragged breath. "Maisie." Grit my teeth on the pain. "Maisie." For a minute I can't think. Then I remember. "Help me … stand."

I want to give her more directions, but I can't get words past the fog in my mind. I want to go to sleep, but the pain is knifing across my guts. I must gather more strength. How long have I been lying here, panting? "Maisie, now."

My daughter gets behind me and pushes. I heave myself up. Together, we maneuver my bulk into a crouch, leaning against the bed. It feels like my insides fall to the floor in a torrent of blood cascading across the planks. I inch my hand down to grasp the baby's foot, tugging gently. He slips out a little, a little more. Finally, almost all the way. "Maisie, catch him."

"He's stuck, Mama. His head—" She looks at me, her eyes huge swirls of chocolate and green.

Some thought batters at my brain. I find the word. "Stargazer. He's a … stargazer. Maisie, you have to put—" I gasp and gasp as the agony cuts me in two. "—put your hand up there and tilt his chin, so he won't … won't choke." I squeeze my eyes shut, push myself to blink them open. I know what I am asking my girl to do.

Maisie's gaze locks to mine as she understands. She bends her head. I feel probing fingers. And the baby wails.

Has it been minutes or hours? Night has entered the room. There is a glare. I look in that direction and see a round blob that might be the lamp. Something is peculiar about the way it is interrupted by black spots, big dots of darkness covering the blaze.

"Mama?" I follow Maisie's voice to where she is standing, the baby wrapped in a blanket in her arms. She has bathed him. I can see his head, his little legs kicking, his—yes, it's a boy. I want to smile, but my face will not form an expression. Maisie takes a step toward me. One tiny fist waves close to my face. At the same time, a look of horror comes over Maisie. A sucking sound draws our eyes downward. The entire bed is soaked with blood, gore trailing down the covers, across the floor, under her shoes.

My sweet daughter takes a deep breath and moves closer, so that I can graze the baby's head with my lips and brush my fingers across her cheek.

At the same moment, I see my mother standing behind her, wrapped in her blue-flowered coverlet. She smiles and holds out her hand to me. Over her shoulder, the moon makes a path. "Longo drom," she whispers. The long road. I struggle to rise.

"Daughter, help me outside." She hesitates. I push all my strength into whispering again, "Outside."

Her face a pucker of fear, Maisie places the baby in the cradle against the wall, and offers me her shoulder. "Don't let your sisters see." As I stumble through the front door, she places her body between me and the room beyond. All at once, I smell rue, wet earth, from the herb garden.

"Longo drom," whispers my mother, with me now in the shelter of wisteria vines. The moon lights a path over the roof and beyond. I am rising and falling at the same time, now spinning like a leaf in a pond.

I struggle to see my daughter, a peak of light in the silvery drizzle. "Maisie, take care of your sisters." I breathe the words to her and hope she will hear everything I don't have time to say. *I love you. I trust you. Remember me.* My own mother again holds out her hand to me. "Ash Devlésa. Stay with God," I whisper to my beloved Maisie.

Evie, October, 1959: Fields of Clay

Friday afternoon, the lunchroom practically vibrated with anticipation and dread. Some girls dropped their voices whenever a boy came near, hoping for a last-minute invitation to the dance. Boys joked about going alone so they could drink more. I walked through the high-pitched chatter as if it didn't concern me. Maybe the word hadn't gotten around.

Wrong. At our table, Veronica and another girl from French class cast sideways looks at me. Then Veronica shoved a magazine under my nose. "Boyfriends cramp your style. Who needs them? I borrowed the latest copy of *Elle* from Madame Duffy. You want to read it?"

I accepted the magazine, smiled, and stirred the spaghetti with sauce that had congealed into wormy orange sludge on my plate.

The other girl whipped a lock of red hair out of her eye and nodded. "Poor pitiful guy has to go to the dance with Rena now." Veronica shot her a warning look, too late.

The smell of onions and overcooked tomatoes pinched my throat. A point above my right eye that had been aching all morning began to throb. "I think I'm gonna be sick." I ran for the nearest toilet. Three steps from the girls' room, I skidded to a stop as familiar voices leaked from inside the gym's partly open metal doors.

"You know I do, but what if my dad won't help us, then what?"

"He will, won't he? I mean, he has to! You're his son." Beverly's voice pleaded.

Tommy replied, "He wouldn't even let me bring the car today. I'll have to walk over to the store to get it. Look, I'll pick you up later at home, and we'll decide what to do. Okay?"

"What time? I didn't bring my things because I thought you were going to drive me home. I'll have to take the bus back to get them. Or should I wait for you?"

"Why don't you go ahead on the bus? That way, if I'm late, you can be getting ready."

"The bus takes forever to get to my place. I'll barely make it there before Mom gets home at four. You'll be there before then, won't you?" Her voice sounded unfamiliar, wheedling, weak.

"Look, just go home and wait for me, okay? If your mom comes, tell her you're packed for the dance and I'll be by to get you later. I gotta go." Footsteps clomping away did not quite muffle sounds of— crying? I put my hand on the door to check on my friend, but a clatter of steps and a familiar voice stopped me.

"Hey, Bev!" Bobby's voice sounded ten times brighter than when he greeted me. How had I missed that for so long?

"You're the guy I was hoping to see!" Now Beverly's voice sounded only faintly breathless. "Bobby, could you take me home after school? I have to get my things and be back here for practice at five. Tommy's dad won't let him have the car till later."

Bobby cleared his throat. "I guess so. But I can't wait for you to get ready. I have to pick up Rena's corsage and make the before-game meeting. Otherwise, I'd bring you back."

"Oh, I'll get my aunt to bring me back."

I heard a rustle, and Bobby's abashed tone. "Okay. Okay! You don't have to be that grateful." Embarrassed, but pleased.

Any doubts I had about Beverly playing games were gone. Here she was stringing Bobby along—for what? Why not have Willeen bring her back, if Tommy didn't get the car? Come to think of it, why had she pressed Tommy to be at her house before Willeen got home?

It didn't make sense. I shook my head to clear away the bitterness and headed for the bathroom. The hammer in my head struck with every footfall.

At five o'clock I sat on my bed in a plain skirt and sweater, trying to decide if I wanted to meet Veronica at the game. My headache had eased, but I was having trouble mustering any enthusiasm for watching my former boyfriend dance with Rena.

From the front room, Mom exclaimed, "Willeen! I'm surprised to see you."

The front screen slapped shut. "Isn't Beverly here? She was supposed to take her clothes with her on the bus today and get ready here, with Evie, but I found them hanging on her door when I got home."

I got to my feet, confused. What the hell was going on?

"Evie? Did Beverly say anything about forgetting her clothes? Or coming home with you?" Mom stood in the doorway, a puzzled look on her face.

Who would believe I hadn't talked to her all day? And what could I say that wouldn't get her in trouble? And why do you care if she's in trouble? said my worst self.

I stammered, "No, no, she didn't. I thought she planned on going home for them after school."

Willeen appeared behind Mom, holding the burgundy wool suit Beverly had planned to wear to the game. Enfolded in the same reused dry cleaning bag, I could just make out the ivory lace of her dress for the dance. Willeen held them both out. "Why would she go all the way back home for them? You're sure she didn't plan to come here?"

Clearly Beverly had given a couple of different versions of her plans. A pressure crept into my throat so that my voice sounded pinched. "Maybe she missed the bus and she's still at school. I'll go with you to find her." I reached for my coat, avoiding Mom's gaze.

"I'll drive, Willeen. No sense in taking two cars." Mom's tone said she knew there was mischief in the air. I determined not to let her see I knew it, too. We waved to Dad, sitting in the porch swing, and drove to school. I wiped the fog of my breath from the window and stared at the cold lavender of the late afternoon sky.

🙥🙟

By the time we knocked on the side door to the gym, the walkways to the field were filled with people streaming in for the game. Popcorn buttered the air. "The cheerleaders' practice room is right down this hall." I tugged on the heavy metal door. "It's locked." I rapped again on the hard surface. No one answered. "I'll go around and through the gym. There has to be someone there."

I told the grizzly janitor that I had an urgent message for one of the cheerleaders. He spied my mother and Willeen behind me, looking ready to scold someone, and let me in. I ran across the wooden floor till I reached the linoleum-lined hall on the other side of the basketball court.

Rena almost ran into me on her way up the basement stairs. "Your friend's in big trouble. She missed practice." I could have smacked her smug face. Instead, I ran back to Mom and Willeen.

"She's not here! She didn't come to practice!" My heart pounded.

For a moment, even my mother looked at a loss. Then she fixed me with a look that said, *time to get serious.* "Evie, what do you know about where Beverly went today?"

I didn't bother to think of another lie. "She meant to go home, but I don't know why. Bobby Baker drove her. I think she intended to get a ride back with Tommy later." I looked around in frustration. If Tommy had brought her, she should have been here by now. I could hear the team in their pre-game pep talk from the other side of the walls.

My mother turned to the janitor, who still stood in the doorway, watching us. "Where is the football team?"

Two minutes later we were knocking on the basement door on the other side of the building. My mother did not bother explaining to the coach, who opened the door. "I need to see Bobby Baker and Tommy Turner. Now." Behind the coach, the team knelt in prayer. Tommy stood tall and faced my mother. His eyes were red, as if he'd been crying. Next to him, Bobby flashed me a look of something so near hatred that I stumbled backward and had to grip the doorframe.

Willeen's hand gently moved me aside. She'd been quiet so far, letting my mother take the lead, but now she took Tommy by the shoulders where the pads tented his jersey. "Where is my daughter?"

Bobby stepped in front of his friend. He looked at Willeen calmly, his voice extremely polite. "I dropped her off at the florist. She said she'd walk the rest of the way." The florist! A good two miles away from the Tyndalls' house.

Willeen turned to Tommy. "Weren't you supposed to pick her up for the dance?"

Tommy paused as if trying to find a good story. "We were supposed to meet at your house, but I couldn't get my dad's car. I called, and—I don't know where she is. I thought she'd come in with you. I caught a ride in with Bob."

Willeen and Mom examined the boys' faces, then turned on their heels as if they were of one mind, leaving the players and coaches staring, and hurried to our Nash. I scrambled after them. Until then, I'd ignored the pangs in my gut that said something awful had happened. Mom flinging open the door, plopping into the seat, and gunning the engine before I had even settled in, told me how bad things were. Willeen's gaunt face confirmed it.

Mom jerked the car into gear and backed out of the space before she floored the accelerator. "Bet Tommy and Beverly quarreled, and she took off. We'd be all day getting the straight story from those two boys. I'll drop you off for your car, Willeen. Frank can take his truck, and I'll go get Mary Alice. We'll all look for her."

As we rushed toward Mrs. Beasley's house, a voice knocked at my memory: "I'll run away to live with you!" But now Beverly knew the way and she had not come to me. Where would she walk on a cold night? And what could be important enough to make her miss Homecoming?

I watched a crescent moon rise, pale against the darkening sky. Too late, I realized Beverly could never be just another school friend. A vision of her green eyes and chortling laugh floated up at me from inside a leafy bower—the garden? How old were we then? No matter. She was the one person I remembered almost as long as I remembered being me. I should have found out what she was planning.

Mom dropped Willeen at our house to pick up her car and find Carl. Then we located Mary Alice as her shift at the hospital was ending. Before Mom had finished explaining, Mary Alice slung her purse into the back seat and climbed in after it. We three drove the bus route toward the Tyndall's. Nothing. Mom had turned the car back toward Mary's Alice's house when I spotted it: Beverly's maroon sweater, tangled on a bush, its white letter blazing in the headlights.

I barely had time to say, "Look!" before Mom slammed on the brakes.

Mary Alice jumped out as soon as the car stopped. I followed, ignoring Mom's sharp, "Evie, wait!" I didn't care if I got in trouble.

Dusk fell as we leapt across the ditch, Mary Alice's white tennis shoes smacking the red dust into gritty clouds that almost choked me. On the other side, a snarl of brambles and snapping branches hampered us. Mary Alice stopped. Over her shoulder I saw Beverly, lying face down, her bare legs sprawled out behind her. Mary Alice turned, blocking my view, and barked, "Go for an ambulance. *Now!*"

I scrambled back toward the car and shouted to my mother from the far side of the ditch, "Mary Alice says get an ambulance! Quick!" Mom looked from me to Mary Alice and back to the open car door.

She hesitated, staring straight into my eyes. For the first time in my life I didn't bother to hide my defiance. Mom reached across to the glove compartment, took out a silver flashlight, and tossed it to me.

"You'll need this." Then she slammed the door. By the time I had scrabbled back across the ditch and into the brush, the car's taillights had all but disappeared. I steeled myself to look at my bloodied friend's ... body? Was she alive?

Beverly groaned, and my knees turned weak with gratitude when her arm moved to clutch her abdomen. But the sight of her bare buttocks and the blood smeared across the backs of her thighs made my stomach lurch. "She's nake—" In Mary Alice's glare I saw a kind of resolve that I tried to imitate, clamping my words behind my teeth.

"She crawled away from the road before she lost consciousness," Mary Alice murmured. In the next breath, she comforted Beverly. "We're here, Honey. We're going to take care of you."

Beverly's hands stretched out through a tangle of thorny blackberries.

Mary Alice took the flashlight from my palm, laid it down so that it shone toward us, and plucked Beverly's tattered white blouse from a bush a foot away. She began ripping it into strips. "See if she has a head wound." Later, I realized this was the one important thing I could do while being directed away from the oozing spot between Beverly's legs. Mary Alice applied a wad of cloth to Beverly's thigh and scrutinized her for more wounds.

"She's been—" I tried again to make my mind grasp the situation.

"Evie, if you're going to be here, help me and keep your mouth shut."

Beverly moaned but did not open her eyes as I knelt down beside her. I felt every inch of her head with my fingers until I reached two swollen, hot places above her left ear. "Just lumps. No blood," I reported.

She came alive beneath my hands. "Awrrgh!" Like a wounded animal, she tensed and tried to rise, then fell limp.

Mary Alice moved swiftly to my side. Beverly's head turned just enough for me to see one blackened eye. "Beverly? Honey, can you hear me?" Her aunt repeated Beverly's name until her swollen lids fluttered, then handed me the blood-soaked cloth.

"Evie, press this onto the wound on her leg. Keep steady pressure on it. She doesn't need to lose any more blood." I moved to Beverly's feet. Most of the blood came, not from her insides, but from a deep gash on her left inner thigh. In the flashlight's glow, I could see scratches running from her knees to a point where her thighs met pubic hair. A wave of nausea clenched my stomach. I placed the cloth against the cut and leaned my weight into it.

Mary Alice's hands passed efficiently over Beverly's head and neck, a much more careful exam than I'd given. She lifted Beverly's eyelids and peered into her eyes, causing a shiver to run from Beverly's shoulders to her feet. "She has a concussion. Took a hard knock on the head." She continued to explore for damage, lifting the elastic of Beverly's bra to run her hands down her ribs. "Sweet baby," she murmured.

I sat back and rubbed my hand down Beverly's calf. "Hang on, Bev."

At the sound of sirens, I stood and lifted my head, for the first time recognizing the persimmon trees writhing around and above us, their limbs waving through the red lights sweeping from the road. Mary Alice continued talking quietly to her niece while the attendants struggled toward us through the brush.

❦

I rushed into the emergency room behind Beverly on the stretcher, Mary Alice at her side. In a curtained cubicle, a doctor performed a quick exam, nodded at Mary Alice, and announced that Beverly would live. I made myself small as possible as the medical team circled the bed on which Beverly lay. When the head nurse learned I was not kin, she pointed me through a set of green-painted doors.

For a half hour, I sat in one of a row of attached plastic chairs and waited by myself, seeing Beverly's sweater waving on the branch, her naked legs snared in brambles, the blood smeared over her. I reached one conclusion: If I had said what I knew the moment Willeen had entered our house, Beverly might not be lying behind those doors.

After an eternity, Mary Alice shoved through them. Some switch in my brain turned on speech.

"I didn't think she'd get hurt! We've walked out there so many times—" I could feel my voice rising as I tried to control my tongue. *You shouldn't take attention away from Beverly*, some voice said. But my mind insisted on processing everything I knew about why my best friend lay in a hospital bed.

Mary Alice sat down in the chair bolted next to mine and hugged me. "Oh, honey, nobody blames you. Girls have their quarrels. You had no reason to think she'd be attacked." How did she know we'd quarreled? I tried to remember what I'd said, but fatigue had built a dam in my head, around which swirled more questions than answers.

When the elevator doors at the other end of the hall opened, my mother rushed out. "Evie! I'm sorry it took so long, honey. I had to find your Dad and Willeen. She and Carl should be right behind us. Dad's parking the car." Mom cradled my face in her hands and examined me with that searching look I'd seen after a thousand scraped knees and hurt feelings. She then turned her attention to Mary Alice. "How's Beverly? Was she—" Mom swallowed so hard I could hear it.

"Probably. I wish Evie hadn't had to see it, but I needed her." She patted my knee. "You did fine." I let myself believe I'd done what needed to be done.

Dad arrived, looked into my eyes, and smoothed my hair away from my face. He whispered to Mary Alice, "They catch the fella?" She shook her head. He leaned against the wall just outside the swinging doors, arms braced behind him, feet crossed.

The elevator opened once more. Willeen limped toward us, her face a mess of red eyes and swollen lips, her hair jumbled in thick clots, as if she'd been tearing at it with her hands. Carl trudged behind, hands jammed in his pockets. A thick fog of argument surrounded them. Carl nodded to my father and stopped to stare through the two patches of glass in the emergency room entrance. His head swung to the sign that said, "Hospital Personnel Only." He pushed through.

When Willeen heard the doors slap open, she turned from Mary Alice's embrace and followed Carl. Mom took a seat beside me. Mary Alice sat down on my other side. Both clasped their hands over mine on the cold metal rims of the chair.

After a few minutes, Carl came bursting through the green doors and pounded his fist on the wall. Without a word, he walked to the end of the corridor, where he stood at the window, like he could find some answer in the gray clouds and parking lot. My dad walked over and crouched down nearby, against the wall, not saying anything, but close enough to catch a whisper if it came.

The doors shut again with a softer swish behind Willeen. My mom walked over and put her arms around her friend. Willeen's big face, hovering at least a foot above my mother's small tan one, crumpled into a deep riverbed.

Mom pulled a white handkerchief from the pocket of her flowered dress and wiped away her friend's tears. "Willeen. Beverly will be well enough to tell us what happened tomorrow, won't she? Meanwhile, it's enough to know she'll be all right, isn't it?" She stroked her friend's back. "They'll take care of her here."

Willeen took the handkerchief and rubbed at her eyes. She jerked her head toward the other end of the hall. "Tell that to him. He says she's better off dead."

"Why do men carry on so?" Mom stepped back just a little from Willeen's side. Then she noticed me. "Evie, go see if there's some

Cokes in the machine, would you? See if Carl and your dad want–" She fumbled in her pocket for change. We all looked down the corridor in time to see Dad and Carl disappear into the elevator. "Well, I guess they have some other beverage in mind." Willeen spun around. "I almost forgot. Evie, she wants you. Doctor says you shouldn't stay too long."

I looked at Mom, hesitated. Mary Alice stood and beckoned, so I unstuck my feet from the tile floor and stepped through the green door after her.

We padded down a corridor painted the same sickly hue to a desk, where a gray-haired woman with soft blue eyes and glasses sliding down her nose watched us approach. Mary Alice leaned over the desk. The older lady patted her on the arm. "I heard she's your niece, hon. I'm mighty sorry."

Mary Alice wiped a hand across her eyes. "Thank you. This is Beverly's best friend, Evalyn Gates. Beverly's been asking for her."

The older nurse searched my face and tucked her chin, so that her glasses slid even farther down the bump of her nose. "Honey, try not to get her upset. It may not be the best time for a lot of questions. She needs to calm down." She turned to Mary Alice. "She got right difficult with Dr. Taylor. He gave her something to make her relax." She paused, checking her next words. "Maybe you can talk her into letting him examine her. 'Cause you know who'll be in there next."

Mary Alice tugged on my arm. "We'll try. Come on, Evie, let's go see our girl."

"Who'll be in next?" I whispered as we hurried away

Mary Alice locked her jaw so the words barely slipped out. "The police."

I stopped, unable to go on. I had never talked to a police officer before. Never been inside an emergency room. The uniformed people rushing back and forth felt like waves bashing me against the walls.

Whatever Beverly felt right now would be a million times worse, but I could only keep track of the fear swirling inside my own chest. Mary Alice propelled me firmly ahead.

She opened a door to a room where the moon, unleashed by moving clouds, inched over every surface. One set of sheets lay empty, like an unwritten letter. From the other, an unfamiliar face turned to us as we entered. I took in Beverly's condition.

Bandages spanned more than half her head and bruised flesh welled into red balloons around her slashed lips. Her eyes were rimmed with purple. I thought of the little girl with locks like sunshine and struggled to keep a sob from escaping my throat.

Mary Alice moved quickly to her other side and bent down. "Sweet girl," she said. Beverly put an arm around her aunt's neck. I felt her squeeze my outstretched fingers. Our sobs mingled like a chorus of mourning swans.

Minutes passed before Mary Alice straightened. The nurse in her took over. "Who made your bed?" she scolded. "You can't rest with those big wrinkles under you. And who knocked over your ice?" She smoothed and yanked while chattering, and I knew she did this every day, for people whose sadness overwhelmed them, who needed time to think, to get a grip. Today, she distracted herself as well.

Beverly blinked and croaked, "I did that. Dad wouldn't stop asking questions. So I made a fuss." So that was why Carl punched the door and Willeen flew after him. Mary Alice swept the spilled cubes into the wastebasket. Beverly reached out to grab her hand. "Dad said the police would come. I don't want to press charges. I won't talk to them. I won't." She licked her split lips between words.

"But he—" I couldn't bring myself to say the word "rape." Inside, some still, small voice said, *Why? Why won't she tell? Can you just not tell and go on?* A glimmer of suspicion surfaced—*what had she done?*—but I shoved it back down. "Beverly, why not?" I searched the rotten fruit of her face for an answer.

Men talking fast approached, their feet clopping on the corridor tiles. Mary Alice looked at Beverly like reading a book. I saw only that steely-jawed glare I'd seen a million times when Beverly had decided on something.

Mary Alice whirled, grasped the door handle, and swung into the hall.

"Gentlemen, sorry, but she's not able to talk now." A voice like tumbling rocks rattled against the door. "It's not clear what happened. No, I'm not sure at all. She's groggy, and all I know is she has lots of bruises and scratches. How she got them, I don't know." The voices receded. I imagined Mary Alice guiding the detectives down the hall. It had never been hard to get men to follow her.

I stroked Beverly's hair. I wanted to lay my hand along her cheek, but her skin everywhere I could see—around the head bandage, the hand lying stiff on the outer sheet, the throat where a terrible thumb print smoked against her tanned skin—was swollen, like a breath would leave its mark. Slowly, I let my bottom sink onto the stool next to her bed and laid my head next to hers on the pillow. We were eye-to-eye. I whispered, "What happened? Why don't you want to tell?"

Her eyes rolled away from my face toward the ceiling. "I can't face all those questions. People will think it's my fault. I can't face him."

"Him? Who?" Did she think I knew who had raped her?

"They'll hurt me more if I tell." Her hand closed over mine in a grip so tight my fingers burned.

"They? Who? Not—not Bobby, right? Not Tommy?" I gulped to hear my own voice pleading with her not to accuse anyone I knew. Beverly shook her head, violently.

Suddenly, my mother's voice floated down the hall. "She won't let them examine her? She must be terrified, poor thing!"

"Beverly, who did this?" I whispered, urgently. "You've got to tell me before I have to go. I'll come back tomorrow, but tell me, quick. What should I know?"

"He said he'd make sure Carl knew about me, me and Tommy. Daddy might kill him. Evie—" She grabbed my other arm with the hand that had been lying dormant on her chest. "I can't tell! It doesn't matter who it is. I can't risk—" Her left hand smoothed the sheet over her stomach. The door creaked open.

Risk what? What could she risk that hadn't already been taken? Her life?

In the next instant my mother appeared, saying a quiet hello, kissing Beverly gently on the cheek, suggesting we give her time to rest. Beverly's eyes glittered as Mom pulled me away and the door closed.

I followed down the corridor, my mind landing like a truncheon on the facts I could not escape. My best friend no longer trusted me. I could read it in her eyes. Maybe it had happened because I resented her for taking my boyfriend. Maybe she was wise not to tell me. Maybe I knew the answers, if I could just think my way through the puzzle.

All the way home, I poured over what I knew of the day's events, but I couldn't assemble a clear picture. As my mother pulled open our screen door, words rose from the coldest part of my insides. "Mama, did Beverly do something wrong?"

Mom opened the door wider. "Come in," she said softly. "I'll make us some tea."

We stood for a minute in the kitchen's bright light, my head on her shoulder, my arms around her waist. I pushed away. "Why does Carl think she would be better off dead? If someone hurts you, why is it your fault?"

Mom stroked my hair and chose her words carefully. "People think rape is about women giving something away, but really it's about having something stolen from you, isn't it? Still, people don't treat you the same afterward."

I stood very still, listening to a bird that had landed on our dogwood tree, glimmering a little in the light from our kitchen bulb. I turned my head, but the branch stretched into such deep shadow that I couldn't identify the species.

Mom kept her grip on my back. "Some people confuse sex and rape. Rape isn't like sex, when you love someone and want to be with them. There's nothing gentle and loving about rape. A man forcing his way inside—that's just meanness. And he hit her. A lot. Hard. And ... maybe she has some injuries inside. So the doctors may have to sew her. That's why the doctor wants to examine her, to see if she needs surgery."

"So how is that her fault?"

A shiver ran down my spine as Mom let go of me. She heaved a big sigh and moved to put the kettle on. "Beverly might have taken a ride from a stranger. If she did, that was a mistake. People will talk mean. You may as well get used to it. Seems people see evil in the most innocent acts." Water from the copper bottom sizzled on the hot stove while Mom stared out the window. "My mother used to say that men want to know the mouths at their table come from their own loins. But why people want to make a religion out of virginity, I don't know, daughter." She turned and lifted the kettle, but then put it back down. Her voice became angry, tough. "And the shame put on women who are raped—like they must have wanted someone to hold them down and hurt them—I never could see why anyone would want that. Even if girls chase after men—wanting sex isn't the same as wanting pain."

Standing in the middle of our blue-squared linoleum, I knew the anguish in Mom's face reflected mine. Dad stepped through the door. "Let me know when you're ready to say goodnight." His voice trilled, soft, like the bird I could now see clearly in the growing light. Its throat pulsed red.

⁂

I settled into my bed, staring at the glass globe on the ceiling. The door opened with a click. Dad padded into the room in his stocking feet and sat down in the rocker in one corner. He moved the book in his hand into the porch light that gleamed through the window.

"'Night, Dad."

"'Night, Baby."

I drifted into a sleep in which birds sang sweetly, while humans hid in bushes.

Evangeline: Blessings

Having no weight in this world is one choice I can make.

When I first came here, into this void, I wondered what it would take to reach across this great distance. I did not know that I could choose to bond myself to this world, at least for a time. Perhaps there are angels who can cross easily, at will. I have learned to make the effort only if absolutely necessary. But how? And why? Even after death, these questions.

There are as many answers as one wishes to find. The breeze teaches letting go; the ocean, purpose and direction. My mother taught me how to catch a thread of being.

At some point, she was there, a familiar feeling in my bliss. She might have floated by. But Roma are always Roma, even in death: Family is everything. She reached out and caressed my thought, let me know she would come at will, mine or hers. After that, I found my father, his busy thrumming not hard to locate, once I knew how. And Tomas, his quiet signature an intense longing to connect. Stephane had been harder to locate, still concussed by the shock of the mine explosion that peeled away his body in the California wilderness. Little Mirela by his side still, carefully tending.

After that, it took little time, learning to think like what I wanted to become. With effort I can pierce the veil and focus myself to any given spot, in any form I understand.

I've been back to this field many times. It settles my thoughts, to walk in soil I've tended. Sometimes, I watch my granddaughter with her sister-friend, their cartwheels and laughter reminding me what was good on Earth. Vinnie and Tally pick these fruits without a thought to my presence, though I have seen them each gaze toward the field where the vardo appeared, always when they think the other isn't looking. My eldest never comes with them. She scurries up and down this road, my busy Maisie, trying to drown her memories in a sea of tasks, though she cannot keep her thoughts from straying toward home. If she only knew, her name is inscribed inside each fruit here.

My visits are short. Never have I wanted to stay. If I did, I would be in their way, a familiar boulder they must travel around, thus diverting their steps. And they have not needed me, or not the things I can do, which is precious little in their Earthly state.

Still, that special thread twitches me back.

Today I felt its tug most strongly. Once I saw what was happening to her, I could not desert my granddaughter's sister-friend.

Surprising, that it had been the little one, the white-haired one, who found the courage to take what he wanted, rather than the tall boy with fish-stink clinging to his clothes. The big one sat in the truck, watching the road, behind, before, twisting in his seat to see his friend first taunt, then leap out and wrestle her. I remained there, disembodied and unable to interfere, the breeze quiet, even the trees holding their breath. No way to hitch a ride, to find a path to her.

I watched while the little one ripped her clothes. Her cries rose like a crow's call over the fields and I thought, surely, something, someone would come. No one did. Maybe the big one in the truck understood the wrong, for he jumped out and pulled at his friend, tried to make him get in the car. But the little one brought out a knife, swiped at his friend, made him go back to watch the road. He grabbed the girl as she scrambled from beneath him, and showed her the flashing blade. She stopped fighting. Her hands took hold of a bush where he had tossed her shirt. I saw the white of her throat as she arched her back, steeling herself.

I thought of every buoyant thing I could remember: sun on water, a leaf on the wind. I stretched myself out, made myself hollow. And the breeze began. Whipping around trees, beckoning me with branches that pointed the way. I leaped, and found the wind willing, fleeting down the hill, gathering force, picking up twigs and branches. Tossing them at the boy trying to prove himself some distorted notion of a man.

Oh, I was thunder. I was lightning. I was the face of God. The boy gawked at the thrashing trees, pulled up his pants, scrambled, tripped, fell, and slid across that ditch.

Lewis came. I knew him right away: the same swagger he had that day on Redding's porch, a rocking big-man gait, and him as short as a stump cut close to the ground. Put him in a preacher's suit, he's still a small man trying to take more space. He peered at the girl like he would a smashed bug, shoved the little one, yelled at the big one, sent them packing, and raced away in his big black car. I swirled around them, pulling at their clothes, driving their hair into their eyes, rocking their cars until they were far down the road.

Then I found the sister-child, softened my hands to graze her face, sent a cooling shimmer from her head to her toes. I whispered in her ear, said her name, again and again, so she would not forget.

Evie, October, 1959: Fortress

A whiff of coffee drew me out of my stupor. The chair where my father had sat last night was empty, draped with a knitted blue afghan. "Thank God it's Saturday," I thought, grateful that I could leave till later the question I knew would be on everyone's tongue at school: who? Not that I didn't want to know who had done this horrible thing to my best friend, but, after the night's sleep, other mysteries plagued me more.

I sat up and pondered. If Beverly had planned to go home to dress and have Tommy pick her up there, why had she told her mom she would be coming to my house, instead? And, since Tommy had said he'd have the car later, why had she begged a ride home with Bobby, instead of taking the bus and waiting for her boyfriend to pick her up? Clearly, she planned on something else, but what? Until I knew more, I couldn't risk asking these questions in front of my mother, or Willeen, or Granny. My feet found the fuzzy pink slippers next to the bed. I padded down the hall to the kitchen. "Can I go see Beverly today?"

Mom turned from the stove. "Not, 'Good morning, Mom?' Not even, 'Why aren't you working this morning, Mom?' The mill's running, you know."

The egg-stained plate on the table told me that Dad had already eaten. Out of habit, I picked it up and put it in the sink. "Sorry. I'll just have a biscuit." I picked one from underneath the checkered cloth and nibbled at its edges.

Mom took two eggs from the refrigerator. "You'll have a proper breakfast. I'll scramble them with peppers the way you like them." She clattered utensils for a few more minutes while I settled my backside against the counter and watched her cook.

She showed no signs of answering my first question, so I tried another. "Will it be in the papers, about her clothes and all, and—"

Mom took the newspaper from the counter by the back door and handed it to me. Only now I couldn't bear to open it and read about what had happened to my best friend. Mom slid an egg onto my plate with a spatula and said in a calm voice, "They said that an unknown assailant attacked Beverly Tyndall, Tallulah High School varsity cheerleader, around dusk last night on the Old Anderson Road. No one saw the incident, and Miss Tyndall is being treated at Municipal Hospital. There is no mention of her clothing or details of the crime."

I unfolded the paper, saw that the article was indeed short, and tossed it on the tiles by the stove. Mom set the plate on the table in my usual corner. I sat down, picked up my fork, and tried to lift the egg to my lips, but the red peppers reminded me of the blood dripping from Beverly's wound. I put down the fork. "Nobody will know she was raped from that article." Maybe I wouldn't have so much to explain on Monday, after all.

"They'll know about it. That girl, Rena, told the police that Beverly talked about hitchhiking." Granny Burnett spoke from behind me. I turned and caught a glimpse of my father going out the door, his lunch bucket in hand. He must have let Granny in. Now she lowered herself into the chair opposite me.

Mom walked over to the coffeepot, poured two cups, set one down in front of Granny, the other at the third chair, where she sat down herself and folded her hands. She could have been waiting for a sermon to begin. She looked pointedly at my plate.

I crunched a tiny bite of toast. It slid down my throat without gagging me, so I took another nibble before I ventured a question.

"Do you think she did that? Beverly, I mean—hitchhike? With a stranger? I mean, everyone out there knows each other. There aren't many strangers."

Granny jerked her head impatiently. "Beverly knew better than that." She looked around the table, spied the round sugar bowl almost hidden behind the jar of hot peppers, lifted the lid, and dumped a spoonful into her cup. Mom and I watched as she dribbled milk from the matching creamer into her spoon before she stirred it in. Her coffee turned slightly less brown.

"Oh, Lordy," she said, rubbing one hand on her knee, covered by a long dress printed with tiny red flowers. "I just come from the hospital. Beverly ain't doing so good. Doctor says can't nobody but the family see her. Mary Alice and Willeen are with her now." She lifted her face to my mother. "Maisie, I'd appreciate if you could set a spell at the house with me today. Lots of company's been coming by and—well, you know Carl ain't good with people."

"We'll go." Mom moved briskly around the kitchen, perhaps thankful to have something to do. "I brought in some fresh tomatoes this morning. Got some ham in here, too." She rummaged in the refrigerator.

Granny cleared her throat. "Folks been bringing lots of food by." Mom stopped searching and sat down again to listen. "Willeen says to tell folks that Beverly doesn't remember much about the man that attacked her 'cept he had a blue car. Don't know how she got away. Sheriff says ain't no way to find a stranger in a blue car without a better description. Probably done gone to Atlanta by now."

"A stranger." I swung my head toward my mother. She looked steadily back at me. Who did she suspect?

"Willeen and the po-lice think so." Granny pursed her lips and shook her head. "And that boy—Bobby What's-his-name—po-lice cleared him 'cause the florist confirmed his story about Beverly jumping out of the car, and he made it to practice on time, with

Tommy, the boy she was dating. Couldn't either of them have had time to hurt Beverly and get back to school in time, they said."

I watched my fingers lace and unlace in my lap, uncomfortable that even for a moment I had suspected careful, considerate Bobby. And Beverly had said the rapist threatened to tell Carl about her and Tommy, so of course it wasn't Tommy. But what could the rapist tell about them? I pushed away my plate with its smears of yellow. "Who around here would do something like that?"

For a long minute, Mom and Granny looked at each other. Granny spoke. "That Allen man hurt the girl a long time ago, Maisie. Never could prove anything, anyway."

The front door slammed. My cousin, Dave, ran in, slapped a steel bowl with a plastic lid down on the table, and ran out, pedaling backward, screeching, "Mama-says-could-you-please-take-that-to-Willeen-she-has-a-luncheon-thank-you-good-bye!"

Mom lifted the lid to reveal a thin crust of toasted cheese covering clots of noodles. She looked at Granny. "Talitha! She means well."

"Well, you taught her everything she knows about cooking, Maisie!" Granny's face relaxed a bit as she chuckled along with us.

"Evie, you better get dressed. We'll head out to Willeen's in a half hour or so." Mom stowed the noodles in our refrigerator. Reluctantly, I stored my questions for later.

The laminate table surface wiggled slightly as Granny leaned her weight on it while she stood. "Thank you, Maisie. I knew I could count on you."

No cars were in the Tyndalls' drive when we arrived, but that soon changed. Mom and Granny were in Willeen's kitchen when the first visitors arrived. Aunt Vinnie got out and Uncle Arthur parked two minutes before Mrs. Beasley drove into the yard in her old, rusted Pontiac. I looked at them and knew that funeral and wedding manners did not apply. I hurried to the door to call Mom.

Within three minutes, Aunt Vinnie and Mrs. Beasley had handed their casseroles over to Granny and sat down in wicker rockers with glasses of iced tea brought out by Mom. Uncle Arthur drifted off to the far side of the porch, and Mom and Granny settled in the swing. I plopped myself down on the stoop.

"Well, well, well," Mrs. Beasley began. "Sure is some sad day. I know Carl must be out of his mind." She kept shaking her head like she couldn't figure something out.

Aunt Vinnie snorted. "Carl ain't known what to do about anything in twenty years. So what's new?" She fanned herself with the cardboard fan she had pulled from underneath the cushion.

Granny said nothing. Mom shifted in her seat.

Mrs. Beasley lifted her glass to her lips. "Man rapes his daughter, you'd expect him to be out gunning for that rattlesnake, 'stead of working. Saw him driving off toward the mill this morning, like usual."

Both Granny and Mom threw their shoulders back and prepared to fire. My mother got first aim. "The police are looking for him. No need for Carl to go along."

Mrs. Beasley bristled a little. "Well, I'm sure I didn't mean—" She took a blue fan out of her handbag, spread its tiny folds, and waved it in front of her face. "Such a pretty thing, that's all. That blonde hair. And those green eyes. A shame, what happened. What will they do with her?"

Mom picked at a cotton flower on her dress as if it might shed its petals for her. This time Granny fired back. "What do you mean, what will they do with her? They'll keep her in the hospital until she's well. She'll be home for a while, I guess. She can keep up with her studies at home."

Mrs. Beasley stopped fanning. "Well, of course. But what will they do *then*, I mean. She can't go back to school. Does Willeen—do you—" and she pointed with her fan to Granny, "—still have relatives in the mountains? Maybe she could go there."

Something inside me flickered and rose in my throat—tears, bile, a lump so big it could burst. Would Beverly have to go away?

Granny half rose from the porch swing. Mom put her hand out to stop her. "Eunice." She had never used Mrs. Beasley's first name in my hearing before. "Eunice," she repeated, "why would Beverly need to go away because someone attacked her? It's not like she did anything wrong, is it?" The way she said it made a challenge. My throat eased a little.

Aunt Vinnie snorted. "Some folks think women rape themselves and go looking for more 'cause it feels so good, I reckon." She looked pointedly at Mrs. Beasley.

"Oh. I never meant to say she done something wrong. Though they say she did get in the car with a stranger."

Mom opened her mouth to reply, but another car distracted us. Out popped a family from Beverly's church, with a boy about eleven. I didn't know his name. As his parents marched toward the steps, he walked around to the tire swing and started pulling leaves off the tree, throwing them toward the tire's center. His father, a tall, lanky man, tipped his felt hat toward the porch and wandered to the far side of the car like the cornfield across the road needed inspection. The woman who stepped onto the porch loomed tall, with graying hair.

My mother greeted her. "Annie Clark, nice to see you."

"Maisie. Mrs. Burnett. Mrs. Beasley. Howdy, Vinnie. Ain't seen you in a coon's age." When she had nodded all around, she paused for a moment, and addressed my mother. "We won't stay, Maisie, Mrs. Burnett. Just thought we'd drop off these pies. All the women from the Missionary Society baked, except Rose Anderson. She's got arthritis real bad in her hands, you know. But she made this afghan before she got it so bad, thought it might come in handy." And she handed over a thing made out of gaudy yarn—red, blue, brown.

"That was mighty nice of you all." Granny took from Mrs. Clark's hands the stacked pies, each wrapped tightly in aluminum foil, and went in toward the kitchen.

"Thank you, Annie." Mom acted like she'd been given cloth of gold, holding the thickly crocheted mass out from her body as she went through the front door. She came out again almost immediately. We could hear Granny clattering inside, making room for Annie Clark's dishes among the ten or so we'd found there, from yesterday's visitors.

Mrs. Beasley rose from her chair. "Set here, Annie. My boarders'll be home for dinner. Got to make something for them." She left much faster than she came. Mrs. Clark looked around, as if deciding if she had time to stay. No one repeated the invitation. Finally, she went quietly over to the rocker Mrs. Beasley had vacated and sat in it.

Aunt Vinnie snorted again as she watched Mrs. Beasley go, then remembered her manners. "Sit down, Annie," she said, as if Mrs. Clark were not already sitting beside her. Then she called to Mr. Clark. "Been fishing down at Saluda lately, Harold? Arthur says he don't believe there's any fish in there anymore. What you think?"

Uncle Arthur let go his grip on the wood railing, stretched his arms, and stepped lightly down the steps to clap Harold on the back, rumbling something about bass being slicker than newborn babies. Mr. Clark agreed, and they wandered off to lean against the cars. The boy joined them, now throwing leaves at the gaps in the cars' hubcaps. The territory they had staked out lay just outside of easy hearing from the porch. I looked at Aunt Vinnie with new respect. She sipped from her sweaty glass.

Mrs. Clark wiped her face with the same bleached linen handkerchief she'd used to wipe her glass. "We came to see how that poor girl of yours is and if there's anything we can do. The things that happen nowadays!" She shook her head while raising the glass to her lips. "Why, me and Harold just said there's too many strangers around these days. Can't tell what kind of mischief they might be up to. Ain't that right, Harold?" She turned back to Aunt Vinnie with the mildest of expressions. "Did she say what he looked like?"

Harold brought out a knife and a short piece of pine and started to whittle. Uncle Arthur watched, maybe trying to guess what he would produce.

Vinnie stood and headed toward the screen door. "There's a pile of folks coming. I'll boil some more tea. Evie, want to help me?" After I followed her through the screen door, Aunt Vinnie paused to wipe her forehead. "Lord, give me strength."

All day, idle but pointed questions lapped around the porch, interrupted by frequent infusions of iced tea. Casually or with direct impertinence, visitors inquired whether Beverly dated lots of boys. No one came right out and said, "Your granddaughter is a tramp," but several managed to work in comments about what young people were coming to these days, or how short those cheerleaders wore their costumes. Every time they did, a little current went from Mom and Granny in the swing to Aunt Vinnie to me.

The afternoon blurred into a parade of guests. I lost track of their names. One lady in a dress edged with lace spat out that push-up brassieres were an invitation for a rapist. Aunt Vinnie leaned over and made a hissing sound in my ear, to my great thrill.

She, my mother, and Granny smiled, poured tea, and rebutted every attempt to blame Beverly for being raped. I tried to memorize their expressions, the way they smiled while disagreeing, the polite but firmly dismissive way my mother turned away abrasive questions with a frank stare and a reminder that the Tyndalls were friends and neighbors.

After Vinnie left, I lingered on the porch while Mom helped Granny wrap leftovers. Some would be stored for Carl, who had not yet returned from work, though the moon peering over treetops accompanied the fading sunset.

A cooling breeze wafted from the river in the distance. I watched the darkness gather and longed to go back. Back to the day Beverly, Tommy, Bobby, and I had lingered in our swing, just a few weeks ago. Or the day George came home, and he and Mary Alice laughed and chatted with the neighbors, cousins tossing balls in the yard. Even back to the afternoon Carl threw the radio. All before Beverly's nakedness in the brambles, her bruised face, the sly comments from Mrs. Beasley and others. Before I had to think about how to explain what I barely understood myself.

A flutter of wings drew my attention to the big oak that sheltered one end of the porch. Reflected light bounced from animal eyes I might almost have imagined. I listened for some clue, but there was no call, no voice to stir the silence. Still, I felt watched. Or watched over?

One tiny seed of bravery took hold in my heart.

I walked to school, as usual, pausing at the big oaks that framed the steps, the way I had on the first day, and the day after I'd broken up with Bobby. This time, I had yet a different set of fears. I stepped off the curb and marched resolutely toward the front doors, not pausing to look at anyone.

Mom had given me some advice about how to handle curiosity about Beverly. "Tell them someone hurt your friend, and she's getting better. What more can you say? Just focus on your work." I forgot how much I resented her strict rules. That day I clung to her direct approach.

If I expected the kids to be nosy, like the adults whose iced tea glasses had lined Willeen's porch banister, the opposite proved true. Oh, everyone in the halls buzzed about Beverly. At least, I'm sure that's what they were talking about. They turned away as I approached, or fell silent until I'd passed. Hardly anyone spoke directly to me, beyond some sheepish hellos and a few necessary questions about schoolwork.

Through a fog of hallway whispers, I made it till the final bell. In class, I followed Mom's advice, sinking my worries about Beverly into work. I almost enjoyed a quiz on quadratic equations, sliding numbers around like slippery puzzle pieces that resolved into a known pattern.

A few kids did venture the topic of Beverly's condition. Protection came from an unexpected quarter. Several times during that first day, I found Veronica Wheeler at my elbow. She smiled and steered me with a hand on my sleeve, glaring at anyone who approached me without a clear reason.

A girl from my biology class sidled toward us in the lunch line and mouthed, "I'm so sorry." Veronica swung her tray between me and the girl with a loud, "Excuse us. We were just leaving." At a table by the window, she chatted about how French women had more style than American women, due to proper accessorizing. In the past, I might not have paid attention to such a topic, but that day it felt like a light breeze I could follow without getting chilled. I smiled at her in gratitude.

And when I stepped out of the heavy wooden entrance doors at the end of the day, Veronica fell in beside me. I answered her greeting with relief. "Well, I got a decent score on that algebra quiz without studying at all, thank heavens."

"Maybe worrying too much makes you over-think your answers," suggested Veronica. *Call me Vee*, she'd said, but I hadn't yet found the nickname comfortable on my tongue. "I never have that problem."

"Don't you worry about your grades?"

She threw her head back with a laugh that echoed like a seesawing violin. "I'm a cosmetology student. As long as I pass Western Civilization and English, the rest of my time I only have to worry about setting curlers and mixing dyes. That's easy." She waved her hand toward the receding school building. "I just want to go to the Fashion Institute. No killer courses for me. Well, except for French. That will be useful for my apprenticeship in Paris."

A memory blazed into color: Beverly sashaying in scarlet lipstick around her room, back when we thought the most important question was, which classes could we take together. Concern for her lit a bonfire in my belly. "I have to get home. I want to call and see if Beverly's getting out of the hospital."

Veronica nodded. "She'll want to talk to someone her own age, I'll bet."

I watched Veronica swing her beige plaid book bag down the block toward her house on Park Avenue and considered what she'd said. Would I be able to best help Beverly by listening? Or should I avoid mentioning the attack, unless she did? And how could I curb my own curiosity to know what happened? I turned toward home, holding on to what Willeen had said when I'd called the day before. *Maybe tomorrow.*

That afternoon, I slipped into a straight-backed chair near my mom and aunts on the back porch, out of the eyes of prying neighbors. The late autumn sun slanted straight across the floorboards to catch us in a stab of light. Idly, I reached into the pot Mom held on her lap and picked out a bean or two, but my ears didn't engage until Aunt Vinnie bristled. "What good will rest do her? Worst thing that could happen to a woman, but best she get over it and go on. We all should act like nothing's happened." She snapped a bean and threw the halves into a bowl.

"These are the last we'll see till spring." Mom tossed another pod onto the teetering pile. "It's not the worst thing." She pursed her lips and shook her head.

"What is, Maisie? What could be worse than having some man rape you, take your virginity, and everybody knows about it?" Vinnie brushed sweat from under her auburn bangs.

Mom stopped breaking beans into bits. She watched motes dancing in the dying sunlight as if an answer might appear in the air. Then she shook her head again. "I don't know. But it's not the worst." Nothing Vinnie could say would change her mind.

Aunt Tally scrunched an ice cube between her teeth. "I think the worst thing would be having everybody ask you about it over and over. Or else them *not* asking you about it, 'cause they think you wanted it."

Mom looked at her sister with the indulgent half-smile she wore when Tally occasionally made sense. I used to think Mom doted on her, but now I realized she merely loved her.

"Mom, did Willeen say when Beverly would be home from the hospital?" My first call to the Tyndalls hadn't been answered. I planned to persist.

Mom looked through the screen at the clock over the stove. "Said she'd be at the hospital right after supper. Wait another half hour before you call again."

Two bushels of beans later, I dialed the Tyndalls' number. "Is, is Willeen there?" Carl's rough voice on the phone threw me into a tongue-tied state.

"No, she's at the hospital, getting Beverly." He didn't offer any more details.

My heart jumped. "Well, maybe we'll come out tonight, for a few minutes."

"Best to wait. She'll be too tired to see anybody by the time she gets here." He hung up.

The women had moved to the kitchen. "What did she say?" Aunt Vinnie twisted in her chair to see me better as Mom looked up from stirring a pot on the stove.

"She's coming home tonight. Carl says she'll be too tired to visit."

Mom reached into a spice canister and sprinkled a handful of her special blend onto the stew. "I thought she'd be there a while. But I guess there's not much physically wrong with her."

Tally harrumphed and shook her amber earrings. "It's not her physique that's suffering the most."

I wanted to tell her she'd used the wrong word, but I was too busy agreeing with the thought etched on Mom's face: What next?

❦

Slowly, over the next few days, the whispers at school built into a crescendo, like a river dammed to a waterfall. I began to hear words tossed after me in the hallways. Single words, like "Tease!" Or phrases, like, "Who wants damaged goods?" Kids knotted together, and smiled with their eyes cutting sideways at me.

On Thursday afternoon, late for my Journalism Club meeting, I watched Rena barrel down the steps toward me, calling out "Evie!" over and over, Sandy at her heels. *She sure remembers my name now,* I thought. Other kids stopped to listen. *That way she gets a bigger audience.* A little spark of surprise illuminated a bitter side of me that I barely recognized.

"Oh, you poor thing. It must be terrible!" Had she mistakenly heard that I had been attacked, too? She grabbed me by the shoulders and dragged me off the sidewalk to a grassy area near the steps. Sandy stepped to one side and averted her eyes, as if she hoped I wouldn't hold Rena's act against her.

Shocked by Rena's touch, I couldn't focus on a response. My silence didn't bother her. "You've lost your best friend! Beverly won't be coming back, will she? I mean, that's just too hard. People are so mean. They say all sorts of terrible things, and I'm sure her parents won't put her through that. They might even have to move to find her another school!" A glint in her eyes told me Rena would find that very satisfactory, indeed. She pulled me farther aside, and practically shouted.

"I want you to tell Beverly that we miss her terribly on the cheerleading squad. But we understand if it's just too hard for her to come back now." She reached behind me and drew forward a short girl with dark hair and slightly squinty eyes. "Fortunately, we have our alternate, you know." I recognized Squinty Eyes as Number Nine, who had stumbled and lost to Beverly at the tryouts. Not sure at all what would exit my mouth, I kept it closed. Rena quickly pecked my cheek with pink, pouty lips. "Well, call me if you or Beverly need anything, Evie. I mean it." She swiveled in her black and white oxfords. "We have to get to practice!"

I wiped her spit off my cheek and turned to go. Out of the corner of my eye, I saw a tall figure standing where four concrete walkways met underneath the flagpole: Tommy. My thoughts rushed backward to the night Beverly went missing, when Willeen and my mother had made him and Bobby tell them where she'd gone.

That same bitter voice that had questioned Rena's motives now whispered intently: Beverly and Tommy were up to something that night, and if Beverly won't tell, maybe Tommy will.

I went after him. I didn't look up to the state and school flags flapping against the metal poles, their grommets striking like bells, but kept my eyes glued to his. He flinched, but let me come, licking his lips and moving his feet a little to get ready.

I snagged one finger in his green polo shirt. "Tommy, why didn't you pick up Beverly the night of the dance?" A taste like gunmetal filled my mouth. I enjoyed his discomfort as he cast his glance down and to the side, where dry leaves skittered across the path. One came to rest against his dark navy tennis shoe.

"I meant to get my dad's car and pick her up at home. But he wouldn't let me have it. Why? What did she tell you?" I watched his hands change their grip on his books several times. Why was he afraid of what I knew?

"She could have brought her dress to school to get ready there, but she didn't. She expected you to take her home in your dad's car so she could get dressed there, then you could drive her back to school, right? Only your dad didn't give you the car. So why didn't she just take the bus home? Why have Bobby drop her off?" I stared steadily at his face. "She wanted to get home faster than the bus would take her, didn't she? You two were planning to go somewhere other than the dance." I didn't know where that idea came from, but Tommy blinked in surprise, as if I'd hit a nerve. But why? Were he and Beverly skipping the game? For what? Or had he never planned to meet her at all?

He worked his mouth but no sound came from it. A deep voice called his name. "Turner!" We both swiveled to see Bobby at the top of the basement steps to the field house, about twenty feet away. "Turner! Come on, you're late!"

Tommy wheeled around, close enough for me to see wrinkles of pain around his eyes. "Evie, I can't." He repeated it softly but clearly. "I can't."

"Turner!" Bobby's voice sliced the air between us. Tommy broke into a jog, all the way to the field house door. Bobby scowled at me and waved Tommy through.

"Wait!" I called, and ran after him.

Tommy turned back, but Bobby shoved him toward the door with one hand, held the door open with the other, and, with a coldness that chiseled through my chest, spat. "You don't need any of that, Buddy. Some girls just drag you down." His lips formed a grim smirk. He stepped through the door after Tommy and slammed it shut.

My improved math skills weren't needed to calculate the odds of getting an explanation if I followed them down the steps. Standing at the top of the metal stairs, I batted away the pain of having once been Bobby's girlfriend, buried his insult somewhere deep inside, and ran to the journalism office.

Heart pounding, I skidded outside the door, spilling all my books in a flood of flapping paper. Lunging for them, I knocked heads with someone who'd reached down at the same time. I looked up and found myself three inches from two deep chocolate eyes that sparkled like the condensation on Christmas fudge. Their owner handed me my books without a word, flipped a wedge of dark hair off his forehead, smiled with a brief nod, and turned back to the other kids slouched in desks or leaning on tables.

"Everybody ready to go over the articles for this week's paper?" Howard Pearson redirected all the grinning faces to the topic he'd been discussing before my entrance. I took a seat in the rear and glanced at the paper someone handed me. How could I be wondering if Howard was being especially nice to me, when my old boyfriend had just cast me into darkness? My mind tried to find a place to stow those feelings. Instead, I buried my head in the story assignment list.

Granny's voice was dim. I leaned over Mom's shoulder to hear better.

"We just called to see if Beverly is okay," Mom said. "No one is answering at Willeen's." She moved the receiver away from her ear so I could hear the response.

"They went to get some medicine for Beverly's leg. The doctor is worried that deep cut will get infected. She'll be all right. She has to stay quiet for a week or two. No school till next semester." Granny lowered her voice. "She hit the doctor a second time when he went to examine her, you know. Don't blame her. I never liked no doctor fussing around me, down there. Poor child don't know nothing about what's happened."

"What do you mean? Doesn't she remember?" My question traveled over the distance to Granny's farm.

"Honey, I ain't sure what she remembers. She's not talking much." Resignation rasped in her harsh sigh. "The police say if she won't let the doctor examine her, they can't prove a rape happened. And if she can't recall anything, well, there's nothing more they can do about the assault."

Mom looked at the receiver as if she needed to remember what was real, then placed it again a couple of inches from her ear so I could hear, if I stayed close. She emphasized each word of her reply. "How do they think she got hurt? She's all bruised and scratched. And you can't give yourself a concussion."

Granny's sigh once again preceded bad news. "They said it might be a lover's quarrel. 'Happens all the time. These girls got a million boyfriends.' That's what one of them po-licemen said."

My mom opened her mouth, but no sound came forth. Finally, she settled on a tried-and-true response. "Evie and I could bring out some food. I made jogray just the other day. Got some going to waste in the refrigerator." It was a polite lie—her jogray stew never went to waste.

Granny's answer might have been blurred by tears. "No, Maisie, thank you. I love your mama's stew, but I got to go over to my girl. Her mama needs some rest."

The receiver had barely clicked into its cradle before I exploded. "But she doesn't have a million boyfriends—she has *one*! And he has an alibi. They're saying she's a tramp, aren't they?"

Mom didn't try to reassure me. "Police always say that when they can't find the man who did it. And sometimes when they can. Everybody knows it's not true, but it's useless to try and change their minds." Her face closed like a gate as she turned on her heel and walked toward her bedroom.

I hadn't thought much about the police catching the rapist, but now that I knew they weren't even looking, I found a stone of despair cradled deep inside my gut. Why should Beverly have to be a tramp forever, while this guy got away? And how long before I would get a chance to talk to her?

That Friday, I sat chewing my pencil, trying to concentrate on my French homework, when Mom knocked on my bedroom door. "Why don't we go over to Miz Garretson's and see about your dress for the wedding? Mary Alice said she saw some beautiful pink tulle over at Reynold's Department Store. We'll get you measured, then go get the fabric, and we'll show it to Mary Alice and Beverly Sunday after church."

I rose from my desk, closed my book, and went to the closet for my coat. Mom watched me scramble around under the pile of things on my bed, looking for my purse.

"Evie, you do understand that you have nothing to be ashamed of?" Mom's worried face watched mine for clues.

I stopped searching and sat on my yellow flowered quilt, stunned. Ashamed? Was that what I felt? Ashamed of Beverly? Yes, that was it. Beverly had now been publicly labeled a tramp— the word kids at school hissed behind the "bad" girls who went with boys to park down by the lake. They wouldn't make an exception for whether you wanted it or not. And if I hung around with a "tramp," they'd eventually call me one, too. It might not be fair, but it would happen, nevertheless.

Mom still stood with her hand on the door. "You can't make people stop talking. So you'll just have to ignore them and go on with your life." I looked at her sharp features, her plain navy dress, her worn leather slippers. My mother would never shun a friend because people talked. She hadn't shunned Beverly's mother.

I swallowed and forced words out in something like a steady tone. "I just want Beverly to come back and have everything like it used to be."

"Daughter—" Mom paused for a long time. "Things might never be like they used to be. But they won't be bad forever. Beverly will get well, and it'll be old news in a month or two."

She tried to offer me hope, but we both knew that people would never forget.

Evie, November, 1959: Truth with a Vengeance

Mom called me to the phone late at night.

"Headlights, have they made you editor of the paper yet?" The familiar nickname made me smile, instead of making me mad.

"Cut it out, Beverly. You know Howard's the editor. How are you feeling?"

A sound like a gust of wind crackled between us. Then her voice, low and sarcastic. "Sick to my stomach. Sore. And pissed off. I missed homecoming."

"Sandy won Queen. And that boy from Toccoa who plays halfback was King."

She chuckled, but her voice was thin. "At least it wasn't Rena. Can you imagine how stuck-up she'd be if she'd won?" No excitement about who wore what, who people talked about in the hall. "Have you seen Tommy?"

Her question brought me to a full stop. Why ask me? Hadn't Tommy done what boyfriends were supposed to do—bring teddy bears and candy to you in the hospital? My heart thudded. Is that what Tommy meant by "I can't"? Can't talk about it now—that's what I'd thought he'd meant. But what if he'd meant, can't have anything to do with her? My insides felt like a milkshake in a blender. "No, not really."

"Not at all?" A sharp tone rang in Beverly's voice. She didn't believe me.

"Well, just for a few minutes. He asked how you were." I scolded myself. *You just made it worse, if he hasn't even called.* Could it be he hadn't?

"Oh." She sounded tired all of a sudden. "Exactly what did he say?"

"He was late for practice, so he said, um, we'd talk later."

"Don't lie. Just tell me what he said. Word for word."

I closed my eyes and pulled air from my lungs. "He said, 'Evie, I can't.' That's all." Seconds passed as I exhaled and waited for her to speak.

When she did, it was barely a whisper. "Evie, I'm tired. I gotta go."

"I'm coming out to see you tomorrow. We'll talk—" The line went dead.

I woke the next morning with a rasp in my muscles and decided to take a bath. Ivory soap bubbles soaked away the aches. Then the phone rang in the hallway.

Mom's voice answered, "Gates residence." Her conversation filled with silence. Then, "Are you sure we can't do anything? Well, we'll come by tomorrow after church. I'm sorry she's not feeling better." Mom knocking on the door followed the click of the receiver settling onto the hook. She came in and sat on the fuzzy pink toilet cover. I propped my arms on the edge of the tub, surrounded by popping, soapy blisters.

"What happened?"

"Beverly had a bad night, crying and screaming. Willeen says she can't leave her. I'm gonna go in and run her looms to keep Willeen out of trouble with the supervisor."

I sank back in the tub, feeling myself dissolve like the suds. "It's all my fault." A few prods from Mom brought tumbling out the story of Tommy and Bobby's comments, and how I'd had no cover story for them.

"Aren't they the gentlemen!" Mom's lips drew a straight line across her face.

I scratched one shin with the ankle of the other leg. "She really loves him. I can't believe he'd dump her like that."

Mom hauled herself up. "I have to get to work. And you have to get out. You're turning into a prune." She tossed me a towel and parked her hands on her hips. "A friend who can't take some heat for you isn't a friend."

I ate the eggs Mom left for me and started in on my chores. She didn't mean me, I knew, but I spent a lot of time that morning stewing over how I could help Beverly.

We drove to the Tyndalls' after church. Folded inside my purse was the swatch of pink tulle I had begged from Mrs. Garretson. I hoped talking about the wedding would cheer Beverly up.

Willeen's beat up old sedan had been pulled to one side of the yard. Mary Alice's sleek blue Nash sat near the battered mailbox.

Dad, as usual, made for the swing. Mom entered the house with a smile, holding a big, tin foil-lidded bowl out in front of her. "I brought this stew, Willeen. The way my mama made it. I thought we could—" She stopped so quickly my nose brushed her neck. Over her shoulder, I saw that Mary Alice sat across from Willeen at the kitchen table, her face flushed and angry. Mom looked from one to the other. "Is everybody all right?"

"I came over to go to church with my sister and my niece, for a little moral support." Sarcasm rang in Mary Alice's tone.

"Where's Beverly?" I looked down the hall toward the bedrooms.

"She's resting. Better leave her alone, for now." Willeen's cheeks flamed red. Was that confusion in her expression?

Mom and I sat down on either side of Willeen. Mary Alice spoke first. "Honestly, Willeen, I don't know why you bother. It's not like you believe anything that old coot says. Why don't you tell Carl—"

Willeen stirred. "I always figured that one preacher sounded as right as another. Till now."

Granny slid in the oak front door, carrying a pot of something that smelled delicious. "'Morning. Evie, set this on the counter for me. It's heavy. What are you two so het up about?" Granny, too, stopped at sight of Willeen and Mary Alice, and waited.

Willeen folded her hands in her apron. "Well, I guess the preacher made us the laughingstock of the whole congregation."

Mary Alice's slap on the table rattled the coffee cups. "Laughingstock? You? Carl is the laughingstock, with his stupid puppy-dog ways. That preacher just called your daughter a whore!" I put Granny's heavy iron pot on the counter. Mom and I locked eyes. None of the women I knew used the word "whore."

"Oh, Lord." Granny sat down next to Mary Alice, her hand to her forehead.

"He didn't call her a whore—" Willeen began.

Mary Alice snorted. "No, he just called her a Jezebel. Is there a difference?"

"He didn't call her anything," Willeen insisted. "He said *some* girls dress in tight clothes and tempt men and parents shouldn't let their girls go acting like those Hollywood Jezebels if we want men to respect them and maybe we should all demand that the school stop letting girls cheerlead and make a spectacle of themselves."

"And tell them what he said about dancing! Like all those kids on TV are doomed to hell for jitterbugging."

"Well, I think he went too far there—"

"What did he say about dancing?" I couldn't keep from piping in, though Mom gave me a scorching stare and held her hand out to stop me.

Willeen stood and took the flour canister down from the shelf, banging it on the counter next to me, so hard I jumped. "He just said—" Mary Alice snorted again as Willeen paused, "— that dancing is the root of all these divorces and rapes we're having, 'cause young people think everything is about sex now and nobody marries for the right reasons and we parents should make our daughters act chaste so they can find a man who wants a good mother for his kids more than a tight skirt and wiggling hips."

"Like you could find a man like that." Our heads jerked toward Mary Alice.

"George isn't—" Mom started, stopped. Her own cheeks turned one shade darker pink. The familiar faces, usually so calm and agreeable, closed as tight as the Bible that lay next to Willeen's purse on the table.

"I didn't mean George. I wouldn't marry him if I thought he was like that. But you know men are a little more ... excitable than we are. That's what I meant." Mary Alice's brown eyes locked on my mother's. I pretended to straighten the kitchen curtain.

"These preachers cause more trouble than a bunch of foxes in a hen house," Granny said. "I wouldn't give a plug nickel for any of them."

"What are you going to do?" Mary Alice demanded, more calmly. "Beverly doesn't need to hear that kind of stuff."

Willeen whirled to face her sister. "I feel like taking a switch to his sorry ass!" Her words struck like lightning bolts that bounced around the kitchen.

A car door closing drew my attention out the window again. "Well, you better cut one. He's here." The preacher headed for the steps, Carl a stride or two behind.

Nobody moved in the kitchen. The men's shoes made scraping sounds on the porch. My dad murmured a greeting. The preacher responded loudly, "How do, Frank? We ain't seen you out our way lately. Come read the Bible with us some time." I couldn't hear Dad's response. A crowd of feet stepped into the living room. One set marched from the front room towards us.

Carl appeared in the doorway. His eyes went straight to Willeen. He gave no indication he saw any of the rest of us as he cleared his throat. "Can we get some coffee for the preacher? He's come to pray with us."

Willeen stood still with her arms folded across her chest, like she hadn't heard him. Carl went over to the stove and lifted the enameled coffee pot, swishing its bottom to see if it was full, and struck a match to turn on a burner. It was as if he'd lit a fire under Willeen. She grabbed a broom from the corner.

"Willeen! What in Sam Hill—you got company!" Granny inquired.

Willeen stalked out of the room. "I got to get some of this trash out of the house."

I ran to the living room just in time to see her bring the broom sharply up against the preacher's ankle. Squealing like a dog hit by a rock, Preacher Allen grabbed his foot and danced backward toward the front door, smashing into a ceramic plaque that crashed to the floor, scattering pieces of a Bible verse across the scrubbed boards. Willeen took another swing at his shins, following through like Joe DiMaggio hitting a line drive. But the preacher scuttled out the door before her broom could reach him.

"Carl, I'll wait for you by the car!" he yelped.

My Dad, who had stood quietly watching the preacher and Willeen, walked back to the porch swing. It creaked as he took his seat. Granny, Mom, Mary Alice, and I stood all bunched in the doorway, watching the preacher walk briskly toward his dark sedan.

Carl strode across the room, grabbed Willeen's arm, and wrested the broom from her. "My God, woman, what are you doing?"

"He looked like a heap of trash that needed clearing away to me." Willeen stood with her arms folded, glaring down at Carl.

"He's a preacher, for God's sake!" Carl's face flamed as red as Willeen's.

Willeen spoke deliberately. "His uncle was a preacher, too, right? He raped his own daughter. Last I looked, incest was still a sin. Should we respect him as a Man of God, too?" Someone behind me—Granny? Mary Alice? Not my Mom, who stood next to me—let out a snort.

Carl's face turned purple. "That happened a long time ago. We're supposed to respect the dead. Can't do nothing about that now, anyway. But we can help our daughter—*Nettie's daughter*—figure out what to do with her life before it's too late."

Willeen put her hands on her hips, leaning over Carl. "What life can she have, when—" and she spat out the next word, "—*righteous* people look down on her?"

Carl leaned the broom in the corner. "She can give her life to the Lord and let him take care of that."

Willeen's voice ignited like gunpowder pouring over a fire. "If she goes to church from now till hell freezes over, Carl, she won't be able to erase what that preacher said today." Her next words came slower. "And nothing we do will bring Nettie back."

Carl's face crumpled, and his voice emerged muffled in tears. "But if we give her to God, maybe she won't suffer the way Nettie did." His shoulders shook. "How can I tell her somebody hurt her baby? Somebody hurt her and left her in the mud to die."

A sound caused us all to swivel toward the hallway, where Beverly stood, a rifle trailing from her hand, its butt against the floor. She said to Willeen, "If you hadn't hit him, I would have killed him."

In two strides, Carl reached her, took the rifle, and leaned it against the wall. Beverly leveled her stare toward her father. "He knows who attacked me, and he helped him get away. And now he's telling the world it's my fault," she hissed.

Willeen grabbed hold of Beverly's hand. "I knew you'd tell us when you could," she said.

"Beverly, who, who got away?" I forgot to worry about what to say and blurted out what I was sure everyone wanted to know.

Beverly turned to look at me with eyes that shone brighter than any leaf gilded by sun. "His nephew, Bud Allen." I shook my head, not placing the person. "You know him. He hangs out with Jim Marshall. He has hair lighter than mine." She pushed her blonde hair back. I tried to imagine lighter hair. And then I knew. White-blonde hair bending over a car wheel in the street. Jim Marshall with his little phone book.

"But how did the preacher help him get away? Was Jim there?"

Words began tumbling out of Beverly like a stream too long dammed. "Bud tried to get me to open my legs. He hit me. He pulled out a knife and cut me. Jim pulled him away, and something happened—I don't know what, but they ran like a lion chased them. Jim flooded the car, I guess, and they were yelling and Buddy said he had to finish me off, or I would tell, and then—" She looked around at us, and we watched the fury gather in her face. "Then I heard the preacher's voice, saying 'What's wrong?'" Her voice went from halting to a deadly calm. "His face appeared over the ditch, and I reached out to him, but then I heard him yelling, 'Come on, Boy, listen to me! You got to get as far away from here as you can! Go to the church, take the pickup there. Keys are under the dash. I'll tell your mama. Let's go!'"

She looked at Carl. "I crawled away when they drove off."

Carl turned on his heel and pushed open the screen door. We all followed, watching with our hands on each other's shoulders as he made his way toward where the preacher mopped his brow by the open car door.

Once you hear a fist smack flesh, you never forget it. Carl knocked the man down and bent over him, striking blow after blow till blood poured from the preacher's nose. My father ran from the porch and grabbed Carl's arm, swinging him around until he had hold of both Carl's shoulders. Preacher Allen didn't need an invitation: He leapt into his car and left in a blur of dust.

Carl's roar ripped our silence. He shrugged off my dad's hands and barreled toward his truck. Willeen called out from the doorway. "Carl! It won't do any good if you go after the preacher. Do you hear me? It won't help Beverly. It won't help Nettie. You'll go to jail. Do you hear me?" She raced down the steps.

My mom caught Dad's eye. "Frank, don't let him get in trouble."

"Wait, Carl, I'll go with you." Dad slammed the passenger door as Carl fired the truck and pulled away. Dad spread his hands out the window to show he was unarmed, but would do what he could. We watched until they were a dot down the road.

Granny turned and strode toward the kitchen. "Well, the Good Lord may be with us, but he forgot to put more coffee on."

The rest of us circled Beverly and Willeen. Mom enfolded them, one in each arm. Mary Alice held open the screen door and we all walked inside. Willeen almost fell into a straight-backed chair, while Mary Alice and I deposited Beverly on the sofa, Mary Alice lifting her legs to lie even with her head.

My mother disengaged herself, went to the kitchen, lit the stove, and placed the kettle on a burner, while Granny measured out coffee.

I slid into a chair next to Beverly and folded my arms around her. Hands reached out and patted us—maybe Willeen, maybe Mary Alice. They drifted into the kitchen, where I heard them talking over dishes clattering. What they said barely registered.

"Beverly," I whispered. "He really didn't rape you? Jim pulled him away?"

Beverly covered her face like she could shut out her memories. "I don't know, Evie. I just don't remember anything except his knife between my legs." Her eyes dulled. "It doesn't matter. Even if the police catch Bud, and he tells them the truth, I'm still going to be a Jezebel. You should have seen those people looking sideways at me, pointing. They believed every word he said. Nothing's going to change what they think. Or what Tommy thinks."

"Why should Tommy think anything bad about you? He loves you."

She gathered herself, stood, and sneered down at me. "Yeah? Where is he?"

I watched her stalk to her room.

Dad came home late that night. Mom and I hurried into the living room, our hair damp from our baths, my bathrobe flying untied behind me.

"Frank, what happened?" Mom took Dad's jacket and hung it on the peg by the front door.

Slowly, Dad removed his hat and hung it beside the coat, his face etched into lines of exhaustion. "We went to the Allens'. Mrs. Allen said Preacher went to visit his sister in South Carolina. Grabbed some clothes and took off without saying much. Then we drove over to Bud's mom's house." He rubbed his knuckles, a habit when he was tired. "That lady ain't got a pot to piss in. Refrigerator on the front porch, door hanging off its hinges. Floor boards rotting—she's had it rough." He shrugged. "Couldn't get no sense from her. She ain't seen Bud in a month, she said. 'Cording to her, he left weeks ago to go in the Navy. Could tell by her eyes she was lying, but—you ever see her?—she's a little bitty thing, standing there in her ragged dress. Even Carl ain't gonna hit a woman. After that, we went to the police."

He shuffled over to his favorite chair, next to the old radio, aimed away from the TV, which he hated, and sat down with a plop. "That Lieutenant Holman acted like he wanted to help. But they ain't gonna do nothing."

"Why?" I felt for the ends of my sash and tied it tight over my pink pajamas. "Now they know who it is, why can't they arrest him? And Jim Marshall, too."

Dad wagged his head from side to side. "Daughter, what's right and what can be done are two different things. The policeman tried to be polite, but he said—" I knew he tried to find words he could say in front of me. "You have to look at it like a lawyer does. The prosecutor won't take a case with no eyewitnesses and his mom giving him an alibi. The preacher ain't here, no more'n Bud is, but, even if he was, how you gonna get twelve people to take a girl's word over a preacher's? And—" He stopped and turned his hands on his knees like knobs "—her boyfriend, that Turner boy, says she planned to meet him. 'Can you imagine what the prosecutor will do with that?' he asked. 'Girl goes traipsing around meeting boys when her parents ain't home, maybe she went with the Allen boy, too. They had a quarrel, and she changed her mind.'"

Though I tried hard to hold it in, I began sniffling. Dad held out his arms to me, but I stood my ground. *You're not a baby*, my new self said. Besides, these were tears of rage. I kept my voice steady. "Why does that make a difference? So what if she went with him— she didn't, I know she didn't, because she's in love with Tommy—but how can he just beat her and get away with it?"

Dad stared at a corner of the ceiling. "Daughter, folks get away with plenty they ain't got no right to. I wish I could tell you something else, but I can't."

A week later, wheels crunching on gravel in our front yard drew me to the window in time to see Granny Burnett get out of her ancient truck and make her way carefully to the grass-covered conduit that marked the path to our front door. I hurried out to take the grocery bag she hoisted in one arm, clasping her battered purse in the other. "Brunswick stew?" I peered inside, puzzled. We passed through the front door.

"No, Hon, it's the persimmon jelly I promised your ma from that batch Tally and Vinnie picked last September. I been meaning to get them over here, but ain't had time, with that back fence needing repairs." She sank into Dad's chair in the living room. "Lord, I'm too old to be good for anything."

Mom came out of the kitchen, drying her hands on a towel. "You ought to relax more, what with the farm being paid for and all." She sat down on the sofa, settled a bowl in her lap, and began to peel potatoes over it, the knife turning swiftly in her hands. I perched on the other end of the couch.

"I'd sell, but don't nobody want to buy that worn-out land," Granny said, fretfully. "That's how we got it. Nobody else wanted it." She fingered the edge of her handbag.

"What's wrong?" Mom spotted Granny's nervousness a second before I did.

"Maisie, children are just about the most worrisome thing. I swear I wished I'd drowned all mine when they was just pups." I knew it was a joke, but I gaped my mouth at mother, who swatted my arm to make me stop.

"What's wrong, Granny?" she repeated.

"Lord, Lord. Well, just say it, I guess. I come to tell you Mary Alice and Beverly is gone. Gone to Atlanta. Ain't coming back, 'least for a while. Mary Alice said she'll write her address to you and George, later, after she's settled." Granny rushed through this announcement and came to a sudden stop.

Someone who didn't know her might have thought Mom didn't seem surprised, but I saw her brace her hands against her knees. "So. Was that Mary Alice's idea? How'd it happen?" She sounded as if she knew the answers already.

I had expected Beverly to leave ever since the day Willeen swept the preacher out, but it had never occurred to me that Mary Alice would go with her. *Did you think she'd go alone, at seventeen?* My sarcastic self prodded with a pointy finger.

Granny picked a fan out of the basket by Dad's chair and waved it around her face. "Well, now, I don't know whose idea. Maybe the doctor's. He told Mary Alice that Beverly needed to get away, it'd be too hard on her going back to school around here, where everybody knew what happened. Mary Alice looked for places to send her, but Carl wouldn't hear of letting her go to strangers. 'I promised her Ma I would keep an eye on her, and I'm gonna keep that promise,' he said.

"One of the people Mary Alice called while she was looking was this friend of hers in Atlanta, who's the head nurse at some hospital.

She needed more nurses, and Mary Alice said, 'I can make more money in Atlanta and Beverly and me can stay with Carol, maybe get our own place in a few months. Beverly can go to school down there.' It took some talking, but finally Carl seen the light. 'Ain't no one knows her down there,' he said, 'so maybe she can start over. Find a new church.' He ain't never gonna give up on that idea. But he knows Mary Alice will take good care of her. She's family. So he finally said okay. They left yesterday."

"What does Willeen say about it?" Mom folded her hands in her lap, her downturned expression anxious.

Granny frowned. "Maisie, that's the thing. Willeen ain't said one word, not one word about any of it. She just set there awhile and then she stood, said, 'Guess it sounds all right,' and walked out of the room. But she ain't happy. I seen her eyes. She's mighty sad, my daughter. That's her baby. But what's she gonna do? Beverly stays around here, and people tell their nasty stories. She's better off down there, starting a new life. Mary Alice is right."

"She probably is," Mom agreed, though the set of her shoulders told me she wasn't satisfied. "But ain't it hard on Beverly, getting taken away from all her friends like that? Away from her mother, too? Willeen's the only mama she's ever known."

"You'd think it would be," Granny said. "She didn't say nothing, neither, except 'I'll get to live in the city!' She packed her bags, and off they went."

Mom rose and wiped her hands on her apron. "Well, I guess that's that. We'll hear from Mary Alice regular, I expect. Stay for supper?"

Granny shook her head and braced her hands on the chair to rise.

I turned from one to the other, not understanding why they didn't have more to say. "They'll come back, won't they?" My skin felt tight as a sheet snapping on a line. The walls seemed to echo. Why hadn't Beverly come to say goodbye?

Mom spoke sharply. "Of course, they will. Mary Alice has a wedding in June. And Beverly is a bridesmaid in it, like you. Come on and help me with the supper. Sure you won't stay, Granny?"

Granny got to her feet. Mom waited till she drove away, then turned to me. "Get your coat, Daughter. We are going to pay a visit."

On the way, Mom tried to justify sticking her nose into someone else's business. "Willeen and I have been best friends since we were babies. Besides, I need to take her these patterns." When we got to the Tyndalls', she left the patterns on the car's floorboard. I picked them up and carried them in behind her.

Pots boiled away on every burner of the old iron stove. The kitchen sweltered, the windows edged with steam, but Willeen stood staring at the Chinaberry tree.

Not until Mom raised the lid on a pan did I smell scorching beans. "Get me another pot holder, Evie." I handed her a square of quilted cloth. "And check the biscuits in the oven."

I lifted out the big tray of fat biscuits, browned just to the edge of burning.

"Willeen, where's Carl?" Mom spooned the beans into an old lard tin, and dropped it all into the big metal barrel that served as a trash can. She pulled a Mason jar of beans from the shelf and emptied it into a saucepan. Willeen finally spoke.

"He's working overtime. When he ain't working, he's on the road, these days."

I wondered where he was on the road to, but Mom seemed to understand. "What does he expect to accomplish with that? She'll never get better."

Willeen wiped her hands on her apron and moved to the table.

Mom gestured to me. "Evie, if there's coffee in the pot, bring us some." I poured two cups from the percolator. Mom sat down across from Willeen. "Drink your coffee," she said. They drank, in silence, for several minutes, while I stirred the beans.

Mom refilled their cups. Only birdsong split the silence, until Willeen spoke. "You know, I can still see her coming up that drive, in that fast walk she had, her hair pulled loose and flying out behind her. And singing that song she loved. How did it go?" Willeen paused, her eyes fixed on her cup, scanning for the memory.

My mother sang in her sweet, clear voice. "Green grows the lilac, all sparkling with dew. Sad, sad, am I, since I last courted you. But at our next meeting, our love will renew. We'll trade the green lilac for the orange and blue." Willeen nodded to the tune.

When I looked out the window, I saw and heard something different: Beverly twirling down the road on her strong legs, singing, "A-wop-bop-a-loo-bop," thrusting her hips out at each swing of the beat, her honey-colored hair flinging to the rhythm.

Regret fluttered around and into the smell of scorched beans.

Willeen spoke softly. "No, Nettie will never come back to us. Some hearts are just so soft, they break into too many pieces to mend." We listened to the birds singing for a while longer.

Mom rose and put their cups in the sink. Then she turned to Willeen. "He took Beverly to see Nettie, didn't he? How did Beverly act afterwards?"

Willeen looked reluctant to speak, but she did. "They went a few days ago. Beverly said, 'I look like her, but she's much more beautiful than me. *Was*, anyway.' She didn't want to talk about it more than that." Willeen repeated, "Something broke in Nettie, something that couldn't be fixed."

Mom murmured, looking out the window to the fields, "How do you take being betrayed by your own mind, over and over again? She hid her illness from all of us."

"We were barely more than children, ourselves," Willeen said, flatly.

A moment later, we stood on the front porch, looking out over the stubbled fields. Late asters, impervious to frost, filled the ditch across the road, their intense blue tinting the crisp evening air. My mother spoke in a tone to be taken seriously. "It's not your fault, Willeen. You did the best you could. Who could have—*would have*—done more for another woman's child? Beverly's got strength. She'll be all right. Mary Alice will see to that."

"I know." Willeen nodded, her eyes on the fields and flowers. "But I'll miss her just the same."

The evening hush resounded across the sleeping furrows. Willeen stirred. "All these years, Carl thought he was doing what Beverly needed. 'I don't know no other way to raise her right than in the church.' He said that, many times. I thought maybe he didn't have to be so harsh on her, maybe we should get away from the hellfire-and-brimstone, come over to your church, Maisie, where there ain't so much commotion going on, but Carl said no, only the undiluted Gospel would do, so I went along." She took a deep breath. Her voice rose, and the wind seemed to swirl in response. "But damned if I will ever let him tell me what's good for my daughter again."

Still, Mom studied the field. "Maybe Carl being so strict made Beverly rebellious, but nothing you or Carl or Beverly did brought this on. Being raised in one church or another, or wearing dresses down to your ankles, ain't gonna keep no good-for-nothing man from acting like an animal."

My mother seldom preached the gospel, but she clearly meant that sermon to stick, even if it was delivered to a ditch full of asters.

We walked to the car across the dry front yard, buckled with ridges of hard clay. My mother opened the car door, looked back once at Willeen, got in, and closed the door with a slam. I slid into the passenger's side.

⸙

On the way home, Mom said, "The way I see it, Beverly will be better off." Rain began to fall. She leaned closer to the windshield, as if counting the drops. "Mary Alice will take care of her. She won't have to listen to that nasty preacher, or twits like Rena." I smiled at Mom's impolite term, but my heart still felt swollen in my chest. "It'll

be good for Willeen to go see her, get out of that house and away
from Carl for a while. She won't need to work so much, now that
Beverly isn't home."

"*Carl.*" I tried to spit out his name. "If he hadn't been so mean to
Beverly—"

"Now, Daughter, think before you start throwing stones. He was
mean, but not because he wanted to hurt her. He just didn't know any
better. He thought Nettie being so beautiful, and so flighty, made her
a temptation to everyone. So he tried to keep Beverly from being like
her mother. Lock her up and don't let her show any spirit—that's the
old-fashioned way."

I could not be convinced. "He didn't stop the preacher and other
people from making it Beverly's fault. He could have—"

"Could have what? Gone after the man who raped her himself?
He did. No luck. Threw a fit and made the sheriff catch him? I guess he
could have. But that wouldn't have changed the lawyers' minds about
what they could prove in court. 'Bout the only thing he accomplished
is no one's seen Lewis Allen around here since." Her one-note chuckle
sounded satisfied with that outcome.

"My daddy would have—"

"Your daddy would have moved heaven and earth to find that
man, you bet, but if he didn't, you'd still be okay. We're stronger than
we look, Daughter. Beverly has to start a new life. She needs new
friends and to find some man who will be good to her. In five years,
she'll be married and have kids of her own, and this won't matter. If
she's lucky." My mother sounded as uncertain as I'd ever heard her.

"If I could find Bud, I would pour hot oil on him till every ounce
of skin peeled off and then I'd push him down in the salt cellar for
good measure." I spat this out with more venom than the guy in the
black hat in the cowboy movies.

"I reckon some of us would help you. But I don't see how it
would erase what Beverly's got to deal with." A grim smile pulled her
lips down. "Then, again, he wouldn't hurt anyone else, would he?"

We fell silent. The sky rained harder, and the rusty windshield wipers groaned louder. I watched drops collide with one another on the glass beside my head. "What if she does find a good man? He won't be able to erase her memories."

Mom sighed. "No, nothing erases bad memories. But having someone to share your life with, that makes a difference, Evie. Believe me."

I examined the raindrops sliding past my face. Clear as glass, wet as water, but if I put my hand up, I would feel only a hard surface. My own voice sounded far away. "You have Dad to share your life. And yet I don't even know my grandmother's whole name."

The instant I said it, I regretted it. My mother's face crumpled from within. One sob reverberated off the window in front of us. Gradually, wrinkle by wrinkle, she straightened out the sorrow into a smooth mask. And that scared me even more than seeing her cry.

"Mama, I didn't mean—I'm sorry. I don't know why I said that." I knew exactly why I'd said it. I'd reopened a wound in my mother's heart because my own heart was cracked in two. Some part of me, a gremlin I kept in a bottle, rejoiced that someone else felt as hopeless as I did. It hadn't helped. Now my pain was doubled, hearing my mother try to suppress her own. I curled into a ball against the car door.

Mom said nothing, not even when we pulled beneath the big oak tree. Miserably, I flipped the silver lever and climbed out of the car. I had to wait for Mom to unlock the front door. No lights inside indicated that Dad had gone to bed.

Mom stuck the key into the lock, twisted it, and finally murmured, "Come in, Daughter. I'll make some tea."

When we sat at the dinette, a cup and saucer set for both of us, only the light above the stove lighting the room, I looked up. In my mother's face, compassion, and something else, something like a light banked for a long time, in her eyes. "Her name was Evangeline

Adriana Lee Grey. Those persimmon trees you've seen since you were little came with her down the mountain." Mom's voice had flattened into an emotionless drone, but I knew better. I could see her eyes glitter with tears. "She delivered babies with Dr. Nettie. She was Romani. A Gypsy."

Her words wove in and out of the pulsing in my ears like a tune you want to hear but can't enjoy. Anger battled curiosity in my mind. The inevitable won. "A what? A Gypsy? You mean like fortunetellers, and—" I didn't want to say "thieves," but people said that about them.

"No!" Now her voice was fierce, a tone I knew well. "They don't kidnap children, either. But that's what our neighbors thought. That's why they treated my mother badly."

"What happened?" My voice sounded small against the wind stirring the crabapple outside the window.

"She died when my brother was born. I tried to find someone to help her, but no one would come. She was so tired, there was so much blood, she couldn't—" The words lay between us, a long spool of sorrow without end. I'd made my mother tell something so terrible not even I wanted to know the whole truth.

Yet there were questions I had to ask, in case the light inside my mother never lit again. "Is that why Uncle Paul doesn't come home?"

"That, most of all." The words fell out of her mouth like stones across a deep pond. "We don't tell anyone about being Roma, Tally and Vinnie and me, because people are prejudiced. I mean, some people think they know, but Mama never told anyone but Nettie. Some people thought she was one of the Italians who came from the quarry. Some called her Gypsy, but most people don't know what Gypsy really means. She let them think whatever they liked, went right on about her business. She taught us to ignore questions. Or laugh them off. It's easier if you don't talk about it. We didn't tell you so you wouldn't have to keep the secret."

"You mean you didn't trust me to keep the secret."

"No, Evie. There are some things you don't understand."

"Then make me understand!" I hadn't meant to snap at her, but the gremlin was rather pleased with the effect.

She looked down at her hands as if they could shape the truth. "All right. Long ago, our ancestors came from India. They didn't want to leave. There were wars and famines and plagues that pushed them out. After that, they traveled because people stoned them, ran them out of town, murdered them. Those folks thought they were Egyptians, strange, dark people, with an odd language, gods no one there had heard of. Everywhere they went, people blamed them for whatever went wrong. Sometimes, of course, they did wrong out of desperation, but no more than any other people did."

"How did our family get here?"

"Different ways. My mother's mother's family were sent here as slaves." She paused and let that tidbit sink in. I felt my mouth fall open. Slaves? Who had heard of Romani slaves? "I told you, people are prejudiced. Back then, Roma could be deported, killed, enslaved, and no one could stop it."

"Yeah, but—I mean—" I really couldn't find words. I knew that Black people had been slaves. And some people thought they still should be, that they weren't as good as white people. And now, my own great-grandparents had been in the same boat? I couldn't tell that at school. Kids would say worse things than Professor Know-it-All. "What about—you said your mother's mother's family came here that way. What about—"

"My mother's father's folks? They came to England because they were burned out of France, and then to America, looking for safety, I guess. They were musicians. My mother's mother's folks were farriers."

Here was a word I could grasp. "Blacksmiths?"

"Yes. But they also were metalsmiths. They could mend or make almost anything. Sometimes they traveled, mending pots and pans, and so on." She looked directly at me and her gaze in the moonlight from the window was as deep as still water. "Evie, no one can know. It's not just us, but your aunts and their families we have to worry about."

On the table, the moonlight lay in a stripe across our hands, like a bright cloth binding us together. For the first time, my mom had trusted me with a secret, a huge secret. That should have made me happy, yet so many emotions, so much sadness, in one day had left me drained of all but a desperate urge to gather as much information as I could. Moonlight could not be depended upon. "Okay. But the language you speak—"

"Romanes. We all know some words from my mother."

Romanes. I fixed on the rain outside the window as I tried to grasp the thread. Through the horizontal sheet of water paraded a vision of musicians and caravans with pots hanging from the roof, making their way to some distant land. "Are there any other Roma here? Where is the rest of the family?"

My mother halted a long time before she spoke. I knew she was editing, choosing what to say. I felt energy draining from me, as if the rain were washing through my head. *Better learn all you can while she's talking*, one voice said inside. Another marveled, *how can you be a Gypsy?*

Through both filtered my mother's voice. "My mother's family didn't like that she married—my dad. They moved west, and my parents didn't follow. So we didn't know other Roma. Except for—"

"Mrs. Garretson." The words flew out almost before I knew that I knew.

"Yes. Evie, I wanted to tell you—" She turned toward the wind lashing the panes. "But it's hard to explain to a young child, and frankly, I knew you would tell Beverly, and—"

Beverly would have told someone else. She loved to gossip.

I lowered my head to the cradle of my hands on the table and tried to absorb everything I'd learned that night. My best friend had disappeared, a grandmother I never knew was from some group I'd never heard of, except as odd characters in vampire movies, and Carl Tyndall had stood up for his daughter. Too late.

Mom whispered something to me about being glad she'd told me. Mrs. Garretson could tell me more about the family history. For a change, I wasn't listening. My room felt like the only fortress I had left. I rubbed my forehead and said, "I think I should go to bed." Before my mother could respond, I was in the hallway, my head throbbing with her words, "She was Roma. A Gypsy."

I flipped on the light above my bed and turned to the mirror, taking in my dark hair, my gray eyes, my skin just slightly less golden than my mother's. India? A Gypsy? What is that? And how could I ever share that with my friends?

Then I knew: I wouldn't. Beverly raped, Beverly, silent, Beverly gone—and now this. I had had enough of explaining things I barely understood myself. Mom was right. There was so much I didn't understand. Though my limbs felt like water-soaked logs, almost impossible to lift, I pulled on my soft cotton pajamas with the yellow rosebuds. Exhausted, I climbed into bed and tried to shut every door in my rambling mind.

My eyes popped open against my will. Why hadn't I asked more? Had Uncle Paul met our family out west? Had my mother ever met them? And what about Dad? How had they come together? Had he thought twice about marrying a Gyp—a romni? What did Mrs. Garretson have to do with our family? Questions tormented me until the first light peered through the window beside my bed.

Maisie, 1935: Branches

Vashti Garretson toted a black valise. She'd pulled her hat so far over her eyes that I didn't recognize her and almost shut the door, but she said one word— "Evangeline"—that made me throw the door wider.

"Your mother is expecting me," she added.

Oh, yes, she knew my mother and loved her so well that she stumbled and nearly fell when I stammered out that my mother was in the graveyard. After she sat for a while with a cup of strong tea, I took her to the top of the hill where we had placed Mama underground in her pine box. For a long time Mrs. Garretson stood and stared down at the stone embroidered with flowers that Papa had bought in town. I thought she would perhaps turn on her heel and walk away. Instead, she reached around to me, then gathered Vinnie and Tally, too, in her arms. "You are my children, now," she said.

Before Mrs. Garretson came, my arms were so tired from cooking, cleaning, and rocking the baby that I fell asleep anytime I sat still. Sometimes, in the garden, I would fall into a trance and find myself at the end of the row, not knowing if I'd planted cucumbers or squash. She took over the cleaning and most of the cooking, so after that I had only to watch my sisters, tend the garden, feed the animals, and make sure that Papa got what we needed on his trips to the store.

No need to ask Dad if she could stay. From the day Mama died, he worked the farm and took the crops to market and fixed anything that needed mending, but, when his chores were done, he stalked to his chair by the fire and sat without joining in our conversations. He did follow us with his eyes and occasionally questioned us about school. If we went to him for a goodnight kiss and hug, he hugged back. Once the little girls were in bed, he'd sit without a word to Mrs. Garretson or me. If Tally fussed for Mama, he'd stalk out and sleep in the barn.

After a while, the three of us made a pact not to cry so Papa would stay inside with us. Even Tally kept her promise. Yet, gradually, Papa slept in the barn more and more often, till I got used to taking his meals out there. He moved his clothes and shoes into the tack room. He hadn't slept in Mama's bed since her death, anyway, just built himself a pallet on the floor, even though Nettie had brought a new mattress to replace the one we burned. The room still smelled of her.

One night, after Papa had taken to sleeping in the barn, Vashti Garretson put on her nightgown in the loft with the little girls, climbed down the ladder, and turned to me at the door to Mama's bedroom, saying, "It will be all right. Don't you worry now. She died outside, didn't she? That was right. And a mulí as sweet as hers would do no harm, anyway." Then she closed the door behind her.

We got along pretty well, if you didn't count Tally dogging my every step, day and night, and Vinnie waking, screaming, in the dark. They didn't want to go to school, wanted me in their sight every minute. Papa never knew if Vinnie went to class or Tally had a fever, or even if we'd eaten dinner that night. He moved like a toy monkey I saw on a stick once at Redding's store, jerking his arms and legs to accomplish whatever task he'd set. His mind wasn't with us, but his body worked hard, like he always had.

So when I found him face down over the well, I thought perhaps he'd been mending the bucket or the rope that turned the handle. Stepping closer, I saw that his face bloomed red and bore impressions of the stones on his cheeks—the stones he carried himself up from the creek, to build the well house.

Mrs. Garretson and I carried him inside. He was so light. I hadn't realized how much weight he'd lost the past two years, his clothes hanging so far off him they trailed on the ground, his arms and legs like brittle branches. No wonder. I couldn't remember the last time I saw him eat.

"His heart gave out," Dr. Nettie said. She washed him and put on his black suit, the one he used to preach in before Mama died. The same way she washed my mama, so I wouldn't have to.

The church people came, a few of them. Lewis Allen took me aside. "As head deacon, I'd be proud to preach your father's funeral," he offered. I looked at him in his blue suit, his hair all slicked down as if clothes made all the difference in whether you were a fool or a minister, and shook my head.

"Thank you kindly," I said, "but Papa left instructions he wants the preacher from the Methodist Church in town." I didn't care if I disappointed him. I remembered how he'd sniggered behind my mother's back at the store.

"Well, all right," he said, and clapped his hat on his head, looked around the room to gather his disciples, and walked out the door. We haven't seen any of them since, to speak to.

I try to have charity in my heart, like Mama used to tell me to do, but I will never forgive that Mrs. Dockhart would not come to help my mama—even after the risk my mama took for her—nor did most of the other women pitch in to help me feed or clothe my sisters in those weeks before Mrs. Garretson came.

Only Mary Avery stopped in sometimes to see how we were doing. "Your Mama was the kindest person I ever met," she said, handing me a pie. But Mrs. Avery kept busy with her own large family and, as time passed, she came less and less. Sissy Applewhite sent word from Toccoa, where her family had moved onto the Starr mill village, that her heart broke for us, and she would be out to visit as soon as she completed confinement with her third set of twins. We never heard more from her.

On one of the last warm autumn evenings, about six months after my fifteenth birthday, a man—a boy, really— ambled up our drive like he was on a walk to look around the world. He squinted at the turkey oaks in their fall colors, at the fields lying fallow on one side of the drive and thick with collards on the other, at the barn poking its triangle of roof toward the September sky. And, finally, at me, as if I might be one of Toccoa County's amazing sights. I dropped the chicken feed bucket at my side and watched him come, wondering if the county had hired a new tax collector. Looked too puny to be anything but a tramp, though. His sand-colored hair stuck up at an odd angle, like he'd been scratching his head and had forgotten to smooth it down. He turned to look at the herb garden and I saw a tiny bald spot on his crown.

I let him get to the edge of the farmyard before I spoke. "If you need a meal, go to the kitchen. Mrs. Garretson's there. She'll make a sandwich for you." I started to turn away. Dark came on swiftly that time of year, and the cows were bawling in the barn.

His scuffling feet made me turn around. "Could use a sandwich," he agreed, when he had my attention again. "But Mr. Redding sent me to bring you this packet of cloth and thread." He shrugged off his shoulders a drab-colored backpack like the one my daddy used to pack his lunch for the field.

I met his eyes. Nothing dangerous there, I thought, but I felt suddenly weary. "Got no money to pay for such frippery."

"Mr. Redding said you'd say that, and to tell you your daddy had already paid for it." He snapped back, short, but civil, then took a handkerchief out of his back pocket, wiped his hands, and stuck one out at me. "Frank Gates is the name. Proud to meet you.'

I was skeptical about my daddy having paid for the package. He'd already been gone three months. More likely, one of Mr. Redding's kindnesses.

Frank Gates took in the farm yard, the hens scratching, impatient for me to get moving with their feed, the wood pile looking low. "Looks like you might need some help. I could come back after work for an hour or two." He stood there, hand out, like he had no plans for that hand anytime soon.

I set the bucket down again and took two steps forward to take his hand, expecting to let it drop and get back to my work. But his hand met mine like a tongue fitting into a wagon axle. I felt my life turn around and set out anew in that moment. Guess that's why I turned my back on him and only spoke over my shoulder, without looking at him. "You can go to the kitchen for a sandwich." His eyes burned a hole in my back, while I threw open the door to the barn.

All the while I nestled against Dulcy, her milk spurting between my fingers, I thought about his face and the way he had looked at me. I liked his eyes, blue—not gray-blue like Papa's, but sky blue like a sunny day—and the rise of his forehead, a bare slope, over them. And the way his hair smoothed back from his forehead, revealing even more of his sunburnt skin. The tufts of cowlicks meant he scratched his head a lot. He looked like the thoughtful kind. Most of all, I liked the dry, warm feel of his skin. I tried not to think about that. I threw some corn to lead the hens and latched the coop for the night.

The kitchen smelled warm with gingerbread. Mrs. Garretson sat at the table, her big hands wrapped around a mug of tea, listening to the stranger describing some flowers he'd seen in the fields that day. She named them for him. Vinnie had retreated with her books to the far side of the hearth, but Tally sat on a stool to the left of the table, drinking in everything the stranger said. She had a look on her face that said she was pretty well smitten with him.

I poured myself some tea from the ironstone pot, and sat a little way away from the table, in the rocker where Mama used to sit.

"Mr. Gates told us about a horse he saw pulling a wagon with a ring of flowers hung around its neck. Who around here do you suppose would take the time to doll up an old wagon horse?" Mrs. Garretson looked expectantly at me, as if it were my turn to take the reins of the conversation. But I only nodded, wanting to take the stranger's measure, and I could do that better if I listened more than I talked.

I'd been working the farm alone since my papa died, and, though I needed help more than I needed anything since, I didn't want to get stuck with someone who would be more trouble than he was worth. I met my friend's eyes and saw that she understood, for she turned back with a question.

"Where did you say you're from, Mr. Gates?"

The stranger laid his hands flat on the table. His fingers were long and thin, the backs browner than his face, but delicate. He's been picking something, I thought, but, looking at the shoulder blades visible through his thin plaid jacket, like two handles jutting from a door, I doubted he'd be strong enough to do as much as Vinnie.

He spoke like he'd heard my thoughts. "I had my raising on a tobacco farm in North Carolina. Folks died in a fire, along with a brother and a sister. Whole house just lit up one night. Nobody knew what caused it."

Mrs. Garretson's hand flew to her throat. "And you escaped?"

He looked down to watch the spin of the mug he twirled in his hands. "No, Ma'am. I had gone to spend the night with my uncle. We meant to get an early start loading his crop for market. Word came through a neighbor that the house had burned down and my folks with it. I don't mind telling you that was right hard to hear." He spoke quietly, not making a big show of it, and that might have been the thing that made me think he would pull his load. His voice did not grate on me.

I had never before heard a man speak about something that hurt him. Even in his wildest grief, my father only sat and stared at the fire. I had wondered if men felt the same way we women feel about things, and here came this stranger with a tear in his voice. I didn't know what to think. Did I want a man around who cried easy?

His face showed no sign he'd really cry, though. He turned to me. "You working this place by yourself, ain't you?" His voice said he knew it, and he knew how hard it was, and if he could do something about it, he would. I found my tongue would not untwist to answer.

Mrs. Garretson answered for me. "Their father died earlier this year. We been making it go, but Maisie here could use more rest, and the little ones need to stay in school a while longer. I ain't much use for more than cooking and cleaning." As if to prove it, she limped to the door, drawing her shawl from the peg in the corner. "I best bring in some wood. Fire's going to be handy tonight, with this early chill."

Frank Gates stood without scraping his chair on the floor and went to the door. "You stay here. I'll get the wood." The door closed behind him. Everyone left in the room, Tally included, knew I'd let him stay.

Vashti Garretson had come to the same conclusion. "He ain't got no harm in him, Maisie. Might be a right nice fella."

I got up and followed him out. By the time I reached the wood shed, Frank had already split three or four logs and turned for more.

"Only place you can sleep is in the tack room. There's no heat, but plenty of blankets, and the walls are good and sound. No holes or chinks to let the wind in. If you could feed the horses and get the cows to pasture in the morning, I'd be much obliged."

"No, Ma'am." He said it so quietly I almost convinced myself he hadn't spoken.

"No?"

He shook his big, square head. "Cain't no single man stay out here with you ladies. I'll bunk in town, with the Reddings, like I been doing, and come out here afore and after work every day."

I swallowed. I couldn't believe he'd work so hard for nothing. "We ain't got no money to pay you. I thought maybe room and board...." I let the words lay there, but tears rose in my throat. All the fatigue of trying to work the farm on my own came crashing around my ears. Of a sudden, I didn't know what I'd do if he didn't come back.

"The board, I'll take. That Mrs. Redding is an awful cook."

We both fell to laughing, relief welling in my windpipe as I giggled like a fool.

And that's how Frank and me started. We worked real good together. So good, that until Allen sicked the sheriff on me, I thought about going back to school.

On a cold morning in winter, the ice snapping off the trees in the pale yellow sun, and the horses stamping in the barn, too cold to care for pasture, Frank and Vashti Garretson and me were drinking a quick cup of coffee in the kitchen, before our second round of chores, when Lewis Allen came to the house with the Sheriff himself. Standing on my porch in his shiny boots, the sheriff announced we didn't have papers on the farm and would have to get out. Frank stood behind me at the door, his hand on my shoulder to hold me steady.

I knew from listening to their talk that my mama and papa had paid the church for every last acre of land—the house, too—but I'd never seen any papers.

Thank goodness Nettie saw from across the road the sheriff's car in our yard and she come roaring up in her own car and set them straight. "You have to give her time to produce the papers," she said. "You can't evict her now."

We turned the house upside down. Nettie found the deed shoved down in Mama's cedar chest along with Dad's discharge papers from the Army. Allen had signed it himself as Head Deacon. My parents had made all the payments, but he bet on me to be an ignorant little girl and run scared. And I was scared. Still, when we went to court and that judge—a little, tiny man, so wrinkled he looked like a gnome in my schoolbooks—asked for the papers, I waltzed right to his bench and handed them over.

They weren't done yet. "She's a minor, Judge, only fifteen years old," said the Sheriff's lawyer. "We got to take charge of her, her sisters and brother. They're too young to take care of themselves." So scared I felt my bladder leak, I looked around for help. Nettie leapt to her feet.

"But Mrs. Garretson helps them!" Nettie motioned for Vashti Garretson to come and join us in front of the judge.

That lawyer unfolded his tall, thin frame. "She ain't blood kin." He pointed one long finger at Mrs. Garretson. I thought she would hit him with her big black purse.

Nettie thought a minute, and said, "Judge, can we have a hearing set so we can prepare a plan for the children?" The judge agreed.

As she drove us home, Nettie said to me, "Maisie, I've gone as far as I can. You need a real lawyer to take it from here."

She took me to a real lawyer, a man with an office on the second floor of the drug store in Toccoa. He said we could try to have Mrs. Garretson appointed guardian for us, but since she had no steady income, he doubted the judge would go for it.

"Isn't there some other way?" I asked.

He nodded, chewing on a fat cigar. "Well, little lady, you could get married. You're old enough, and there's no parent you got to get permission from. You got a groom in mind?" He smiled like he'd made a big joke.

"Well, actually, yes, I do," I said. I didn't even stop to think if it would work.

Frank was out pruning in the orchard when we got home from court that afternoon, so he missed Nettie's tires popping on the gravel. The sun fell slant through the cherry branches as I brought him some water and a sandwich.

He saw me coming, climbed down from the ladder and met me on the ridge. "What happened?"

I shook my head like I had no hope. "Judge says Mrs. Garretson ain't kin, and there's only one way we can stay together here, me and Paul and the girls."

"What's that?" He wanted to know.

So I told him. "I got to get married."

He studied on the shears in his hand for a minute, then bent and drove them tip-down in the ground. "You got anyone in mind?" He said it quietly, like he couldn't hardly stand to hear the answer.

"Yes, but he don't know it yet."

I saw his Adam's apple bob once, as if he were shoving words down from the inside. "Maisie, you got to be straight with a man. A man always wants to know where he stands." He jammed his hands in his pockets and looked away as if he were figuring out his next move.

I couldn't help but smile, a little. "But I don't know if he'll have me. He might not feel the same way about me. How do I find out?"

"Maisie, can't no one feel but one way about you." He'd turned around, studying my face. In about three steps he stood right in front of me. "If he ain't willing, I'd like to apply for the job."

And that was that. You could get married in Georgia at fourteen, in those days. I had that and some to spare. When we went back in front of the judge, I'd become Mrs. Frank Gates, the wife of a grown man, and that judge had to let the girls and Paul stay with us. I reckon Lewis Allen had never been so surprised in his life. He glared at me and stomped his cigarette out in the marble-floored hallway. I went walking by, my arm linked in Frank's, like we were out on a stroll. And I ain't never been afraid of him or the law since.

I figure what we can't handle together, my husband, Mrs. Garretson, and me, the good Lord doesn't mean for us to have.

Evie, December, 1959-May, 1960: Spring and Pink Tulle

A few weeks after Beverly and Mary Alice left, we had a surprisingly balmy day, for December. The sky loomed a pale, distant blue and the air held a false hint of spring. I was relaxing in the swing, on a break from my Saturday chores, when the mailman delivered a postcard. I took the card from his broad-fingered hand and turned it over while he crunched through dry grass toward the house next door. Mary Alice's round, cursive initials appeared below the message.

> *Have time to write just a few lines. Beverly and I are*
> *both fine. Sorry we couldn't say good-bye, but I needed to*
> *start work right away. Wrote George to explain. Going*
> *to work now. Hope to see you soon. M.A.*

And at the bottom of the card—which showed a skyscraper on the front—she had scribbled an address: 14 W. Peachtree Street, Atlanta, Georgia.

Inside, Mom flapped her hand when I offered the card. She had set up the ironing board in the corner, next to the fireplace and the TV. A basket of Dad's work shirts, neatly pressed and folded, rested on a kitchen chair she'd arranged within reach. She turned back the collar on one of my blouses, iron poised. She looked down, so that I couldn't read her expression. "What does she say?"

"Not much. Apologized for leaving so quickly. She wrote George. They live on Peachtree Street. That sounds nice." I scanned the card, back and front, once more. Not a word from Beverly. The iron hissed.

Had Mom heard me? She made a vague murmuring sound as she maneuvered the steel tip into the blouse's collar.

Disappointment hacked a familiar hollow in my chest. Since our talk in the moonlight, Mom had gone back to her usual dark-closet approach, though now I had a clue to the contents. What good would it do me to know more about being Roma, when I'd been sworn to silence? You can't be something you can't admit to. Can you? Not if no one really explains what it means.

Still, whenever I entered the room during my aunt's visits, they would switch to English. Oh, Aunt Tally once in a while would explain an overheard word, like, "Kushti means 'good'." And Vinnie told me a little about the idea of purity: Keeping the house clean was a part of being spiritually pure, because the home was sacred space. What did that have to be do with me? It did not help me stare down the gossipers at school. If anything, it gave me one more thing to hide from them.

And nothing I'd learned explained why there was a perpetual tinge of sadness around my mother's eyes, while my aunts seemed perfectly normal. I would never understand her. So I concentrated on holding onto the one thing I could look forward to: George and Mary Alice's wedding. Beverly would be better, and we would be bridesmaids together and life would be something like it used to be.

I flopped into Dad's chair and watched Mom fold the blouse and lay it on top of the stack. "When can we go get my bridesmaid dress? It's almost January."

Mom made a sound, half chuckle and half "humph." "And the wedding's not till June. Mrs. Garretson said she'd be ready to fit it for you sometime in March. She has two others to do, you know, Beverly's and Carol's."

"What does a matron of honor do, anyway? Veronica said it's supposed to be your sister. Why didn't Mary Alice pick Willeen? Why Carol?"

"I am not in the habit of asking people why they choose others, Missy." There it was, the mind-your-own-business tone. "Maybe Willeen didn't want to do it. She's not doing so well, you know."

Back to our cat-and-mouse game. "What's wrong with her?"

I thought my mother would ignore me again, but she pulled the iron's plug from the wall and delivered some news. "Willeen left Carl. She lives with Granny now." I stopped swinging my foot, unsure about whether to feel happy or sad for Willeen. Mom turned her back and lifted the basket. "Guess she didn't see any reason to stay out there, with Beverly gone."

I thought about what she'd said long after she had put the laundry away and gone into the kitchen to start supper.

All my childhood had been spent with the Tyndalls and the Burnetts—those I loved, like Granny and Beverly and Mary Alice, and Willeen, whom I'd liked but not understood, and the one who just seemed unknowable to me, Carl. I depended on them being there, gauged everything I knew by what they said and did. With them gone, my life was a listing ship, out of balance.

I stepped to the screen door, looking out at the corner of the mill village I could see from our porch. Everything seemed gray now, faintly fused with the deceptive blue of the porcelain sky. Empty.

And, always, another hole to fall into.

Unlike the photos of models she cut from extravagant *Elle* ads, everything about Veronica Wheeler was understated, but still noticeable: her black eyes accented with dark pencil around the rims, and her nails, white tips over pale pink polish that matched her lips. She was so cool, she reminded me a little of Mary Alice. So when she invited me home to meet her mom and see her collection of hats, I accepted.

We strolled across the marble-tiled floors of their hallway and entered her ivory-painted bedroom. On the way, we'd passed in the hallway a photo of a man in a hard hat with our mill spitting smoke in the background. It seemed out of place alongside a black-and-white photo of a graceful dancer and a brass lamp with a brocade shade.

"Is that your dad—" I gestured back toward the hall.

"Oh, Mom keeps begging him to take that down, but he's so proud of being Supervisor of the Year. Tacky." She flipped her schoolbooks onto her white desk and pointed me toward a seat on the rose-colored cushions framing a windowed alcove.

"You could look like that." Veronica tapped a photograph on the wall: a woman with auburn hair piled high, eyes rimmed with a cucumber color. She twirled in a silver silk dress that barely skimmed her figure, thin but ample in the right spots. "You have the bones, nice hair, if you'd cut it right, and a swan neck. The angles of your face are almost —" she twisted her head to see me from a different perspective "—exotic."

I ducked my head, acting too modest to answer. Really, a faint resentment flared in my chest. Exotic. How do you get exotic from being chased across three continents? *If you only knew,* I thought. Instead, I squelched my indignation and admired the wall of "chapeaus" that she'd collected on her family's frequent vacations abroad: wispy, jewel-colored treasures with lace, veils, and a panoply of feathers. From Paris, she said. And Rome. Barcelona, as she pointed to a fiery red number. She was the only person I knew who had been out of the country, so I asked her where she liked best of all the places she'd been.

She laughed. "Well, definitely not here." Veronica did not plan to stay in Toccoa County. "Women can earn good money in fashion. And you get to live in New York and go to Paris for the shows." Her black-rimmed eyes glowed with confidence. I wanted to soak in her offhand manner. As if anything were possible, but the choice was hers.

Choices. My own future loomed as a grey mist with nothing approachable, nothing real enough to touch. After twenty minutes of looking at her penciled dress designs, which she was confident would make her famous, I realized I'd be late getting home. Veronica made me promise to come back and let her make a chignon from my bushy hair. "I can tame it. I promise you."

On the way out, she introduced me to her mom, who had just come in with a grocery bag in each arm. I helped put the groceries away and lingered for "just one" chocolate from a beribboned box, even though I knew I'd never make it home in the "no questions" zone. I watched Mrs. Wheeler flow effortlessly around the kitchen, opening drawers while she questioned us about our day. She was shorter, lighter than her daughter, who was built a bit square, like the man in the photo.

"She used to be a dancer," Veronica murmured. "On Broadway. She still practices every day." It occurred to me that Veronica wanted to remake everyone into some version of her mother, since she'd never squeeze herself into a small frame.

Mrs. Wheeler didn't wear obvious makeup—less than her daughter—but I could imagine sequins on her lithe body and in her black hair, like the dancers on the Ed Sullivan Show. All the way home, I wondered what it would be like to live and work where people went to the theater in diamonds and furs.

❧

On the day in mid-March when I got my bridesmaid dress fitted, early spring flowers were blooming. The roads were wet from a sleety rain, so Mom kept her attention on the slick pavement. I felt almost happy, describing our neighbors' gardens to her.

"Look at those camellias blooming along Mrs. Avery's porch. Wow! Can you see the size of Mrs. Garretson's tulips? They're tiny, pink and white. What are they called?"

"Little Miss Muffets, I think. And those big white tulips are called 'Queen Anne.' Let's hope a late ice storm won't kill them before they bloom good." Mom peered for just a second at our seamstress's side yard before pulling into her drive.

Since my talk with Mom about her mother, I'd been wondering about Mrs. Garretson, who'd been Gramma's friend. I stole glances at her face while I stood on a chair so she could measure the hem. Why hadn't I noticed before her golden skin?

But the mostly-done dress stole my attention. I stared down at my new dyed-to-match pumps and imagined dancing in the pink orchid color Mary Alice had chosen.

"Be still, Missy. If you wiggle, your hem will be crooked." Mom suppressed a grin at my antsiness. Mrs. Garretson kept pinning for what seemed hours. Finally, she stepped back. I raced to the mirror, tripping in the unfamiliar high heels.

Mom had pinned my hair high on my head so that the loose ends would not get in the way. The off-the-shoulder collar, a yard or so of translucent tulle folded into a loose shawl, tinged my neck and shoulders with a rosy glow and threw red sparks into my hair. I was no longer a "mouse," as George liked to call me.

Even Veronica will like this, I thought. *And she can do my hair.*

"You look positively glamorous." Mom beamed with approval.

"I do look good, don't I?"

"Sweet." Mrs. Garretson tried to agree.

Above her head, I smiled at Mom, who winked back at me in silent complicity. I looked a little more than sweet, and we both knew it.

"Come on, Princess. Take it off. We have to get to the grocery before it closes." Reluctantly, I followed Mom's directions and pulled the satin skirt over my head.

Mom fiddled with the old, rusty Pontiac trunk lock and lifted the lid. "Please get these potatoes and the milk jug for me, Evie. I need them for supper. I'll have Dad bring in the rest when he gets home. Lord, April starts tomorrow. June will be here before we know it." She headed for the porch, but stopped. I peered around her shoulder.

"Dad's not home yet. Will I do?" George grinned, pleased with his surprise.

"Oh, you'll do!" Mom agreed. She rushed to throw her arms around his neck.

He tried to reach out to grab me, too, but I grinned and stepped back, socking him playfully on the arm with the milk jug. "You ready to get married?"

"Ready for launch!"

Mom slapped at George's shoulder while ordering him to be useful and lug in the groceries. She watched, smiling, hands on hips.

George came back to the supper table, shrugging. "I left a message with Beverly." He ran a hand across his buzz cut and rested his other hand on the back of my chair. "Bev had homework to do, Squirt, but she said she'd call you soon."

I struggled to keep my lips from turning down. I'd talked to Beverly twice since she'd left. Both times, she'd sounded like she was in a tunnel, and it had been hard to hear. And every time I'd suggested going down to see her, she'd had a school project due, or Mary Alice had weekend duty. I'd begun to think that getting away from Toccoa County meant getting away from me, too.

George took the saltshaker from Dad's fingers and shook it over his plate without looking at it. Mom frowned. George grinned at her and wiped specks off the table with his hand, tossing them onto his plate. "Mary Alice won't be home till about midnight. She isn't expecting me yet. If that fella hadn't cancelled and the duty officer offered me his place—I can't wait to tell her they're sending us to California! She's gonna like that—palm trees and sunshine! You won't mind if the phone rings real late, I hope?"

He looked earnestly at Mom and Dad. Dad did not like the phone any more than the TV. He often said that if people wanted to talk to him so much, they could get in their car or wagon and drive over to see him. But for once he did not bristle at the suggestion of a call. He used his biscuit to clean his plate.

Mom shrugged. "Reckon we can get back to sleep. What will you do to stay busy till then? You're nervous as a tomcat." After a second, she blushed, realizing what she'd said. George made a wail like an alley cat and allowed that he knew how tomcats felt.

I looked around the table. When we'd last been together like this, six months ago, I had been a baby. Now even George looked at me approvingly and said, "You're growing up, I see, Sis. Which boys do I have to beat off with a stick while I'm here?"

It was my turn to blush. No lines of boys stood outside the door, waiting to take me out. But earlier that week I had overheard a comment from one of the football players. I had hurried past the boys gathered at the foot of the school's front steps—glad neither Tommy nor Bobby was with them—but not so quickly that I couldn't notice an uncomfortable silence—uncomfortable for me, because I knew where their eyes were aimed. "Not bad, for a brain," one voice said. A chorus buzzed in answer.

And that wasn't all. I was keeping another bit of good news to myself, not ready yet to share it, even with Mom.

A black-haired girl named Rose, whom I knew slightly from Journalism Club, had invited me to sit with her and her friends at lunch. I was grateful. Veronica rarely ate lunch any more, working on her hair dyes or sketches, instead. When I saw Howard Pearson place his tray down at the far end of our table, I tried to focus only on the kids seated around me.

At first, they seemed an odd collection. Two girls were art majors and a boy with curly hair worked on the school literary magazine. Howard was deep in an earnest conversation with a fellow I recognized as one of the leads in the fall production of "Oklahoma!" It wasn't long before I was engrossed in listening to them talk.

The actor called out to my friend, "Hey, Rose Tattoo!" causing Howard to look in our direction. His eyes locked with mine for just a second. I smiled. He smiled back. To distract myself, I asked Rose about her nickname. She giggled, bent over and whispered to me, "You'd make a dynamite Laura in *Menagerie*. Think about it." I gulped my tea to wash down the fry that clogged my throat.

Curly leaned over to set me straight. "Rose keeps begging our drama teacher to put on one of Tennessee Williams's plays. 'So we can get everyone out in the open.' Can you imagine the storm that would cause?" He snickered through his fingers.

I had no idea what he was talking about. Later, I went to the library and looked up Tennessee Williams. I read, "*The Rose Tattoo* opened on Broadway in 1951. A film adaptation released in 1955 starred Anna Magnani and Burt Lancaster in this story of a girl raised in the slums of Rome by her maternal grandmother." A picture of the show's stars showed a busty woman who looked a lot like my friend, down to the jaunty red scarf she liked to wear around her neck.

All that spring, I ate lunch at Rose and Howard's table. The others talked about films and books and theatre and, occasionally, politics. They might argue which teacher taught best, but there were no cracks about who cheated on whom, or which freshman girl had the best chance of making the cheerleader squad. Somehow, though I knew so much less than they did, I relaxed.

After a couple of weeks, I began to notice that intellectuals weren't the only denizens of Howard's table. Sandy dropped down in a vacant chair one day to talk lighting with Rose, student director for *Annie Get Your Gun*, in which Sandy would star the next week. A boy I recognized as a player stopped to crunch baseball scores with Howard. I looked down the table at my editor, chin propped on fist, cowlick tipping over one brow as he concentrated on the baseball talk, and felt a twinge. That same bitter little voice that warned me when Rena had been about to waylay me, told me to keep my distance from Howard now. *He'll be gone next year. Don't get so wrapped up in him.*

Curly leaned from two seats away one noon to remark, "Hey, great piece you wrote on the old courthouse fire, Evie." I thanked him, but kept my eyes on my plate. Howard had assigned me the article two weeks before, and, after I'd handed it in for last week's edition, had waved it at me, grinning, from the other end of the newspaper office. I didn't want to admit how much his approval meant to me.

Rose swiped one of Curly's chips. "I liked her article on cheap trips to Paris better. I'm going after my junior year in college, if I can save enough."

I slowed my words in order to sound casual. "You're going to college? Where?"

A wave of dark hair covered her face as she sipped a Coke. "I got accepted at Swarthmore, but my folks can't swing it. So I'll go to State and try to transfer to Pennsylvania my junior year." Her voice sounded cool, but I thought I saw a glint of excitement in her eyes. "What about you?"

I tried to match her confidence. "Well, I thought North Carolina. Chapel Hill. They have a good lit mag." I waited for someone to smirk or snicker, but no one did. Around the table, I saw bobbing heads. "But I'd really like to go to school in New York. Maybe Columbia?"

Curly swayed around Rose to question me. "Do you write fiction, by any chance? I have a lot of poetry for our own lit mag, and not enough good short stories."

"She does." Even I turned to Howard in surprise. How did he know I'd been working on a short story, my first?

"When you dropped your papers that day, I saw the first paragraph. Wish I could have read more." He looked directly at me. My skin felt like it sizzled. I managed to stammer out a promise to drop a story off at Curly's box in the office.

Rose leaned my way. "Howard likes you," she whispered. My skin burned hotter.

She was right. Howard Pearson asked me to the prom, standing in front of my locker one afternoon after Journalism Club, when no one else lingered in the hall. He was jittery, jamming his fists in his pockets. I looked into his brown eyes and gratefully accepted. Maybe he wasn't the school heartthrob—only football players made girls buzz as they passed, it seemed—but I thought he looked as handsome as any of the other letter sweater guys. And I would be able to talk to him between dances. If he danced at all.

I occupied myself with how to find this out, without sounding like I doubted his abilities. No one I talked to, not even Rose, remembered seeing him at any proms.

"Maybe you bring out the beast in him," Veronica laughed.

While I was making my bed that Sunday, waiting for my chance to talk to Mom about a dress for the dance, car wheels crunched the gravel out front. Mom met me in her bathrobe as I hurried out to answer the door. She put a finger to her lips and nodded toward her room, where Dad still slept. "Dad's sleeping till church time. He got called in to fix a loom last night. It's for George, anyway."

I was suddenly and completely curious, but Mom had her don't-ask-me-any-questions look on, so I went back to my room, where I looked out the window. Mary Alice waited at the top of the steps. She wore a crisp navy blue dress with a white collar. A white leather purse and white gloves rested next to the porch railing on the top step. Maybe she came to go to church with us? Why didn't she come in? I wondered. I wanted to go out to greet her, but Mom stood guard in the hall.

George's voice sounded surprised. "You drove all the way here so early after work?" Something made him stop. I waited through what seemed like a long silence before I realized that Mary Alice was speaking very softly. I peeked out my door to the hall. Mom's face seemed anxious as she waited in the kitchen doorway.

"What's happening?" All of a sudden, a lump clogged my throat.

"Come in the kitchen and we'll make tea," Mom said. We only had hot tea, instead of strong coffee, if someone fell ill or catastrophe occurred. Or she needed to tell me something difficult. I sank into a kitchen chair. Mom was not too preoccupied to note my faults. "Don't dawdle. Set the table." I got the cups and saucers. Then she set me to peeling potatoes. I knew she was trying to keep me busy and out of George's hair. I found the paring knife, pulled potatoes from the basket on the counter, and waited until Mom went to her room before sneaking a look at what was transpiring on the porch.

My brother and his fiancée were sitting close together on the top step, not touching, Mary Alice's skirt wrapped neatly around her, hands in her lap, her voice urgent. George was silent, but I could tell by the tautness of his muscles that he listened closely. I could think of nothing I wanted to know that fit what I saw. I ran back to the kitchen and the potatoes, pausing to listen when Mary Alice's car rumbled away.

George came inside a few moments later, but I did not hurry to find out what had happened. I kept busy in the kitchen, straining tea and finding the creamer and sugar bowl. Mom and George talked, voices low, in the hall. Then came the snick of George's bedroom door closing. Mom went back to her room. I heard Dad, sleepy and surprised, and the rustle as he dressed. He passed swiftly in the hall to knock on George's door. No answer. The screen door slammed and the swing creaked as Dad settled into his favorite spot.

Mom finally came into the kitchen. I turned, my back to the sink, hands holding onto the counter for dear life. "What is it?" I said. But I knew before Mom spoke.

She came over and put one hand on my shoulder. "Mary Alice called off the wedding." She looked out to the garden, where our crabapple tree bloomed in bright white flowers, red-tipped stamen bursting through their centers. "Be good to your brother. He's taking it hard," she whispered.

I sealed my lips tight and refused to let out any sound. Instead, I stood with Mom in the kitchen and listened to the birds singing. After a minute, she swiveled her head to me. "There's one more thing."

"What?" As the moment dragged on, my mind raced to take stock. No wedding. No sister-in-law. And now something else—

"Beverly's pregnant." For long minutes more, the birds sang their insanely happy songs, and the clock over the stove ticked. When I could hold back my sobs no longer, I ran for my room. Mom did not follow.

❧

"I'll wear my bridesmaid dress." I kept setting the table, avoiding Mom's stare.

"Why? We'll find a new dress. Maybe Mrs. Garretson can use the same patt—"

"No. The pink dress will be fine." I laid the last knife into its place and wheeled slowly to face her. "There's no sense in wasting the fabric."

My mind buzzed slightly, as it had since Mary Alice deserted us. *I don't care. Do I?* No response meant full speed ahead.

Mom gestured with her spatula. "Evie, it's your first prom. Let Vashti make you a special dress." I didn't know whom she meant for a minute, until I remembered one of Mrs. Garretson's chattering remarks.

"Vashti is Persian, from the Bible. She was a queen who refused to parade her beauty before the king's guests. That name's been in my family for centuries." Centuries had seemed like an exaggeration at the time.

I walked toward my room. "No. It will be fine. Call me when dinner's ready."

❧

"You're lucky. Not every sophomore goes to prom." Veronica spat words out around the bobby pins clamped in her teeth while she teased my hair for the dance. She grinned—or, rather, grimaced around the pins—to let me know she felt happy for me. I knew she didn't have a date.

"Anyone can go to prom. Our school's too small to have separate dances for upper and lower classes." I held up strips of the pink ribbon Veronica planned to weave through my locks and recited what Howard had said when he invited me.

She studied where to place a long strip. "Yeah, but hardly any senior boy is going to date a sophomore. Especially not one as cool as Howard."

I twisted my head toward her so fast I jerked a strand of hair out of her hand. "I didn't think you liked Howard. You said high school newspapers are for pretenders." Veronica's black eyes met my gray blinkers in the mirror.

She sighed and started over, then smirked with subdued red lips. "Yeah, well, his paper won first place in the regional rankings. I guess he's a cut above."

"*Our* paper," I corrected her. At the same time, part of me wondered why Howard wanted to bother with me.

He arrived right on time, in a white sport coat with a deep pink rose in his lapel, carrying, for my wrist, one perfect white orchid with a pearl-studded band. "You look marvelous," he murmured. He shook my father's hand, promised my mother to look out for me, and waltzed me down the sidewalk to his father's waiting Buick. *This can't be real*, I thought, as he closed the door. I looked down at my lap, covered in pink satin, at my wrist, encircled by blinding, exquisite perfection, and thought suddenly of two girls dancing in a field beneath a blazing blue sky. *Beverly would have loved seeing this.* I thrust out my chin to keep from crying.

At another time in my life, it might have been a complete romance from fairytale beginning to triumphant ending. The moment Howard put his arms around me to slow dance, I felt a charge that brought me alive and zapped me into a magic circle. When he held me close, I could feel my blood rushing, light flickering from one internal nook to another. I thought I must be glowing from within like a lantern. When we moved apart, the numbness returned underneath my rose-pink facade.

I said hello to friends, including Veronica, who leaned against the back wall in a short black dress and hoop earrings, like a bored model, and Rose, lingering by the punch bowl with Curly. They were a perfect match: she wore a white lacy dress, and he sported a dark Charlie Chaplin suit.

I was watching balloons trailing on the ceiling, not listening to the Prom Court announcements, when the principal suddenly read out my name. Howard gently nudged me onto the stage. I stood next to Rena and another girl, looking out into the auditorium's bright lights, reading the expressions on the upturned faces watching us, as Sandy and Mike were crowned. Approval, that's what I saw. Admiration. Afterwards, during the special waltz for the Court and our dates, kids and teachers followed us with their eyes.

The dance ended, yet when Howard drove me home I floated onto the porch. A sting, a mild buzz jolted me pleasantly as his lips brushed mine. *So that's what a kiss should feel like*, I mused. *Light years away from kissing Bobby.*

Not even Howard confirming what I'd heard spoiled my wonderment. "You know, I'm leaving next week for a summer internship. Then I'll be starting college out of town. But I'll write," he promised. I nodded in a daze. He grasped my hand, said, "Thanks, Evie. That was wonderful," and disappeared into the mist that drifted across our lawn. A little disappointment filtered through the gauze as I watched him go, like a cut that would hurt more later.

How could I be dissatisfied with the night's results? My mother greeted me as I stepped inside. I unfolded the white sash emblazoned with gold lettering—"1960 Prom Court"—and accepted her congratulations, then walked through my bedroom door, closed it behind me, and went to the mirror.

Something Veronica had said buzzed around my head: "You could be a beauty queen." With my hair up, my face seemed leaner, more bare, cheekbones scraped back to the tips of the ears, neck long and vulnerable and taut, like Veronica's models, with their bored eyes. She had been right. I did have a swan neck.

Standing in front of the mirror after my first prom, I remembered the poster I'd seen the week before in the window of Maple's Department Store: "Miss Toccoa County Pageant. Winner receives $1000 scholarship and the right to compete for Miss Georgia. Must be 17 years of age. Inquire within. Toccoa Chamber of Commerce." Was this my ticket to college, punched?

A new girl looked back at me in the mirror, a girl with darker eyes—no telling what color they were now, but they still shone. I unpinned Veronica's careful chignon and let my hair fall in waves to my shoulders, which curved inward to breasts that weren't so large as to be awkward, but also not too small to catch attention. Like watching an actress in a movie, I thought, *This person could walk down a runway and not mind people gawking at her.* Her eyes said she knew secrets that may or may not be worth much, but they were hers. Because no one she knew was who they said they were, anyway. *What if life is about caring more about yourself than others? What if it's about not loving too much? Or maybe it's about not feeling too much?*

The strange creature blinked at me, a big, gray-eyed, glassy stare. On the surface, cool determination. Underneath? Something shifted, a quake-like quiver. Well, maybe this rosy façade could contain what lay beneath.

I wasn't seventeen yet, but in another year, I would be. And I could learn by entering the Miss Tallulah High contest first. Then, when I was seventeen, I would go get that application. What could it hurt to try? If I couldn't conquer the despair I felt inside, at least I could cover it up with an attractive lie.

Evangeline: Windblown

Animals come to me, offer me their wings, their voices, their powerful haunches. I find I most love the freedom of the birds. In spirit as in life, the same question: stay or go? Birds answer that with their wings.

I have ridden the updrafts with an eagle, soaring over the bones of my distant ancestors— now no more than relics to me, for I can call their souls at will, and they, mine. Precious still is the turning of the earth, the ceaseless rhythms of the tides, the molten heart beneath the core. All the corners of the Earth are familiar treasures. There are other worlds to see, far bigger plans to comprehend. And yet, here I stay.

I nestle in the eaves of the house we built. Some part of me flickers along the road, tosses restlessly in the branches of the persimmon trees, wings with the barn swallow along the sweep of firs—some little glint that cannot leave just now.

I did not see, at first, the hole in my Maisie's heart. She did well. I knew she would. Held onto her sisters—not her brother, for he preferred the road, like my father—found her life's companion, planted the seeds that carry us forward. Maisie holds the family close, sings them lullabies and hymns, but she hears our long sorrow songs, that make us a people apart. It is a sadness I am powerless to lift from her, and I do not try.

With her daughter, there is a break that begins with the things my girl cannot say, about my death, and the difference between one moment and the next. Grief sinks its talons deeper, the longer you hold on. Now, my granddaughter wants to fly.

Truth shapes itself to the heart that holds it. Even love can't change that.

Yield

Eve, October, 1971: Wild Persimmons

Piercing my third-floor classroom window, the mill whistle is a faint warning. "Fifteen minutes" I announce and turn back to the clear blue sky I've been dreaming myself into, like a leaf floating into crisp air. I could be anywhere, any country or city, Paris, even—A snicker pulls me back. Without looking, I can guess the cause: Lacey Reeves is winding up the boys.

I spin. Sure enough, four sets of eyes cut her way, watching her, slack-mouthed, like she's a rocket defying gravity as she arches backwards, breasts standing out taut against a thin yellow blouse.

I lift myself from my perch on the wide sill, slip between the rows into the peepers' line of vision, stare at them long enough to make them duck their chins to their tests. Closer inspection reveals sheens of sweat glimmering along their temples. Last spring, the School Board declared air conditioning out of the question due to the extra costs required by the desegregation plan. Now that I've spoiled the boys' fun, the least I can do is to see that the swing-out windowpanes are open as wide as possible.

A second whistle blast causes the entire class to shift in their seats. Two forty-five p.m. Their pencils race through the final essay questions, making up for minutes spent dawdling earlier in the period. I walk over to the tall windows. To my right, the mill's stack sends up a stream of glitter that trails off to the north. North. New York and museum openings, canvases splattered with staccato ideas, bookstores where people snake through lines, hungry for a new way to talk about love and death.

If only—

I correct myself and tug at the first window's iron hand pull, which leaves red crescent-shaped imprints on my palms. About a hundred coats of paint have puddled into the sashes. While I shake my hands, encouraging blood to rush back into fingertips, I remember there'll be very little free time tonight. Over breakfast, with a determined glare, Mom announced that she's going to make meatloaf and a pie for dinner. Her left arm is numb since the second stroke, and still she wants to act as if everything is normal. So I'll twist open all those jars of spices and ingredients, corral the mixing bowls, maneuver so it's my hand that reaches for breakable objects. Then washing up and two or three hours of grading tests. At least, when I finish, near midnight, it will be a tad cooler.

My peripheral vision snags on Kathy Waters, in the seat at my left hip, chewing her pencil, face wadded in concentration. Any other day, she'd be sitting with her hands folded, waiting for the rest of the class to finish. A chipped blue barrette clings, a tattered butterfly, in her drab brown hair. I lean over to see what's troubling her. A question that should be a snap: "Henry Fleming has strong opinions about war in *The Red Badge of Courage*. Are his views relevant today? Why, or why not?"

Think, Kathy. We're fighting a war in Viet Nam. Folks are rallying in the streets. Maybe she received my message. She goes back to writing, her earnest script steadily taking shape on the page. The other kids call her "Miss Brains" and her skittish brown eyes say she's accepted exclusion. I know that life right well, down to the choice of the wide lace collar on her blouse. It looks poetic, she would have said to herself—I would have said to myself, ten years ago, at fifteen.

What saved me from being a wallflower? A tiara. What a surprise for everyone, including me. Miss Tallulah High in my junior year, then the Toccoa County pageant as a senior. Some desperate notion of changing my fate urged me on. Feeling like a fraud every step of the way, I pulled off the runway strut long enough to get my scholarship. What an innocent in my rose-colored tulle, thinking that college meant escape. Four years at the University of North Carolina, then New York, literary capital of the world, here I come--that was the plan. Now, here I am, nearly twenty-seven, teaching in the same school where I graduated, living in the house where I was born. Even Her Majesty the Queen would chafe at the collar of my blue linen suit.

I stifle a sigh and detour around the standing globe to reach the middle windows. At the end of the fourth row, Lacey is at it again, watching from the corners of her wide green eyes as two heads, this time, swivel toward her. One glimpse of me and their hands are suddenly busy forming letters in jerky movements. Not Lacey. She laughs, head tossed back, then casually picks up her pencil.

I swivel away to hide my grin. No encouragement. She has a brain. Let her use it.

Last week, we read an excerpt from Carson McCullers' *Member of the Wedding*. Lacey got it all, every line that McCullers crossed in her story about a girl who wants to transcend womanhood. She asked one question: "Miss McCullers didn't live in the South when she wrote this stuff, now, did she? Didn't she spend her time in Paris and New York?" Those huge eyes narrowed to slits, waiting for my answer.

I suppressed the urge to say, Yes, and I long to follow in her footsteps. Not many of my girls will get the chance to see anything outside our stamp-size grid. How to explain how dangerous it is for a woman to be comfortable in her own skin? Girls like Lacey, aware of their beauty but oblivious to the consequences, are in special danger of being labeled trollops, or worse. Especially here in the Bible Belt. The only thing more dangerous is for a teacher to talk about sex with a student. The best I could do was to inquire after class, "And what is there here for you, Lacey?"

She shrugged, nonchalant. "Don't worry, Miss Gates. I'll figure something out. I won't be wearing an apron with my first name on it down at Kroger's." And she had flashed those green orbs at me. Eyes like the wet underside of leaves.

Out of the blue, my mind telegraphs *Beverly*. I swivel to the window, brushing away the image of my friend—my *former* friend—dancing in our orchard, eyes flinging emerald sparks. I know what comes next: the picture of her crawling through blackberry brambles, the night we found her, beaten and bruised. Bad enough that I have to walk every day past the girls' bathroom where we had that last quarrel—the one I'd take back if I could. I won't let myself walk down memory lane. I can't. It's a bad idea to cry in front of your students.

Instead, I pull the sleeves of my suit away from my armpits, sweep back the tendrils of hair that have escaped from my ponytail, place my fingers again under the curved metal grips, and yank. Instantly, Steve Ames is out of his seat, reaching carefully across my breasts to replace my thin fingers with his sturdy, flat-tipped ones, zipping open the window in a second. He moves down the long row of tall window frames, pushing the panes up further at each stop. I smile and wave him back to his test. The class president and future Chamber of Commerce leader. Dependable as a sundial.

On my way back to the front, I step past the shelved reference books lining the far wall. The four black students in my advanced lit class sit nearby, all in a row near the classroom's rear door. For protection and a quick exit, most likely. Last month, tacks miraculously appeared only in *their* chairs. Untraceable, but I moved the likely culprits to the front row.

Last year, at the start of the school's second year of desegregation, I thought a match struck in the hall would have lit a bonfire. Now, instead of a blaze, there's an uneasy simmer. The students are settling into "territories" that include basketball for the best black athletes—

boys and girls— football and cheerleading for the white kids, and so-so grades for almost everyone.

Except MaeEtta Stewart. Her head with its carefully relaxed curls is bowed right in front of me. MaeEtta is all business, all the time, her clothes pressed, her papers to the point. She takes in everything that happens with a steady, assessing gaze. I'm betting she plans on hopping the "Big Apple Express" straight out of Toccoa County. I doubt her parents will object. Her father is the former principal of the black school that used to exist in that tiny building out past Mrs. Beasley's house in the country. These days, I hear he teaches in Atlanta, driving a hundred-mile round trip every day.

"We can only absorb so many new teachers," the School Board President said, primly. As if the district's black staff were some sort of invading army.

I scan the rows once more for signs of distress, and, seeing none, move closer again to the long sill, leaning over the edge to see if I can catch a cool breeze. Hot, gritty air crowds into my face, instead, stinging my eyelids.

In a snap, my mind travels a circuit from grit, to stifling heat, to Beverly, swiveling her hips, arms flung to the sky, dancing on an August day. *Beverly.* Mostly, I manage not to think about that time. Only sometimes these instant replays flicker.

The bell buzzes. I straighten my back and march toward the front. "Papers forward." The stack on my desk grows and leans in the direction of their flight.

I hadn't intended to come home at all after college graduation. Columbia University had offered me a teaching assistantship in the graduate literature program and a rare internship at their prestigious *Journal.* I planned to visit briefly with my parents and aunts when they came up for the Chapel Hill ceremony, then hightail it to the city, stay in a student hostel, and get to know the subway system before the fall term. Ahead of me loomed a future of travel and success as a literary phenomenon.

One week shy of the ceremony, my mother's voice crackled through the phone: "Your Dad is ill." I gripped the receiver to my ear, tuning out chatter from other girls passing in the dorm hallway. One invited me for beer and pizza, but I waved her away.

"He had a heart attack. He's stable now. Finish the school year. But come." With her usual economy of detail, my mother forged ahead while I tried to grasp the situation. "Doctor says he can come home in about a week, and we'll set up a bed in the living room for him. Now, I've sent you a beautiful white linen dress that Mrs. Garretson made for you. Tally and Vinnie will take pictures so Dad and I can see you get your diploma. I called George in California. He'll be here soon. So, bye, don't worry, and have a safe trip." Another girl tapped me on the shoulder to ask if I were finished with the receiver that dangled from my hand.

Compressing anxiety into action, I packed up my books, my Indian print bedspread, and my boxes of spicy teas. No question, I would go home. The only question was how long I would stay. In the meantime, my brother would be there.

When the big day finally came, my aunts, Tally and Vinnie, took turns snapping Polaroids, beamed as they hugged me, and fed me turkey sandwiches on the lawn from a hamper they'd brought. Then they herded me to the dorm to pick up my things, which we crammed next to Uncle Milt's bowling bag in the trunk of Tally's light blue Cadillac. I waited till Aunt Tally settled into her groove before peppering both aunts with questions.

"Congestive heart failure," Tally intoned, making sure she got the syllables right.

"Yes, but how bad is it?"

"You'll have to ask your mother," Aunt Vinnie replied.

"How long has he been sick?"

"I'm not sure," Tally muttered, wiping a speck off the windshield in front of her.

I tried another question, and another, knowing I would get little more information. The sisters' stone wall, again.

❦

Dad slept more than he woke, and when he woke his eyes searched frantically for Mom. Whenever he stirred while Mom was sleeping, I read whatever he wanted to hear. Mostly favorite Bible passages, like the Sermon on the Mount. Sometimes, the classic stories he'd read to me: *Kidnapped* and *Black Beauty* and *The Three Musketeers*. For hours, the oxygen compressor was the only sound. I felt my muscles begin to cramp up from inactivity.

George came and went, but I couldn't make myself leave. How could I enjoy settling into New York, knowing my Dad could go at any time?

Aunt Vinnie made a suggestion. "Your Mom needs you mostly when she's tired, in the evenings. Tally and I can look in on her during the day. Maybe you could sign on at the school as a substitute teacher. It will keep you busy and also let you save a little money for when you go up North." My ever-practical family.

For many years Dad had scrimped on shoe polish and shaving lotion to grow a small account to supplement my scholarship—"Because a girl who starts reading at three ain't gonna stop at high school," he'd said, with his shy grin. I didn't want to leave him for a moment. But as the months wore on, and he hung on, I knew I had to focus on something besides waiting for him to go.

Principal Baker hired me right away, pending receipt of my transcripts, on the strength of my continued presence in the hall trophy case, grinning in my glittery sash. "You'll be a great role model for the girls," he'd exclaimed.

I doubted that. But I discovered I rather liked urging kids to consider Jane Austen's heroines, rising above circumstances. Even on the days there were no lit classes to teach, when I simply babysat detention class, or struggled through a French I lesson, I enjoyed trying to point students toward the world outside our five square miles.

Early one morning, before class, I brought my coffee to Dad's bedside. Though he breathed steadily, one of his hands reached out to clasp mine. The other lay along Mom's forearm as she dozed in the wingback chair next to the bed. Catkins on the oak guarding our front window had caught my attention when I felt his grip on my fingers go slack.

Mom must have felt the same loosening. She lifted her head, her face already set in a tight mask. Then she brought his hand to her cheek, where it rested until the undertakers came to take him away.

Six weeks later, arrangements already made for fall at Columbia, I was grading papers for the French class, laboriously double-checking myself with the teacher's manual, when a racket from the kitchen sent me flying. Mom writhed on the floor, one hand clutching her head, eyes wild as a trapped animal's. I followed her gurney through the same green doors where they had taken Beverly, so long ago.

After the stroke, the doctors said she had maybe a year of therapy ahead of her. One year stretched to two and a full-time job for me. A third year to make sure she could manage on her own, and then the second stroke hit while she shelled peas at the kitchen table. She shouldn't live alone, the doctors said.

c⁓⁓⁓

I nose my 1964 Barracuda into the unpaved driveway, step out into the shade of the big oak tree, and lift out my satchel of quizzes. Except for the four years I spent in Chapel Hill, I have always lived in the house with the green-painted porch swing, two from the corner. Today, the swing is occupied by my Aunt Vinnie, who lifts a glass of iced tea to greet me.

"How is she today?"

Vinnie shrugs. "Fretting about those darn persimmons. There's maybe a bushel left on the trees." Her auburn hair glints as the sun threads its way through the latticed butterfly vine that shades most of the porch.

"Persimmons." My foot finds the spot on the step that creaks. Memories rush at me, distract me from Vinnie's remark. How many days I leapt up these steps to tell Dad about my day at school. All my life, he'd been the honey in my comb, eyes beaming at me with pride. My mother is proud of me, too, but she doesn't like my "New York" attitude—that's what she calls my disdain for small-town life. Or did, before the strokes induced her to parcel out her words.

I sink to a perch on the top step as a cane taps lightly on the hall floor. Mom totters out the screen door. Leaning back on the post, I look her over out of habit, checking for any sign of droop in her mouth, fatigue in her face, another stroke waiting to take its toll. She stares back with a steady eye, knowing what I'm doing. "You working tonight?" Her voice is still slightly slurred. Not badly. You wouldn't know if you didn't remember the crisp delivery that used to keep everyone jumping.

I struggle to shake off my fatigue. "Yes. Tests to grade."

"Good. You can go with Vinnie to check the persimmons this Saturday. You won't have papers to grade if you've just given a test."

My smart, scheming mother. I blink at the halo of the dying sun, flaring around her head. Maybe redirection will work the way it does on my kids. "What's for supper?"

"Meatloaf. Remember, I told you this morning? Vinnie snapped green beans for us. Gonna make a pie from those last berries." She looks triumphant, as if I'm the one with occasional memory lapses.

Which gives me an idea. "Oh, yes! I'm really hungry. If you start mixing the meat and crumbs, I'll come in and help with the rest, as soon as I catch my breath." If some of the beef and bread ends up on the floor, so be it, as long as I can have a few more minutes of rest before the evening's challenges begin.

It works. Mom totters back inside, the door flapping shut behind her.

Vinnie isn't fooled. "You don't have to go. Tally and I can handle the picking and clean-up." She kneads her knuckles where arthritis has raised them to knots.

I groan my way upright and flop into the swing beside her. "No. I'll help. It's only—it used to be such a special place to me. Now it's ruined."

One glance at Vinnie's crinkled face shames me. "I'm sorry, Aunt Vinnie. I don't know much about my grandparents, so the orchard means Beverly to me, and that's, well, a nightmare."

Vinnie pats my knee. "You get over bad times, eventually."

I nod, but I doubt it. "I don't understand why Mom goads me into going there, when she wouldn't go herself. Why—"

Vinnie interrupts, studying her pearly finger tips. "That's Maisie's story to tell. She'll tell it when she's ready. And maybe she wants you to be braver than her. Have you thought of that?"

"Yes. I have. If she told me the truth, we could be brave togeth—" A crash of glass slashes across my thoughts. "Oh, Lord! I've got to get in there." I run to the screen door and yank it open. When I glance back at my aunt, she is bent double, hauling herself out of the swing. How can I let her pick persimmons by herself? My heart rushes into my throat, unwilling to let the words out. Duty wins. "I'll go, Aunt Vinnie. I will."

She looks at me with her usual calm demeanor. "Tally and I can handle the picking and clearing. Maybe you should start with something easier. Go and see that old tree you and Beverly were so fond of. Start with the good memories." A windblown kiss floats behind her down the steps.

Guilt tweaks my dry throat. As I fly inside, I try to wrap my mind around her suggestion. Can I really go there? Am I ready?

One sight of the kitchen blanks out everything else: gleaming shards embedded in a carpet of ruby ketchup. Mom stands in the middle of the carnage, hands twisted into her apron, a sure sign of distress. I take her hand, gently glide her into a chair.

With a dustpan and an old towel from the cupboard in hand, I kneel to the rubble, grumbling silently to myself. What is so special about those darn persimmons, anyway? Why can't we let the birds eat them?

My dad's words when I was seven float into sound: "Now, don't you go asking her about it. It makes her sad to talk about that time."

⸎

The floor at last is clean. I take Mom's hand and gently pull so she rises from her seat. Her face has settled into resignation, which scares me more than indignation or sadness. I speak as softly as possible. "We have another bottle of ketchup. I'll open it and pour some into a cup for you. The mustard, too. And I'll get out the mixing bowls and ingredients for the pie."

She walks with stuttering steps over to the stove, then turns and hugs me around the waist. "I'm sorry you're stuck here taking care of me," she mutters.

I've grown used to my mother's contradictions: sharp words, soft heart. I hug back. "Nonsense. You're recovering. Columbia isn't going anywhere." I hope it's true.

As she scoops tidbits from jars, mixes and stirs, her body settles into something like the old Mom, she of the steady hand and the quick step, as if the cooking rituals she's performed thousands of times restore her to herself. But her gaze does not follow her hands. She stares out the window, her face a map of sorrow. Missing my father, his step worn into the ridges of the broken tiles? Or some older grief, some echo of black eyes blinking from her past? My heart lurches toward her, jerked by the cord that runs taut between us. My outwardly serene, inwardly volcanic, complicated mother. I swallow my own heartaches and prepare to rescue whatever else needs rescuing.

Eve, Spring, 1972: Howard's Promise

Tallulah Falls is a postage stamp on the map, not much bigger in real life. The square is ringed by one row of shops, a one-story elementary school, Tallulah High, the Tallulah Worsted Mill and its company-built village, and four stacked blocks of other housing that ranges from grand to miniscule. From the middle, a broad canvas of farms stretches out in various directions, interrupted occasionally by a crossroads church or store. In order to buy a book or a magazine that doesn't have casseroles or cars on the cover, we have to go to Anderson, over the South Carolina border, fifteen miles past our orchard and thirty miles from the courthouse steps.

At Tallulah, I'm the only high school teacher under thirty, besides the new speech teacher, who so far has kept mostly to herself. Hardly any of my classmates stayed after graduation; most escaped to Atlanta or other cities with more opportunities.

Judy Vickery stayed to manage her family's restaurant. Last month I tried having dinner by myself there. The pitying stares were punishing, especially when the pony-tailed waitress leaned over and said to me, while her lavender-polished nails pushed back my $2 tip, "I hear there's some single men hanging out down at the American Legion on Friday nights."

Sure. What would a Viet Nam vet want with me once we finished our argument about protest as patriotism?

When they handed me my roses back in 1961, the Viet Nam war had barely tinged our consciousness. Now, in my purse, folded, is a picture from *Life* Magazine of Miss Montana, 1970, in full tiara and crown, her fist raised. She lost her crown and her scholarship for saying what she thought. Someday, I'll tell her what her photo means to me. Bet she's not in Montana anymore. No, that kind of notoriety would be hard to maintain, here or there. Small-town fame is hard to handle.

Lately, I've made a habit of walking the mile downtown to the bank on Saturdays, where I cash my paycheck and withdraw spending money for the coming week. Invariably, someone along the way asks about my pageant days.

Today, inside Toccoa Mercantile, the curly haired teller looks at my signature. "How are you? And your daddy and mama?" Her smooth forehead puckers in concern. I don't recognize her. The simple diamond ring on her third finger is a poor clue. Being gone four years means I missed a whole generation of teenagers. Girls still marry young here. Somebody's baby sister?

I give her my nicest close-lipped smile, in hopes of getting my money soon. "Fine. Thank you."

Mrs. Earle—it says so right on the plaque—beams with pleasure as she hands over the bills. "I remember when you almost won Miss Georgia." She bends over the counter, blue eyes sparkling like they'd called her name instead of mine. "You remember Sandy Hennessy?"

I let my pleasant expression freeze, like a leftover one has no intention of reheating. My magic mind eraser swipes away the memory of Sandy, with her sharp widow's peak, carefully looking away as her pal, Rena, tells me how Beverly must be too ashamed to return to school. Still, I have to acknowledge the question. "Head cheerleader?"

"That's right!" The teller's smile, broader now, grants me the prize. "She's my first cousin—took me all the way to Atlanta to see you compete. I loved that one-shoulder number you wore for the evening gown competition. Classy! Sandy said she always knew you were special." She makes a sad face. "She's not real well since her divorce. Now there's a story!"

Clearly, she plans to tell it. So I back away, using the bow, smile, and retreat move I learned as a beauty queen to escape hangers-on. The teller waves and turns to her friend, pointing and chattering, no doubt, about my one-shouldered evening gown.

I turn, push open the revolving door, and step through to the pavement. So Sandy drove to Atlanta to see me compete? What am I to do with that piece of information? Betrayal, followed by a display of loyalty? There's something about friendship I can't get, as if I've missed a vital lesson. Still, I chuckle a little at the teller's enthusiasm. I myself had loved that black dress with the white bow and floating chiffon tie.

That night was a cascade of flashing cameras and TV reporters, microphones, and stupid questions designed to get me to gush about being number two. Too much of a crush to say a proper hello to the people who called to me from the crowd. And, underneath it all, satisfaction that I could grab my scholarship check and not have to perform the winner's duties. I was most grateful when the new queen served out her term without eloping or falling ill with mononucleosis, leaving me free to enjoy my first year in Chapel Hill.

I pause on the sidewalk, close my eyes, and conjure Chapel Hill. Lively bookstores, cafes glorious with spicy scents on a rainy day. Jazzed-up bulletin boards, art galleries, hand-lettered flyers stuck up on poles swimming with ideas about how to change the world. A rising tide of revolution in the air—civil rights, the women's movement, vegetarianism—all of it a million firing synapses from here. There, no one cared where I came from or how I got there, as long as I could latch onto the language of the moment. In those days, I was sure the swelling sea would sweep me to new horizons.

My eyelids crack open to the yellow-brick courthouse still squatting in the middle of the square, a buoy bobbing among the surrounding shops. I know the name of every shop owner and most of their kids. Their customers and *their* kids. I have read nearly every book in the county library in the courthouse basement and have a standing order for anything new. In the midst of this never-changing vista, one place always provided stimulating conversation. On a whim, I decide to make a right turn down College Street.

The *Democrat's* brownstone looms ahead. I stop in front of the clear expanse of glass to read faded galleys from the archives, mounted on wood and propped in the windows. A photo of Harry Truman, fists raised in victory: *Democrat gets it right!* Tall teenagers, elbows and knees akimbo, in a vertical pile: *Yellow Jackets Win State.* I blink at the next galley—the black and white gown, the grin and wave, the sparkling sash: *Eve takes first runner-up!* shouts the headline. These are the highlights of the past two decades?

Mr. Anderson, the quietly ironic *Toccoa County Democrat's* editor and owner, taught me, his cub reporter during my senior year, how to write succinct heads and pithy sentences, and how to look behind the quotes I was given for more story. He coined "Eve" as my pageant name. "Evie is too cute for a queen," he'd said, his bushy brows puckered over wire rims and a spare smile. My heart pings with sadness for him. Last I heard, he'd had another heart attack and the paper had been put up for sale. Someone else is gathering the news that plops on our doorstep every day.

I remind myself to send him a card, if the drugstore has a decent—Bells jangle behind me. Ashamed to be caught admiring my own clipping, I scoot down the pavement, halfway to the cross street before I realize that someone is calling my name.

"Evie? Eve!" I spin to face the music and wobble on a crack in the pavement. My one high school crush, Howard Pearson, holds open the door with one hand and waves me in with the other. "Want to come in and visit your old stomping ground?" That same boyish cowlick falls over his eyebrow.

I look down at my shoes, half expecting to find them mired in freshly laid tar. What to do now? Howard's huge chocolate mocha eyes always sent me someplace where I was unsure of my footing. We went out exactly once before he graduated, but what a date: I have that gorgeous orchid pressed into my high school annual. Dazed, I manage to step inside, onto the forest green carpet, without raising my face. "Well, maybe just for a moment. I have to get back to my mom."

One hand on my elbow, Howard guides me past the startled, steel-bouffant-haired receptionist while he inquires about my family. I chat politely about Dad's death and Mom's health, stealing quick glances as we walk. Yep, he looks fine. And he sounds genuinely sorry for our loss as he leads me into the office labeled "Publisher and Editor."

I skip backward to check the nameplate. Yes, Howard's name in brass.

He settles behind the desk and waves me to a trim Danish chair next to it. "Surprises me, too, every time I see it. It's temporary, though, till Mr. Anderson gets better and I start my next job." Squaring his clasped hands in front of him—ringless, I note—he fixes me with a look that makes me cross my legs. How can he affect me this way, after—well, a few men in college, and one or two after, but nothing serious?

"I haven't seen you since—" He clears his throat, giving me time to recollect.

I squeeze my eyes shut. "The petting zoo. Don't remind me." During my local "reign," I had been scheduled to show kids how to feed a goat at the Toccoa County Fair. Dressed for the job in jeans, flannel shirt, and a crown, I held a bottle to the smacking lips of a three-month-old kid and squatted by the side of a five-year-old admirer. We both looked up and smiled for the camera. Who should be behind the lens but my date for his senior prom? Too surprised to understand what he mumbled—something about filling in for a friend on his vacation—I froze, mid-crouch, and fell on my tush, knocking the goat to its butt while I scrambled to retrieve the goat's breakfast and my jeweled headpiece.

I return from my reverie to Howard's grin. Apparently, he still makes me fly out of myself. My fingers explore the smooth edges of the chair's upholstered seat.

He moderates his expression. The stapler on his desk comes in for careful scrutiny as he opens and closes its hinge. "Sure was great to see you again. Wish I hadn't had to leave so soon for my next year at school. We always seemed to have bad timing. I was lucky to get that assignment in Georgetown after senior year, but—" He puts down the stapler and spreads one hand to make the point. "Covering the big fishbowl, Congress, was a high school editor's dream. I wrote you."

"Yeah, well, two postcards do not a romance make." The trite syntax makes me wince.

Howard swivels his desk chair. Is he impatient? Should I go? I should go. His eyes remain locked on my face. He spreads the other hand, in full explanation mode. "Before I knew it, you were Miss Tallulah High, and it didn't seem right to expect you to wait for me, when every man you knew probably wanted to date you. Then you went on to bigger things—" His shrug indicates his helplessness before fate.

I brush my hands along the chair's metal arms. "Actually, I didn't date much in high school. Lethal combination: brains and a tiara. Had to advertise for a date to my own senior prom. Mr. Anderson ran it for me, as a joke."

Howard has a baritone laugh, rich and deep, like a cello. "I heard about that." He continues, chuckling. "Something about 'must be alert to lipstick on teeth.'"

"Actually, it worked. Five brave men applied, and the one I chose avoided stepping on my ball gown." Nerves scrape along my chest and score my throat. "Well, my mom...." I rise and head for the door.

Any thought of a quick escape melts as Howard murmurs to me around the glass. "Think we can put that bad timing jinx behind us?"

Yes! I want to scream. Instead, I deliver a stern talk to myself. Why start something here, now? You want to move. Come on, force the words out. "I ... have a lot to do. As soon as Mom is better, I'll be on my way back to graduate school. Then I hope I'll get a publishing job in New York. Besides, I have lots of papers to grade."

He parries my excuses. "You have to eat. You have school vacations. And recreation provides energy, did you know that?"

It takes five minutes more for him to wear me down. Okay, we'll do dinner.

Afterwards, I stand on the corner and swear. Damn. Damn. Damn. This I don't need: another reason to stay.

Late Saturday afternoon, I pull onto the roundabout, where encountering another car makes negotiating the steep curve by Vickery's Cafe a guessing game. Nobody here needs signs. Everybody knows that if you want to go to Elberton, you move into the right lane by Belk's. If Lavonia is your desire, you hug the lane nearest the Courthouse and continue on around until you reach the corner of College Street. If Beverly's old neighbor, Mrs. Beasley, is in the other car, you guess which way she is going and pray she remembers, too.

A right turn brings me into the café's side lot. I climb out and turn my back to lean against the car, waving at our version of the Courthouse Sages, who loll on stone benches in the building's shadows, their bright hat bands and varicolored suspenders distinct against the dormant azaleas. The heat has faded into a crisp pre-Hallowe'en balminess.

Howard pulls into the lot in his Karmann Ghia and parks at the far end, under a red-tinged maple. As he climbs out and starts walking toward me, that forelock of deep brown hair bobs in time with his long-legged stride. A tall, impossibly graceful, yet distracted, giraffe: hands in his pockets, eyes aimed toward the ground, no doubt re-writing leads and opening paragraphs in his head.

By now, our sixth date, we have a routine. Dinner together, then he returns to put the morning edition to bed. Later, he swings by and we go for a drive, during which furious kissing erupts at whatever scenic spot he hasn't managed to "show" me yet. We can't meet at his place, because leaving my car parked in front of his rented apartment over the *Democrat* office would have the school buzzing the next day. I can't take him to Mom's house. Frustration isn't the word for the desperation that has led me to bury, under the lipstick and tissues at the bottom of my purse, the diaphragm I had fitted in college. In case I get up enough courage to suggest a motel room halfway to Athens.

Meantime, there's been no indication Howard is leaving anytime soon, though Mr. Anderson is home from the hospital. Anyway, even if we manage to solve our privacy issues, where would our relationship, literally, be going? Watching Howard cross the restaurant lot, I take myself prisoner, locked away between walls that read "Grab him!" and "Run!" Holding onto the doorframe, I stand my ground as he advances.

He plants a kiss at the corner of my lips. "Hi, Orchid."

"Hi, Stub." His familiar smell, graham crackers and spicy cologne, overwhelms me. Bracing against the car, I smile back. "You free?"

He shakes his head. "Not yet. I'm waiting on a feed from the AP on that highway bill. Maybe later." His hand on my back, a squeeze on my waist. Tingling everywhere it counts. But is that a promise I hear?

I pretend I didn't notice. "Well, okay, but first—food! I'm starved."

"Right! Let's go put on the feedbag." His lame jokes hide the fact that he's really Superman. Which isn't lost on our hostess. "Madame Proprietor! How's the world of wine and roses?" Judy Vickery smiles sweetly at Howard. A little less broadly at me. I gamely return a grin, knowing she thinks I am crazy not to sweep him off to the altar this minute.

By the time our sauerbraten and beers come, he is in fine form. "Did you hear about Sue Denton starting a jazz dance class in the basement at First Baptist? She calls it Sanctified Movement." And he's off on stories that cross his desk, all reminding me that small town life has its ironies.

We're halfway through our meal when Judy wanders over. "Say, Eve, Sandy Hennessy was in the other day—well, she's Sandy Reeves now—and she asked me if I knew what happened to Beverly Tyndall. Do you two stay in touch?" Her big blue eyes blink at me, perfectly innocent. She has to know it's not a welcome question. And what the hell does Sandy want to know for? I flash again on her standing aside in the Quad while Rena made her utterly uncalled-for remarks and realize I am shredding my napkin under the table.

Howard is on his feet before I can react, handing me my purse from the table, slipping some bills into her hand, and pulling back my chair. "Judy, sorry, but I have to get back to the paper. Deadline, you know. See you later." And before I know it, we're through the tiled entryway and out into the nippy air. I didn't even get a chance to see her mouth fall open.

I take a deep breath before turning to Howard. "How did you know I wanted out of there?"

He smiles and puts his hand under my elbow, guiding me toward the parking lot. "For a teacher, you don't have much of a poker face. Listen, I have a nice bottle of Italian wine in the office fridge. You could tell me about your friend." He pauses, and I feel him gazing at me.

I stall, examining the maple leaves turning orange overhead. Am I ready to share my biggest heartaches? Where would I start?

"Or not," Howard adds, steering me toward my car.

I stop with a scrunch of gravel and try not to frown at him. That would indicate I am not pleased. And I am very pleased, I discover, underneath my panic. My choice. No pressure. And I'm curious. "Where did you get Italian wine in Tallulah Falls?"

He grins now and shrugs, mopping the hair from his brow. "The Wine Connoisseur mail-order club. One of my vices."

Satisfied, I nod. "Wow. Okay." I stir the gravel with the toe of my navy leather pump. "So, how about around nine—"

He interrupts me by reaching out to take me in his arms, in the middle of the parking lot, in full view of the sages and diners leaving the restaurant. It takes me a moment to realize that the couple staring as they pass are my dentist and his wife. "Dr. Harrison, hi, Mrs. Harrison, hello. Hope you had a great dinner." They wave, big smiles on both their faces. I speak into Howard's collar. "What are you doing?" I try not to hiss, because, well, this feels wonderful.

Howard whispers back, "You know, if you leave your car in Jim's Garage lot next door, you could always say it was there overnight for some work. In case anyone brings it up." He plants a light kiss on my neck. "I'll only be a few minutes with that story."

"Yes." A one word answer is all I can manage. His steps crunch away from me, punctuating the whirling tango in my mind. No need to worry any more about who's going to make the first move. I duck into the Barracuda and twist the key in the switch. The engine knocks into rhythm. The side exit provides a quicker getaway.

As I round the corner from the garage, Howard is waiting for me in the doorway. He waves me in, plants a kiss on my nose, then disappears into the back room. Ten minutes later, we are tromping up the back steps to his apartment, which is cool and dark. I look around at the comfortable leather furniture and a collection of hardbound books in the two bookcases that line the back wall. A Scott Fitzgerald fan. Figures. I take three sips from the glass he hands me. Crisp, juniper-flavored.

Howard reaches over and gently disentangles the strap of my pocketbook. He lays the purse on the coffee table, leads me to the sofa, and takes my hand, leaning back so he can see my face. "Do you mind if I ask, how did you make the choice to be a beauty queen?" His gaze is direct. I'm not a prize he's won. Or an object of disapproval. I am flummoxed. He lifts my fingers to his lips. "You always remind me of a hummingbird. Small. Delicate. And...." He pauses, pupils darting in a search for words.

"Gaudy?" I throw out the suggestion, hoping to make him laugh. He does, a deep, chesty rumble. Good. I don't feel like an example of graceful womanhood tonight.

"Dignified, that's the word I'm looking for. You never seemed to be all that into yourself. Maybe I'm off base." He sits up, folding his long arms at the elbow, resting them on his knees so he can prop his chin in the hand that isn't holding mine. "Beauty queens aren't necessarily vain, I know, but—"

"No." Smoothing my skirt over my knees makes ripples of fabric across my thighs. I have never tried to explain this to anyone before, not even to my parents, who stood back and let me take all the limelight I wanted. I open my mouth, not at all sure what will come out. "When Beverly left, I needed something different to be. I mean ... she is the first person I remember, after my parents and my brother, and we kind of fell into certain roles, you know? She was the social butterfly, always flitting around—"

"A blur in the hallways. And at pep rallies. That's what I remember about her." His smile encourages me.

"Yeah, a whirlwind, really. She was good at having fun. I was— well, 'bookish,' that's what my Aunt Tally calls me. I felt awkward around people my own age." I force my tongue to shape words. "After the ... attack, people—grown-ups, really—asked lots of questions, what happened, what was she wearing, and so on. They thought I should know. Kids mostly left me alone, talked behind my back, but I knew they were thinking the same thing, that she asked for it, and I knew what she'd been up to." I told him briefly about Rena exulting in Beverly's humiliation, and how Sandy had stood by and let her play to the gawkers around me. I wanted no part of anyone who had taken part in that drama, then or now. "The thing was, I didn't know what was going on with Beverly then. We had quarreled right before that, and things weren't the same. She left suddenly, and I haven't really talked to her since. A few awkward phone conversations...."

A soft, warm sensation floods my right palm. I look down. Howard's big, warm paw encases mine. It almost makes me swallow my story, but I persist. It's now or never. Maybe I need to say this.

"So there I was, alone. You know how high school is. You have to have some ... facade, so people feel like they have you slotted. Otherwise, they pick at you. And what did I have, besides a stack of books to hide behind? It didn't feel like enough camouflage, so—" I am floundering now, because I don't want to admit how much enmity there was in my decision. What if he thinks less of me? I try to pick my next words with great care. "I thought, what other kind of mask is there that no one pries behind? You can be popular, or a leader—both of those took more strength than I thought I had—or you can be...." I stop. It all sounds so ugly to me now.

"A beauty queen. Because that's something people value, but they don't expect to get too close to one." His words take my breath away.

I can't even look at him. Instead, I curl my fingers around his. All I can manage is a whisper. "Was that terrible of me? I needed some sort of disguise till I could pull myself together."

He leans back, still holding my hand. "It's never wrong to defend yourself." He smiles. "I'm Jewish. We're born in a defensive posture."

"Yes, but—" The half-drawn curtains behind Howard reveal snowflakes: sprinkles, a mere dusting, but they remind me what it felt like to be buried under a torrent of lies, and half-truths, and agony. My throat burns from squelching tears. I can't lay all that before him, not yet. "I think it made me kind of numb, so—well, it was a relief to focus on how I looked, what I wore, how I walked and talked. Putting one foot in front of the other saved me from thinking about terrible things. And then Beverly's aunt, Mary Alice, my brother's fiancée, broke off their engagement. I loved her, too. It felt like I had nothing left, as if—"

He fills in for me. "As if the rug had been pulled out from under you, I imagine." Slowly, he reels me into his arms, where I snuggle into the hollow of his throat. I realize I've only scratched the surface. The bigger shocks—what happened to Beverly's mother and my grandmother—were the hardest to bear, and they're too much to share so soon. My lips feel like a bubble about to burst. *Not telling everything you know isn't the same as telling a lie*, Aunt Tally had said. But there's one more thing he has a right to hear. I push myself upright and look at him. Better to know now if he's going to reject me. "If we're going to keep this up, you deserve to know all my secrets."

He sits forward so that his elbows are on his knees again. "And then we can start on my family, if you like." He takes my hand again, kisses each finger separately, then lifts me to my feet. "It's not like we have to tell everything tonight, though."

I reach into my pocket for a tissue. "No, but there's one more thing I need to say. My grandmother—"

"Was Roma. I know."

Now he has thunderclapped me into silence. He runs his hand through my tangled hair, touches my cheek, and grins at my astonishment. "My father knew her. She used to come into the store when he was a boy. Always brought him something. A piece of gingerbread tied up in cheesecloth. A truck she had made from baked dough and painted with egg dye for him. She was small and delicate and ... she reminded him of a lovely bird, he said. One day when she caught some boys teasing him and calling him names, she bent close and whispered to him, 'It's okay. I'm an outcast, too. I'm a Gypsy.' He was a little in love with her, I think."

Those deep pools of brown are centered by a twinkle that makes me think of a star's reflection in a stream. "I know how he felt." He takes the wine glass out of my hand, sets it on the table, and strokes my arm from the wrist to the lace that edges the short sleeve of my blouse. His finger feels like a thin trickle of water quenching my parched skin as he traces a path from my shoulder across to my collarbone. He whispers in my ear, "I've waited years to touch you there. I'd wait years to do it again, if I had to." He slides both arms around my waist and stops me from talking in the best possible way.

૮ᑐᕪᧁᑐᕪ૭ ૭

The week of my birthday brings a squall that drives icy rain across the streets in sheets. Unused to heavy clothing, we can't find hats or gloves, and so walk quickly, heads down, anxious to shelter behind the newspaper's heavy oak doors. Before I can dash inside, Howard grabs my hands from my coat pockets, his face flushed with emotion. "I want to talk to you."

Oh, no, I think, he isn't going to—What will I say?

He lets go of my nearly frozen fingers long enough to produce a shiny key on a silver ring. "Mr. Anderson made me an offer I couldn't refuse. I bought the building. And the paper."

One flake would have knocked me down. Dizzily, I follow him inside. My smile feels like a drum skin stretched nearly to breaking. "I didn't think young reporters made that kind of money." What I was thinking was, *how will I ever leave now?*

He gestures toward the bristly mat at the door. "Welcome home," it says. "A gift from my Mom. My parents helped. And Mr. Anderson, like I said, made me an offer I couldn't refuse."

It takes everything I have to pull off a dazzling smile. "Now I understand why you kept talking about that new press. Did you see it while you were in Atlanta?" His answer rolls over me like mist, unheard. I focus on getting my feet to move forward.

"Take your coat?"

"What? Oh, yes." I fumble my way out of the sleeves, watching our shadows cast against the wall by one small lamp across the room.

"It needs some brightening in here. I keep meaning to. ..." My eyes light on the round walnut table, where a huge vase of Daybreak lilies and Sunrise roses glimmer in the near-dark. My favorites.

Howard flicks on a sconce behind them so that the flowers blaze into flame. His arms steal around my waist from behind as he rests his head in the crook of my shoulder. I am always amazed how he manages to bend his tall frame to my height.

"Wherever you are is bright enough for me. Happy Birthday." He kisses my nape.

Does he mean that? I wonder as he grabs me by the hand and leads me toward the bedroom. No need to turn on the light in here. Candles blaze in every corner.

He kisses me hard enough to rattle my rib cage. Shit, I think. Damn him to everlasting fire.

༄

About midnight, I roll the Barracuda into the yard and step as quietly as I can onto the porch. I'm almost to the swing, when I realize Aunt Tally is there, smoking a cigarette.

"Where's your car?" Even as I ask, I spot her Cadillac across the street.

She flicks ashes, holding the cigarette away from me, and pats the seat beside her. "Good to have your man home, hm?"

I step over a roasting pan at her feet. "Aunt Vinnie made dinner?"

"Pork roast."

My mind readily retrieves the scent of Aunt Vinnie's spicy roast stewed with peppers, onions, ginger, and eggplant. I sit down, gingerly. "I don't know if he's my man, exactly."

Tally pokes me in the ribs. "What have you been doing for the last two hours, if he's not your man?"

I attempt to give her the evil eye, but it isn't very effective in the dark. I settle for a lame joke. "Planning to live on the Left Bank and have platonic affairs with men who demand nothing of me."

Aunt Tally harrumphs. "If men don't demand anything of you, you can't count on much from them, if you ask me. Besides, how long do you expect him to wait?"

I huff under the weight of trying to explain. "Howard wants to live here. I want to live in a city that has at least two bookstores. Maybe it's as simple as that." An inadequate explanation, but as much as I can round up. My insides feel bruised, like I've been holding back an army.

Tally sucks her teeth to let me know what she thinks of my explanation. I try again. "My choices here are to be a former beauty queen, getting older and losing my looks—" An even louder explosion escapes from Tally, but annoyance makes me talk over her. "Or I can be the best little English teacher in a town under 5000 in population. I'd like to be valued for something besides my ability to walk in high heels and grade tests."

How can I expect Aunt Tally to understand? She's lived in Tallulah Falls her whole life. "Well." She rises and scoops up the clean pan. "One can either be a big duck in a small pond or a small duck in a big pond, Sweetie. Your choice. Toodle-loo."

While I watch her get into her car and pull away, I consider that. Losing myself in some big sea of humanity might be exactly what I need.

Eve, Fall, 1972: Lessons

Laverne, the speech and theatre teacher, has rooked me into cuing the students who are trying out for parts in the fall play, *Love's Labours Lost*. To my surprise, Laverne has done an excellent job of adapting the play to high school tastes. She stripped out the more obscure wordplay and some of the subplots, but left lots of nonspeaking roles for the more awkward teens, who just want to hang with the cool kids. I admire her economy in the script she's handed me—only 80 pages.

The sun stabs horizontally across the auditorium through the clerestory windows. Students strut across the stage, reading bits of dialogue and trying to find just enough passion to make the grade, without becoming targets to the stage crew. "Ignore them. If they had the guts, they'd be trying out, too, not hiding back stage, making wisecracks." Laverne, her Cleopatra cut swinging over one eye, urges on one of the baseball players, who does a passable job as Costard, despite his friends' muffled catcalls from the wings.

Everyone, including me, is surprised when Kathy reads for Jaquenetta, the country wench. We're all blown away by her swinging hips and lusty laughter.

"Who knew Kathy could strut her stuff like that?" the Jock mutters to his friends.

It's Lacey's turn, and she takes Rosaline's part, toning down her walk and her hair-tossing enough to be a respectable lady-in-waiting of the sixteenth century. It's like she and Kathy have decided to switch real-life roles for the play's duration.

While the teachers who will decide on the casting huddle in back of the hall, I hang on the stage with the clumps of would-be actors. Kids needle each other with the usual rumors and innuendoes about who's with whom, who can't get a date, whose clothes are too tight, too loose, or too outdated.

A girl from my sophomore lit class, her bright hair blazing in the klieg lights, distracts the group. "Miss Gates, do that wave thing." Almost everybody else picks it up. "Come on! Please!"

I am hungry, and I hate revisiting pageant days, but there's no sign of an end to the gesturing and audible whispers from the back of the auditorium. On the stage, anarchy looms close. So I pop up from my seat on a half-wall at stage left and hit my mark— twisting and turning my cupped hand, exaggerating a long stride as if hampered by an unmanageable train, a ditsy smile plastered on my face. The kids chuckle, then some guffaw, and a ballplayer is on his feet, pretending to stomp on my imaginary skirts.

For once, I am not at all concerned about maintaining my authority. We are loose and finding new embellishments, students competing to offer their own silly versions of stage manners, when I catch sight of a couple deep in the shadows at stage right. Their bodies are inches apart. Groping each other? No. Something strikes me as odd. I hand Lacey my imaginary scepter and tiara. She swishes across the stage as I exit.

Steve and Kathy are so preoccupied they don't hear me approach. I halt three steps away and clear my throat. In the silence that follows, there's a muffled sob. Steve snaps to attention and tries to shield Kathy with his body as she puts her hand across her mouth, wet eyes blazing at me over her clenched fingers. I am stunned. These two, a couple? Usually, I know who is going with whom—it's part of my job—but this pairing takes me by surprise. Kathy is a mouse. Steve, very self-confident. And Kathy and her mom, a divorcée who struggles to hang on to a waitress job, are not exactly in the Ames's league at the Country Club.

Everything about their body language says I've interrupted something serious. A quarrel, a make-out session gone awry, or something else?

First rule of discipline: break up the conspirators. "Steve, why don't you see if the late activity bus is in the circle yet?" He shoots a silent question at Kathy. She replies with a nod. He hesitates, still, but his habit of obedience kicks in. He stalks off toward the front doors.

Kathy straightens her downturned mouth into a more neutral expression and shutters her blue eyes. I'm about to turn away, my mission of preventing fraternization during school hours complete, but I recall that she told me in an essay that I'm her favorite teacher. And she let Steve leave us alone. Maybe this is as close an invitation to talk as her pride will allow.

I beckon to her. "Let's go back to the dressing room, shall we?" With a hand on her shoulder, I lead the way to the drafty back room, wave her inside, and peer into her face. "Did you two have a bad spat?"

Kathy bobs her head, but glances to the left and down instead of looking at me. After five years of teaching, I'm not the innocent I used to be. She's lying. I decide to pry a bit further. "How long have you been going together?"

Kathy still doesn't look at me. "Since last summer." Resembling a mouse tortured by a cat, she shoots me another desperate look. Does she want my help, or not?

"Oh, really? I hadn't heard that through the grapevine." We both know there's no way the Class President's choice would go unremarked by the gossips who sit dead center in the cafeteria every day, watching all entrances and exits for fodder. If they're an item, it's under wraps.

Kathy's teeth go to town on her lower lip. She looks everywhere but at me. Still, she hangs on for one final gambit. "His folks don't like my mom." This is believable, for more than economic reasons.

I met Mrs. Waters last year on College night. She breathed bourbon into my face and pumped my hand, sputtering her thanks while I praised her daughter, then bolted from the room. On my way home, I spotted Kathy turning down the street where she lives, on foot, alone. After that, anytime I've required a parent's signature on test scores, I've ignored the fact that the name on Kathy's paper matches her own neatly looped handwriting. Not a problem, with her usual grades. Suddenly I remember that I wanted to ask Kathy about her test score. Now doesn't seem the time.

The girl who holds her mom at arms' length doesn't strike me as likely to go bonkers if Steve's parents don't cotton to her mom. Unless—Georgia has recently changed its marriage laws so that people under eighteen have to get their parent's permission to marry. I lean forward and rest my arms on my knees. "You're pretty young to be worried about your parents meeting. What's the rush?" I fix her with a steady eye and watch her poise crumble like an underdone cake. Her sobs break with a force that rains snot mixed with tears down her face.

I fish a tissue from my pocket and hand it to her. Her shoulders are shaking so hard I move to put my arm around her. Her head burrows into my collarbone. "Miss Gates, I'm pregnant."

My breath catches in my throat. "So have you two told your parents?" I expect a long story about their reactions, but Kathy says nothing. Putting my hands gently on her shoulders, I move her back so I can see her eyes. They are huge, bright, and soaked with tears. "Have you?"

She turns away from me. Her voice is soft, but clear. "I don't want to have the baby, and I don't want to get married." She flinches a little. Expecting blows?

"Why not?" I know the words are a mistake as soon as they leave my mouth.

Kathy flashes the full force of those blue eyes. "That's what everybody says—my mom, my friends—why don't you marry Steve? He'll be rich, a good provider.'" Her fists clench as she breaks away from me. "But it's me who'll take care of the baby. Well, I've been taking care of my mom and my little brother all my life, and for once I want to take care of myself." She lifts her chin, challenging me. "I'm going to college and I'm going to be a scientist. I'll spend my time in a lab, where it's quiet, and nobody has any reason to bother me, and come home to my own house where I can do what I want to do. If I'm lonely, I'll get a cat!"

I stand, too, and spread my hand to reason with her. "Well, of course, you have a future. But what are you planning to do about the baby? You can't just wish it away."

Wasn't that exactly what I'd hoped for Beverly, that wishing would make the pregnancy go away? The postcard flashes through my eyes: *Beverly had a baby girl. All fine. Her name's Antoinette. Love, Mary Alice.* All those months of wondering how she could bear to give birth to her rapist's baby. This is Kathy, I admonish myself. She hasn't been raped.

I squint to make the girl in front of me come into focus, knowing I will lose her if I don't show her respect. "Will you go away to have it?"

She opens and closes her hand, and takes a step toward the door. "Miss Gates, it's best you not know what I'm going to do."

Her answer makes me weak in the knees. "Kathy, don't do anything rash. There are dangers—please tell me you're not going to some back alley doctor." Again, I bat away memories: *There's something you can do about it if your family has money.* How naïve we were! And Kathy's Mom doesn't have a dime.

She opens the door and tilts her chin. Defiant.

"Kathy!" Anxiety makes my voice squeak a pitch higher. I try to drop it down a tone. "Promise me you won't do anything until we talk again."

She squints. "You'll tell. My mom, or maybe the principal. They'll make me leave school."

"Did I tell your mom you got a 75 on that quiz?" I know we're both seeing that rare low grade, and next to it, the fake signature.

Kathy nods her head. "Okay. But I'm not going to change my mind. And don't worry. I can't do anything until I save more money."

My hands relax the grip they've had on one another, and I realize I have nail marks in my palms. "Okay. How about we talk after school on Friday?" I'm calculating if I'll have a career by Friday, if word gets out what we've talked about. Our principal has made it clear that all family problems should be referred to counselors, immediately. But I can't live with the chance she won't talk to a counselor. At least, she's talking to me.

With a quick jerk of the door and an almost-smile, she's gone. I sit down and breathe my way back to calm, until I hear Laverne's voice onstage.

When I make my way to the footlights, Steve is there, on the edge of the crowd. Kathy's not in sight. He doesn't even give me a brief inspection. Did Kathy tell him our deal? From the way he's waiting patiently for the role announcements, his hands resting lightly on his knees, I'm guessing she hasn't even told him what she plans.

I settle onto the half-wall, breathing like I've just run a marathon in sprints. Meantime, my teacher voice is taking me to task. *What the hell do you think you're doing, letting a student decide something so dangerous without telling the principal?* Some other voice, one I'm just barely acquainted with, answers: *I'm keeping a trust, so she has someone to lean on.*

The group begins to scatter. I haven't heard a single name attached to a role. But I can see by who's happy, who's dejected, which students got the part they wanted. Laverne stands at the door to the auditorium with her arm around a sobbing student's shoulder. Putting a smile on my face, I grab the nearest sad kid and prepare to console.

❧

At home, I head straight to my room with a damp washcloth clamped to my forehead. Aunt Tally's high heels clomp onto the porch, and soon her voice and Mom's mingle from the porch swing. I get up and go to the phone in the hall.

When I tell Howard about "my student"—deleting her name— his deep voice is tinged with caution. "That's illegal in the state of Georgia." I clamp the receiver tighter to my left ear, keeping the other ear open for any breaks in the chatter outside the door.

"What is—having an illegal abortion, or knowing about it, but not reporting it?" It's hard to keep from whispering. For just a moment, I hate Howard for being a man, able to walk away from this dilemma, if he chooses.

"Well, having an abortion isn't illegal. Performing it is. The School Board might fire a teacher who kept one secret, but they'd have to prove you knew about it."

"Thank you, Mr. Newsman. Am I being interviewed for the next edition?"

Howard doesn't like it when I challenge his impartial reporter line. "If I were interviewing you, I'd want to know her name. Anyway, the abortion situation is about to change. Maybe. And, besides, I want to know if you can go to the Chamber dinner with–"

"You mean that Supreme Court decision? What's it called—Roe something? About overturning the state laws restricting abortions. Did they decide?" My question cuts across his invitation.

"If they did, don't you think I'd put it right there on the 'National News' page? Even if it did offend the sensibilities of the local clergy. No, the Court heard the arguments last month. They'll decide sometime early next year."

A memory worms its way into my worries: a World Lit classmate sliding numbly into her usual seat at our table in the cafeteria, tear tracks on her face, voice shaking as she describes finding her roommate on the hall bathroom floor, pools of blood spreading to the shower drain. "I knew a girl in college who had an illegal abortion."

"What happened?"

"She died." My tongue circles my mouth, trying to find moisture enough to speak. "The next evening, my own resident advisor, this tall, pale lady with a scratchy voice, called all the girls in my dorm into the downstairs parlor. 'There will be no gossip about this, none! Anyone who speaks of it will be suspended. We want no repeats of this shameful behavior! Does everyone understand? Lasciviousness will not be tolerated by the State of North Carolina!'" Until now, I hadn't realized how mad I'd been. Lascivious? Word was, she'd been cornered at a party by one of the football players.

Howard's gentle, "Evie, you still there?" patters through the phone line. I shake my shoulders to focus my thoughts.

"Sure. No matter what, the Court's timeline will be too late for my student. If she goes to one of those back alley 'doctors,' who knows if they'll give her antibiotics to avoid infection, or use sterilized instruments instead of rusty scalpels?"

"It may be someone's aunt with her knitting needles." Howard made a guttural noise. "Sometimes we get word about a death at the hospital in Anderson and in the process of checking it out we learn the woman died from a uterine infection. Doctors won't go on the record about a specific case, but they tell horror stories about what happens. Some have colleagues up North they'll refer women to."

I twirl a strand of hair, yanking tight enough to wince, remembering Emily Glassinger, the girl in my brother's class who'd gotten an operation. At college I'd heard about the flyers advertising legal abortion clinics in Greenwich Village ladies' rooms. "My student's mom can't spare a thousand dollars—or whatever it costs to get a doctor's help up North."

Howard's baritone softens even more. "Eve, do you think maybe this isn't a problem you can resolve? Isn't there someone else you can refer her to?"

"Like who? Her mom won't be much help."

"You could refer her to the school counselor."

My turn to snort. "Old Man Taylor? What help would he be?" I try to picture the counselor's brown-spotted hands and squinty eyes while he listens to Kathy's tale of woe. My imagination can't even get her through his door.

"Losing your job won't make things better for the girl, either. If there's anything the School Board hates, it's any scandal that smacks of sex."

He's right, and I know it. "Well, I'm going to talk to the girl on Friday. If I think she's about to do something dangerous, I'll talk to the principal. But I'm not going to rat her out if I can find another way. It would be nice if adults could be less scandalized and more helpful."

Howard clears his throat. "Listen, I don't disagree."

I change the subject before I obsess again about why Mary Alice didn't help Beverly find a doctor. "Are you covering the School Board tonight?"

We chat for a few more minutes. Afterwards, I step outside to check on the coughing fit I heard from Mom's end of the swing. She drops her hand from her mouth as if I've caught her doing something wrong and asks about my phone call.

My aunt shakes her bright red curls at my answer. "Girl, you better grab that man and get on down the aisle. He's the sweetest fellow I ever met. You won't do better."

"I'm not looking for better, Aunt Tally." I perch on the end of a rocker, like a bird unsure of its territory.

"Still looking for a bigger pond?"

I trade glances with Mom and stand. "I think I'll take a nap before dinner."

I hear Tally say, "I thought she woke up a few minutes ago," while I flee to my room.

Eve, 1972: The Fruit of Queens

Mom hands me the basket of wet clothes and grabs the clothespins from their hook by the back door. I open the screen and wait for her to limp through. We negotiate one step at a time down to the yard area nearest the garage, where the clothesline swings between two crabapples. She has refused all offers from my brother and me to buy her a dryer to go with the washer we gave her last Christmas. I plop the basket down atop a few blades of crabgrass, lift and hang a dripping sheet, while Mom pins.

We're nearly finished hanging the second load when she says, "You've been nervous as a cat lately, Evie. What's gotten into you?" She's never called me "Eve."

I tell her about Kathy's dilemma, leaving out her name and the part where her plight makes me think of Beverly. "She didn't show up to talk to me last Friday. She promised she would." Mom's thoughtful expression probably means she hasn't missed the link. She nods while I wind through the tale, but offers no advice. I hand her the last pillowcase, which she pins. Then I help her back up the steps. She speaks as we're standing again in the kitchen. "You feel like taking a ride?"

"Sure. Where to?"

"You drive, I'll lead." She grabs her purse from the hall table and hands me my shoulder bag. "Don't forget to lock the doors." By the time I've locked both doors, she is sitting on the warm plastic seat covers, waiting for me. "Head out to the old hospital." She points the way.

We pass Beverly's country grammar school and the Tyndall house with no comment, though I cut my eyes to see if the Chinaberry still stands in the back yard. It's there. A child's Big Wheel rests in the front, its plastic tire aimed to the sky. I press my shoulders into the seat. This is not making me less grumpy. The persimmon trees loom.

"Mom, where are we going?" I manage not to sound pissed off, but can't keep a warning tone out of my voice.

Mom raises her finger to point again. "Turn here."

I slow to a crawl. Ancient oaks touch hands over ruts overgrown with jimson weed. A tangle of honeysuckle and bittersweet weighs down fences on either side.

"Aaron Applewhite still uses this path to get his bales back there. Your car should be okay." Mom sits straight in the seat, thin hands holding her purse squarely in her lap.

Surprisingly, we bounce only once or twice over the deepest ruts before I see a paved highway ahead. I look left and right and recognize the road to the Burnetts' old place. "That way is the store where Dad used to buy me Cokes and peanuts when we went to visit Granny."

Mom nods. "Redding's, it used to be. It's called Wriggly Pig or some such now." I smile at her refusal to learn new names for things. "Take that drive."

"What drive?" I peer through the vines and finally see another rutted road of sorts, sharing with the cowpath an angled entry from the pavement. My muffler dings a few times on rocks, but nothing falls off. Through a copse of turkey oaks, blazing like grouped orange flags, a roof appears. Suddenly, I know where I am. "Gramma's house?" I feel like a kid taken to see Santa Claus. "Why are you showing me now?"

"Seems like you're ready to listen." Mom refolds her hands in her lap and leaves me to decipher her cryptic comment. I don't have a clue what she means, but, then, she's always a mystery to me.

I drive on and stop beside a neglected cottage. The porch tacked on to the back appears surprisingly sound, its thick beams unbowed, though the roof has lost some shingles and its floor is littered with wind-strewn piles of leaves. In fact, the house itself is not that bad, hewn logs showing underneath a mostly-missing layer of splotchy plaster.

The passenger door groans and Mom is out, placing her walking stick carefully on the mud humps in the wasted yard. I follow her. She barely pauses to look at the house, moves on into the back yard. To the left lingers a barn with its roof caved in several places and a tool shed in barely better shape. The east side of the porch opens onto some kind of walk, its stones partially hidden under another layer of leaves, sticks, and one or two fallen birds' nests. I look overhead at the eaves. Yes, there are the telltale wisps of reeds and feathers. Doves, or maybe swallows.

A few minutes' examination reveals the outline of a garden. I can see a gap-toothed, rusty wire fence, a gate made of one-by-twos knocked aside and missing its top plank. Inside and outside the fence, an invasion has erased the planted patterns: mimosa, with its long dry pods, and a dense shrub layer of autumn olives, leaves upturned to reveal silvery undersides. A dozen kinds of ferns have migrated under the huge oaks. Tallow trees add their heart-shaped, orange leaves to the mix. Dangling in various places over fence, shrubs and vines, is the most beautiful invader of all: wisteria, dripping lavender tendrils, gorgeous as an Impressionist's brushwork.

Mom limps to the gate, steps over, and swipes aside the piles of weeds. There, in small patches, green and abundant, I see a wheel-shaped bed of mint contained by brick, and other herbs less familiar, each set apart by stone or clay. One patch of fern-shaped leaves—

rosemary? No, not rosemary—has been circled with river stones. My mother cups a frond, then rises and pins me with her deep-pooled eyes. "Your grandmother, you know, was an herbalist. She made tonics and medicines for everybody hereabouts."

I cock my head to access the memories. "You told me she was a midwife."

Mom bobs her head. "Yes, that, too, later on. She began healing folks before Doc Evans and Dr. Nettie came." She stares over the lilacs as if expecting to see someone round their curve and holds her hand out for me to grasp. "Let's go to the orchard."

I'm about to make for the car when Mom pulls my arm. "This way."

She starts up the hill. A quick calculation of our position informs me that the orchard must be on the other side. Haphazard swatches of evergreens, maples, and heavy brush stand between it and us.

"I hope you recognize where you're going. There might be snakes."

My mother pulls her sweater closer around her and tosses her head at the sky. "They'll be slowing down by now in the cool weather. You'll be faster than they are."

"Yes, but I can't carry you."

I intend a joke, but Mom twists her neck to take in my face. "Honey, it doesn't matter so much about me any more. Save yourself."

A chill unzips my spine. Never has my mother spoken of her own death, not even in the hospital with tubes crawling from her nose and arms. I peer into her face for some familiar toughness. She digs her stick into the hill and begins to climb.

The terrain is much steeper than it looked from below. It takes us minutes to mount the knoll to a point where we can look down, and when we do, I am surprised by the extent of the plantings. Far down below, there are the familiar writhing persimmons, backed by apples trees with their broad open reach. Higher on the slope, peaches curve across the mid-section of the hill, mixed with cherries in a diagonal weave. At the very top, pines crest the rise, guarding the lot. On this side of the slope, thick evergreens grow in a semi-circle, almost like a formal garden, though knee-deep in under-brushed ferns and fleshy weeds.

Mom struggles to the center of the firs' arc without letting go of my arm. She uses her cane like a scythe, releasing rustlings and ripples in the tall grass as small animals flee to safety. In one slurring rush, a family of partridges scurries away from her swinging stick. "Snakes appreciate a little warning that you're coming," she explains.

A curious bird, redheaded and blue-chested, flits to a teetering reed and flicks her head from side to side to watch our movements. Mom stops and observes the creature. "Barn swallow. Your nest is nearby, no doubt." The bird calls a quick *su-seer*, but doesn't budge, though Mom swishes ever closer. She lets go of my arm and parts the brush near the center of the arc.

"Mom, careful. What if there's a skunk or something? What is it you're—"

"Ahh!" Glee overtakes her face. "Some survived!" She breathes heavily from the exertion, but draws me close to examine what she's found. I gaze past sweeping balsam branches, expecting to see a flower, or perhaps a tall herb she remembers from long ago. Instead, I'm shocked to see long graceful branches bearing oblong leaves and about a dozen roundish red fruits with nubby ends, glowing against the deep shadows under the firs, like red lanterns in a circle of light. Their color is so deep, so perfectly flame-like, I am drawn to touch one. It is firm, but plush, as if you could palm the color red.

I inhale a scent at once fruity and tart. There's something intoxicating about it: Such lushness would surely lead to sleep. "What is it?"

My mother reaches into the sun-speckled shade and snaps off a globe, raising it to my nose. "Pomegranate. Your grandmother called it 'the fruit of queens.' Come on, let's go down and cut it." She leads the way back down the hill to the porch.

We sit on a lower step and Mom takes out of her pocket the little knife she used for years to cut threads in the mill. Scoring three deep cuts from stem to crown, she breaks the fruit open and hands it to me wrapped in her handkerchief.

Inside, large sacs of seeds cluster between strings of pinkish pulp. The seeds themselves are the attraction: every one is a slick promise of sweetness, a juicy kiss. Mom nods and I lift one to my lips. "Umm! Where have you been hiding these?"

She jerks her head toward the hill. "They don't grow just anywhere. Need protection from the frost and too much rain. My mama experimented for years before she found that spot, sheltered by the firs, but in their own little meadow where they can soak up the sun. I didn't think there'd be any left. But I hoped." She fixes me with a look that says I should know what she means.

I don't. I'm too busy slurping the wet seeds from their transparent bags.

"It's a good thing you're not trying to get pregnant."

I stop and look at the globs of seeds on my lap. "You mean—" I switch my eyes to my mother's face.

"You ever notice that Tally, Vinnie and I are all around three years apart? None of that stair-stepping you see in lots of families. And Paul, he came along when I was thirteen and little Tally was almost seven. Mama decided she'd try once more to give my Papa the son he wanted." She speaks her next line to the trees. "That's what killed her, trying to give him a son."

Once more, I gauge how many questions are too many for my mother. Today, she seems ready to talk, so I chance it. "What was she like? You told me some of what happened, but not much about her."

She fishes inside her blouse and brings out the oval locket I haven't seen in years, snaps it open to reveal two portraits. My grandfather still looks mild, slightly surprised. Today, I note a bit of Aunt Tally in his light-colored eyes. What a world of difference from my grandmother.

Her dramatic dark eyes and glossy hair sweep into you, pose some question you are inclined to answer.

Wit-witt sounds a bird, startling me into looking overhead. A twittering and rustling under the eaves says the barn swallow has returned home. I peer back down at the sepia photograph.

"She's like you, don't you think?" Mom pats my hair in its swingy bob.

"Prettier," I say. I feel the raised etching on its cover and turn it over to examine the design. "Why, it's—" I raise my eyes in astonishment.

Mom smiles and reaches for the locket, lifts its chain over her head, and lets it drop to her breast, not bothering to tuck it away. "Yes, pomegranates. She used to say all women are queens, with or without kingdoms." Her chin points toward the trees. Now I can see them, gleaming from the edges of the firs on the slope. "My Aunt Juba brought my grandmother cuttings from a Spanish romni she knew. Pomegranates grow wild in Spain, but they come from the Mideast. Persia, perhaps, where Queen Esther came from. You remember your Bible stories." She flashes me an amused look, no doubt counting my many excuses for skipping church. She is quiet for another moment as she smoothes her hand over the porch railing. "I guess the trees had grown too tall to bring in the wagon, like they did the young persimmon trees, so she brought cuttings, instead. What we have there on the hill are grown from suckers. Don't know if they'll make another winter."

I want nothing so much as to save those trees. Except to know more about my grandmother. "They called Grandmother Eve, like me, didn't they?"

Mom nods, licks her lips and brings her arms across her chest. I ask if she is cold. She shakes her head, an emphatic no. "I thought to name you Eve, but the preachers carry on so about Eve and original sin. My father said some preachers like to make everybody feel so sinful the human race might as well quit. Thanks to Eve, we kept going. I thought Evalyn fit better with Evangeline, anyway." She twists her head and hangs her shrewd eyes on my face. "My mother was brave, like you, when you want to be. She used that fruit for other things, too."

I look deep into my mother's eyes and see something I have missed there: a challenge. All these years, has she waited for me to tell her who I am? "Do you mean you can stop a pregnancy with this?" I lift one section of the pomegranate and watch its juice run down to my elbow like a thin trickle of blood.

"She used another part for that, not the seeds. It's dangerous. It can kill you if you take too much." Mom reaches inside the pocket of her cardigan and retrieves a handkerchief, handing it to me. "Pomegranate juice will stain."

"Mom, are you telling me to—" I watch her with confusion as I dab at the purple stains on my arm. Will it work, I wonder? I imagine handing Kathy a piece of fruit.

My mother shakes her head, another emphatic no. "We don't know the secrets they knew in those days. How much to use, which parts to use. But my mother knew. I watched her dry the skins and the seeds, crush the pulp into a drink. I don't know which parts she used for what, or what the dosages were."

"Then why are you telling me?" My head hurts with the effort to understand my mother. A mystery, yes, always: her moods, her secrets, her stern warnings.

Now she shifts her whole body to face me. "Eve,"—for the first time, just like that, she calls me by my grown-up name, "—I'm telling you that each generation gets more chances, more knowledge. Some say it's this here—" and she hefts a piece of fruit from my lap—"that's the fruit from the Garden of Eden. It's this knowledge, how to give life, and how to stop it, that Eve gained from the serpent. Some say that knowledge is evil. Some say the serpent was evil. I say it's just an animal, with its own facts and ways of knowing. I say it's what you do with what you know that counts."

She raises her head in a sweep of the barn, the shed, the garden, and the hills above. "I lost my mother, most of what she knew about herbs and tinctures. All she had to tell me about our people, how they came across Persia and Europe to America on those slave ships and steamers." My mother rises.

For once, my ears are overflowing. "What are you telling me—slave ships, Persia where did this come from?"

The edges of Mom's lips flip into a tight smile. "I have a lot to tell you, but first let's go home. It's cold out here."

On the way home, she dozes in the passenger seat while I lick pomegranate juice from my sticky fingers and peer through the dusty windshield, the sun setting in a smeared glow across my vision. I keep glancing at mom's face, wondering why now, why this moment, to let go what she's been storing for years. I see the deep lines etched around her lips and nose, the pallor of her cheeks, and I think, as always, that there's something she isn't saying.

It's gloomy, early evening. I light a fire under the gas burner, set the teapot on to warm. Mom sits at the table, looking out at her garden, while I fuss with cups and saucers. We sit sipping our tea for a few minutes, no sound but the clock ticking over the stove and a faint wind come to stir the leaves outside. *There'll be rain next*, I think, and no more have I thought it than I see and hear it flicking against the pane. I turn again to face the kitchen and Mom begins, as if that is the cue she's been waiting for.

"When I was eleven, my uncle came to take my mother away." She nods her head slowly, in that way people do when they are feeling the truth of their story. "She wouldn't go. But we lost her, just the same."

I hold very still so she will go on and tell me the story that I know she has held back for many years. And she does.

Maisie, 1972: Breach

When you are standing covered in your mother's blood, you cannot think past that moment. Mama and I were in a tunnel together, moving on shafts of light to some faraway place, where it did not matter if we were on time. Outside, I could hear a lark trilling in the lilac bush, and a dove under the eaves cooed. I wanted to close my eyes and drift off to wherever I was before she pushed me into this world. This world, where your mother could suddenly leave you.

The seconds ticked by. The baby cried in my arms. I could not get my feet to move. When I wavered, just a little, my soles made a sucking sound. I looked down and found myself standing in a pool of her blood. I did not let myself look again. Instead, I locked my eyes on her face, her lids closed almost all the way, just a glint of shiny eyeballs showing through the brush of her lashes, but that glint fierce. I knew what to do. The baby kicked as I held him closer, but when he felt her lips on his head, he stopped as if frozen, his brown eyes opening wide.

Mama looked past him for a moment, as if she were searching for someone. She tried to raise her arms, but fell back against the pillows with a deep exhalation. "Out, outside," she breathed. I glanced around. Of course. No one should die in the house, she'd told me, so that the family could keep living there, free from the mulí's desire to rejoin the family. But how could I lift her? I couldn't.

When I looked back, I was aghast to see her half-standing, crouched between the bedpost and the wall. "Outside!" she whispered, fiercely. I put my shoulder under hers and steadied her, drawing a quilt around her shoulders against the chilly rain. "Your sisters—"

When we entered the front hall, I angled my body so that, if my sisters looked, they would think I was taking soiled bedding out to the clothesline, maybe. Would not see my mother huddled like a ragdoll against my chest. Somehow, we made it past the herb garden, to the sheltering wisteria shrubs that bordered the yard.

And then I could hold her no more. She seemed to curl inward, even as she reached out her hand. I thought she wanted my hand, but I understood when she breathed, "Mami," and looked past me toward the moon looming over the house and barn. For a second, her attention shifted back to me. "Maisie, watch out for your sisters."

I clamped my eyelids shut, ignoring her hoarseness, pretending it was any day, Mama saying that to me before school, after school, whenever someone came to visit. I tried to close my ears, too, so her last words would never reach them. Some part of me clung to her voice, a part that wanted any scrap of her still left to me. When I heard her say, "Ash Devlésa," I knew what it meant. She had said that when she told me about her mother dying. Ash Devlésa. Stay with God.

I could have stayed there, blind, in that dark of my own making, and might have kept my mother with me. But my baby brother cried, a wail of desperate need. I made a choice. I opened my eyes.

Gone. My mother's beautiful black hair still shone. Her golden flesh, which always reminded me of a pear reaching ripeness, gleamed in the moon's rays. Yet after a few seconds, her face became paler. Oddly, I felt her still with me. I could hear her voice, choking, trying not to cry, urging me to hurry, whispering fiercely. Saying those last words to me: Ash Devlésa.

It was not with God that I wanted to stay. My brother wailed again. Nothing was ever harder than to cover my mother with the quilt and to turn my back on her as she lay there in the soft rain. I returned to the house.

The whole time I cuddled the baby, while he beat his little fists against my breast, I trembled with the effort to find a way, any way, to make Mama live again, or to go with her down that long tunnel. Desperately, I searched my mind, and in thinking how to do it, I began to look around.

My eyes lit on her carved wooden chest. Inside, the buttons from her Papa's vest, and her locket, nestled in velvet. And that's when I remembered: She did not want me to follow her. She wanted me to take care of my sisters.

I was thinking about this when a voice came from behind me. Tally. I ran to shut the bedroom door she had opened only a crack. Her whimper slid beneath the door. In a few minutes, it would become a full-scale roar. Suddenly, there was Vinnie's voice, too.

"What's wrong? Is Mommy okay? I want to see the baby!"

When you are standing covered in your mother's blood, you cannot stop to think. And if your baby brother is crying, just minutes after he's been born, and your two little sisters want to know what's wrong with Mommy, you can't pause to weep, yourself.

I did not want to wash off her blood, because then I knew she'd be dead. That I would not be going with her. But, since I could not follow her and still do what she asked of me, I had no other choice. When I placed the baby on the far side of the bed, he turned his head toward Mama and wailed.

I ran to the pail in the corner, the same pail I had drawn from the well earlier that day—it seemed days ago—when mother and I were making breakfast. "Maisie, I'm relying on you." I heard her voice say that again and again, while I scrubbed my hands and face. I tore off my dress, listening all the while to the baby gasping for breath and knowing my sisters were huddled on the hearth, frightened. My clothes were upstairs, in the loft, so I threw on one of Mama's flowery dresses. Her scent enveloped me as it slid over my head. I had to steady myself on the straight-backed chair beside the bed.

I lifted the baby, opened the door, and stepped into the hallway. "Tally, get me some towels from the closet. Now! Vinnie, go draw more water from the well. Mother's tired and wants to sleep, but we need to clean up." My sisters scampered to do what I asked, while I took our little brother to the cradle by the hearth.

I had no idea if rocking would quiet him, but I wanted them to have something more to do. Tally stuck out her lip and whined, but she did it. She moved across the floor and put her foot against the cradle, sending it rocking, hard, at first, then more gently as she steadied it with her hand. The baby still cried, but sounded less desperate.

"Vinnie, stroke him. Tell him it's going to be all right."

"Is it going to be all right? Will Mama be all right?"

I closed my eyes and drew breath deep into my lungs. "It will be if we all do what we should." I wanted to believe it was not a lie.

About an hour later, I opened the door for Dr. Nettie.

She looked me over—her eyes lightening with relief—untied the rain hat beneath her chin, and slipped out of her wet coat. I hung them on hooks to dry.

"I came as soon as I could, Maisie. Papa needed me to look in on the Mayhews' baby on my way back from town. She has a terrible fever. They live on the other side of the creek and Carl just now got through with the horse."

She waved behind her at Carl, who sat astride Jenny. He clucked to the horse and took the drive at a trot. Had Dr. Nettie ridden behind him? Would my father be here to take her home in the car? No time for such details.

"How's your mother?"

I was fine until she asked me that. Suddenly my tongue felt glued to the roof of my mouth.

"Maisie!" She spoke more sternly. "What's wrong?'

Still unable to speak, I moved aside and pointed to the bedroom.

She stopped just inside the door and stifled a cry. I did not want ever to enter that room again, but I made myself go and stand beside her on that sticky floor, because Mother would have wanted me to.

"What happened? Where is she?" Dr. Nettie's voice was harsh and urgent, and I wanted to cry, but I tried to explain.

"She didn't want to die inside. She told me before that it's hard on the family, to feel the spirit of the mulí who wants to rejoin them. So I helped her outside."

"Show me!"

I thought Mama had bled every drop from her insides before, but the clean quilts I had used to cover her were now blotched with blood. *At least you are not seeing her with her eyes bulging and staring,* I thought. I had gently pulled her eyelids down with my fingers, so that if Tally and Vinnie came out they would believe she was sleeping. I know it made no sense for her to sleep in the rain, but I was moving in a fog of fear and fatigue and worry. As it was, I had a time of it keeping Tally from going into the bedroom and finding Mama gone.

Dr. Nettie breathed loudly through her nose for several minutes. A change came over her: I watched her reach deep inside herself and find that calm she used with patients. She drew it on like a cloak. Her voice took on a brisk tone.

"Maisie, when is your dad due home?" She drew a pair of rubber gloves from her pocket and put them on.

"Tonight, I guess. He would be here, already, except for the rain."

"We must make sure he doesn't find her this way." She turned to me. "We'll have to lift her. Can you help?" She watched me closely as I opened my mouth without a sound, battling my urge to say no. I managed a nod. "Good. Get on the other side of her. We'll take her to the barn." I did not question her. If we had carried her inside, we would have drawn my sisters' attention, and I did not want them to see Mama until we could make her look beautiful again. As it was, it was all I could do not to stare at the blood that caked her legs and soaked her nightgown.

I've often wondered if we would have fared better if we had left her like that for my father to see. Would my father have taken better charge of us, if he had seen Mama in that horrible state?

I only touched her briefly as we made a sling of the soft quilt, but I will never forget that touch—an icy rubberiness that told me Mama was not there. Her beautiful feet looked like wings of marble propped against my shoulder. Her face was peaceful, but still, so still

Once we reached the mound of clean hay in the barn, we set her gently down and Dr. Nettie waved me away. Ernie hung his long face over the stall and snuffled softly, but Espero seemed to shy away, a shadow against the far wall. I lit a lantern for the doctor and hurried back to the house, returning once to the barn to bring a clean pink nightgown for Mama. Then I rejoined my sisters inside, around the hearth. We huddled there all evening, passing the baby between us, feeding him from the sugar tit I made, while the doctor bathed Mama, dressed her in the fresh gown, and folded her hands on her chest. The girls did not attempt to see her, which told me they knew she was gone and were pretending they didn't.

By the time we heard the truck rumble into the drive, Mama lay like a sleeping princess on the hay. The doctor greeted Papa at the door with his son in her arms. He pulled the blanket aside to see the boy, and tears of joy spilled from his eyes.

That became the last smile I ever saw on his face. He looked at Nettie. She said nothing, but he must have wondered why she and not Mama presented his son. Without a word, he stalked to their bedroom in his tall boots. I crept behind him. He stood for a moment staring at the empty bed, then turned to me with a fierce face. I pointed to the barn.

When Papa stepped through the door, Mama's hair lay shining, spread out around her like a deep patch of night sky. The animals were silent, respectful. He stood, stiff and unbelieving, his hat in his hands. Then, with two long strides, he fell at her side.

The sound that echoed then through the yard and around our house shook my sisters from their watchfulness and sent them wailing. It wound around our heads like a wolf's keening, and, I swear, it made the dishes rattle in the cupboard. Never before and never since have I heard such human anguish.

Vinnie and Tally went shrieking into Nettie's arms. I slid down the kitchen wall, somehow released by my father's grief into exhaustion so deep that I do not remember hitting the floor. But as I slid, I remembered what Mama had said.

"Maisie, I am relying on you."

Eve, November, 1972: Reap What You Sow

The whole time she's talking, Mom keeps her grip on my hand, tightening her fingers on mine when she reaches the hardest parts. Now she stops, takes her handkerchief from her pocket, and wipes tears from her cheeks.

I cannot even begin to imagine what it felt like to pull her baby brother into this world, then watch her mama die, but I see now the edges of my mother's fiery determination. How she bends to a task, why she tells only what she thinks I need to know. How she holds to life like a book that calls her to account.

Still, I have to ask. "Why are you telling me this now? Why not earlier?"

She lifts her eyes, and I see in them colors I have not seen before: the usual threads of deep green and brown, but also gold, and gray, like my own. I mark the red sparks in her hair, and how her neck arches with hardly any sagging skin, long and thin and elegant. Do I look like her? I know I do and yet until now I have spent so much more time thinking how we are different. All those long years, butting up against her sternness, it never occurred to me it was made of the same flesh that sheltered me.

I am so busy noticing that I forget to listen for the answer to my question. Mom waits. When I look up, a glint of amusement in those deep pools of green says she has not missed a thing. Her smile turns grim.

"When would I have told you? At three? At six? A little girl shouldn't hear such pain. And when you were nine, your body was getting ready to change. I didn't want you to think that ahead of you was certain death. When you were fifteen, you struggled to find out who you were, what you wanted, how to make your way. I couldn't saddle you with my pain. After that, Beverly's assault. So much anguish. Your father's death brought more sadness, and you had to nurse me. When could I have burdened you with all this?" She shakes her head and takes another sip. "It's hard to carry the knowledge that people let your mother die because of their fear and ignorance. That's the worst of humanity, it makes you wary, and I didn't want you to be chained to the past. But you're older now. To understand what a woman can go through and come out the other side, how she can be lost in a moment's flicker, to forgive—that is work for a woman. A mother." Mom keeps her eyes focused on her garden.

"I'm not a mother. Maybe I'm not old enough yet." My weak effort at humor does not deter her.

I watch her profile swing toward me. "Really? I think you have 120 children in your classes. You can choose to be just their teacher, I suppose, but it seems you're thinking otherwise. Otherwise, you wouldn't be so troubled by your students' problems."

Now it's my turn to examine the garden. "I don't know if I'm up to the task. Sometimes, fear and ignorance wins. How did you forgive Mrs. Dockhart? How do I forgive someone like Buddy Allen? What did he have to fear, that he needed to break my friend's body and spirit?"

Of course, my mother has an answer. She tells me about Lewis Allen's family, how his father beat him for plowing a crooked line and left his own brother caught in a trap. How Buddy's father, Lewis' brother, continued the family's cruel streak. "Misery can catch up to any of us, but some people carry it around inside, like a pot about to boil over. My mother knew the worst in people and still helped everyone, even those who were cruel to her. 'No point in adding a drop to an already-full cup,' she used to say."

I shook my head in admiration. "You always seem so sure of yourself." It dawns on me that maybe that's what I resented the most, the one thing I couldn't copy, the thing I most admired in Beverly and my mother. "How do you know what you want, Mother? Most times, I haven't a clue."

She examines the shadows forming where the sun has deserted the hillside. "I was fifteen when Papa died and I married your father. A year younger than you when you helped Mary Alice rescue Beverly. I didn't know any more than you. I *felt* it was right." She jerks her head, as if we could fly like crows back to the fields. "Your heart can only tell you if you listen to it."

I smile at this sentimental postcard from my mom, maybe the least dewy-eyed person I know—and now I see why. I glance down at her hand, clutching mine again, and remember her sitting with my father in the swing, their clasped hands folded together like an ongoing prayer. I hear her voice saying on a long drive home from Willeen's, the day I knew that Beverly was gone for good, "… nothing erases bad memories. But having someone to share your life with, that makes a difference…."

Mom pats my hand, rises, shuffles to the stove, puts the kettle on for more tea. The last of the sun glints in the windowpanes, and a bird perches on the clothesline. The flash of blue at its neck fools me at first into thinking it's a blue bird, but as its head swings and tilts with its call, I see the patch of red farther down its throat. Another barn swallow.

A memory bubbles from my childhood: It is a Sunday in fall, and my father and I have come to the persimmon field to gather fruits for mother. He points to a swallow in flight. "His mate will be nearby.

Look for her." We scan for the smaller female among the branches and reeds at the road's edge, and he adds, "Swallows mate for life."

I watch my mother pouring water over tea leaves and realize how much loss she's suffered in her life. Yet still she managed to love us all. And in that moment, something springs free in my chest, like a coiled wire that's been tied down. How did I not see her sacrifice, how hard she worked to keep the road open for us?

Another question pops up. "How did you find Dad? You had to quit school to work, right? Did you meet in the mill?"

An instant smile graces Mom's lips. "Oh, no. We met at the farm."

"I want to hear about it. Unless you're too tired?"

I can tell by her drooping eyelids that she is tired, but she shakes her head and straightens her back like she's on a mission. "I don't know what I would have done if Vashti Garretson had not come." She sits down, the teakettle in her hand, and pours more water into our cups with the teabags hanging over the lips.

I shake my head in astonishment. "Our Mrs. Garretson?"

"Well, she came for a visit, not knowing my mother had died, and became my guardian angel." She sits down and tells me about raising an infant and two girls and caring for her farm after my grandfather died, with only an elderly woman for help.

I can feel Mom's relief when my dad walked up that drive and into her life, can see how his quiet strength bolstered her own. *They were made for each other*, keeps repeating in my head. Listening to that loop, I let the silence go for a minute. I see her reflection in the window, gazing out at the now-empty clothesline. "Did you ever think of going back to school, when Mrs. Garretson and Dad came to help?"

She swings around to face me, her eyes still caught on something in the distance. After a minute she shakes herself into the present. "Lord, honey, things just kept happening. They tried to take back the farm, you know, that bunch at Papa's church." She explains a tale I can hardly believe: Nettie Evans helping her battle for her land and custody of her siblings in court, against the sheriff and Preacher Allen.

"You mean Brother Allen tried to take the farm? And your sisters and brother? How could Carl work with him, knowing that?"

Mom waves away my spasm of anger. "Oh, Carl's one of them who believes without question, whether it's God or some preacher he's listening to. I never tried to convince him otherwise." Her mouth stretches in a straight line. "Maybe I should have, and then he wouldn't have been such a fool about Beverly. But if it hadn't been Lewis, it would have been some other minister. Carl needs to believe something." Her sharp eyes lift to mine. "Some folks don't trust what's in here—and here—" She taps her head and her chest "—so they look for something outside themselves to carry them through."

I think about what my mother holds on to. Family, God—one maybe a little too busy to help those who don't help themselves—my father's love for her, and hers for him. Evidence of that love I'd seen all my life.

We both turn our cups round and round. It's a thing Mom does when she's puzzling things out. Until this minute, I hadn't realized I'd adopted it from her.

She grins, watching my hands. "You should have seen Lewis Allen when that judge dismissed the sheriff's petition for public guardianship. He ain't been so surprised but one other time in his life and you seen that one yourself."

A vision of the preacher dances before me, him hopping backward on one foot, holding the ankle Willeen has just swatted. I grin, too. "Mom, I wish I could have seen that first time. But didn't you want to hold onto the farm, after all it took to keep it?"

"Well …" Her mouth pinches and she shrugs her shoulders. I've learned new signs today for how my mother really feels. I see she's resigned herself to holding onto only what she can manage to keep safe. "For all his hard work, Frank never liked to farm, and with Doc Evans dead and Nettie gone so much, and us having beat Lewis Allen in court, him and his group out at the church found ways to make us miserable. Nothing we could trace to them, but things kept going awry. One night, it was a hose left on in the near field, all our young seedlings drowned. Next it was our well house knocked down. When they set a fire in the barn one night, we thought it time to leave.

"So I offered our land to Aaron Applewhite. His dad farmed by us as a tenant. Aaron had come back home, bought twenty acres or so, then took what he could of ours, most of the good bottomland, on credit—and made every payment on time till he paid it all. I couldn't bear to part with Mama's orchard and he couldn't really afford it, anyway. 'Glad to have this land, Mrs. Gates,' he said. 'Never could get this place out of my mind.'

"Truth be told, I would have sold it to the devil before I would have sold it back to that bunch at the church. We found out all Allen's legal shenanigans were really about getting our place for his parsonage. He certainly wasn't concerned for our welfare. He wanted to take all the work my daddy put in to make our farm pay—and most farms didn't pay in the Depression, you know—and he would have run it into the ground. I wasn't about to see my daddy's farm go that way, no sirree."

I have to laugh at the thought of my mom in a rare display of temper. She would have been a lot to reckon with. "All those years, you were so polite whenever you ran across each other. I never knew about all this stuff."

Her chuckle sounds like real glee. "That's because every time I met him, I remembered what he tried to do to me, and my family, and I let him know I remembered by holding my chin high and acting like the good Christian he ought to have been. Good thing Carl finally saw through him, but that was his to find out." She sighs again. I know she's regretting not making a bigger fuss about Willeen and Carl taking Beverly to Allen's church. My grandfather's church, I realize with a sudden lurch in my breast.

My mother's first rule of life: tend to your own business and let others tend to theirs. I wonder if she's ever wanted to just walk away from it all. "So when you left the farm you could have gone anywhere. Why did you stay here? I mean, I know it's a different set of people out there and in town here, but gossip travels pretty far. Wouldn't people be just as prejudiced in town? Seems to me they are."

Mom cocks her head to examine this thinking. "They are, I guess, especially toward blacks. But you ever notice everyone on the mill village has a story about their family? The Johnsons and your uncle Arthur's family, they're part Catawba, you know. You don't know your Uncle Milton is part Romani too, from that group that live up at Lancaster. You've lived two doors down from a family your whole life, bet you don't know the mother is from one of the Italian families out at the Elberton quarry. People used to treat them as bad as they did my mama. Mr. Tilman is working his way back from a crime he committed when he was just a boy. Probably some have African blood and don't tell it. Everybody's got something going on and don't nobody bother each other very much.

"Oh, some folks at the mill called me 'Gypsy,' till they got to know me, and long time ago some of the men used to ask me to dance for them. But the foreman said my weaving's good as theirs, and he don't care where I come from, long as my looms run steady. Besides, I learned something from my mother."

"What's that?" I reach to refill her cup from the pot I've brought to the table.

"A romni never tells everything she knows. Most folks don't have a clue what the Roma really are and what they don't know won't bother me. I let them keep their secrets and I keep mine." She purses her lips and lifts her cup till the steam closes her eyes.

I ponder this trait. "That's one habit I reckon I didn't get from you."

Mom confronts me, eyes open now, head lowered. "No? Then why have you been eating yourself up all these years about why Mary Alice and Beverly left? Why not go ask them?"

I'm embarrassed that I can't let their names cross my tongue. "Have you heard anything about them, lately?"

Mom's focus shifts downward to her cup. I wonder if she still regrets the wedding that didn't happen, even now, with George and his sweet Ginny settled out in California. She lifts her face. "You know that Mary Alice married a doctor, a few years back."

I did know, at the time, but mostly I had tuned out the few details Mom had let drop from her conversations with Granny and Willeen. Now, I'm listening intently. "They have three kids now. Beverly bought her own beauty shop in Atlanta this past fall. Granny Burnett and Willeen go down to see them both. They've invited us along, several times. You kept saying you couldn't go." She looks sideways at me.

"I know. I guess I should go, though. Why not?" I move the sugar bowl from one spot to another, listening to its clay bottom clatter on the dinette table. Mom rises and puts our dishes in the sink. I carefully push the bowl back to its usual place.

Since that moment in the persimmon field, when I held my best friend's hand while she bled and decided to keep her secret from me, I've packed my own heart away so tightly, that I don't know if I can find enough room for the man who loves me, much less for old friends who disappointed me. Suddenly, ferociously, I want to try.

"I think you want to go." Howard slips me a reassuring smile, then moves his attention back to the road. We are on our way to the Swamp Guinea, which sits in the middle of nowhere, with a murky view of the river and fabulous fried catfish.

I frown at the pines slipping past my window. "But she...." I stop, hearing the whine in my voice. After all these years, even I am tired of the soundtrack. Instead, I focus on unfinished business between Howard and me. "Never mind. I'd like to hear about your mother and father. I mean, I know she lost her family in the war, and that your father was a G.I. How did they get together?"

Howard's voice fills with the deep affection I saw when his parents invited me to dinner. His mother hovered, not overwhelming, but attentive to everything Howard or his dad—or I, their guest—could possibly need. And they returned the attention, Howard getting up to refill her water glass, his father, in his crisp blue suit, jumping up to slide her chair out when she rose to bring dessert. They reminded me of my parents, finishing each other's sentences. But there's something more now, a note of gravity in Howard's baritone as he elaborates. "My father was assigned to work with death camp survivors while they received emergency treatment and waited for hospital beds or visas. He met Mother when she came to find her parents and her brother."

I reach for his shoulder, knowing from the few family pictures on their mantel that she did not find them. All the pictures are of Howard, his mother and father. No people with her dark hair and almond-shaped eyes, frozen in young adulthood. No brother, a round-cheeked toddler who didn't get older. I wonder if somewhere there's an album filled with images from before the war. Could she bear looking at them? An image flashes into my mind: my mother's face as she opens the locket for me.

So softly I can barely hear, Howard says, "They said the Kaddish together."

His story envelops me like the night rushing by outside the car. He has listened to the family sagas I could tell, mine and Beverly's. Two nights before, when I came to the part about my mother standing in her mother's blood, and again when I told him about the night we found Beverly in the field, he encircled me with his arms until my tears stopped. Now as I watch slipping by the trees that stand sentinel over the landscape of my youth, he tells me the story of his mother, sent to England alone on a boat as her family remained to settle their affairs in Germany. Of his father falling in love with her and bringing her to America. His voice remains softer than usual, but it is also matter of fact. He came to terms with his family's history long ago, I think.

The car crunches into the parking lot underneath the Guinea's colored Chinese lanterns. Howard kisses me on the cheek and walks around to open the car door, the only sign of sadness a certain slowness in his pace. On our way into the restaurant, he pauses to speak to one of his stringers. As his hands shape the story he wants her to write, he turns to make sure I'm not too cold or too bored. I ask myself, how much more do you need to know?

I'm far less confident on Saturday as I aim the Barracuda for Atlanta. Granny and Willeen, comfortably ensconced in back, chat with Mom, who sits in the front, looking back most of the way. They are talking about old friends I don't remember hearing about before. "Which exit to Mary Alice's?" I interject, watching the green signs loom long before I can see the city's skyscrapers in the windshield.

Willeen sits forward to direct. "Smyrna. Look for the hospital. You turn there. Then three streets to the east."

We arrive in front of a long ranch house with green shutters at the windows. To one side, I can see what appears to be a sunroom. Keeping to a smooth stone path that meanders around the house, through some sort of blooming ground cover, we follow the sounds of children playing. The path leads out onto a concrete terrace ringed by azaleas and camellias, sloping down to a second concrete apron around a kidney-shaped pool.

On the deck, a woman in a green and blue coordinated pants outfit is kneeling over a child. His stubby legs, his red tennis shoes, stick out in front of her. Two older kids toss a ball near the water, the girl squealing whenever the ball comes her way, the boy laughing while she leaps to reach it.

"Mom! He's throwing it over my head on purpose!"

The woman stands and turns her attention to the older kids. The little boy in the red tennis shoes has thick, dark brown hair curving around his perfectly shaped head. He looks over his shoulder with huge brown eyes and sticks one finger in his mouth.

"Come here, Sugar," Granny coaxes, holding out her arms. He pulls himself to his knees, then to his feet, and totters toward her.

Mary Alice whirls. Her bright eyes dance. "Willeen! Mom! Maisie! And … Evie?" She walks quickly toward us, touching Granny's shoulder, hugging my mom and putting one arm out to me. If she notices that my hug back is not enthusiastic, she does not let on. Another squeal diverts her attention.

"All right! Stacey, Stephen, go in now and wash your hands. It's time for lunch."

Mary Alice will not listen to Mom's protests that we didn't mean to arrive for mealtime. We sit around a glass-topped table and eat cold chicken salad, crisp greens, and French bread, drinking lemonade, while the children have their sandwiches and Kool-Aid at a little table on the patio. "You can change your clothes after lunch. Before your nap." Mary Alice's voice says there's to be no arguing.

The two oldest kids look through the screen at her with downturned mouths but quietly eat their sandwiches. I watch as the little one steals grapes from his brother's plate, the older boy half-heartedly pushing the tiny hand away every few minutes.

Mom asks polite questions, which Mary Alice answers cheerfully. Granny stares besottedly at the handsome children, and Willeen keeps her thoughts to herself. I listen. The conversation is generally about Mary Alice's children and husband.

"Yes, they are handsome children. I mean, even if I am their mother, I think so. No, Tom is sort of sandy-haired, but, well, Granny says they look like her Dad. Right, Granny? And, of course, like me." I watch her smooth hair shake softly around her serene face and wonder how much of the self-possession I had so admired was actually self-absorption. I want to believe her selfish so I can hate her. All the heartache I felt that spring morning long ago wells up. I chew carefully to avoid choking on her food.

Mom's pointed look says it's my turn to show some interest. I push an ice cube away from my teeth. "So you and Tom met at the hospital?"

"Oh, yes. He's a pediatrician. Thank heavens!" She rolls her eyes toward the children, now playing quietly with trucks and blocks on the patio. "Stephen, watch your brother!" She swings back around to face me. "George and Ginny—how are they?"

"I didn't know if you knew—" My voice trails off.

Mom takes the thread. "Fine. They have four kids, now. The oldest is really good at music. He takes those Suzuki violin courses, you know? Gets it from my mother's family, I guess." She sips her tea, watching me over the glass.

I sit back and fork another leaf of lettuce. Mary Alice asks her mother if anyone on their side has musical ability, because so far her two oldest are interested in nothing but sports and TV. It is a way to let Mom have the upper hand. I have seen the *Let's Learn Spanish!* books on the coffee table, next to drawings of Mexican pottery.

I know Mary Alice will eventually turn her attention to me, and she does. "Evie, you're a teacher now? How wonderful! I'll bet you're terrific."

Crumbs spray onto my plate as I bite into a piece of bread. When I have thoroughly chewed it, I reply. "Not so terrific, maybe. The kids call me *Mister* Gates behind my back. Guess that means I'm tough."

Mary Alice gives me the look of calm reassurance I remember, the same look she must have given patients a thousand times a day. "They need tough. As long as you love them, too. And I bet you do."

We look at each other, and no one speaks for a beat or two. Even the kids on the patio are quiet, and Mom and Granny and Willeen chew, maybe trying not to disturb this moment. I look into those bright, unblinking brown eyes and know that I am not going to hate her forever.

Later on, in the kitchen, I help Mary Alice scrape plates. The kids are tucked into their beds under slowly moving fans. Willeen sips a cup of coffee on the patio, while Mom and Granny exclaim over photographs of Mary Alice's wedding to her doctor. I marvel at Mom's ability to push away the past.

Mary Alice and I work silently for a time on the short stack of dishes. "Evie," she begins, "I always hoped you'd come see me. I wrote, asking Willeen to bring you down."

I look out the wide window, across the pool and the green lawn. "I guess she mentioned it to Mom, but, well, college kept me busy, and, after that, grading papers and school activities—time flies, you know." I don't even try to avoid the cliché.

"And guys, I imagine." She smiles warmly. "Granny brought me your senior picture and those news articles about the pageants."

Tears sting my eyes at the thought of her looking at my photographs, while I believed she never gave me a moment's thought. I will not cry here. I straighten my back and lean against her clean Formica counter. "No, the boys thought I was a little too smart. Except for Howard Pearson."

"Oh," Mary Alice smiles knowingly, like we share some conspiratorial knowledge of men. "And now?"

I take a deep breath. "There's still Howard Pearson. He owns the local paper and writes a decent editorial every week."

"And is that good?" She takes a clean dish from my hand and dries it. There's a brand-spanking new dishwasher in the corner. I wonder if she just wants to do things as we used to. In this cool, pristine house?

The sparkling glass fixture shaped like an array of candles over the dining table holds my attention. "Well, I'm thinking about it. Maybe we'll be engaged soon."

A long look from those deep brown, unreadable eyes. "Good for you." We finish the dishes in a not quite comfortable silence. Mary Alice wipes the counter, then braces her hands against the edge. "Beverly would like to see you. I'm sure of it."

I blink. "I don't even know where she is." Mary Alice lets my evasion linger in the air. My neck muscles ache. A memory intrudes: a hospital room with green walls, Beverly's purple-flowered face, the feeling of fear and sadness gathered in each corner.

"What did she tell you back then, about what happened to her?" With that same calm I'd once admired, but which now seems maddening, Mary Alice takes a pad and pen from a drawer and writes something.

My nails are pink and glowing from the warm water. I curl my fingers into fists. "Not much. She didn't want to talk about it. What I never understood is, why did she keep the baby? Couldn't you have ... found a doctor for her?" It takes an act of will to make myself look at Mary Alice.

Her eyes are steady as the brown dirt under oak trees. They move toward Mom and Granny, still with their heads together over the photo albums. She leans her midriff on the counter, staring out toward the gleaming pool. "Why don't you ask her yourself?" She pushes toward me the note she's written. *1574 W. Peachtree Street. Atlanta.* At the bottom she's included a telephone number. "Maybe then you can forgive me."

I can find nothing polite to say in response.

Mom rescues me, coming into the kitchen with her purse. "Mary Alice, thank you for making lunch for us. We need to get home. Evie has to take me to church tomorrow." She walks over and without hesitation puts her arms around Mary Alice, who hugs her back, her arms wrapping around my mother's thin shoulder blades. Either sun or tears make Mary Alice's eyes shinier than ever. I stretch my lips across my teeth in an almost-smile. It's a start.

Granny steps onto the white tile from the living room. "I'll get Willeen."

We all look out the window to the patio. The children are awake and gathered around their aunt. I can't hear what she's saying to them, but her smile is the closest thing to cheerful I've seen on her face all day. How hard it must have been for her to raise Beverly, with no hope of having children of her own, listening to friends talk about their own broods. No wonder she lost so much steam after Beverly moved away.

A few minutes later, Mary Alice smiles, waves, and closes the front door. I help my mother into the front seat.

"Wasn't that a nice visit?" Granny slides into the back seat with Willeen. I walk around the car and look back at the house. Mary Alice stands in the plate glass window, her hand upraised against the glass.

☙❦❧

Granny and Willeen's yard, swept clean and planted with zinnias, dahlias, and pink and white roses, fades in my rearview mirror. I take a left on the old hospital road, toward the turn that will bring us into town, but I wing left again, pull over and stop on the gritty roadside. Mother says nothing. I check my mirror for oncoming cars and slide the car another inch or two, carefully, toward the ditch I know is there. Pinpoint-size stars glimmer between dark-armed trees through the windshield.

"What makes a woman give over the man she loves for her niece? And why?"

Mom sighs and does not declare I'm wrong. "Maybe she knew that George would find someone else, but there was no one but her to rescue Beverly."

I know she's right, and the truth spins my world. I peer into the dark at my mother. She chuckles, not exactly amused. More like she wants to soften the blow. "Not all wisdom comes from books, Daughter," she says, softly.

I breathe deeply, gathering lungfuls of wild rose, cow dung, and dry, dry grass. "George is happy enough, now, I guess." I picture my muscled brother, playing football with his sons by the lake. "Is Mary Alice happy?"

Mom turns on her tiny hipbones to look at me. "How did she seem to you?"

I know what she's doing and I resent it. This is another way to tell me to mind my own business. "Happy enough," I say, at last.

"Evie, when will you concentrate on your own happiness?"

Finding no answer I want to discuss, I release the parking brake and drive home.

∞

It is Monday morning in my classroom. Sunrays pick out students passing their papers from hand to hand as the bell rings. I watch Kathy sweep her books into the crook of her arm and decide to take action. "Can you stay for a moment after class?" I murmur.

Her neck stiffened, she sits, arms folded, like a toddler kept in a corner. She has avoided my eyes for days. We wait for the room to empty.

I lean on my desk and try to keep my posture open, welcoming. "How are you?"

She digs her arms deeper into their nest against her ribs. "Fine." The second bell rings. She stirs. "I've got to get to math class, Miss Gates. We have a quiz today." She looks at me, expectantly. I don't say a word, just hold her eyes till she gives in. "I'm okay. You don't have to worry about me. I took care of that situation."

Now it's my turn to cross my arms. "And you're all right?"

She pulls her books into her chest. "I'm fine." She takes a step toward the door, and pauses, her back to me. "My mom knew someone, a doctor."

Mildly surprised, I hesitate. I guess waitresses have a lot of information the rest of us don't hear. If Kathy's head weren't turned, I could read her expression, gauge her state by what I see there. But her whole body, poised to escape, doesn't want me to know.

My mother's words about letting other people keep their secrets echo in my head. No good can come from prying further. I sink down in the chair behind my desk. "If you need to talk, I'm here." I reach into a drawer, pull out a pass, and extend it to her.

Howard asks me again about Kathy as we pull into the Courthouse Square Café in the Karmann Ghia. "Say, what happened with that student, you know, the pregnant one? You were so worried about her."

I wave to the Sages and slump against the seat. "She did what she intended to do all along, I guess."

The newsman snaps to attention. "You mean she had an abortion?"

I shrug, consciously noncommittal. "All she would say was, 'Miss Gates, I took care of that problem. You don't have to worry about me.'"

"So how's Steve taking it?" He slips the car into park. It takes a minute before I realize I haven't said the name of Kathy or her boyfriend. Howard grins, gets out, and calls back through the door before he swings it shut. "I'm a newsman. You think I can't find out who took the train to Athens recently?"

"But they might have been going to a game at the University. Did you think of that?" I watch him through the windshield as he crosses to my side of the car.

"Nah. It was mid-week." He snaps open my door. "Steve went with her. Fine upstanding young man that he is. In Athens, you can get married at sixteen, or—the other thing. I wasn't sure which they chose."

I climb out. "Where do the young get that whole 'I'm invincible' thing? She never seemed to consider that something might have gone wrong."

Howard brushes my favorite shock of hair out of his eyes. "I don't know. The most dangerous thing I ever did was try to crash Dick Nixon's press conference with my college credentials. It's a good thing I'm not a woman. I'd be a real wimp."

I congratulate him on his superior sleuth skills, pondering how I'm going to keep secrets from him in the future. A balloon of sympathy for my mother floats in my chest, for all those years she struggled to decide what to share.

She's right: What good does it do to burden the young with dire warnings? Better to steel them with love and respect. A memory of my parents at the kitchen table, patiently explaining the rules of dating, slips to the surface.

What would I have done if Kathy had asked my help? How much of my grandmother do I have inside? I like to think I would have found a way. If I keep teaching, I know it won't be my last opportunity.

June comes, along with the prom and chaperone duty, which Howard relishes. I find I don't mind it as much as in the past. Walking into that gym again with my arm hooked through his, I recall gazing down from the stage, my first ribbon spanning my chest, his exquisite orchid on my wrist. A little nub of pride blossoms in my chest, not for being a beauty queen, but because I managed to get out long enough for a peek at the wider world. Underneath, there's the familiar hunger for a fresh vista.

Howard's warm eyes scan the room for information even as he pulls me to the dance floor. His gaze comes to rest on me, waiting for the music to swell. He knows something's up. I put my hands on his shoulders. "How'd you like to take me to Paris this summer?"

He folds me into his arms as a slow number begins. "Is there a special occasion?"

I shrug and smile. "Maybe."

It's rare that I surprise him. He grins like a dog who's pulled off a clever trick. "Sure. The summer after that, Venice. Or Madrid. Or Morocco. Wherever you want to go, milady."

I tilt my head back. We are terribly mismatched in height, but maybe that doesn't mean much. "Do you have to try hard to be perfect? Or does it come naturally?"

He begins to sweep me into a turn. But there's something else I have to say. I step off the floor into the alcove by the stage. "You know, are you sure your mother will–"

He spins me back onto the floor. "Mother would like you and your mother to come to dinner one Sunday soon." He smiles and steers and my feet manage to keep up.

We twirl past a group of kids standing in the shadows. "Miss Gates—go for it."

Howard sweeps me into a spin, his hand against my back, gently pushing me through the turn. A cheer follows us across the dance floor.

Right then and there, I decide that I will, indeed, go for it.

Eve, June, 1973: New Buds

The shop is a brightly lit salon of the trendy boutique type, along a stretch of Peachtree that is coming back. Green ferns twirl below a blue neon sign, reading simply "Beverly's." I stand across the street in one of those early spring showers that will leave as quickly as it begins. My grip on the umbrella tightens while I watch customers enter.

Along the window ledge, softly-tinted posters depicting models with impossible hairstyles mix with glinting gold objects I can't identify from this distance. A woman comes to the glass to see if the rain has stopped. She has blonde, highly-lacquered hair and long, red nails that she presses against the window. A little cleavage shows where her black blouse hugs her body. Can it be—? Movement catches my eye. I'm confused to see Beverly striding along near the corner, swinging one arm cheerfully, books clutched to her chest, her short pleated skirt flapping with each long stride. Wait—not Beverly, but an almost too-real image of the girl I knew. The teenager enters the shop. The blonde woman throws an arm across her shoulder and they walk away.

I pretend that it's curiosity about the objects on the ledge that draws me across the street, my umbrella shielding my face, and stop in front of the shiny display. Several trophies are from hair styling competitions, but one tells me something: *Carolina Shag Champion*. I imagine Beverly at the beach, gliding saucily along, twirled by some grown-up boy, her heavy gold hair lacquered now, long legs pumping in a style that is now old-hat in the age of British rock, but was all the rage when we were younger. She married once, Granny said. It hadn't worked out.

A middle-aged woman with a well-preserved smile and a lot of brunette hair piled on her head steps toward the shop door and almost knocks the umbrella out of my grip. She apologizes profusely and steadies me with her hand.

The door opens. "Come in, Denise. I've been waiting for you. Let's do something that will rattle Cancun on your cruise." The voice, bright and full of energy, hasn't changed. I sidle away, struggling to keep the umbrella over my face. The wind lifts it.

A tap on my shoulder. "Evie?" I turn. "It is you!" I had forgotten how green her eyes were. And, really, the hairstyle is not quite over the top. In fact, she looks fabulous, tan and fit and bouncing on her toes, as always. "Oh, my God! Mary Alice said you came to see her! I hoped—come in! I've got a customer right now, but I'll see if one of the other girls—" She gestures toward the brunette, who smiles and nods and enters the salon. Beverly holds the door open.

I find my voice. "Oh, no, I don't want to interrupt! I'll come back, I'll—"

"Nonsense! Come on in. I'll make you some coffee—or tea, maybe?—and we'll talk. Let me get Denise under the dryer first."

All the times I've been propelled along by the sound of that voice come to mind. I am pleased to feel a tug of resistance in my chest. "No! I'll come back in an hour."

Beverly grins like she knows exactly what I am thinking. She leans close, and I prepare to wince. "There's a good coffee shop on the corner." She points. I trot away, happy she hasn't called me "Headlights."

☙❦❧

Beverly doesn't try to dismiss thirteen years of silence with small talk. Instead, she leads me to the back of the shop, pulls out a dark blue leather album from underneath a marble counter, and hands it to me. Aware of the silence in the narrow room, lighted now only by sconces of a vaguely modern design, I look down at the manila pages. She has kept clippings from my pageants.

I've hardly recovered from my surprise when she hands me another album, this one pink-ribboned. "There's pictures of my daughter in this one." She mists one of two auburn wigs on the counter, and begins setting it on huge pink rollers. "You don't mind, do you? I have a customer coming for these early tomorrow morning."

I sit in an aqua leather chair and examine photos of a blonde baby that could easily be Beverly. One, of a two-year-old happily splashing in a tub, stabs my heart so suddenly that I slap the album shut. Instead, I focus on a photo hanging over the counter. It's a young ballerina in arabesque—the girl I saw enter the shop.

"Antoinette likes to dance, too, I see."

"Toni. Yes, she'll be Clara in the Nutcracker this year." Beverly beams.

"And you? You still shag?" I jerk my shoulder toward the trophy in the window.

There's maybe an edge of brittleness to her laugh. "Well, I like to keep up with the times." She does the Jerk for three quick side steps and twirls back to the counter.

It almost makes me smile. Right then, steps pound down a staircase I can't see and a heavy door flings open to reveal Toni in bellbottom jeans and a light sweater, a jaunty newsboy cap on her head. "Mom, I'm gonna walk over to Janet's to study for our science project. Okay?" She tosses one book and catches it in the same hand, stuffs it in the backpack dangling from one shoulder.

Stretching one fake strand between her fingers, Beverly nods toward me. "Say hello to Evalyn."

"Oh, my mom's friend? I'm glad to meet you." She touches the brim of her cap.

I blink rapidly and manage a smile. So her mother has told her about me. The girl turns back to Beverly, too polite to note my breathless silence.

Beverly's cool gaze switches to her daughter. "Okay, but call me as soon as you get there and again before you leave. Right?"

Toni wiggles her shoulders with impatience, gives her mother a peck on one cheek, smiles at me, and is out the door, bells jangling.

"Wow! What do you feed her?"

Beverly grins. "Hot dogs and Kool-Aid, like we had growing up." Her smile softens. "She's a great kid. Straight A's, unlike me. Don't know where she gets it."

I open the album and turn to another photo, this one of a bubbly seven-year-old, red headband framing large, dark eyes. I have turned the page to more dancing snapshots, when it hits me. I turn back. Our glances meet in the mirror. My mind spins the last thirteen years of notions around till a new interpretation snaps into place. "You said—" I swallow hard. "Buddy Allen has pale blue eyes."

She puts down the comb and backs onto a stool in the corner, twists to the side, and pulls a bottle out of a cabinet. Holds it, label out, towards me. *Cabana Boy Rum*, touts the print. I nod vigorously.

While she's mixing rum and coke, I try to count how many people had to know that Tommy Turner is really Toni's father. I figure Mary Alice, at a minimum, but probably Willeen and Granny, too. My mother? She would have guessed.

I accept the glass and swallow a third of it before I can speak. Beverly sips her own, waiting. Finally, I find my voice. "Why didn't you tell me?" I struggle to sound less pissed off than I feel. "Were you afraid I'd tell?"

She flicks a glint of humor toward me. "I couldn't take a chance Carl would find out. He'd have hurt Tommy. No offense, Evie, but you aren't the best secret keeper."

I bob my chin. She's right. Mom would have read the secret on my face and told Willeen and who knows what Willeen would have done.

Beverly twirls the glass in her hands. "Tommy and I were going to run away the night of the prom. That is, I thought we were running away, until Bobby told me Tommy wasn't coming. I couldn't believe it. I slammed out of Bobby's car and walked towards home, so I'd be ready as soon as Tommy came. Then those—those thugs stopped me." She takes a sip of her drink and lifts her head. A long, level stare. "I didn't have many choices. You figured it out, when you saw her photo. Everyone else would have, too. What do you think they would have called us?"

"So what? Did you think I wouldn't stand by you?"

A rueful smile takes the place of her frown. "Evie, you were headed away. Everyone could see that. And there I'd be, the town slut. Where would that leave Toni?"

"I understand now why you left, but not why you walked out without a word." I stubbornly pin my lips together.

Her eyes plead with mine. "I was seventeen and pregnant. The love of my life had abandoned me. I couldn't think. I needed to get away. Mary Alice offered me a way out. And I took it."

Abandoned. The one word I'd always felt belonged to me. "You never wrote."

Beverly lifts her palms. "I thought about writing, many times, but it's not something you put in a letter. At least, not if you hate writing, like me." She looks at me, her eyes keen. "I know you'd have tried to keep the secret about Tommy. But you'd have more questions—you always do—"

She's right. I would have asked a lot.

"—and at first I didn't know what I wanted to do. Mary Alice got me as far as a doctor's office, once, but I couldn't go through with— you know—" I watch her struggle to find words. Good. At least she's not passing it all off as glibly as she used to. "Going to see Mama Nettie changed my mind. Did your mother tell you what they did to my mother?" Beverly searches the reflection of my eyes as she picks up her comb.

I nod. Even now, I try not to think of Nettie's lobotomy.

A vein in Beverly's neck jumps like something small has burrowed inside. She stretches out a long strand of hair and holds it for a second. "We were sitting in the sun room one day. All of a sudden Mama Nettie reached over and patted my belly." Beverly lets the curl go and stands still, bush-green eyes meeting mine. "To this day I don't know how she knew. I mean, I didn't show much, then. But that moment I knew I wanted to keep the baby. Like I could complete a circle or something. Have something my mother was never allowed to have." The shop's air conditioner clicks on and a cool wave sweeps over us. I can't look away from Beverly's image in the shining glass.

"Honestly, Evie. It's like I was in a trance. My body felt strange to me. The only thing that brought me any peace was sitting with Mama Nettie. Every time I went, she did the same thing, patted my belly and smiled. Soon as I could after Toni was born, I took her out there and put her in my mother's arms. She cried and rocked her for an hour. Nearly had a fit when I took her home. Now she looks forward to our visits. The nurses say she keeps Toni's picture—" She gestures toward the photo of her daughter in ballet costume, "—in a plastic frame, and shows it to everybody. Even sleeps with it."

I smile, thinking of Nettie finding a little peace. I'm glad I came, if only for that. "So Toni knows her grandmother? Nettie, I mean. And what about Willeen?"

Beverly pauses with her comb in mid-air. "She's a good girl, my daughter. Reminds me to stop for flowers for her grannies every time we visit either of them." She puts down the comb and faces me. "After Toni's birth, I thought again about writing you. But Mary Alice had just broken up with George and I figured you'd blame me."

I marvel at how our reasoning twists in on itself, leaves us chasing shadows till our whole world looks topsy-turvy. Beverly is right. I was mad. I did blame her. Would I have understood, at sixteen? I can't answer that, even to my own satisfaction.

I have a lot of questions. She answers every one. Explains that she begged Bobby to take her home because the bus might not get her there before Willeen arrived. They planned for Tommy to walk to his Dad's store after school and take the car, after which he'd drive out to get Beverly. He'd leave a note Mr. Turner wouldn't find until well after prom time, since he worked late. They figured somebody would miss them when practice started—hence the hurry. In two hours—less if he floored it—they'd have driven to Augusta and gotten married. Tommy had already enlisted in the Army there—the Air Force wouldn't take him. His dad could find the car at Fort Gordon, and, if he was mad, well, they wouldn't have to see much of him.

I gasp. "Bobby might have been blamed for the rape. Do you realize that?"

She grasps the edge of the counter as if keeping a grip on facts. "Evie, I didn't plan to be raped. I planned to elope."

After storming out of Bobby's car at the florist shop, she'd walked toward home, still expecting Tommy to meet her there, and been stopped along the road by Bud Allen and Jim Marshall. Those two had seen Beverly and Tommy out at the shoals, where Beverly had talked Bobby into taking them for some "alone time," and they taunted her, saying they'd tell everyone about what they'd seen, unless she went with them. They tried to drag her into the car, but she had twisted away and run into the field. The rest of the details I remembered from that day at Willeen's, when Beverly had told us about the preacher's protection of his nephew.

One part I didn't know: Tommy had come to see her one night, late, in the hospital, and had repeated a version of the words he'd said to me: "I couldn't." He had never gone for his dad's car, as Bobby knew he wouldn't.

"Jerk! Whatever happened to him?"

"The Army, for a while. Now he's a lawyer, I hear."

I down my rum. Beverly smiles and raises the bottle to refill my glass, but I shake my head. "I'm driving."

She sips her drink without speaking for a moment. "I understand why he didn't come. With his mom dead, his dad is all Tommy has. So he hoped I'd get a ride to the game—mad as hell, of course, that he didn't show." She chuckles ruefully and leans her head on her fist, her arm propped amid the bottles and brushes on the counter. "He probably thought he'd talk me down, eventually we'd tell his dad about the baby, Dad would be happy, Tommy would support us on his Army pay, and all would be well."

I keep my voice neutral. "Do you think that's how it would have gone?"

She flaps her hand at me and takes a gulp. "Hell, no! I think his dad would have called him a chump for throwing his future away on a millworker's kid, instead of going to college. He'd have forbidden Tommy to see me again."

I look down to keep her from reading in my eyes that I'm pretty sure that's what happened. By the time I saw Tommy in the Quad, right after the attack, Daddy had already dangled his future in front of him.

And if Beverly had let the doctor examine her, the pregnancy would have been discovered and revealed to everyone. Mary Alice whisked her away to protect her and give her time to get over Tommy's betrayal. Why hadn't I seen that before?

I wince, realizing selfishness is not in Mary Alice's toolkit. Once she'd taken Beverly away and made a home for them, no one could take her place. My brother might have married Mary Alice anyway, but she wouldn't have wanted to make him take on the burden of a niece and grandniece, instead of a family of their own. What if she'd given him the choice? I guess she knew him better than I did.

Beverly leans forward to get my attention. "It wasn't that I didn't trust you, Evie. I had that one shot to get away. Here, in the city, no one asks me questions about Toni's father. I tell people I'm divorced— which I am, by the way, got out after a few months of drunken excuses from a louse—and no one condemns me for being a Jezebel."

She spins the stool closer to me. "Evie, listen to me. We both wanted to get away from town, but we were headed in different directions. I wanted to dance, and live, and enjoy myself. It didn't matter where, so long as no one judged me. You wanted to see places and understand things, make sense of the world. I've never thought the world made much sense beyond this: Everybody goes after what they want. Sometimes we get it, sometimes we don't, and sometimes we butt heads with each other in the scramble."

She sits back and flings her hands wide to indicate the shop, with its gleaming fixtures and sea-toned upholstery. "I'm queen of my domain. I have no one telling me what to do, and I have a daughter who loves me. I'm happy! Quit worrying about me. Think about yourself."

Everyone wants me to mind my own business, it seems. I bristle, and this time I don't worry about being polite. "Everybody in our hometown thinks you're a slut. That's what they think about any woman who's been raped. Your mother's in an institution. Your daughter has the wrong last name. How can you be happy?"

Beverly stands and narrows her eyes, smiling. "Honey, it's not about what other people think of you. It's about what you think of yourself. Why aren't you married by now? I hear Howard's asked you a bunch of times. Unless, of course, you still plan on living in Paris, in which case I'd think you'd be wearing couture."

I rise so fast the album tumbles to the floor. I retrieve it and set it on the counter. "Right! Well, since when are you Pollyanna? You and Mary Alice ruined our hometown for me. Anyway, it's all a façade for dirty little secrets." I am surprised at the depth of my own bitterness.

Beverly slaps her hand on the counter with a chuckle. "Faca—ain't that what's on a building, Evie? What folks have are *feelings*. And sometimes those are mean, and evil, sometimes they're sweet and clean. Whether you're in a small town or a big city."

I shake my umbrella. "Right. Which one are you, Beverly? Which am I?"

Those snapping green eyes challenge me. "Evie, we have never been anything but Ivory Soap pure. If you're not sure about that, you'd better throw Howard back in the pond. Plenty of women would like a chance to catch him."

"Well, I'm glad we had this chance to clear the air."

"You can't clear the air and still carry a grudge. Even I know that. So make your choices and live with them."

"Yeah, well at least my choice wasn't to lie to my best friend." I spin on my heel and head for the door, but not before Beverly throws one last dart.

"Everybody lies, Evie. Even you, a little. It's who we do it for that matters. I did it for my daughter, not to hurt you."

I run to my car and throw myself into the driver's seat. I want to rush back and hug her. I want to smack her. I realize that I have always wanted to do both. So I cry for a very long time, before wiping my eyes and nose on a tissue from the glove box and pulling onto the highway. I-85 whips past in a blur, in silence. No talking to myself, no radio, just listening to the wind whistle past the window.

The next day, I watch the sun creep across the back porch to rest at the tip of Mom's slipper as she peels apples for pie. "How is Mrs. Garretson?" I ask.

"Fine. I took her some yarn to keep her busy. Her eyes are too dim to sew much." The fruit skins make long spirals that fall over her wrists into the steel bowl she holds clamped between her knees.

"I'll go visit her soon. Maybe she'll tell me more about Uncle Stephane and the rest of the family." Mom continues peeling without comment. I decide to make a guess. "Uncle Paul found Paolo and the kumpania, right? How did he do that?"

She looks at me and puts down her knife. "Mrs. Garretson knew where they were—she'd lived there with my uncle and Mirela. Paul needed to find a man he could look to like a father. Paolo, Mama's cousin, took him in."

"Why don't we hear much from him?"

Mom sighed, resting her hand on the bowl's edge. "Well, he trains horses, you know—Paolo taught him—so he travels a lot." She rubbed her forehead, sat back in the metal chair, and lifted her shoulders. "The most traditional Roma, like Uncle Stephane, think we aren't really Roma because your grandmother and I didn't marry Roma. To them, Paul isn't supposed to speak to us, even. But he writes a note to me now and again and he says some of the younger Roma are less … separate."

I absorb this so deeply that my skin tingles. "Do you think things have changed enough that he will talk to me? I want to learn what it means to be Roma."

Mom gathers the peels and apples in separate bowls and rises. "There's always hope, Daughter." She goes inside, and I watch through the window while she lifts something from a small tin on the windowsill. She reappears and hands me the locket that passed from my great-grandmother, to Gramma Evangeline, to my mom. To me. "When you go, take this with you." In my hand, it feels familiar, like something I have dreamed. "Paolo will recognize it." My mother's voice is very gentle. "And how is Beverly?"

I look deep into her swirling eyes, see the patience she has always had for me, and curl my fingers around the chain. "I wish I had known before that she chose to keep the baby. She tried to protect her the whole time that bastard was raping her." Now I'm sobbing, holding onto my grandmother's locket, completely unable to add what I want to say. *And I wish I'd understood how much pain you were keeping to yourself, too.* My mother pats the place where my neck, my shoulder, and my spine all come together. She understands. The cool metal warms in my palm.

Eve, August, 1973: Full Bloom

Heat still rises in waves through the orchard and up the hill, though a stiffer breeze blows to silver the undersides of leaves on olive trees nearer the road. I stand at the top of the orchard and look out over the landscape below.

Watching the crow on the wing, I remember the rest of the childhood rhyme: *Eight is a kiss. Nine is a wish. Ten is a chance never to be missed.*

Thank heavens I didn't miss my chance to come to know my mother.

Turning at last, I lift a sweeping balsam branch in Grandmother Evangeline's secret garden and find orbs hanging from upright stems. They glow like a banked fire.

Memory plays a moving picture of Beverly, twirling with the sheer joy of being alive, despite all the heartache she's had. Evangeline herself found love with a man she barely knew, who was willing to bring the persimmons and pomegranates and plant them in this new place. I think of Mirela, nursing my Uncle Stephane back to health. And my mother, so careful in her decisions, maybe because she paid so dearly to conquer her feelings as her mother lay dying. And Beverly, again, choosing to protect her baby, even if it meant protecting her rapist, too.

Such choices are bought dearly. Maybe love makes the price worthwhile.

And there's my student, MaeEtta, looming, firm-limbed, over my desk. *What shall I do with this paper, Miss Gates?* Her wide smile shows me that she is not at all worried about her grade, or about finding her place in the world. Next year another girl of unknown description, but equal promise, will replace her. Will she leave this place or will she stay and flower in native soil? I have stopped trying to predict my students' futures.

Wind rustles the trees, and I remember girls hiding in a Chinaberry, the soft leaves imparting some comfort, refuge from the adults who will any moment come, with their ridiculous demands, their rules against blood, and lust, and innocent yearnings alike.

I close my eyes again and feel girls ripening in the soft Georgia evening. On the wind, the scent of fruit, earth, and slightly acid girl-sweat. In their beds, on sheets never quite cleansed of the soil deposited by days of play in yards of hard-packed clay, their cheekbones begin to hollow, their breasts to strain against nightgowns of thin batiste. I feel the swirl of all the dreams inside their heads, their hands clasped around the smallest treasures—a barrette, a piece of smooth marble. Salty flesh mingles with sweet perfume of geraniums and mock orange, scents flowing back and forth through windows flaked with old paint. The tears they have stored for those even smaller, lighter in the scheme of things—lightening bugs smashed against screens and butterflies with broken wings—flow from my own eyes. All of the joy and sorrow they will confront as their bodies ripen and decline to old age, traces like a vine through my core.

Girls dance to catch men's eyes, yes. But also because their hearts require it. When I lost Beverly, I thought I lost my invitation to dance. Mary Alice took with her—or so I thought—the only route to escape the dullness of small-town life. I made my own way, but only by hardening my heart so much that I muffled its beat.

I turn again. Right in front of me, persimmons lift their twisted arms. I focus instead on their strong trunks and think of my mother, holding a place for all of us, and my grandmother, trying to knit the old and the new into a home. What gardeners they both were, like the crows who drop seeds and reap their fruit.

And me? Am I swallow, or a crow? A little of both, and something else, perhaps.

The late summer sky glimmers its fading luxury. Stars wink on.

Below and to my left, down the hill, workmen have piled their tools on the porch that my grandfather built. When the weekend passes, the bedroom floors will have been replaced with clean, fresh oak planks, and my mother and Mrs. Garretson will move in.

"You sure you want to sleep in the same room where—" I couldn't finish the sentence, couldn't say the words that had haunted my mother and clouded my understanding for so long.

"Where my mother bled to death?" Mom's gaze was the same steady, opaque shield that I had resented for years. Now I saw that it constrained her sorrow, while holding it near, like the clear bottles of herbs in water that she placed on her windowsill. Nothing spilled onto her family, not one drop of cruelty or selfishness wrought by despair. She shook her head as if acknowledging something deep inside. "Nothing can erase her presence here, that moment when she left me in charge. I have done what she asked. I will think of that every night I rest my head in this room." Her next words made me shiver, like an angel brushing by. "She would be so pleased that you have come to stay here, in her garden."

On my right, at the very end of the row of persimmon trees that pinwheel below me, where a vardo once stood in the orchard, sits the cottage I have built and will share with the other gardener in my life—though he might have more in common with mynahs than crows. Its sloped roof houses a chimney for warmth and gathering. Its front windows are wide and bayed for cozy reading. The cottage of all my teenaged romantic fantasies.

Tomorrow, Howard and I will marry in the old Methodist Church where my parents have been members since before my birth. My brother, George, father of four, will walk me down the aisle, but he will not give me away. No one will give me away. My father's love will pour down through the old windows, love not in Technicolor but in soft greens, yellows, and blues. I will feel my mother's eyes on my back as I hand the bouquet to my best friend—her hair a smooth blonde helmet, green eyes shining with happiness for me—then turn to face the man I have known since I was a girl, trying on roles like I tried on scarves, knotting and re-knotting my life till I got it straight.

I will stand before the altar and nothing I say will be a lie, though the words were written by someone who never knew what it's like to see your best friend lying in a hospital bed, bleeding for the crime of trying to dance her way through life. As I take Howard's hand, maybe it doesn't matter if I cannot say amen to every word. I will believe in the man who stands next to me and in the people who sit in the pews. And around my neck will rest the locket my mother opened for me, so long ago, its precious portraits still cradled inside.

I lower my eyes once more to the red globes near at hand and to the persimmon trees twisting below. Every day, for many years to come, I will walk the path over this hill, through the fruit of queens.

Howard's promise about Paris and Venice convinced me that saying yes to one place might not prevent me from loving others—or even enjoying the open road. I finger again the envelope in my pocket: my teaching contract. I'll mail it on our way to dinner. I haven't promised to stay forever, but I am willing to give this hybrid life a try.

The swallow flits overhead. I acknowledge it. "We're all just passing through."

It flies on toward the horizon. Overhead, the Milky Way, speckled with light and dark, is luminous in our vast sky. From family I don't even know yet, music rises, a bubble of pure joy, thrumming up from the earth beneath my feet. Night frenzy! I think, and let it sweep my body into motion—feet awhirl, head thrown back, arms flung wide to gather them all.

Latcho drom, I whisper. Safe journey.

About the Author

Glenda Bailey-Mershon grew up in the Appalachian South in a family with diverse roots. A former bookstore and small press owner, she has taught women's studies, anthropology, history, writing, and GED preparation. Her publications include *Sa-co-ni-ge: Blue Smoke: Poems From the Southern Appalachians; Bird Talk: Poems,* and *A History of the American Women's Movement: a Study Guide.* She has edited or co-edited four volumes of Jane's Stories' anthologies by women writers, including *Bridges and Borders.*

Links to her blog, Weaver's Knot, and to her book reviews at Women and Books can be found at www.glendabaileymershon.com. *Eve's Garden* is her first novel.